CROCODILE BLOOD

ALSO BY GEORGE MANDEL

NOVELS

FLEE THE ANGRY STRANGERS
THE BREAKWATER
INTO THE WOODS OF THE WORLD
THE WAX BOOM
SCAPEGOATS

HUMOR

BEATVILLE, U.S.A.
BORDERLINE CASES

CROCODILE BLOOD

BLOOD

GEORGE MANDEL

ARBOR HOUSE / NEW YORK

Manufactured in the United States of America
10 9 8 7 6 5 4 3 2 1

Library of Congress Cataloging in Publication Data
Mandel, George.
Crocodile blood.
I. Title.
PS3563.A436C7   1985   813'.54   85-11211
ISBN 0-87795-742-8

Minor elements published earlier have been
reshaped for inclusion here. It is hoped they will
not induce in some readers a feeling of *déjà vu*
except where intended by the author.

—G.M.

For Sam II and his brother Rome

CONTENTS

PANORAMA ONE / MIDNIGHT PREY   1
COLLAGES 1–8

PANORAMA TWO / DEVIL'S EYE   179
COLLAGES 9–13

PANORAMA THREE / THE DISBELIEF OF
CHRISTIANS   271
COLLAGES 14–20

PANORAMA ONE

MIDNIGHT PREY

MAJOSEE COWAYA, who gave me Storyteller as my good soul name, to her lost good soul I give this panorama of eight collages. They include biases and excesses her passion inspired me to catalogue as habitually as I've always filed away in bin drawers the topical newspapers my craft assembles eventually into visions of enormous conflict.

My own excesses fill the next panoramas, which follow on my attempt to help this great city of crisis with a confession I made to the Mayor some while before he held that office. We were once great friends. That changed back then, when he was Metropolitan Attorney. I had to betray a moral lapse in order to describe a far greater trespass I had witnessed in the course of it, and thereby alert our people to the most hideous of dangers.

I brought him out on the Gulf of Mexico for that civic confession, and he took it harder than the Cuban crisis, radiating its threats of World War III not far away. It was that long ago. But older beginnings vexed my intimate government official.

That morning of sunny salt breezes on the Gulf, an eagle was in his memory, tracing circles high above five human predators who never left his conscience. He spared me the grisly past of Majosee. We had no warning it would beset us for a lifetime.

We were the best of friends.

COLLAGE 1

Twilight was overtaking her, but it could have been morning, the swamp lay so still. Gnats hung motionless wherever the sun hazed through. Scorched in journey, the north wind was no more than a scent in the pines and palmettos, a message of imminent rain. Majosee knew better than to advance in the danger of rain, yet paddled on, to find a safer haven because snakes often hid under the palmetto spears. She wanted no contest with a diamondback.

The rains, horrendous in season, still frightened her as they used to in childhood. But she could tolerate fear, and pain too, having been trained to endure those rigors by the Trail Indian side of her family, which still observed the old ways. She remembered her grandmother pinching her thighs till she wept, as the way of teaching children not to cry out while hiding from government soldiers. Only her father's objections had kept the old woman from piercing her with fish bones for the same purpose even though the white men no longer hunted her peo-

ple down. Now her father and her mother's mother both resided in heaven, their souls at peace, she prayed.

Little rain had fallen this early in the season. Even so, the watercourses had risen enough to float a small dugout canoe, encouraging her to go visit her reservation grandparents as she did each spring with her father while he lived.

The sky, a baked clear blue before the stream carried her through the pine copse, was all at once smeared with cloudy mists. The parched air weighed heavy on her. Majosee hastened her paddling until she discovered a fork that branched off through the spikerush bog toward marshes of a cypress strand she knew. Its friendly tall dome beckoned visibly, and soon she could see the glistening mud of a slope that some hardwood paraded up to the dry ground of a hammock, an island of trees for her stopover during the cloudburst soon to come.

She saw the towering royal palm that stood near a familiar lettuce lake on that dense shelter, and in the first hint of thunder she dismissed the concern of her mother, the bogus scorn of her mother's uncle, who knew Majosee could navigate a canoe as ably as any man. He even took secret pride in her, and she called him Grandfather as her mother usually called him Father, for as clan elder the old uncle had fulfilled his parental obligations devotedly all their lives.

Seminole marriage tradition, requiring the groom to dwell in the family region of the bride, had obliged her father to abandon the cattle breeding of his family for the planter's humdrum life. Thus he would always be longing to voyage home by dry winter's end. With the spring planting done, nothing could keep him from revisiting his saddle, an Indian cowboy once again. Until, with the coming of summer, the Green Corn Dance brought those of the family who had not gone with him to the reservation in the first place—the busk, the festival of new fruits for a fresh new year.

Her brother went to herd with him whenever early leave from the mission school was convenient. Chores held her mother back until the summer celebration. Majosee, inspired by her father's enthusiasm, always accompanied him, and this year when the season was ripe, so was she—for the family visit and

more. Eighteen at last, her education completed, she must start attracting suitors to her mother's appraising eye. It was time to display herself at the horse races and ball games of the reservation.

Up on the hardwood hammock, Majosee lashed the canoe to a stout liana vine for security against storm winds powerful enough to blow her away with the vessel. She streamlined her dugout in the course of the north wind, just as all the long hammocks of Big Cypress Swamp obeyed the southerly path of the drain currents, all the tree islands that lay like giant canoes afloat in the grassy bogs. Then she turned the canoe bottom up to wait beneath it for the swamp storm, hard against a live-oak tree.

An odor came to her, not sweet or spicy like the verdure but heavy with animal yearning. She smelled the lusty signal of the male. And at once the ground shook to the mighty roar of an alligator, quickening her heart. Small animals scurried away in fear: she heard them go. Alligators sometimes came to mate here in the lettuce lake, her father used to tell of the ecstasies they trumpeted, and he was gone and they were here to let her share in their exhilaration. Far-off thunder rumbled with the excited pulsebeat in her ears.

Five boys walked the link road back a piece after the station wagon that had carried them to this wilderness returned to the highway, where their boss was to show up in the morning and truck them into Naples with his Negro and their catch. They had let the accommodating driver overshoot their hike point to keep him from guessing the exact hammock they were heading for with their cumbersome supplies. Not that they suspected the young lawyer might betray them to some game warden, though he knew why they had asked him for the hitch. It was just that old Jessup always insisted the less people knew the better.

They had even implied their campsite was nearby, whereas plenty of grassy peat lay ahead to bog through. All five had the boots for it, and brimmed swamp hats, yet complained in grumbles when they stepped off the packed marl road with all that gear they had to port through the furnace of afternoon sun.

Spikerush tall as their hip boots bristled in glimmering ripples of heat before them. A ways into the plain, Brady Wiley paused to sniff the rank air. "I smell a 'gator hole," he said, already winded. "Somebody git ready a prodder."

Without slowing down, Chuck Stowell said, "Be hooking them tonight. No use studying no fishy mudhole."

The others all came along, Brady muttering, "Bound to be one." The eldest and biggest of them, he tended to dissemble resentfully when overruled. "Ain't seen enough rain yet. Fish die of the scum till the rains raise them ole 'gator lairs."

"Must be poontang you smell," Price Fenton said, and one or two of them gave lazy sniggers. Stringy, not yet full grown, he was the youngest, but noted for wit. "Them fish ain't dying for rain. Must be some hand's got the farmer's wife out here somewheres."

"'Gator poon all you be sniffing out here," Brady tagged on, and the whole crew, sun weary, let his bruised pride have it end there. Nobody spoke again in all the slog through oozing peat.

When at last they gained the hammock, their swamp buggy was parked hard by, and beside it up on dry ground stood Jessup's gaunt Negro waiting in the shade of bushy cabbage palms. The boys could be sure he had poked his deer rifle around for killer snakes beneath the palmettos.

A man over forty, Ole Black Junn had come up from the runaway slaves, those who fled to these Everglades during the Seminole wars a century ago and found asylum with the Indians. Though black as peat, he bore himself with dignity, wore the simple cloth bandanna some of the Indians still used as a turban, and practiced typical swamp native reticence in the presence of whites. But any demonstration of interest in Seminole lore made him as loquacious as most Negroes of the region tended to be. Unlike most, however, he could be provoked by derision to serious (if restrained) animosity.

Junn had driven the swamp buggy in for them from the Sunniland rental, and would return it in the morning for Jessup to pick him up there. He indicated the galvanized tank of beer on ice in the shade of low palmettos, and turned to a shelter he was constructing for himself of canvas lashed to the palm trunks.

As soon as they dropped their heavy gear, the boys all punched open beer cans and took long swallows with demonstrative gasps of refreshment. Each sank down in the grass and drank ecstatically before any of them thought of offering Junn a can. When chunky Lambert Cordhall did so, the Negro declined with a quick salute of thanks, and continued to work on his shelter.

It made a conversation piece for Guy Helker, who had just dug a bottle out of the supply sack with a mischievous wink at Chuck. Despite the cloudless swelter he said, "Rain coming, Junn?"

"Storm. Smell him northways."

"Naw," Price said, crawling over to a palm trunk, "that's just a field hand's quick ass making breezes."

"Got the farmer's wife out there," Lam drew forth as they laughed. "Don't you smell no poon, Junn?"

The Negro paid a laugh and worked on. Propped back against a tree trunk, Brady said, "Beats me how you can smell a wind sign in this sun."

"His Injun nose," Guy resolved in a drawl even more sluggish than Lambert's, and lazily fended off an insect.

They were all in shade spots, comfortably asprawl. Chuck said, "That Injun sniffer catch any 'gator poon, Junn?"

To their surprise, for it was meant as jest and taken so with laughter, the stooping black man came erect in his threadbare open shirt and turned to point northeast. "Last night they be mating out that way. Echo hanging on the air."

"Sheeeee," Brady exclaimed in irritated disbelief. "You *hear* them hooting and kicking up water *last night?*"

"No, smell. Couple days musk, I shit you not. They be mating around here all week, maybe."

Chuck, creeping on all fours for another beer, stopped to say, "We can catch them mating out that way?"

"Sure, you look for deep water. Maybe a pond some animals dammed up. Streams ain't deep yet."

They all sat up exchanging glances as Junn went back to work on his shelter. "Why," Brady demanded, bristling a little, "didn't you say so right off?"

"Ain't my place if you don't ask."

Price grinned. Placatingly he said, "Soon's a 'gator farts to-night, Brady, you hit him with the spotlight before he can slip it to his poon."

All of them laughed at that except Junn, who had his main sheet lashed horizontal like a roof, and was erecting side flaps of canvas in unanchored fashion. Noticing, Lam said, "Hey, Junn, how come you're fixing to sleep with loose flaps if there's a storm due tonight?"

"Ain't fixing to sleep so, I'mo set so. Best build her like a chickee for storms. You ever hear of hurricane blowing Injun house down? Nosir. Loose walls. Hurricane blow through, all you white men's house blow down."

"Yeah?" Chuck retorted, enjoying the banter. "So how come you go set instead of sleep tonight, you ain't belly scared to blow down?"

"No, I'mo sleep tonight, go set this evening. That be when we gits the storm. Maybe sooner."

"Huh?" Guy was the first to react with words, though all of them had with falling faces. "You mean a big rain's coming and we just setting here?"

"That's it."

"Why'n't you say?" Brady shouted in flushed indignation.

"Ain't my place—"

"If you don't ask," Chuck and Price both finished for Junn, just as simultaneous in their scramble to stow the tank of beer under shade on the swamp buggy deck.

The others were toting equipment to it, Brady saying, "We got to find that mating pond before night, or this growl-ass ole engine scare the 'gators burrowing under. And that fucking coon just lets us set here!"

Junn glanced up with knifing eyes, then turned back to work, with all watching as he said, "You don't own me, mister."

Abruptly, Brady Wiley quit bundling the gear to turn and glare at him gleaming with sweat and affront. He had not yet noticed, but did now, that Junn's rifle lay cradled in the fork of a palmetto log at his elbow. The other boys noticed too, all beady with perspiration. Lambert, arranging supplies in the buggy,

shifted over to interpose himself between Brady and Old Black Junn, Guy joining him in the same precaution, grunting, his color sallow. Chuck laid in all their three rifles distant from Brady, who was stowing the grapple hooks and quarreling with himself. Price sidled over to Junn and said, "Where you guess we best look for alligator ground? I'm asking."

"Out that way I pointed."

"Come on," Chuck said, approaching, "we can bed down early and chow up later." He looked for a hint of approval from Junn, wiping sweat as he said, "We can lash to the buggy and the trees, like we've tented in rains before. We'll just sleep the storm through and be up for a nice night's work."

The Negro kept to his own task without looking up. Price said, "Mr. Jessup gave us these army C-ration cans, Junn. They any good?"

"Vienna sausages my favorite."

"Let's go," Brady called from the driver's seat, with Guy and Lam climbing in. When he gunned the engine, blue herons flew off in the distant sawgrass, two of them soaring from some obscured waterhole in which they had apparently been fishing.

Price hopped aboard saying, "You know any particular place them 'gators poontang in? Sure be nice to surround a whole parcel of them."

Chuck scaled himself up into the buggy one-handed and turned to address Junn, who remained speechless at his work as they got rolling on the bloated huge muck-defying tires. "Folks around here say every Trail and reservation Seminole knows all the mating water in these glades."

Junn looked up to say, "I'm just a coon, myself."

He watched without expression as Chuck hurled his beer can at him in quick fury. It tumbled glinting in the sun but fell far short, where other empties lay for someone to clean up. They made haste to anger, these poor whites, high strung from too much blame to bear for their misery.

Guy hollered, "Get our breakfast early, hear?"

That was the boy he had seen sneaking a hand into the provisions gunny a short while ago, the one who looked sick, as if with a hangover or haunting bad thoughts. Nobody who needed

food had to filch any, so it must have been something else he took. Junn wondered what it could be that made people so dishonest so young. He kept staring after them and beyond at the sultry cypress reaches of the swamp. High over the rattling swamp buggy, egrets swarmed in flight like a sudden blizzard.

Abstracted, Junn said again, "I'm just a coon, myself."

The rain came crashing down. The slender canoe was her umbrella in the storm. Hidden in her poncho under the sheltering live-oak tree, her skirts cradling the supplies compactly between her knees, Majosee remained dry beneath the inverted craft, which deflected whatever the meshing treetops could not hold back of the torrent.

Lightning sheared the air plants branched high up, crackling before her eyes to fork the lettuce lake with a perishing hiss of weird green light, the alligators in that tree-shrouded lagoon electrocuted while mating. She had smelled musk before the freshening rain erased all aromas but its own, and the beasts lay cooked in their passion by the angry sky.

Tumultuous thunder shattered the swamp, and now alligators roared again, several in unison, so they were still alive. Either the lightning had struck a runnel and not the long pond of floats and flags or the great armored reptiles were elsewhere. They barked and they blasted. In the deluge their thunder soared, and as it rattled off to echoes an excited fervor urged her to brave the storm and go investigate the lettuce lake.

But her anchored canoe pitched dangerously above her till the gust passed. Against the trunk of her broad live oak, she yearned to go running in the downpour. But again the wind screamed, the rain lashed, and she had to resist the impulse. That thrashing gale could spin her into thickets of jungled confusion and leave her lost amid giant fern and mossy vine, blundering into trees with all understanding of direction gone.

Even when the gale died out at last, and the rain was a rhythmic drumming on her makeshift roof, she kept herself from venturing forth. The alligators were hooting out their lungs in exultant blasts, and she was anxious to watch them splash through the rites of courtship that dated with them from prehis-

tory. But Majosee compelled herself to wait until the rain only whispered on the overturned floor of her canoe, reduced to a tender sprinkle.

Only then did she dare to lower the vessel over her bundled gear. The storm had passed. It was safe to leave her supplies that way. Though dry inside her poncho, she felt a chill all the way up her legs. But the sun had not yet sunk in the Gulf. She could tell by the light that still haunted the forest floor, and knew the returning heat would soon comfort her.

An alligator bark gave her the way. Raising her skirts, she crossed the wet humus ground with soundless care amid the undergrowth to keep the wary beasts from vanishing. Just as cautiously, she squatted in her tenting poncho at the wooded bank of the lake, and waited, thinking of dreams to occupy herself while the drizzle sang on the lush lettuce floats.

Her father often visited her in dreams, sweeping down as a pelican sometimes, or staring upriver at her as a moonlit boar with sharp young tusks agleam, but he always heartened her before the Milky Way swept him off again and left her to mourn on.

A splash disrupted her reverie. Musk floated heavy over the orchid fragrance of the grove. Another splash, and iridescent foam churned a path of alligators at play, two of them in graceful circles around each other. Then, farther off, another splashing grew turbulent, the near pair swimming toward it, abandoning her to loneliness as the dreams of her father did. He had died of pneumonia in the dry winter bleakness of the swamp. Neither Seminole medicine-bundle dances nor the hospital at Imokalee could save him. She had dreamt of swamp fire raging, to wake and learn of pines actually aflame nearby, the morning the news brought grief.

Shadows stirred on the far bank, crawling animal life that she could not make out clearly. Water rippled there. Then sheet lightning poured an eerie silence of illumination through the treetops; she saw the coy face of a deer—and something more before the blanching light dimmed away. Across the lake two alligators lay half out of the water, side by side on the leafy flags, and one of those animals was stroking the other.

Her fleeting glimpse of a foreleg in short motion told her what it meant. A male was courting a female with strokes to stimulate certain glands. That exercise was common knowledge among swamp people, but she had personally witnessed it never before. Again the water tossed under nearby lettuce floats—another pair, an earlier stage of courtship.

She rose to leave on noiseless feet, making her way tree by vine-tangled tree around to the other side of the pond. There in the gloaming she found the breeding couple (male so much larger than female), and stopped behind the trees to lean on one, watching. Stolidly the engrossment proceeded in utter stillness, where not even an insect chirruped, one rough beast fondling the other with strokes on the gnarly rump from time to time.

At length, when the light was sinking away to purplish gloom, the female arched her heavy tail, raising it out of the water. Twice the distant sheet lightning flashed pale radiance over this astonishing spectacle while the male elevated his tail to press it against the female's in a deft slide that turned her slightly toward him. With both forelimbs pressing her down by the neck, he drew back his tail, the great length of it slithering down under, then came around to face her in a closer flash of lightning soon followed by a frightful sizzling crash overhead.

In that brief light the female threw her jaws apart, and creaking groans escaped her. At once the male seemed to lock his jaws with hers. There was a splash in the half-lit lettuce lake, a thrust, and they were engaged below as well, the female arching her tail higher, the male sinking deeper beneath her with booming roars that reverberated through the forest like a clatter of tin pans. In burbling froth he lurched to better penetrate her, and roared again. How exciting nature was, the world in its millions of years! Dusk was gathering a blue mist around the animals where they lay copulating in the shallows. Fireflies danced in the heavy-hanging vapors of musk.

Briskly the other pair of reptiles swam closer by. In a flash of lightning, silent with distance again, she saw one of them blow a necklace of bubbles around the other's head in primitive ritual before the lake fell altogether still again. She could see the slightest activity, and in a while more of it at the embankment as the alligators came apart, the female to crawl ashore, the male to

turn half around and splash shallow water seeking a comfortable place to rest.

The light rain had stopped, but remote thunder suggested a possible mere lull before another storm. Still, she held her ground between the trees, waiting to see if there might be further mating to tell her aunts about. She was warm again. The chill was gone.

All at once the reposing couple grew active, the big male lunging to splash away under water, the female spinning around as swiftly into the lake. Lettuce floats exploded, and the next moment there was not a ripple in the leafy spread. The other courting beasts had also disappeared, the surface of the lake completely calm, as if no life had moved there all this evening long. She had heard nothing in the somber flavor of the grove, but the ears of alligators were said to be acutely sensitive. They had received a message of danger.

Majosee was cold again, but now with fear.

The boys came upon a cabbage palm with its heart torn out, evidence that black bears were about. They were sure because bear craved palm bud more than anything, so the five bypassed that hammock though hints of musk cloyed the air.

Their rifles could handle the big blacks, but much as they relished hunting down a quarter-tonner, there was just no time with a storm coming. "Besides," Brady admonished, "we're here for business, not sport."

So they growled on at a crawl in the pitching swamp buggy, through plashy open cypress marsh until they heard an alligator roar beyond a piney copse. Dark cumulus roiled toward them south across the glowering sky, and thunder erupted nearby. With dry wood to gather in a hurry, they stopped on high ground to look amid the outer trees of a hammock, and that was where they pitched their tent to bed down through the rainstorm close upon them. Again alligator voices sounded, heartening them before they fell off at last in beer-heavy slumber.

There was still some light when Guy, his sleep made fitful by the storm, roused everybody digging around for the bottle of corn whisky he had stolen from Junn. The western sky burned with flaming sunset streaks of cloud, which reflected light

enough to show them good ground for their campfire. In the bathed air not even the vanilla perfume of orchid laced the green bouquet, much less the exuded scent of musk. But they were only minutes awake, still comparing erections, when the earth shuddered to multiple roars that meant a colony of alligators for sure, deeper in the jungly groves.

"Man," Chuck said in his exuberance, "I'd sooner fuck one than cut her belly off. Swamp's enough to make a toad horny. You all hold her down for me, I'mo put it to a 'gator tonight."

"You won't be the first," Price took down the whisky bottle to say. "I hear they're good jelly."

In the laughter, in the drinking, Brady Wiley muttered something hostile. None was sure, but all of them later agreed it seemed like, "I'mo kill that uppity nigger Junn."

They boiled the C-ration cans in marsh water, using a kettle that was Government Issue like their tent and everything else old Jessup provided. At his age he was no ex-serviceman, but army surplus was still available and cheap, those short years after the war. Everybody in the region took advantage of that, even the Indians. Even Majosee, at the other end of this dense hammock, had a little GI gasoline stove to pump up for cooking her *sofkee* coontie meal.

After the chilling storm, she cared for something hot to go with the dried venison she must eat in the absence of fresh fish, and supposed she could chance the modest stove light to eat by in the night the trees had enclosed around her.

It was just as well, she reasoned, that depths sufficient to fish in were not to be found that day. The abrupt fright of the alligators had cautioned her against more complicated cooking. Probably the beasts had reacted to an engine cough from some swamp buggy or airboat passing far off, but if people were indeed nearby she wished no part of them. They were likeliest to be white men (if not the mad swamp derelicts whose presence disobedient children were threatened with but never managed to see). Majosee was not about to spice up the air with frying odors or noise it with busy wash-up chores to attract the deceptive pale ruiners.

Instead she decided to turn off the burner and have even the coontie porridge in darkness with her pemmican. She was long accustomed to the Big Cypress hushes, but this night the occasional slither of life gave her a start. Underbrush and fallen buds were so soon dry around her, as though it had not rained for hours. But rather than chance a misstep, going to the lake, she used drinking water to wash her pot and brush her teeth.

Then, bedding down in the canoe, she kept her cane fishing spear with her in case of danger. The breath of the green night was minty. She looked up at the oversized orchid air plants that dominated the aromas, and listened for the life they teemed with. But not an insect sang, no lizard or bird made a flurry. The night was a canopy of tiny blue windows through which she searched, hoping to see the bright moonflowers bloom.

Long before the moon rose, however, she was fast asleep, dreaming of children and swamp birds until there came a scream, followed by an angry splashing of water. By outcries in frenzy, in wild laughter. By gunshots that told her she was no longer dreaming. The moon was high. The flowers had blossomed red and yellow by the dozens. Echoing back, the exchanges were in harsh clear American.

"He snapped at me, the fucker! Git a rifle, a rifle!"

"Hee-hee, you dronk, Chuck, hook him!"

"Hook him? He's gone under. Shoot! Shoot, I tell you! Gimme that rifle!"

Then the shots. More drunken laughter and raillery. She saw the beam of a spotlight sweep past, and suppressed a compulsion to leap from the canoe and escape. It would be a mistake to run. She would only go stumbling through the brush until vines seized her for the hideous poachers. But it would also be a mistake to stay and let them find her. She tried to still the heavy pitch of her breathing. Their coarse shouts crashed and echoed. She clutched the slender spear at her side as the intruders laughed.

"Prod here," Brady Wiley said with the spotlight on a runnel the storm had raised out of the lettuce lake, and Guy speared a long rod down to dig around while the others prattled and

laughed. "He's stirring, stirring," Brady called out, "bring that hook!"

Price brought the grapple. Chuck came along with the rifle, babbling. "Don't nobody git in that water. Maybe the storm drove them all stark. Other one tried to eat me in that lake, I swear."

"This one's tame," Brady said evenly. "This one just sucking hook. Feel him, Guy? Don't you have him yet?"

"No, ain't no—yeah, hoo-hoo, I do think—lookee!"

An alligator heaved huge and slow in the stream. Brady blazed his spotlight full in its face, leaping the freshet. The reptile froze in paralyzed confusion, blinded for the second it took Price to sweep the grapple hook under and pull. A roaring tempest blared out of the cavernous open jaws, and blood gorged the watercourse.

The prey was perfectly captured by a pair of the four tusklike prongs up into the throat. Guy withdrew the prod to drop it and help haul on the grapple as everyone gibbered in excitement. With a skinning knife in one hand and the corn bottle in his other, Lam said, "One more swig and I'll carve his vest off."

They hauled the beast ashore, belly up in the light Brady kept on it, Chuck saying, "Wiley, you getting brains the size of your balls. You all see him reckon they'd be trying to light out of that lake?"

"You just sucking up to make me let you fuck it."

Easily a dozen feet long, it was obviously a male. "Let's see his cock," Chuck said, and fired a shot that penetrated the brain from below.

A shudder traveled down the length of the animal, and it fell still. "They keep it right in their sink hole," Brady explained. "Turned inside out, till they gits horny. So you can fuck this great big one, little brother, if you're still a mind to. Don't matter he's a boy."

"No wonder I never could find their cock," Majosee heard, trapped in the narrow canoe. Lying there, she heard the same sleepy voice say, "Start skinning, Lam," and with nausea she pictured the knife entering flesh to emerge with a gush of blood, flashing in and out in the fixed beam of light, in and out around

the rim of the scaled crocodilian belly until all the thick under-skin was carved away to the tip of the huge long tail.

She had seen Seminole trappers skin them and bury the remains, but these would be left for the sun and buzzards in the white man's heedless way. And the same awaited her body once they were done with it. In a blend of visions that seemed like madness she saw the alligator give its seed to the female and its skin and its life to the white men. The candy sweetness of the grove seemed like madness. A thousand animals crawled secretly in the air plants, witnessing in silence overhead, and it seemed a madness in the drunken laughter of men who now had another animal trapped. She heard a mighty creature roar in agony and extinction. She must escape and yet must stay unmoving. She was Seminole hunted by whites once again and must not cry out. She heard their speech coming nearer. She watched the moonflowers bloom, in a madness of waiting breathless for calamity.

They surely had the run that alligators were using to escape the lake, and a third one was on their hook. Guy and Chuck gave a simultaneous heave to ground it, then Brady almost lost the spotlight in a lunge to keep Price from pumping a shot at the lumpy head. "Not on top, little brother. That could ricochet. I've seen that happen."

Laughing, they flipped the beast over to writhe in painful frenzy till Price shot it. All of them laughed, but none so explosively as Brady, who went whirling around in a circle that shafted light every way in the grove. "Man, I bet we haul in a dozen! We be richer than ole—"

A heart-stopping shriek pierced the night, an animal reaction to light abruptly penetrating its refuge, and Brady whipped the spotlight beam in that direction as Guy cried, "Cougar! Come on, we bag us a swamp lion! Git the rifles!"

"Now I told you," Brady scolded, bringing the light around in Guy's face. "We here for business, not sport."

Warding off the light, Guy shouted, "Don't be third-degreeing me, you fucker! That skin'll sell too."

"Git the rifles," Brady said. "Long as it's business."

*　　*　　*

She heard them laugh, the menace of it receding. So was the beam of light. Risking a look, she rose up just enough to flip herself out of the canoe. An owl had screeched, not a panther, but that was just as well: it had drawn the men off. The ground was dappled with moonlight in random patches that she evaded with a tread of grueling delay to maintain silence. Only a slow probing step could guide her around the pitfalls of the dark.

An animal came crashing by in panic, a deer no doubt, and terror goaded her to run as well. But she knew better. The voices were returning. Sudden light flung her shadow on a tree so she dropped straight down. The spear was in her hand. They had rifles. Seated there in the dark of the forest night, she took the spear in both hands and held its point at her heart.

Someone said, "That cat's in there. I seen her go."

Bullets—they might start shooting at shadows. She fell to her back with the spear at her breast, and shrank low to keep the prying finger of light from discovering her. She was afraid for her life, yet to take it aimed the spear. Life and death were fighting for her body, her two souls in conflict. She was Seminole, a history of persecution by Americans, but unlike them aware one had two souls.

Majosee cast the spear aside even before the ominous quiet reached her consciousness. It was her unvirtuous soul that wished to escape through suicide, the weaker side of her without heed of the grief it would cause her loved ones. The silence dawned on her then, and its meaning seared like flame. They had fallen quiet, the treacherous whites, because they sensed a life at bay.

Light burst upon the nearest trees, and vanished. What had alerted them, she did not know, but her mind saw them stalking, signaling each other for quiet.

Again light flared, then the dark returned.

Something heavy plunged by, a raccoon perhaps, making its own escape from the lake. In a vision she saw them skinning her, and began to pray. She prayed to the Great Spirit for deliverance, by the Seminole name Fishaki Omechi and by the name Jehovah, called God of all by the white mission school, and

prayed to His son in His name. And a supreme light suddenly enveloped her like the whitest center of heaven.

But it was not deliverance.

"Hoo-eeee!"

"Poonnnn-tang!"

Those were the kinds of cries they blew out.

"Wawww let me at that swamp meat!"

"Hey, ain't you just a mind for business no more?"

"Hee-har, out the fucking way, little brother!"

Those were the barbarities Americans fumed in violent light before their hands and their odors overwhelmed her.

Poachers barked at her face the stench of sweat and alcohol. Her screams were of rage, their wallops acknowledged that. She sank teeth into them and their mouths bellowed and their knuckles cracked her skull. A shout brought the dizzy lamp reeling back to blind her till her own skirts covered her eyes, the finger of light searching under to stab inside her.

Majosee screamed at groping hands that clawed all the parts of her in a lashing cold waterfall of evil. All the many colors she had sewn with her mother shredded in their hands. Gouging fingers cleaved her thighs, she was apart, and that made the white men laugh.

Without breath she heard them quarrel in wet gurgles. A tree fell on her in the maelstrom. A gigantic animal called her a split-tail and threatened her life. The beast shoved a serrated knife inside to skin her. A blade for alligators went thrusting inside her, shearing in and out and in, and they were cheering. Majosee was in their laughter in the eddies. She was a grotesque reptile being skinned and seeded by them all. Majosee closed her jaws on devil men who beat her face while seeding her in and out and in. Weird birds came beating down, foul smelling, the vultures now for her remains beneath the sun.

With her last breath she prayed to Satan. Only for vengeance she prayed in the ebb of her life.

Whisky revived her. Majosee retched and they laughed in the callous lamplight. They went inside Majosee again on her blanket. They kept drinking and skinning and smelling vulturous in

and out of Majosee all night until the owl said, "Bawk," remotely, "bawk," somewhere far, "bawk," as always, the barred owl, "baw-coo."

Another replied closer by: "Bawk . . . bawk . . . bawk . . . baw-coo." That meant the night was over. Someone called away the demon still seeding her sleep.

"Bring that swamp meat over," Lam Cordhall said. "Brady wants her."

"Can't you see we're busy?" Guy Helker complained, half in slumber as he worked his hips at the girl.

Lam turned away to Brady Wiley who, leaning back on a poisonwood tree with the corn bottle dangling empty from his hand, gave a weary moan and said, "What we go do with her?"

The hulk of a man looked strange, as if his mind was off, so Lambert said, "I don't feel all there myself."

"Make sense, will you, Lam."

"That was a crocodile," Chuck Stowell said, coming behind them from the lake with a rifle. "Wasn't it, Price?"

The other two looked but saw no Price Fenton. All three of them stood scratching their heads in speechless awe till Lambert said, "I think chloroform was in that booze."

"No, that was a crocodile, not no alligator, chopped at me in the lake. We just seen it, I tell you."

Price came along then, saying, "How you figure a croc to be up around here?"

Brady said, "Why'n't you hook it or shoot it, one?"

"Well," Chuck earnestly replied, "we had no grapple, was scared of ricochet, and couldn't seem to aim this rifle, neither one of us."

"A croc, sure enough?" Brady murmured, then stood there musing with them all. At length he said, "Go git him off of her. We soon see if that's a croc."

Lambert took Price to help him yank Guy down by the ankles, the chunky youth saying, "Eat some, fucker, and tell us how swamp jelly tastes."

Chuck stood by with Brady, who said, as Guy stood up, "Just haul her along by the blanket. Let's go."

Guy left that for the rest of them to do and lumbered along

with Brady, rigid like him at a sleepwalker's pace in front of the others. "What you carrying that empty for?"

Brady looked down at the bottle. "It's just in my hand." He meditated a while as they neared the lake. "I think maybe there was chloroform. Look at you, your cock's still out. Where'd you git this panther piss?"

"Took it off of Junn," Guy said, putting his fly together. "His Injun blood, booze bad for him."

"Worse for us. I'm sure go kill that smart ole nigger now."

"Shee, Brady, it never doped us off of this here poontang. Must've fucked her five times myself."

"That's just it. Now we got her on our hands, thanks to that ole Injun coon."

Guy, disinclined to reason that out aloud, stood rubbing his face briskly where Brady paused to stare at the lettuce lake with the bottle dangling in his hand. When Price called his name he turned slowly, and gazed the same bleary way at the naked girl on the decorated Indian blanket. Her breasts rose and fell in the heaviest rhythm of sleep, though the three had dragged her all the way. Her face showed severe abrasions.

"You all know," Brady Wiley said, "we can't let her just go and tell her tales."

They all hung there stupefied in the morning fog, immobile with a drugged kind of lethargy. Chuck said, "Over there's where the croc was."

"Hold it," Price said, "don't nobody move, there's a rabbit."

Amid the purple hyacinths crowding the opposite bank, a stout rabbit scampered to nibble at lime-green flags that climbed the shore. It seemed odd for a grown rabbit to be so courageous, even at the far range it enjoyed from the boys, but the entire morning had the disoriented quality of nightmare for them all.

They watched in common stupor. As they did, there was motion in the water, so noiseless and smooth that the rabbit, the most high-strung mammal of the swamp, failed to sense the open jaws that rose to go sawing at the shoreline and scoop the creature away for a meal. The crunch of its skull was audible over the lake.

"You see the narrow snout?" Chuck said. "That's a crocodile. That's a man-eater, like to chop me up in there last night."

Turning for the reaction of Brady, they found him kneeling between the swamp girl's legs. He was committing an act there with the bottle that none of them could excuse, and they protested with sleepy disgust. "All business last night," Price Fenton said, "and just an ole playboy now."

Heedless, Brady stood up and heaved the bottle across the lettuce lake where the crocodile lurked. "Let him whet on that man sauce." He began to haul the girl on her blanket. "Some of you help. We got chores. Hides to pack, a tent to strike. Let's go. That black Injun better have breakfast fixed, we gits there."

Chuck helped. Guy and Lam too. Price went along with the rifle as they made a sack of the Indian blanket and carried her in it, dead still, to the other side of the lake. There, without a word between any of them, they heaved her in.

The instant she splashed water all of them turned away, Brady dragging the blanket as he led them back around to the equipment. There they turned to watch her stir and rise up on her hands and knees. They watched her creep that way through the shallows, to fall at last in the greens choked by hyacinth at the shore. She lay there unmoving, unconscious.

"This ain't right," Price said.

Nobody responded. Soon the water splashed amid the lettuce floats. A mammoth length of armor streaked toward the Seminole girl. The five boys stood in frozen witness halfway around the lake as the great crocodile crawled ashore. It stopped alongside the girl lying naked on her face. The beast was immense, close to three times her length, though half of that was tail.

All watched jaws the length of her torso open wide and take her head. The crocodile pinned her down with a foreleg. Her head lay lost within the huge meaty gullet of scales, which throbbed obscenely in the haze of rising sun.

All of them stood rooted like the trees, in a pitch of disquieted breathing. The beast lay poised, as if too wary of probable interference to start eating her down from the head. Yet it seemed an animal strangely without caution, unafraid.

They could see the ravenous teeth at the flesh of her neck. Price lifted the rifle, but lowered it when Brady and Chuck turned to look. Then all watched the lake, uttering not a word.

The crocodile could take her as it did the rabbit, at a swallow, but moved not a sinew in its massive body.

They heard the owl go "Bawk . . . bawk . . . bawk . . . baw-coo."

Nothing more could be heard in the forest of hazy green murk until the answering call came dolefully and faded off to lasting silence. "Bawk . . . bawk . . . bawk . . . baw-coo."

Then they saw, all of them later said they saw, the colossal reptile sweep its tail under the girl in the shallows. They said they saw the lettuce leaves flutter in the lake around her, some kind of current rolling her body slightly about to face the scaly monstrosity. And they saw her moccasined foot sail out of the water. Her upper leg rose, dripping water, right out of the lake with a dancer's unhurried grace. Supporting it, the great gnarled tail uncoiled and swept behind her, the rump surging after it between her legs in a broil of foam. They were sure they saw this, and saw her knee bend, sliding up to rest on the armor mass.

The jaws of the crocodile yawned. Her head emerged, and the Indian girl seemed to glance around as a stormy low rumble came up from the bowels of the beast. She curved her arm over the gross gray reptile just as it gave a lurch beneath her with a roar, and they thought she spoke to it, holding on, gripping the crocodile in the haze where moths and butterflies fluttered.

Her hand had touched none of them all night, but she held the enormous prehistoric monster, her hips moving on a current in the shallows, back and forth.

COLLAGE 2

Under the dawning sky, where night lingered amid the dense broadleaf trees, animals drew near the bacon crackling in Junn's skillet. The aroma brought even herbivores close, one deer staring until a panther came with cat eyes glinting.

"Every creature aspires," Junn mused aloud in his campfire glow. "I think they like to be men if they could."

A raccoon scurried through the brush, anxious to pick at any garbage set aside. Junn loved the swamp. And he loved the unmeddling night, its chill and its danger included. He loved his days too, but less well. The night teemed with living mystery. It whispered the final secret of nature, in a voice no one could hear.

The swamp buggy came growling to a stop in the bog beyond. Soon the five boys emerged from the darkness, glum and wary like the forest beasts their noise had scattered. Crouching around the fire, they had nothing to say, and Junn sensed trouble.

Jubilation should attend a catch like theirs, he thought, hauling utensils out of the buggy to wash. Yet they ate their fruits
and passed the scrambled eggs around in silence. Even if they
had drunk down all the devil's eye that Guy had stolen from
him, there were enough of them to have spread thin its possible
effects. Still, they were young, and might have suffered frightful
hallucinations. All through breakfast they exchanged not a
word.

Coffee brought talk at last, and it was addressed to Junn.
While most kept their eyes down on the fire, Guy Helker said
they had a favor to ask him. All but the biggest one kept their
eyes averted. With the single-purpose glimmering eyes of the
panther a short while back, Brady Wiley watched him as the
other boy continued: "You just got to help us, Junn. There's a
man-eating croc up in there."

"It nearly got me," Chuck Stowell looked up to say as Brady
stared. "Like to kill me with one chaw right in that there lettuce
lake."

Junn detected malice in the attention Brady kept fixed on him
as Price Fenton said without looking up, "He ain't just whistling, Junn. That was a crocodile. We all seen it."

"We all seen it poon a swamp girl," Lambert Cordhall added,
poking a stick at the fire.

"We seen it eat her too."

Brady's voice at last, the malice unmistakable. While the others asked Junn's forbearance and belief, each on a humble note
in his voice, the big fellow's contribution was a challenge, daring Junn to contradict. Accustomed to the naked arrogance
some kinds of white people resorted to when in the wrong, he
carefully avoided giving any skeptical sign, but allowed himself
to suspect that some or all of them had committed a serious
infraction. Why they should care to invent a crocodile in these
hammocks he was willing to wait and see.

"We seen it drag her down under the lettuce floats," Brady
went on—growing angry, it seemed, as Junn stared. "It ate her
down under there."

"Well, we didn't see that for sure," Chuck said. "We seen it
drag her under, but we didn't see no eating down under."

That brought a resentful grimace from Brady. But Chuck, while not quite the same powerful size, looked almost as dangerous as Brady, who swung his hostile gaze back on Junn as Price offered, "We just reckon that. She never did come up."

"Nor did that crocodile," Brady said, glaring. "No doubt it ate her."

Junn had eaten earlier, but poured himself more coffee to stay busy as they circled up to what they wanted of him. He saw Brady becoming angrier, but said nothing.

"We seen it split her tail," Lambert put in, glancing at each of them over his cup. "Ain't that so?"

"Sure seemed that way," Guy said. "Didn't it, Chuck?"

"Ain't you go speak when you're spoken to?" Brady demanded of Junn, his eyes aswarm with venomous lights.

"Ain't you all sure of what you seen?"

All of them turned now to stare at him. Price Fenton said, "Junn, that was a croc for sure. And by God I do believe we seen it spread and fuck that Injun gal."

"Little bitty croc?" he ventured.

"No, big as a plow horse," Guy said. "Still and yet it put the root to her. Least it looked that way."

"You right close by?" Junn asked. "In good light?"

"Well, no," Price admitted. "Across the lake. In dawn haze. But it ain't likely to be otherwise if we all seen the same."

"How you sure you all seen the same?"

"We told it the same," Chuck said, losing patience. "All of us said the same."

"You all of you drink that devil's eye of mine?"

"What difference does that make?" Brady shouted, his impatience blistering, as the others gave contrite smiles.

"Difference, potion go in devil's eye. Difference, you got cactus and Injun black tea, other stuffs too. Make you see goats talk, and your mama come back from heaven to say hey, her face close enough to kiss, you a mind to. Put you in a rainbow, you never seen such colors on this earth. Difference, you see what a body tell you to, he been drinking devil's eye with you."

They all traded bewildered glances. Then Brady engaged him with a slow, deliberate malevolence. "I was fixing to kill you, nigger. Still a mind to. What you think of that?"

The others, to a man, cast down their eyes. It plainly meant that, while none was taking part in the threat, all were standing behind it, or at least out of its way. Something very dire was afoot, and it didn't take much thought to recognize that the swamp girl was at the center of it. Fearing the worst for her, whoever she might be, Junn said, "Well, Mr. Brady, can't say I thinks too highly of that."

It brought weak laughter from all but the big Wiley boy, who went on in a chilling tone of pure white hate to say, "You the most uppity, black-bellied, mammy-hopping coon I ever did see. You think you something. Well, I'mo kill you, Ole Black Junn, sure as peat burns in winter. Less you do us a chore we needs real bad, hear?"

"I hears you," he said straight out, not bothering to grab at straws by looking at the others. "What can I do for you genamens?"

"Junn," Price came up earnestly, "we got to be sure no part of that girl shows up in that lake."

"Don't ask no questions, Junn," Chuck said. "Just you please go and see that croc ain't let no arm or foot slip out his jaws to go floating around."

"We trust you," Guy said, "to see to that for us."

"Especially no other part of her," Lam Cordhall snuffled, and Junn knew they had raped an Indian girl. He knew they had brutalized her and were fearful the evidence might show in her face or pelvis if their own butchering surfaced or the beast they represented as a crocodile left remains.

"Sometimes a crocodile come up from the mangroves," he said. "Heard tell of that. Sometimes they spawn in a woman, so the Alachua used to say. Alachua make this legend, say a reptile man be coming back to make war again on white folks, animal and Injun go against the whites. But Mikasuki say that type all gone to Oklahoma, they own legend say that."

Wagging his head in irate disbelief, Brady said, "What the damn hell you going on about?"

But Price was quick to say indulgently, "What's Alachua, Junn, some tribe? Heard of a county, that name, town too, I think, away upland."

"Yes, old tribe in these parts. Thems, and Mikasukis, some

Creeks, others too, they all come to be called Seminole. That word mean hankering for freedom, something like that."

Brady Wiley stood up. "Let's go. You drop us and the catch on the highway, then take the buggy to Sunniland as usual."

"Only you stop off at that hardwood first," Chuck instructed, standing up with the others, "and poke out the lettuce lake."

"And Mr. Jessup," Price finished, "be waiting at the rental to pick you up and come take us all to Naples, git our cash, as usual. Nothing to it, Junn."

"You dead man 'less you do," Brady said in cold simplicity.

"Nothing to it," Junn echoed like the good nigger they needed so badly. He had no other choice. Not at the moment, anyway. They had raped that girl and killed her. He believed they had made up or hallucinated the crocodile.

Some mourning doves skimmed away before him, pink and gray. They were the only life Junn saw aside from insects after pitching through the cypress head in the snarling swamp buggy. Yet, along with a thin metal prod, he took his deer rifle up into the hammock, because there were wildcat tracks in the bog.

It was good to be distant from those boys. The morning sun baked a candy flavor to the air plants. He hoped his lot would not be to discover the dismembered parts of that girl. He hoped he would not have to bury human remains. And even as the thought reared in his mind, an odor came to weigh down his heart in disgust. It was decay, so soon in this oven of a swamp.

But that was alligator flesh decomposing. He saw the scatter of carcasses, and looked up to see if the scent had attracted vultures yet. He could not find the sky, however. Even there at the lake the overhead was too dense with spreading fronds and new broadleaf. Junn peered along the surface of green floats, but saw no sign of life or death.

Musk was faint in the air, shrouded by the sweltry breath of orchid and fern and mulberry spice. Halfheartedly he tried the prod under some lettuce floats. Five criminals overtaken by a horror of justice on their way back to breakfast had imposed an impossible job on him. Something else vexed Junn too, and he quickly surmised it to be the absence of animal life that would normally be astir near the lake.

Not a lizard or turtle foraged anywhere. Only the flies and grasshoppers were visible. (He heard a katydid.) Alligators were probably lurking under the floats. Maybe there was a crocodile in fact. And the possibility of water moccasins lurking made him all the more afraid of the lake. Yet he went wading in.

Something shifted in the lettuce floats a ways off. He believed his eyes had caught something, and forded in its general direction, holding the rifle high, his prod with it, though not in the way of the trigger. Then he saw it for sure. Life was there beneath the floats. Quickly he speared the prod to the shore and prepared the rifle for swift shooting at the eye of anything that came on. The presence of a crocodile did seem farfetched, but he could not gamble to see if it was only an alligator, should some saurian blunder his way.

And there it came, a long gnarled sweep of armor bearing leaf and foam toward him. He aimed, but the beast went under, spinning away. Junn backed off, and still it made a pass his way so that again he pointed the rifle. Again the reptile dived, spinning away remotely to its original hiding place. Junn turned to get out of the lake in haste. But before he was full around he saw something that made him cry out with a startled gasp.

A girl's face had raised itself to him, then fell out of view again like a hideous ghost beneath the drifting verdure. And just then a cat screamed and the air thrummed to the beating of wings, branches snapping overhead, air plants erupting in a shower of insects and petals and fragrance.

Chilled to the heart, Junn hauled himself ashore, conscious without seeing them that buzzards were descending, and then he saw them over the lake. The girl was dead, he reasoned, and an alligator was feeding on her jealously enough to ward him off with sallies. Or a crocodile, for it was a monster of a beast that leaped in a high splash to scare off three ugly vultures. He thought he saw a head too long and narrow-snouted to be an alligator's. But the angle was an underbelly one: Junn realized he might be seeing what the story of the boys suggested he see. The vultures kept circling out of curiosity, then swept away and plummeted to vanish among the carcasses.

He had seen a girl's face, and it was hard to back away. There was nothing so ghastly in his memory as that death

mask in dripping lettuce leaves. Impulse pressed him to defy the boys and leave them to the judgment of fortune. But he looked again for signs of the girl in the lake. Not in obedience to their command that he erase the evidence of murder, he knew it could not be that, yet he looked. The animal might indeed be a crocodile that, in strange vindication of legend, had spawned in the girl and was compelled by instinct to safeguard her pitiful remains.

Junn got his rifle set and, without knowing why he should do battle for the corpse of a stranger, forged into the lettuce lake once again.

The girl was alive. She was whole. There were no open wounds to be seen. It was time to go against those boys.

Junn felt strong enough to do so. The reptile had retreated from him and surrendered her. Even the flock of buzzards, grown to six among the carcasses, had soared in grumbling flight from him when he carried her past to shelter. He could face down five boys. As long as he never let them surround him again in the swamp at a distance from his rifle.

Such boys were harder to understand than the animal. Whether crocodile or alligator, it might have kept the girl from sinking in her misty lettuce bower. It had not mauled her at all. Thus, with the big reptile having made slithery long passes against him twice, she was clearly something more to it than just a meal. What, he could never more than guess, but it seemed unreasonable to dismiss the mysterious just because fathoming it was beyond him. Junn wrapped the blanket around her.

In cowardly flight like the buzzards, they had left her blanket on the shore. They had overlooked her canoe and supplies, evidence enough to incriminate them had she vanished in fact. But they had their nigger to send back to pick the area clean like the vultures returning now to carrion. Only he was delivering instead of burying her, and took pleasure in that. As they waited on the far highway for Jessup to bring him from the rental, he could ravish her ripe young body to their blame, but he was a man and not a buzzard. Nature had made him so without teaching him why, yet he took pride.

Junn cooked her a porridge on the little pump stove. Let the white boys make carrion, and let the buzzards partake. Not Junn. She was not yet back in the world when he fed her the hot *sofkee*, but her eyes tried to make sense of him. It was hardship for her to take the spoon, but her eyes were knowing, and trustful. She could tell he was there to help.

But when memory attacked her she sank to hysterical tremors. Torment came back to her before his eyes. The white boys were upon her again and there was little more he could do than pat her hand to assure her the incident was over, little more he could have done had he been present at the outrage. "I would have shot them dead," he heard himself cry out, and though horror remained in her eyes, she fell calm at the sound of his voice.

She was not about to start screaming like the abundant birds. Huddled in the blanket, she held onto his hand with both of hers —soft long hands as chilled as river stones despite the swamp heat of morning. He poured coffee into his tin cup and placed it in her hands to warm them. Then as she drank, propped up against his side, he got the response of a nod when he showed her the pieces of varicolored fabric he had found nearby. But she shook her head when Junn said he could make her skirt complete again.

Thinking her confused, he said, "I got stuff to sew with. Made of so many pretty cloths, it come apart natural at the seams."

The blouse, he told her as she sipped coffee, would be more difficult, but he could sew that too, if not as neatly. The day was too hot for her poncho, and she would not want to arrive home wearing a shirt of his. Again she shook her head. He told her of the swamp buggy he had for an easy ride to the reservation or the Trail, wherever she lived, but she shook her head. It was just to soothe her that he spoke at all, but she raised a troubled glance.

"No." Her voice was hoarse, as if with a cold, and frail. "Not to my family." Her lips were cut, swollen. "I can't."

"Why is that, little friend?"

"They see me, they'll know."

"Well, you bound to tell them. They ought to know."

"No. You remember bad time once about cattle ticks? I tell them without bad men in jail, and maybe a war start."

A swamp buggy in Keyport, the county seat, was an uncommon sight. It could only mean some kind of emergency, grinding down the pretty boulevard. Of those who were up and about, so early in the morning, an old woman waiting for the post office to open and the bread man beside his truck were moved to go over and inquire. They discovered a reticent Negro and a badly bruised Indian girl who, hiding in her blanket, said right out that five boys had raped her in the swamp and she needed the Sheriff's Office.

"Oh, my goodness," the bread man said.

"White boys?" asked the old woman.

"Animals," Majosee replied, her mind still drowning in lettuce leaves and reptiles.

The white people provided directions to the courthouse, asking other questions next, but with an apology Junn drove off. "That's what you get," the bread man called after them, "for poaching bird feathers, you Injuns!"

Junn was not inclined to dispute her, yet Majosee knew he thought her unwise. Or too muddled by the atrocity to think right. Her mind kept floating in time as though in a pool of oil, but she was not deranged. They had left a serpent of bitter fear within her, but she would not let it consume her.

He had advised her to rest deep amid the gumbo-limbos and myrsines of the dense hammock, where she might sew while he fished and gathered provender to replenish her. But she wanted her clothes in shreds, and explained that.

With wary eyes he pondered it, knowing she had no intention of bringing evidence to her people. "You mean," he asked in awe, "to tell the white folks?"

"Have to see those evil boys arrested."

"You expect the Sheriff do that?"

"We been made American citizens a long time now."

"Not so you'd notice, little friend."

He was black and had meant black. She was Seminole and had meant Seminole, not citizens as long as the black people, but

more with the strength of it in their unity. It was from this same Keyport that white men recently invaded the reservation with guns to kill the deer they blamed for the cattle-tick infestation, and armed men of her people had stood them off. Indian men had risen to defend their chief game, to save their sole insurance against hunger from being annihilated on a suspicion, until the U.S. government itself brought proof that countless animals as well as the deer harbored the cattle-killing tick. The Seminole were respected as citizens. The Sheriff could not deny her recourse to the law and tempt a reaction from her people.

Junn had insisted on remaining to protect her if she wished to stay in the wilderness until well enough to see the white authorities. Too clouded to fathom how he knew all that had befallen her, she presently got the answer from him, with the very names of those who had let on their crime to him. It made her sick to hear what she already knew. It made her dizzy to rise and climb aboard the swamp buggy. Then, on the way, when the crocodile returned to invade her dozing, he mentioned the beast. Or maybe it was his mentioning it that brought the gigantic reptile back to mind with a roar of lust that she answered with horrified whimpers.

"You see any crocodile?" was what she had heard him say, driving the swamp buggy here to Keyport.

"I dreamt one had me in its mouth. Oh, God, how you come to know that?"

"Crocodile sure enough? Not no alligator?"

"Crocodile. So big. They talk about one in the night. Then they all go together in my dream, they all turn into crocodile inside me."

She felt herself fainting away. He offered his Swamptown shack to recover in, but she said no. She was shivering, they were driving in Keyport, he said, "You take any devil's eye? You drink they whisky?"

"Devil's eye? Yes, they put whisky in me. They woken me with some, splash it down my mouth." The quaking intensified, with nausea. "Devil's eye? Why you say that?"

"Kind of whisky we calls that in Swamptown. Who keep you from going under in that lake?"

"Why, that was you," she said, though she remembered praying to the Devil and seeing his enormous eye in the lettuce leaves. She remembered praying to Satan for vengeance when God failed her plea for salvation, but she said, "You," and began to swoon beside him in a vaporous well of confusion. Why did he ask? He had rescued her from the crocodile lake. She recalled that very well, and went drowning in the rainy slough of her mind.

But that was not Junn before her, asking, that was a white pair. So she tried to tell the man and woman the kind that had raped her, but heard herself blaming crocodiles instead, or reptiles, or animals, and heard somebody blame bird feathers as Junn drove off in escape from white vituperation.

There were girls as sweet as Majosee in Swamptown. Even some who, having worked as maids in towns like Hammerhead and Wildcat Point, knew what it was to be criminally abused by white men. That was Sheriff Polsen's term for the defilement, and she took to it enough to trust the florid big official and undergo the required hospital examination. She took to Junn's assurances about Swamptown too, and afterward let him drive her to his shack, to rest there while he returned the swamp buggy to Sunniland. He drove out deeply concerned.

He would have been glad to carry her home on his way to the rental, roundabout to her Tamiami Trail village or directly to her kin on Big Cypress Reservation, but she had that apprehension of showing herself to family. She had to get over all that abuse first, the criminal one and also the humiliation of her medical inspection. But there was more to it than that, and he kept his rifle with him up the marl roads to Sunniland.

Junn had never dreamed the Sheriff himself would see them. Expecting a deputy, he was amazed by the famous presence of Dexter Polsen. Then, expecting contempt and ridicule, he was elated when Sheriff Polsen declared that, given positive findings at the clinic, Junn's testimony would probably suffice to back up the girl in court. The burly pink man was so tactful that Majosee, huddled faint in her blanket and sick with the memories, trusted him enough to mention the crocodile, no longer sure it

was just a dream shape she had formed of the ravaging boys.

Junn had meant to ask her not to, but it was too late, and he had to give the full version he got from the boys, including the eerie fornication they were sure they witnessed across the lettuce lake. Majosee sat abstracted through the detailing. Junn felt hot sweat ooze at the edge of his headcloth. No breeze came by, though a big fan was droning high behind the Sheriff's desk as he regarded Junn icily, then said to the girl, "You drink any, miss?"

In the pocket of heat that enclosed them, Majosee said, "Whisky. They forced some on me."

That was all, nothing about the liquor being devil's eye. Yet as if the Sheriff knew its properties, he said, "Could you been imagining crocodile, that there whisky?"

"How could that be real?" she murmured, pale and trembly. "I guess maybe I was dreaming. But I wasn't dreaming what they done. I know what they done was real."

When the Sheriff eyed him, Junn said, "All's I know, they tell me crocodile. They say it done that, and ate her. They duties me to go hide what it maybe left over, this gal."

"They seen it do that?" she said, her trembling severe. "Then I ain't dream that part neither." She had taken in the details, all right, but their impact was just beginning to affect her. "Oh, God," she cried, "I call Satan, he come into me a crocodile."

"Time we got you to the clinic," Sheriff Polsen said hastily, up on his feet. To divert the whimpering girl he said her torn clothes in evidence were registered by his own attesting entry and could now be repaired for her use. An officer had to come help the Sheriff lift her. Majosee seemed near hysteria, but went willingly along for the squad car ride to the hospital.

The clinical report was positive of course. Right in front of Majosee doctors told the attending Sheriff's deputy all about injured tissue and traces of semen that the attempt to drown her had failed to eradicate. But that was the least of her embarrassment, she confided on the way to Swamptown. It was not just the invasion of her privacy, reminiscent of the rape itself, that put her to such humiliation, but also the vulgar insinuations of suspicious doctors. Junn was so preoccupied with retribution

from whites higher up in the poaching than the five boys that her misery didn't fully reach him until he had delivered the swamp buggy and was headed home. Eager to get back, he hitched a ride with some truckers hauling produce to Hammerhead.

In a fierce sun he rode amid the crates with his rifle on his knees. Those boys must have guessed he was not their nigger any longer, once Mr. Jessup came by himself from Sunniland to meet them. They were bound to estimate the danger Junn now posed them. It could be they were already under arrest, but old Jessup would doubtless raise their bail. There was also the problem of Jessup himself, and his connections up in Naples.

"Look out for big Wiley leastways," he muttered, then smiled at the young burr head on a melon crate and shook his shoulders to pretend he was singing as they rumbled along. When the boy smiled back and looked away, Junn whispered, "Got this funny feeling to wish she never said nothing about that crocodile."

The truckers dropped him off at trolley car switches where the congested slime and foulness of Swamptown began spreading out thinner toward the marshes. He was across all the tracks before he made out a truck parked under the palms that nestled his shack. That was Mr. Jessup's rig. Junn shuddered at the idea that any of those murderous boys might be inside with Majosee. It was all he could do to stay on the slat walk and not bog down in the wire grass, hurrying there.

No one was in sight, but that could be due to the noon heat. It sucked sudden oily sweat out of him. He pulled off his headcloth, not to feel the cool difference but to make an unfamiliar sight with his hair springing free, a silhouette not quickly recognizable to anyone with something aimed at him from the truck. He hoped no one had ventured into his shack. He hoped the girl was safe in there. With his headcloth he wiped the rifle dry, then the palms that had left wet stains there.

At the first door in his street, he softly called, "Bowie?"

Small voices sounded inside the shack as the door pushed open, and Dora Pratt lit her sweet smile. "Hey, Junn. Say hey, Mr. Cavalo here."

Two small greetings sang out, the kids home from school. It

was lunchtime, that was why the street lay deserted. "Bowie not home, Dora?"

"Trying out down the depot," the tiny woman said cheerfully. "Come on out back and see how he fixed us that bean trellis."

"Not just yet, Dora. You see that truck pull up, my shack?"

"Yes, I did," she said, the smile waning. "Half hour ago. Ain't that your Mr. Jessup's rig?"

"Yes. You happen to see who went inside?"

"Didn't see nobody git out that truck. But truth, I ain't watch it, seeing it's your Mr. Jessup. Anything wrong, come on in and stay here, Junn."

She was glancing at the rifle apprehensively. He dropped it down on its heel. "Nothing wrong, nothing wrong."

"Bowie be back in a little bit, I expect. Junn, you want me go down and see it's okay there?"

"No, thank you, Dora. You notice I took some Injun gal in there? She been hurt by white boys. Criminally abused."

"I could tell. From way up here. Her in that blanket."

"Yeah. Well, I think I will git me a peek at that bean trellis."

She led him around the far side of her shack, knowing he meant to cut home the back way. At the trellis laid up against a sabal palm, he gave an approving wink and she said, "Go on, Junn, I be watching from the window. Bowie be along."

The bog grass was firm enough there for human weight. He went hidden from the truck's line of sight by the next shack over, which an elderly couple tenanted. Then he crossed open grass to a palm grove, and went on behind the shack of three sisters who were special neighbors he meant to count on for help with Majosee as to clothes and keeping shoddy riffraff off. And that was it, there just was no one on this side but Bowie to help him out.

Junn could see the rear of the truck. There seemed to be no one in it, but he could not be sure because of the deep sun shadow. He advanced to his side window and peered in. There sat Majosee on his cot, wearing the hot blanket and busy with her sewing. She should be asleep, regaining health. Probably a knock on the door had roused her. But that was all right: how-

ever many there might be, sitting in that truck to patiently await him, they had not shoved brutally into his shack.

Drawing close with the rifle up, he looked inside the canvas-top van and found it empty. No skins, nothing of the camp gear he had left on the highway with the boys. There could not be many in the cab with Mr. Jessup. No question that the old man was bound to be there himself: someone not accustomed to the limestone road channel under the topsoil would have bogged the truck down. He went around on the driver's side to prevent anybody at the wheel from firing a shot at him with ease.

There sat Mr. Jessup alone in the cab. He turned a wrinkled smile on Junn, the kindliest-looking old man. All weathered and peeking over the tops of his frameless glasses like Old Farmer Jones, he said, "They go string you up, Junn."

"Who that, them boys?"

"Well, that depends. Maybe the boys, they stay out of jail long enough. Then there's the folks up in Tampa. But maybe you ain't said nothing about no alligator skins."

"I ain't said nothing. Never studied no Tampa folks. My worries ain't went up no higher than Naples."

Mr. Jessup laughed. "Then there's me. You got me to worry about, Junn. See, anything happens, I'mo be out on bail, and sure enough I'mo kill you no-good motherfucking coon."

The old man kept smiling over his glasses, his hat back, his sandy hair dangling. Junn could not see what his hands might be holding, but neither could Jessup see the rifle pointed up at his face. "That mean I ain't work for you no more?"

Both of them laughed. They had laughed together on occasion. They had disagreed at times, but nothing so hateful had ever come from Mr. Jessup before. Laughing on, he said, "I'mo cut your cojos off, Ole Black Junn. Anything happen to me, you dead nigger. You think twice before you testify for some no-account Injun split."

"But them bad-ass boys went and raped her."

"Them that gits it asked for it, fool!"

"They done their best to kill her next, and told me go bury her or be murdered myself, one." He could kill them, he felt to say, but held it back. He was a fool to let himself get exercised

here, where any act of his own or others who came to help would only bring white reprisals down on Swamptown. People were venturing out at both ends of the street. Swift glances showed them all to be smiling at his smiling. He smiled as broadly as he could, but felt his eyelids hanging heavy as a lizard's. "You never done nobody harm, though. I never said your name to no one."

"Damn fool, you go have to, they gits you on a witness stand."

It occurred to Junn to wonder how this man just showed up knowing he had visited the Sheriff with Majosee. This man, whose pale color could scare an entire street of people indoors until they saw laughter, no doubt had a connection in Keyport to keep him informed. That could be anyone from the bread man to a hospital attendant—possibly the cordial pink Sheriff himself, with a share of his own in the poaching to protect. "I been hiring to you some years now, Mr. Jessup. They can't make me say 'gator skins about you."

"Sure they can. Testify them boys in the Big Cypress all night, and you same as saying 'gator skins about me."

"How's that, Mr. Jessup?"

"They go have to say what they been doing out there all the night long. Then they go have to say who they been doing it for."

The Sheriff never made Junn say what they were in the swamp for. "Who go make them say all that, Mr. Jessup?"

"The blame Prosecutor—who you think, fool?"

The man reddened and blinked, no trace of laughter remaining. He had apparently said more than he meant to. On a forced note of humility, Junn said, "Here's you scolding me, who done no evil. Them boys say they been out camping, ain't have to say who for. That be so, I think."

"Who asked you to think?" The flush had disappeared. The lined old face was white as death. "I always let you have your say, all that Seminole shit. Now you shut your nigger mouth. Don't Injun me no more. Don't try my damn patience with no split Injun tail ain't worth two hoots."

Junn met his gaze, then said, "Don't bog down, now."

He eased away sidewise around the back of the truck, Jessup

sputtering angrily for him to get on back there. Rifle up, Junn backed away to his door, and Jessup's door slammed, there he came at a hop around the front of his truck, digging a hand in his suit pocket, shouting, "I ain't finished with you yet!"

"Yessa you is!" It was self-defense—he would say that or go hide in the swamp like his forebears.

"I got your money. You got pay coming."

Not steel in his hand but white, it was an envelope. The smile was back, the sunny old man a benefactor again in washed-out seersucker. Junn set down the rifle and smiled back, but quit smiling when he felt a thickness to the envelope. "This ain't no seven dollar no way."

"That's right, Junn. I'm buying your shack."

"Ain't mine to sell."

"It's yourn to leave."

"Where I'ma go?"

"Down the Keys? Miami be nice too. Lots of work there, some good nigger."

Junn remembered to smile while he sat thinking inside his head. He had a poor raped child in there behind him. This man was buying the shack to burn it down though it belonged to a landholder neither of them knew. The polite Sheriff was not the man to appeal to. But likely the blamed Prosecutor was.

"Yessa. I thanks you, Mr. Jessup."

"You git out before dark."

Jessup turned away to his truck, striding gingerly over the bog grass. Junn pushed inside and shut the door. In the shadows he acted just in time to deflect a glistening blade that flew at him in the hand of a naked wild devil.

She came at him like a devil, her teeth bared with hate, her eyes insane, and though he had her by the wrists she kept trying to stab him, even when she saw his black face and heard him say who he was. Junn sent her tumbling down on the dirt floor. Outside, the truck growled; he heard it roll. Majosee sat up gleaming wet, and reached to the cot for her blanket. Modestly she pulled it around her.

"I didn't recognize you without no headcloth."

"White man come to the door?"

"No. But I seen him and got me the knife. You looked a stranger, all that bushy hair."

A sudden wallop shook the thin board wall and the sound of it was swallowed up by a second thud, a gunshot as Junn threw himself down and the truck powered its engine to roar away. He glanced up to locate the hole left by Jessup's warning bullet, but went blind behind the blanket she threw over his head to cover him protectively with her body. Majosee smelled of sweat perfumed by youth, like fern.

"Don't you worry none," he whispered, rifle in hand. But Junn, lying there with her in the dirt, imagined his shack on fire around them.

COLLAGE 3

An eagle flew over Gulf Glade that day. Barry Christian recalled
it when the ugly news reached him hours later from Tate Fenneran. A majestic bald eagle, right over the town, not long
before the five Bayfront boys did their job on the Indian girl.

It was not rare for eagles to range that far out of the swamp
for their game. A profuse variety of fish still abounded in the
Everglades despite a vast dredging blunder that had seriously
unbalanced the water table, but otters fished there too, cranes
and egrets, other beasts and birds of prey competed.

So the foraging sometimes extended as far west of the great
sawgrass plains as the Gulf creeks and the canals that branched
through the towns of the sandy coast. Christian took notice of
that particular eagle because of a predatory glint he detected in
some of their eyes as the young men climbed into his station
wagon with their grapple hooks and rifles. Somewhere in a
corner of his mind he had likened those boys to the ruthless wild
bird overhead, little realizing how close to the mark he was.

None was older than twenty, but already they were out poaching for a Naples trucker. Christian abhorred it—the arrant butchering, the illegality. Married a year, with a child on the way, he had strong feelings about communal decency and cared about the security of this region to which he was native. But war experience had toughened his mind, and practicing law in a young, ambitious town had taught him to mind his own business unless there was profit in doing otherwise.

Besides, it was good politics to have people in his debt, especially in a county so plainly destined for growth. So, to be accommodating, he drove the boys to Big Cypress Swamp with their clutter of rucksacks and shafts. They had heard he was heading for the swamp to represent Tate Fenneran in some land business deal at the Seminole reservation, and the turn-off to their campsite was not much out of his way.

Now he felt in some degree responsible for their vicious offense. His wife, however, deemed it merely ironic that he should have been the one to transport the agents of such outrage on an Indian girl while en route to the Seminoles himself. Marge commiserated, but insisted he was unreasonable to blame himself.

"I suppose you'd call it mere irony too," he said in their jalousied Florida room, "that I went there intending, at least figuratively, the same pillage of her elders."

"Barry, what are you talking about? They savaged that girl."

"And just what do you think dredging a canal link to Hammerhead right through Big Cypress Reservation would do?"

"I think you'd best stop drinking out ahead of me. You lapse into courtroom oratory—and exaggeration."

"I said figuratively, didn't I? It's small consolation that they had good sense and refused to lease us the site."

"Is it small consolation that your little foray was against property, not person? And at a client's behest, not your own? I'm just not drinking with you."

Marge Christian rose from the couch to set down her cocktail glass. Slender, tall, for all her pregnant bulge serene with characteristic grace, she let her husband draw her down on his lap, and responsively comforted him.

Yet he continued to feel a taint of immorality, not least for having acquiesced when Tate Fenneran asked him to keep thinking about the Seminole deal. Barry said nothing to Marge about that, but resented the position he found himself placed in by Fenneran, who had admitted having financed the Naples trucker, hence (if unwittingly) the alligator poaching as well.

Not only was that indecent, any assault on nature surely seemed unwise. Three keys lay off Gulf Glade, still largely in a primitive state just ripe for development, one of them boasting powdered-sugar sand that numbered its beach among the famous five greatest in the world. The Wildcat Bay front presented a natural site for water-sport marinas, once prosperity cleared out the poor-white slum dwellers there. And swampland already reclaimed in an agricultural fiasco two generations past seemed ideal for housing and industrial subdivision.

Barry Christian had visions of his children—two of them, three of them—languishing in sun-drenched good health on the beaches of those keys. He pictured them water-skiing around the two bays in a sunny drone of motors and echoing laughter. He was home among loved ones that war had put him in fear of never seeing again, and the future was upon him, too bright a prospect to be undermined by illicit depredations like poaching and shortsighted ones like further encroachment on the magnificent wildlife savannahs of the Everglades so close by.

Tate Fenneran appreciated such factors somewhat less, perhaps, being from out of state and connected to heavy commercial power through marriage into Key County's preeminent Brisburn family. But he was clearly a brilliant man, and persuasive, in various ways that included letting his new lawyer in on a sound land investment above Hammerhead. So Barry Christian had agreed to at least think about continuing with the Seminole lease proposition for Fenneran, because that was business, and to at least consider seeing the five rapacious boys for Fenneran's trucker, because that was politics.

At the end of a long private road from the highway that ran through the grassy outskirts of Hammerhead, and past a grove of coconut palms, a capacious old house full of gables towered,

a relic, in perfect repair, of elegant times past. Songbirds whistled in the magnolia trees of the yard. Prairie warblers and meadowlarks harmonized, until a windstorm of them swept away at the sound of an approaching motor.

Beyond the hedges of the broad green lawn, snarls exploded like a gunpowder charge, and an incensed fangy mastiff leaped forth, a slavering bitch with a small but muscular Negro clutching its leash, to meet a county police squad wagon that wheeled up the paved circular driveway to a stop. Sheriff Polsen got out and deliberately opened his back door, allowing the animal to leap in with a satisfied growl.

The morning sun had climbed over high swamp cypress domes away off in the swamp, but Polsen wore comfortable dark glasses. Amid screams of horror he casually walked around the front of the car and let his two prisoners fall out at his feet. Blood glistened on their stupefied faces.

The mastiff came rounding the car with malevolent roars. Fearfully the black man, at sight of the whimpering toughs where they lay handcuffed together winded and hurt, struggled to hinder the dog and cried, almost as canine in his hoarseness of voice, "Oh, Sheriff, ain't like you to punch folks up that way."

"These aren't folks," Polsen said, "and I never touched them. These are maniacal, homicidal sex perverts. They punched each other up in the car."

"Oh, please gittem back in the car, Sheriff. Can't hold Sweetpea off too long. She hongry and she horny."

Sheriff Polsen stood watching the frightened pair writhe helplessly, lying there on the ground. At a sign from him they leaped up to scramble back into the squad wagon, tripping and bumping awkwardly because of the handcuffs. He kept the door wide open, but positioned himself before it to hold off the bitch. "Why don't I just take Sweetpea inside, Prew? You can guard these killers for me with your snake."

"Oh, don't make me laugh, Sheriff, I'mo lose holt!"

"Please, we bleeding," Brady Wiley bubbled, lips split and swollen.

"Just a minute, boy. Here, Prew, let me hold her for you." He gripped the dog's heavy collar, and that subdued her to a low

growl. "Now you can shake loose your snake and show them what they're up against."

"Please, Mr. Polsen, maybe something's broke."

The larger one of them again, blood in his nostrils. He was really scared. Watching him bring a handkerchief to his face, the Sheriff soberly said, "Just how long is your snake, Prewitt?"

"Funny you should ask, Sheriff. I just happen to be measuring it when you drove up."

That cracked the gravity Polsen had labored to maintain; he had to laugh as Wiley mouthed entreaties until the dog gave an angry bark that silenced him. Irately Chuck Stowell rapped out, "Sheriff, you look here! We could be bad off!"

Indignation was often a bully's last resort, but seldom had Polsen witnessed such ruthless self-absorption. It had kept him amused all the drive from Wildcat Bay. Enclosed by the grille behind him, they had kept him also informed, thanks to the hidden microphone that brought back-seat conversation clearly into his radio receiver. He could tell them apart by Wiley's craven whine.

"Oh, sweet Jesus, Injuns put fishhooks in, hamstring and quarter us. Oh, sweet Jesus, mercy!"

Polsen had hoped they would notice the long easterly detour he was taking to the county jail up in Keyport, and sure enough they had succumbed to arguing whether that indicated a trip to review the remains or delivery to Seminole justice. Big Wiley had lunged forward so impetuously that he dragged the other along by his handcuffed wrist.

"Please don't take us that there reservation, Sheriff. Just some ole swamp gal, we never meant to kill nobody, we—"

"Idiot," Stowell had shouted, and must have punched his friend, since they were screaming curses next, each smashing the other with his free hand while struggling with the locked one for some token of defense until Polsen hit the brakes for a screeching long stone-spitting stop on a highway shoulder.

"That is a confession," he said through the grille, then watched them gape with dumb horror. "And me feeling so sorry, all those sweet little brothers and sisters, like to set you free for your mama's sake. Now I got you pinned dead to a confession."

First Stowell demanded a lawyer. Then he made the classic attempt to get all possible distance from complicity in the crime by ranting loud above the radio pick-up, "Shit, we just turned her over, Injun gal, just sport her some, till somebody say we best throw her to this crocodile and see it—"

"Chuck, you shut your hole!"

"Some playboy stuck a hooch bottle up into her, then throw the croc a taste to whet—"

The loudspeaker erupted to a blow, and the Sheriff heard their foul expletives, each cursing the other to his roots with accusations of every vile act from incest to bestiality. Polsen drove on with composure, not even bothering to see if the advantage he had allowed Stowell of his right hand left free was adequate to keep the bigger youth from wrecking him. The Sheriff just took radio communication from headquarters as the two slum characters wasted each other one-fisted in the rear.

And now they sat there nursing bloody noses tenderly with handkerchiefs. Striking one another, they had believed the girl dead, yet bawled their slanders with hysterical self-pity and not a whit of conscience. Polsen was tempted to lock them in the car with the pitiless, snarling dog for the same savage measure of torment they had visited on a helpless female.

But his oath of office frustrated such fond impulses. Hard put to contain himself with criminals as nasty as these, he scratched Sweetpea under the jowls until she fell silent but for the heavy breathing with her tongue out. "This bitch got the hots bad. Since you two have shown a particular appreciation, that kind of appetite, one of you can sport her like you all did the little Indian girl."

Stowell took his handkerchief down to display amusement in the mottled blood on his face and Wiley imitated the pretense, though both were obviously suffering pain and anxiety.

"I ain't just whistling Dixie. Which one go service poor hungry Sweetpea? You all decide between you while I'm inside with Mr. Fenneran. Because ole Prewitt, his snake bound to stand up awatching, other fellow go have to take it up his shaft for ganging up on that girl."

"Injun gal," Stowell reminded the Sheriff self-righteously, bloody nostrils flaring.

Polsen eyed him coldly, slamming the heavy door shut. "They get out the car, Prew, you cut Sweetpea loose, hear?"

Prewitt fidgeted, not relishing the chore. "Don't let this ole sun fool you, Sheriff. See up over the pines, that misty? See how she make a point, she stop there? That mean rain, but not much. Told my old woman take down Missus wash, then put him back up in ten minutes time."

"Hear that, boys? I'mo have to bring Prewitt and the dog inside. But I will leave these doors unlocked so's you can get out and let the swamp storm wash down all that bloody. Or you can make a run for it, them rushes yonder. In which case it be my pleasure to go after you, shooting to kill."

"This man serious?"

"Shut up, Brady."

"We white folks, Sheriff!"

"You white trash. Disgrace me in front of this boy. Give us the measure of your snake, Prew, thick and all."

"Well, say wrist thick and just about the foot stick."

"Gosh, Prew, you sure do make a great big fellow feel ashamed with just an ole six-inch pecker."

"Ah, well, Sheriff, thems is nice too."

Choking back the laughter, Polsen rested a hand on his pistol grip. "Toss a coin, boys. One of you gets to stick it in bitch heat. Other guy go bend over for big black snake. Else I hand you over to that poor Seminole girl's folks. I expect they know how to keep you big brave sports out of jail."

The prospect of such alternatives clearly shocked them. Tate Fenneran was one hell of an effective man: he had wanted the Sheriff to bring them here scared, and these boys were terrified. Polsen had always regarded Fenneran as strong and wise, possibly a great man, certainly a complex one. Despite the cruel disillusion inflicted on him by his wife during the war, he had cut a park out of the swamp for Hammerhead practically single-handed. That had increased the value of his land holdings there, of course, but a park existed nonetheless to lure adolescents in wholesome paths. It even boasted a Colored extension, and Polsen wondered if that sort of forward looking, had it only been there for this unholy pair, might not have helped reorient even youngsters so malicious.

It was Fenneran too who got the newly started bridge under-written for Ceremony Key, bullying past conservative resist-ance on the County Board (including that of his powerful father-in-law), so that Gulf Glade was bound to mushroom as a tourist hub, once the beach hotels went up. Not even the conservation-ists could argue with the jobs his endeavors kept bringing to Key County. And if a major airport in the Everglades ever cut through the perennial opposition to it, there was little doubt that Tate would prove to be the man who had won it.

But he was too complicated to trust unreservedly. Fenneran seemed susceptible to the harm of a possible blind spot in the maze of his complexities. That left Polsen feeling threatened politically, morally, even legally, and never more so than by the use Tate intended to make of this sadistic pair and the other three that deputies were bringing in. The idea of controlling such people was so foreign to Polsen that Tate Fenneran seemed alien too, and not for the first time since they met as students at Armistead so many years ago.

The excellence of the local university had lured Fenneran down from his native Georgia, and marriage had kept him here for good. They had rushed the same girls at college, including Dolly Jane Baltley; when she became Deejay Polsen after all the football and prom dating was over, no great passions of jealousy were stirred. The men remained friends, and were moved even closer when a first cousin of Tate's wife married Dexter's sister. But a hint of something possibly transgressive in Fenneran's nature always left Polsen uneasy. Now that vague sense of am-bivalence was almost unbearable in connection with this pair of vile felons.

Raindrops tapped the Sheriff's hat. Getting in the car for a final communications check, he saw the two brutes trading anx-ious whispers. Poor Todd Brisburn was about their age when he enlisted and went away to die. Lightning flashed. The re-ceiver was full of static. In it he heard the deputy report a car theft in some city jurisdiction, and a street fracas for the She-riff's Department to settle in Swamptown. There was also an-other gambling dive just reported on the Imokalee Road, and that bothered Dexter Polsen. He called in an immediate shut-down order, telling the deputy, "Have the men look for cots and

that stuff." The last raid had uncovered marijuana and prostitution, which called for strong precautions. "See they carry shotguns, hear?"

Clearly, when he switched over to the back-seat microphone, he heard whining Wiley say, "I'm fucking the dog. Say you are, and I'll rip your damn head off."

The Sheriff took pains not to laugh, getting out. He and Tate had not been all that older than these hulks, but fatherhood had spared them the war that killed Loker Brisburn's only son. Ironically, now both owed their prosperity to Hillary's father. The tough old aristocrat stood considerable strength behind his dynamic son-in-law, and Fenneran always remembered his friends. That devotion had spurred Polsen's election as Sheriff, and now it promised to make him rich. If it didn't ruin him first.

Massed overhead, purple clouds burst open as Dexter Polsen bounded up the lawn after the loping dog and laughing handyman.

The rain passed with thunderous sheet lightning, leaving the air refreshed. From his screened patio Tate Fenneran showed the Sheriff sandhill cranes wheeling over a sweep of misty approaches to the Swamp Everglades, high and dry pineland optioned from his father-in-law, which Fenneran was parceling out now to friends.

"You'd expect those birds knew their way by instinct," he said, an engrossed man unconscious of his habits, like the self-satisfied one of rubbing his fuzzy chest with the flat of his palm when stripped down; he was doing so now in his khaki shorts, his face startling in its handsome pugilistic cast, his voice deep as a gong. "You'd think just fish and mating drive them, but that's not so. They run on fear."

"All the lower animals do," Polsen observed, "even humans."

He took a corner of the white all-weather couch, and Fenneran sat down at the other end, saying, "You put the fear of God in those boys not a moment too soon." His eyes were abstracted. He was usually that preoccupied. One could never be sure where his principles ended and his machinations began. "When I said we needed buffers, should anyone of the same

· breed be set against us, I didn't realize how urgent the threat already was."

"Are you sure it's the right thing to go their bail?"

"I'm sure we need people like them right now. It'll be through their boss, of course, just as settling with his Negro was. It'll be just fine."

"I mean what you're grooming them to be. Organized crime calls guys like that—"

"I didn't anticipate organization. Just trying to look ahead, but those gambling shacks are sprouting too regularly to seem less than organized. Some hardheads are interested in the potential of this raw gold of a Gulf Coast. No doubt they could drown us in legalities, and I don't want to see you ever forced to use the power of your office for anything more than legally keeping the peace."

His unashamed gravity amused Polsen. But before he could ask for clarification of that pregnant remark, Fenneran bent to the telephone on its low end table and dialed a number. Tate had this offhand way of making him feel trivial, even childish, at times. Polsen trusted the man's judgment enough to have complied when asked for a prompt report, should the rape complaint be lodged by his trucker's Negro—a possibility this Jessup fellow had apprehended, once the black man failed to meet him in Sunniland after being sent to do the five boys' dirty work in the swamp.

The old man had perceived the danger that would place him in as an abettor of poachers. There were bearskin poachers and bird-feather poachers and more varieties in addition to the insatiable alligator thieves. Polsen was glad they were the burden of game preserve wardens and not his affair. Still, he felt it his responsibility to assist in upholding all of the law. His kin were in trade, like him no better than well off, and his family's single hope for real station was Fenneran. But looking the other way in an instance such as this was as far as the Sheriff meant to go, even for the future of his children.

A dark mist rose far over the pines as Fenneran spoke on the telephone. "But, Barry, everybody poaches," he cajoled. "The Indians—anyone who needs a dollar. I didn't know any better

than you that they were about to rape some poor Indian girl. Nor, for that matter, that they were out poaching for my trucker."

Donny Fenneran came in carrying a coffee tray, his mother radiant behind him. Seven years old, he paced as if he were carrying nitroglycerin, half smiling with the tip of his tongue stuck out. Polsen took off his hat and got up.

Still the most beautiful girl in all Key County, Hillary was in bleached linen, as ever golden fresh and tailored to the time of day. As ever uncertain too in her tentative smile, and furtive in her glances, apparently resigned to the doubts that kin and friends must seem to have about her since the bereaved escape she took to cities of wartime intemperance when her brother Todd was killed. Eyes on this younger of her two sons until he set the tray down, she handed Tate a shirt she had brought out for him, then greeted Polsen with a hopeful, brightening smile.

"Kiss me quick." She smelled of lilac, giving him her cheek as Fenneran asked his young lawyer to keep visiting the Indians about the land-lease proposal.

"You might teach them how influence can work in their favor to get the reservation incorporated. The Tribal Council is as keen on that as we are on the canal."

Watching Hillary pour from the steamy carafe, he reminded Christian (and Polsen as well) that their pineland value might well depend on the canal link he was seeking. "Remember, they have not yet been proven guilty," he said in a shift back to the rapists, Christian evidently balking at any consideration of the case. "And I'm confident in you enough to believe you'll see they are not. For my trucker's sake, put it that way."

That shameless public relations manner constantly surprised Polsen in a man so worldly as Fenneran. And persisting, he took Polsen into the admonition with a glance. "Barry, doesn't everyone have the right to a defense? Aren't you sworn to that principle?" To conclude the call with grace, he murmured, "Call it a personal favor to me," and got up with his attention all at once on his wife serving Polsen. "Drive out the back way, Hill. Dexter has some hoodlums wetting his back seat scared, out front."

Hillary whispered a scolding, "Tate!" Shyly she asked him to

put on his shirt because there was a chill. Far-off thunder rumbled and she said, "There, see?" though the heat was up again as if no rain had fallen at all. It simply bothered her to see even a man so trim as Fenneran that bare at home in company, but the mark on Hillary's past made any decorous gesture from her seem an act of compensation. Life trifled with her in that. For all the power of her sublime beauty, she was so delicately vulnerable.

The irony touched Polsen. He laughed to disguise his sentiments as she sang, "Send love, Dex."

Sudden rain clouds hovered ahead. He said, "Darn old Prew. Hillary, you better have Sissy take down your wash again."

"If you say so," and she was gone with her wistful smile to see Donny off to school. The Sheriff put on his hat.

Fenneran sat drinking coffee in silence till they heard her car pull away. Then he said, "We share a vision of growth for this county. I'm glad we both have the decent people at heart."

Polsen raised his cup in a toast. "Namely, us."

"I'm serious, Dexter. I have no intention of giving in to any pretensions of false cynicism."

"False modesty will do."

Fenneran refused to smile. "I have some redistricting surveys waiting on me, then a state senator to lunch with. You have three more scoundrels to scare in their jail cell. So let's stick to business, shall we?"

Polsen felt himself redden at Fenneran's display of strained patience. "Those three are plenty scared already, Tate. Once they learn who's providing them a lawyer, all five of them are bound to trust in you to the bitter end. Just wish I felt easier about doing things this way."

"My concern is to let nothing stand in the way of constructive social progress for Key County. Nothing. Hardworking people deserve no less. Why do you doubt me?"

Now the Sheriff flushed even more—at his own need to equivocate through jest, as compulsion drove him on to say, "Okay, I'm with you all the way, as long as there's enough to it for the hardworking people of Polsen and Fenneran counties too."

"There's enough for all if we persevere. We can turn this dull

society beautiful and life enhancing by a simple, if hardheaded, process of enlightened order. It's worth every effort. That's why I want you to stay Sheriff forever."

"What? See here, will you put on that shirt? Your milk of human kindness is gushing me right in the eye."

Fenneran suppressed his laughter, but spilled a bit of coffee. "Dexter, I declare!"

"Looky, we're all for law and order, but why me? Your connections, I could make Governor one day, by God."

"Connections like mine exist in every county in Florida. You can spend a lifetime eating out your heart. But my intentions, Dexter, you can telephone the Governor and tell him just what you want done and when." A bolt of lightning opened the sky before them, but he spoke right through the bombarding thunder that followed. "Business build up so rich, they'll be coming to us for help. Mayors, governors, senators be owing it to help us expand even more. That is free enterprise."

The rain came crashing down in torrents. That swiftly the heavy clouds had spread over. Tate Fenneran found his shirt and put it on, saying, "But right here's where we do our growing. Right in the confines of Key County. No use diffusing ourselves for the sake of holding public office. Let Christian do that. We'll pave his way and keep the power at home. Key power, shall we say? State officials will be our men, and Key County will be our empire. How many chairmen of the board, the corporations in this nation, break their hump to become governor? Make their kid brother governor. We'll just make Christian our kid brother."

A charge of concern stood Sheriff Polsen up with the reflection that his own inner nature as well as Fenneran's was subject to doubt, his own drives and real purposes. "All that is something to ruminate, sure enough. But random pieces disturb me. For one thing, I don't know this Jessup guy, and you're setting store by him. How reliable is he, Tate?"

"His skin's on the line, if you'll pardon the unintentional alligator joke. I'm sure Jessup did his best to reason with the swamp girl's darkie. Go right ahead and give the case to our County Prosecutor fair and square."

"Fair and square? Harmon Wilmont is an earnest public servant. He deserves respect and honest cooperation."

"Dexter, I said give him the works. Is providing a lawyer for the boys unfair to Wilmont?"

"No, but buying off the witnesses was."

"You have their signed statement to give him. And five miserable, maladjusted boys have Barry Christian to defend them."

"I thought you had more important work than that for ambitious young Christian."

"We have drainage directly into Okaloacoochee Slough. What need have we, really, for that Seminole lease?"

"But I heard you sending him there."

"To fail, all right?" Fenneran guided him inside the house. "Now don't go troubling yourself with complications you can leave to me. We're saving that Negro and swamp girl a whole lot of trouble *and* keeping the peace this way. I doubt they ever saw fifty dollars all at once. I *know* folks'd burn the coon out, he appear in court to charge white boys."

"White scum, you mean."

"Scum or cream, white better stay on top or the whole puddle of civilization will spill over. Equality is a fine ideal, but give it to primitives and they'll give back chaos. Society'll never work again."

"Could that be the deeper reason you're rescuing that white trash? Am I hearing Hill's daddy more than you in it?"

By a wall of portraits Fenneran said, "Heeding Loker Brisburn is far from unsound. But that's not my deeper reason."

"What's become of all we used to say about raising our black folks from primitive to fellow man?"

"That remains a practical goal. Worth our sincerest effort. But until we see any sign of such a possibility, we'd best cling to old Locker's traditional wisdom and avoid disaster. That's the pragmatic way to real progress."

Sissy drifted through in her housekeeper whites, a silent immaculacy in her wake, the aura of lilac in Hillary's where the imposing central stair rose from polished hardwood flooring under the Diana newel statue Fenneran had transported from Chapel Hill. The Sheriff put on his dark glasses.

"Nevertheless," he said, "I'm not about to let anyone get burnt out, this county. That includes coloreds." From the front door he could see his two thugs paralyzed with fear in the squad wagon. "There's just got to be a limit to what we do and permit, Tate. And to the kind of people we associate with."

"Dexter, people with our reputation for integrity need not worry about the seemliness of our motives."

The Sheriff mulled that over with amazement. He had never found a serious fault in Fenneran's character, yet always felt obliged to stay on guard. The elaborate nature of the man had once left Polsen in doubt that no more than good-night kisses ever passed between Tate and Dolly Jane, until the fearful pride she took in her honesty and virtue finally reassured him.

The rain had stopped. In the scent of blossoming magnolia a pair of beasts sat out there in cowed surrender to any command that might come from the hand that fed them. And among the dregs that were their people the word would pass that Tate Fenneran defended their whiteness, their one flimsy delusion of worth.

"Much as we deplore it, Dex, what's one isolated rape against all we have to accomplish for Key County?"

This man could envision a force of brutes to fight brutes off, and Polsen did not know what to make of it in a moment. He took off his dark glasses. "Say that again. People with our reputation for integrity . . ."

"Need not worry," Fenneran appended, nodding tutorially, "about what others may make of our motives."

Signaled by Dexter to follow, Fenneran reluctantly hung back, but his pause was brief. Down the stairs he went after his friend, across the lawn and the magnolia yard. Polsen yanked open the squad wagon door to display the murderous youths. They were wet, they were bruised, they were pale with fear and submission. The Sheriff spoke to them in a country patois he could attain with the merest inflection.

"Sorry I put you to the trouble of tossing a coin, boys. Sweetpea won't be needing you after all. Damn bitch dog jacked

herself off on a saddle horn. Of course that leaves you both to service Prewitt, he been hankering after you all."

The Sheriff glanced at Fenneran, then walked around the back of the car, leaving him to face the demoralized boys. He looked down on them impassive as a god, and they stared up at him in limp supplication, two burly clods with no apparent intelligence or humanity between them, just an innate toughness that he could control as effectively as Prewitt controlled the mindless power of Sweetpea. Polsen jerked open the opposite door, and they turned to him like a two-headed toy.

"Ain't brought out any hung black boy, however, to bung you two. As it suddenly hit me that the likes of you might *enjoy* taking that big snake up your shaft."

They hung on his words uncomprehending for a while. Then one of them licked his crusty lips and slyly smiled at the other, who said, "Don't say nothing, fool."

"This is your lucky day. That gentleman is Mr. Fenneran. Don't know why he pities snailshit like you, but he means to see you get a lawyer, and the bail to spring you out of prison."

They traded perplexed glances, then slowly became vociferous with gratitude, not sure at which of these benefactors to direct it. In revulsion, Fenneran slammed the car door shut and turned back to the house, aware that Polsen was enjoying this display of umbrage with relief, and probably affection.

The heat was climbing rapidly. The Sheriff's car swept away, and somewhere Sweetpea snarled as Fenneran entered the office extension that was once an idle sun porch. Mrs. Needles had calls for him to return, from his father-in-law and Jessup.

Plump and prim in her marcelled bob, she tittered, guessing just what Loker wanted. "I think it's about Billy's birthday."

Family events were customarily celebrated at Buenaventura, the Brisburn estate on Wildcat Point, yet the old privateer liked to make ritual of every preparation. Ever since Todd was killed and Hillary's grief debased her.

Five years now, that soul-sick debauch of hers, shattering their lives back then. Fenneran still bore the pain, but it had grown continually lighter as forgiveness proved to be his best expedient, so chastening Hillary that she was thereafter as im-

mune to impropriety as the inoculated were to disease. And with psychoanalysis—her depressions less frequent, disorientation no longer recurring—his wife's great beauty was to Fenneran the quintessential work of art in its value as a business asset.

At his desk across the sizable room, he asked his secretary to ring Nat Jessup for him and then go fetch his daughter. The woman twinkled. "Miz Fenneran's daddy next?"

He mimicked her doting smile, and strummed a light chord on the eighteenth-century French dulcimer he kept there to admire. Every aspect of the handcrafted instrument fascinated him. This was one that probably marked the end of utilitarian art in society. He traced its gilt-blue decorated border while organizing his mind for the call. Jessup often forgot he was not to make chargeable remarks over the phone, so Fenneran prepared to deflect any allusion to the fact he had known about the poaching all along.

Mrs. Needles snapped her fingers to signal him, and departed with her sparkling smile. Then Jessup, remembering to be cautious, managed with coded allusions to the courthouse and peat fertilizer to convey that the black man had gone to the County Prosecutor rather than flee with his fifty dollars from the harm that must otherwise come to him and the Indian girl. Fenneran reminded himself that his goals, being worthy, justified the many distasteful steps required, and said he'd appreciate a delivery of some peat or humus himself, ample instruction for the trucker to take necessary measures.

Unhappy about the consequences of this development, Fenneran diverted his attention to the dulcimer. Factory-stamped tools and instruments saddened him with a sense of extinction, something lost to life. Conversely, the dulcimer never failed to charm him. Nor did he ever tire of its primitive counterparts from Africa, upstairs in his den, the Mangbetu split-gourd harp and Ethiopian *kanogeb* with its thick horsehair string and bow. Their hewn wood shafts and animal-skin bodies were positively inspiring, like all the pride-perfect handicrafts he collected— and a comfort without which he doubted he could endure Mrs. Needles, back now with Cassandra just in time to catch the telephone on its first ring.

His golden girl was three, product of the reconciliation as Hillary recovered from the war. When Cassie reached up to him he laughed out loud (her hilariously tiny jumper) and lifted her. "Ready for that horsey ride? I'll sit up there with you."

"Promise?" Cassie said in a peal of his secretary's fawning laughter. The obsequious woman had at least known enough to put off whoever it was that telephoned at this moment of sweet preoccupation. He sent her to have his horse made ready.

Over by the palm grove, Fenneran found Mrs. Needles in distress with a handkerchief to her face. In their high-heeled pumps her tiny feet seemed ridiculous under the weight they supported. Likely she had blundered on Prewitt urinating in the stable, and the sight of it had overwhelmed her. Fenneran set Cassandra down to run on ahead. The woman faced him pale and horrified. Prewitt had shocked her indeed.

"Oh, Mr. Fenneran, he has a cat in an onion bag." Her painted lips were trembling. "Hanging from the eaves on a bed spring. And Sweetpea—" She looked away, sick, the handkerchief over her mouth. "Sweetpea was attacking it ferociously."

"Well, it's his dog," he said lamely, not really comprehending. Prewitt was the gentlest of people. Fenneran patted her shoulder. "I'll see about Prewitt." She leaned over on him, so that it became her fleshy bare back he was patting. Embarrassed, he added, "Call the town engineer for me, please. I'll speak to him after my canter."

Mrs. Needles clutched at his shirt front with a shaky hand, muttering unintelligibly into her handkerchief. Fenneran had to support her by one elbow and the other arm. She was profoundly affected. So was he, that instant, by the spongy heat of her arm. Recovering, she looked at him, no longer pale but flushed in the morning glare, and stepped back, stammering inaudibly, until she managed to say, "The cruelty. Why are we so?"

"Frustration breeds excesses," he said to send her off, and turned away as mystified, as breathless, as she. Beyond the grove he found Prewitt walking the tall bay mare with Cassie already up on the saddle, looking as cautious as an Indian in church.

Fenneran reassured her with a hand firmly on her knee, and

turned to say, "Hear tell you've been matching Sweetpea against a cat. You aim to fight her?"

"Hoo-hoo." Prewitt hid in laughter. "Like to knock down the stable door. I *tole* Miz Needles Sweetpea in training."

"But dogfighting's against the law, Prew."

"Nawsa, not in Swamptown. Nobody fuss."

"But I thought you cared about Sweetpea."

"Sure enough. I clawed the cat, he shoot bald paws out the onion sack, ain't hurt my Sweetpea none."

"Come on, Daddy."

"Prew, she'll be scarred to disaster, any dogfight. I've heard of some hurt so seriously they passed their intestines."

"Yessa, well, they just dogs after all, you know."

"That how you feel about Sweetpea?"

"Naw, shucks, I ain't fight her, just she show them how. What I mean, she in training for to train other dogs."

Running sweat and laughing without point, Prewitt was trying to weasel out of it. But that established a condition he could be held to, and Fenneran was satisfied he had saved Sweetpea thereby from atrocious agony in the pit fights that were staged on occasion by the rabble of Swamptown and Wildcat Bay.

"Daddy, Fawn wants to go and me too."

"All right, Cassie, here we go now."

He swung up behind her, weighing a notion that this weakness of Prewitt's might be applied for some advantage. There surely was substance to the pastime of cruelty, judging from the extreme emotional reaction to it by a woman who had never betrayed intensity of any kind before—and from the reaction she triggered in him. The beast of life dwelt in each of them and all their world just as it dwelt in those abject Bayfronters and theirs. How absurd to squander the probable usefulness of such boys on a point of law that made no allowances for their wretched conditioning.

He might just as well have rejected Hillary out of hand for her one dereliction, without considering the dementias of grief that compelled her. Her father, blaming himself for Todd's fate, had taken Tate into his confidence to wonder about bad seed, confessing an envious brother who, degenerate to the day of his

death, ended every lapse by mercilessly beating his only child. *Frustration breeds excesses.* That had come out of thin air to Fenneran, quite likely the sum of all he had pondered during his crisis over Hillary. But his restraint had bred instead this angel singing on his lap as they rode the trotting mare. He kissed his daughter's hair.

Strategic employment of delinquents, not punitive retribution, seemed the practical way to cultivate one's environment, populated as the world would anyway be forever, Tate Fenneran was sure, by no more than a Bayfront rabble dissimulating in masks of sanctimonious good behavior.

COLLAGE 4

Released on bail, the five Bayfront rapists arrived at Barry Christian's office resembling eagles no longer. All cringed, chalky with fear of the testimonial evidence against them, though they kept remarking it was only an Indian woman.

Apparently the Sheriff had shown them none of the racial partiality too many of the local people tended to expect. That left the five of them shaken enough to recount the incident in full revolting detail, once convinced Christian needed it that way if he was to help them contest the charges.

"Everything?" one boy addressed his uneasy reluctance to the larger boy beside him. "Even about the crocodile?"

"You mean alligator, don't you?" Christian interjected, since the swamp no longer bred crocodile life this far north of the mangrove wilderness away below Everglades Park.

"No," a third boy replied, "it was a croc we threw her to, sure enough." The largest of them, he flushed at Christian's incredulous gaze, and added in blinking self-consciousness, "Maybe the rains drove it up here, I don't know."

With stolid sunken eyes and gutted cheeks, this Brady Wiley looked like a beast. Something seemed abnormal in his evident physical strength, a sort of sickening ugliness in the very muscularity of his forearms. Carefully attentive as they spoke, Christian was glad to have the distance of his desk from them all.

They were murderous, abysmal people, worse than anyone he had ever encountered in all the brutality of war. He felt like kicking them out of his office. A rangy, big-fisted man, he had to restrain himself as they searched their memories for details. The drinking beforehand seemed a hollow excuse in this enormity. Not even their shiftless family backgrounds or arrested educations could mitigate such guilt. There were other youngsters just as deprived in the Wildcat Bay slum below Gulf Glade. These were animals. It was all he could do to keep from bashing their heads together right where they sat before him.

The muscles of Brady Wiley's forearms remained in tension even with both limbs relaxed on the armrests of his chair. This phenomenon was vivid as the fellow rambled absently about their hard night's work in the swamp without sensing the ghastly ambiguity a couple of the others detected with foolish smiles. The hulk really seemed more animal than man. Yet Christian would be obliged to deal with him and them all. Anyone starting a family had broadened responsibilities to meet; he would have to take their case though unable even to regard the five as people.

Like Wiley, another boy showed severe facial abrasions. For the kind of brutality that suggested, Sheriff Bull Peacham had been voted out of office in this enlightened county. "Did any law officer," Christian asked, "beat up on you two?"

The bruised pair glanced at each other. Brady Wiley said, "Not exactly," and that made Chuck Stowell laugh.

"Sheriff to blame," he said, enjoying it. "Taken us out on U.S. 41 instead of north. Ain't no jailhouse that whole Tamiami Trail. Scared us to Jesus till we start hitting on each other."

All of them laughed but Wiley.

Junn was seldom awake when one of the three sisters next shack over came calling in the dead of night. But he was up this

time, sipping devil's eye for calm despite the roving patrol car and its long pauses at the trolley switches every night.

There was no way into the bog stretch of Swamptown other than Track Switch Road. But he did not trust the Sheriff, who had assigned the car out there, and was not sure he could trust the Prosecutor, though that was the man who had turned the Sheriff to it. And even if both those authorities were sincere, they could not protect him forever—or even until the case came up in another week or so.

Majosee, asleep on his old pallet (having refused the cot), was not awakened by the sister's stealthy visit. Junn took the woman outside. He was surprised by her call with the girl there. All three McFees knew about Majosee. All the street did, but most especially the sisters, who saw to a good deal of his chores in return for his help with repairs and improvements on their bigger, two-room, shack.

"Been worrisome," he told her under a moon that revealed too little to tell her apart from her sisters. "White folks coming."

She made a sound to silence him. All three were lanky but woman-full and up near his own age, twins and a sister ten months younger. They looked alike, all dainty in their manners and churchgoing, so he was never to know which McFee it was that called some nights, or if it was more than a single one of them that came to share his cot and save him from the squabbles of abandoned women full of children on the crowded inner streets.

"I knows," she whispered, and that surprised him too, because customarily she only gave voice to her sensations in the night, aside from the sound she always made to silence him whenever he expressed a thought at such times.

"Can't you take her in?" he asked. "I could maybe spend the night with Ramsey and his old woman."

"Shhhh." She caught his hand and led him to her back door. Inside, one of the others was snoring on her pallet. He bent in obedience to the hand in his, and touched the unoccupied pallet. She had him drag it slowly with her to the doorless kitchen room. There she left him to pass the pallet through and went outside.

From the window Junn saw her go across to enter his side door. A frog croaked. Junn found a chair and sat rigid with tension. Dream fears had awakened Majosee the first nights, but she had toned down somewhat to sleep better. Visions tracked her days in sudden Indian abstractions during her house chores, but she kept that to herself and only spoke out her continuing amazement in questions to the air, like, "How can someone do evil to anyone like they done me?" and, "Why so strange, so terrible a thing come to me?"

Junn hated to see her roused from sleep, but it was a necessary precaution, he felt that in his soul. Soon the sister came outside with her, both of them spectral in their baggy shifts beneath the moon. As they approached, he realized they were not going to enter this McFee shack. She was taking Majosee to the Ramseys, to wake the old couple and explain the danger that hung over Junn's shack, the need of shelter for the swamp girl. That would take some time. He considered going back for his jug, but lazily dismissed the idea. More frogs croaked afar.

How simply the eager woman had turned it around to have him stay here and Majosee there. The devil took him to observe that only one of the sisters was snoring in the main room. The other must be awake with itchy curiosity. He thought of lying with her until the busy one returned, and began to swell at the sheer mischief of it. She might even giggle at the prank. But on the other hand she might start screaming and swear she never bucked to him before. And that could be the truth, for all he knew.

Junn had to laugh, the fear running out of him, and he sank down on the pallet murmuring, "A man mostly crazy."

An even greater fear had gripped him, and maybe craziness too, when he brought the fifty dollars to Mr. Wilmont and asked him to please find the landlord of Swamptown, whose money it rightly was. But the Prosecutor, a slight fellow seemingly without eyelashes, assured him he had nothing to fear, and though Junn little believed that, it did relieve him somewhat. To his surprise, the Sheriff had already informed Mr. Wilmont about the rape, first thing after going out to arrest the five boys.

"You show real courage in coming here, John, and I mean to

see you won't regret it. Things are changing in south Florida. We surely intend to have decency in Key County for all."

He displayed the Sheriff's report, all that Majosee had testified and Junn had backed up, all typed out in precise, important lines. Except, Mr. Wilmont explained, it would be just as well not to mention the parts about the crocodile in court. The man really meant to prosecute this case.

"They kill me first," Junn said, and told of the threats by Jessup, the warning to get out, the money to seal it all with a purchase of the shack for which one paid some nameless agent rent. It made the Prosecutor think. At length he said, "John, it shames me to say this, but if I arrested your boss it would be your word against his. He would say you're just an ungrateful Negro, bitter about getting fired. He would be upheld in court. Unless we catch him at a crime. Do you understand, John?"

He nodded to that and to all Mr. Wilmont said next about the old man who owned both Swamptown and the poor-white Bayfront. And Junn might have trusted in the assurance of police protection that followed, had the Prosecutor not said it was out of kindness to the poor that the landlord kept those tracts the way they were.

The way they were was dismal and forlorn, without sewage or water except for street pumps, and shacks going up to pay rent on by the dozens down the inner streets. Soon those shanties would be reaching these outskirts, shooting up between his shack and this one of the sisters, and the stink of cesspools, without adequate chemicals, spreading out from the central reek.

White mind, black mind, one seldom understood the other. Even among the same kind, folks were eternal mysteries to each other. Even these three sisters of his own blood let him know them but poorly. His blood met the Indian girl's too, some part of it down past the Town Clan line of his grandmother, yet they had word-meaning trials between them. It was a while before he realized her thoughts were on the Green Corn Dance, her talk going beyond his comprehension about gourd rattles and assemblage seats.

And date sticks—he could not imagine why she should dwell

on southern cookies when they had serious food to gather. Then on his own he recalled the bundles of sticks the Seminoles dispensed traditionally for their clan chiefs to count the days by until the new-year festival of ripened corn. Sticks of wood, she had meant, not fruit.

As he must judge the white men with guesses, so he had to divine the girl: by her calculations her people had already met to designate makers of the new pottery, and met again to determine the seating for ritual and council, and a third time to foretell the first new moon and distribute the date sticks to count until its arrival and the beginning of busk celebration. Her heart was returning home. That much he could tell, but not the reason, whether to seek redress there as reflections on history lessened her faith in white justice, or simply to relieve the possible concern, by now, of her family and clan.

Junn had spent these last days taking food with Majosee from the bordering marsh—turtle and fish and some crane eggs—and wondering if she could see in visions (being Indian so much more than he) the danger he could only feel like a sickly mist. He must get her distant from it, to a camp deeper in the swamp or to her people, as she wished. Little difference to him. A black man could not stay anywhere too long, and it was always getting time to leave Swamptown behind as he had left Pahokee on the big lake five years ago. He would miss these McFees, the one or all who visited him of an occasional lonely night.

The one crept close beside him now so noiselessly that the pitch of her breathing gave him a start. He had just begun to ponder the belongings he wanted out of his shack by morning, and there she was, rippling with shudders. She had never come on him before with such hungry breathlessness. She had never shown such open desire to begin with, and he wondered if it might not mean the first time this one had ever tried him, or if the presence of her sisters was responsible, or the danger of white assault, which waited out there in the silent night.

Or a dwelling on the plunder of Majosee. The beastliness of five white boys. The idea of crocodile lusting to woman.

"Small means," he whispered, "poor folks got to pleasure us."

"Shhhhh."

*　　*　　*

The burning of Junn's shack was nights later. In Swamptown the result was unrest, until word circulated that no staked cross had blazed with the single abode. Thus assured the incident was not a warning to others by the racist Ku Klux Klan, the people went their uninhibited ways, loud in the streets and gin mills, laughing or contentious in the stark emotional manner of that muddy shanty district.

The *Key Journal* printed no story, so discussion of the fire was minimal around the county towns, though women who let little go by without comment heard about it from their day girls. There were lots of fires in Swamptown.

It caused a brief stir in Keyport due to courthouse gossip that Sheriff Polsen had brought in white boys. But few people linked those suspects with the alleged rape of a swamp girl. Everybody knew about that because the newspaper had carried it in a story about Prosecutor Wilmont's futile attempt to have high bail set after the arrests. The people stood behind him all the way, deploring the crime of rape on religious grounds, and knowing the culprits to be Bayfront trash who lived on conch and swamp game. But no one complained about the court granting bail so low as to set vengeful criminals free.

Public attention in Gulf Glade that day was on the first piles to be driven for a bridge at last to Ceremony Key. The Mayor and Town Board were there, several county officials, their wives, and a big brass band. Tate Fenneran had been invited as prime mover of this expansion, but important business had removed him to Tallahassee for three days, and he sent a congratulatory wire from the office of State Senator Duncan Doran.

County Attorney Wilmont telephoned Barry Christian to inform him in a routine way that his five clients were being held for questioning. Christian trusted his word, knowing the older lawyer well from their roots in the same county town of Tarkey, so he was stung with apprehension by Wilmont's statement that no trace of the Negro or Indian girl remained when Sheriff Polsen reached the demolished cabin (as shacks were alluded to by white people).

That the two souls might have burnt to cinders was too shock-

ing a possibility for Christian to bear. It deepened his feelings of blame for the swamp girl's misfortune, and for having gone back to bargain with her people again for a canal route, only to fail a second time. Told about it, Fenneran had graciously insisted on buying back from Christian the pine acres devalued by his own inability to win the reservation lease. But now that display of generosity seemed a possible atonement for bad conscience, as if Fenneran had known the incorrigible Bayfronters to be guilty of yet another, this latest, inhumanity.

Telephoned on his return from Tallahassee, however, Fenneran absolutely vouched for the five boys as innocent of that cabin fire. Surprised to hear about it, he was unhappy to learn the colored witnesses were missing, and invited the Christians out to dine at Key County's newest luxury restaurant, the Harvester.

That hardly set Christian free of his fear for the Indian girl and black man. He could not resign himself to their possible death as Fenneran and everybody else apparently could. In a matter of days the two unfortunates were forgotten, not only by the white community, but also by the blacks who served it. He had no way of knowing if the fire had brought grief to the Seminoles, or how they might react to such a tragedy. One small shack could prove a tinderbox for a people so long oppressed.

"O fierce Asi Yaholo, who led us to doom but glory too . . ."

Visions often awakened Chitto to pray, but this one had come at the worst possible moment for Cose Emathla. She cursed her mother's brother. Her daughter was away at the reservation. Her son slept nearby, soundly, as usual, despite the loud insect songs. But old Chitto would soon have the entire camp awake, frustrating her respite from widowhood.

"Asi Yaholo, who sat by the right hand of Micanopy the mighty Alachua and sits now by the almighty Maker of Breath . . ." Foolish man, he was searching back more than a hundred years for the warrior Black Drink Singer, whose head the white enemy took to revile and whose name to memorialize with an important city called Osceola. "O Asi Yaholo, as you passed noble Tallahassee seed to the Mikasuki womb, so send

your devotion to the Great Spirit in our behalf. Are we not all of us Seminole?"

What old-fashioned nonsense. Cose laid the mosquito net aside. She climbed down from her chickee platform and hitched up her shift to hurry across the wet guava garden to her uncle's chickee. If he roused the camp it would be impossible for her to slip undetected to the kitchen chickee, where Sint Itcho of the Bear Clan should be waiting. She could not endure three more years of widowhood. The four-year mourning period was a cruel imprisonment. She would be forty by then.

"Oh, intercede for this powerless remnant you left behind to hide forever in the swampland, the armless, the warless, the hopeless, who inherited your doom but without glory."

Cose reached the old man's side weighing an idea of departure for Imokalee, where with menial jobs she and Sint Itcho could marry free of shame among other Seminole migrants.

"Breathmaker, give audience to fearless Chitto. Was my blood line not proven in the endless wars against the Americans?"

"Father, pray tomorrow, when all can admire your visions."

He continued unheeding, seated at the foot of his pallet with his head thrown back in trancelike absorption, and Cose quailed with fright to hear him say, "Has she a mother's brother to defend her? No, all my nephews like my sons are married out to other clans. She has but me."

"Father, what threatens her?" Cose whispered desperately. "Tell me. Don't wake up the camp."

"O Fishaki Omechi, make me fixico to save my graceful flower. Give me the name Fixico to my name."

He was pleading with God to grant him absolute fearlessness of conduct for war, and she had to summon all restraint to keep from crying out for her daughter. Old Chitto fell back on his pallet with a groan. Insects were screaming everywhere. An owl hooted, and Cose wailed, "Father," forgetting now to whisper, "tell me what you dreamt!"

"My dream? It woke me with fright. Awake, I saw Majosee's canoe burning. Not a dream, it was a waking vision of soldiers."

In dread she cried, "Soldiers—what does that tell you?"

"What do I know but visions? I have grown old like all my race without hands, without arms."

"Oh!" She knew he was being evasive to spare her the dread of his interpretations. "Is my daughter not on the reservation with old Emathla?"

"I always liked the man," he said without relevance. "As one grandfather to another."

"Let's wake the others! Let's go to Fish William!"

"No, let's call up the reservation," he said in sudden reversion from Hitchiti to American. "I know it's near about midnight, but they all got some electricity there. Come on, ain't too far to the highway phone booth."

The Harvester supplanted with elegance a stretch of levee wilderness between Gulf Glade and Keyport. Nothing but modulated chamber music flowed from its hidden loudspeakers, and the same good taste emanated from the lighting and appointments. Fenneran had seen to that.

As soon as they met at the bar he noticed Barry's quiet anguish and Hillary's delight with the Christians. Gratified to see her blossom so in their presence, Fenneran was eager to reassure his young lawyer about the Swamptown fire. But he chose to first unsettle him further by revealing the position of control he held in the sprawling, splendid restaurant, having brought banking influence and some family money into the financing.

Christian reacted at a loss to understand why he had not been consulted, or at least informed, about so large an investment venture, but gladly abandoned that subject in favor of the other. While Hillary was still acclaiming the cosmetic refinements of Marge Christian's pregnancy, Fenneran swore he had it from the Sheriff that no evidence of casualties existed in the charred ruin. He assured Barry that his five malignant clients had nothing at all to do with burning down the cabin of Ole Black Junn. Christian would not have to appear for them in that.

Fenneran gave every affirmation save the fact that old Jessup had induced the Fenton and Cordhall boys to enlist the one's brother and the other's cousin for the arson. If *nothing at all* amounted to exaggeration, he could forgive himself because it was all to good purpose in the long run. Watching the younger man grow rosy on his second martini, Fenneran said, "Don't you think boys like that can be rehabilitated, Barry?"

Christian weighed the question solemnly as Hillary, in better spirits than she had been for weeks, exchanged courtesies with the maître d'hôtel. Fenneran could tell that his guests were charmed by the attentive service at their table no less than by the magnificent view of the lighted old mansions of Seashell Key across Key Bay. "I'd like," he murmured, "to fly Maine lobsters down and be done with these Florida crawfish."

"That's a good idea," Christian said, "but I doubt the other. Your suggestion that those boys can be redeemed. I respectfully beg to differ."

"Barry, please order." Alert in her casual glances, his wife seemed a provident, ambitious young woman of intelligence. "Those drinks—you sound in court again."

"I didn't mean it as a suggestion," Fenneran yielded. "I merely asked your opinion. And I accept it." He ordered Caneton aux Pêches while the others were still vacillating over the soups, and said, "No, kids like that can only be helped along, I suppose. But those coming up behind them, Barry, I think they can maybe get a chance at life through—now don't laugh—through better housing."

Christian stared at him. "I'm not about to laugh at that, Tate." His wife asked him to suggest an entrée, but first he said, "I'm all for that."

"Good." Fenneran recommended some other poultry dishes, and some of the meats, and without pausing went right back to the point. "I want to put all those Bayfront families into the pines development. It doesn't have to be platted in two-acre plots. I'm pretty sure we can get a variance for such a purpose."

They were all silently watching him, Christian blinking a while in confusion before saying, "That's why you let me off the hook regarding my pines acreage. I had no idea you were pursuing such an ambitious scheme."

Actually, the ambitious scheme was to replace the entire Bayfront slum with a turnpike, but that would not have impressed Christian as profoundly as a commitment to low-income housing. And with the swamp girl and her Negro missing, Barry would not have to defend the atrocious boys at a rape trial *or* an indictment in the arson. He had to be savoring that as both

wives voiced their admiration for the ideals so explicit in the Bayfront plan.

They were really stirred by this display of Fenneran's public spirit, but not nearly so much as Christian, despite his silence amid the praise they repeated throughout the sumptuous meal. He seemed as contented as Hillary, whose beauty kept magnetizing his self-conscious glances. His age was about the same as hers. Older by no more than eight years, Fenneran felt almost paternal in their awe at his commitment to the progress of Key County.

A bitter thirst for vengeance filled the swamp heat around Majosee with visions of evil. In the crackling hot blaze that awakened the neighborhood, Junn had told her how his home was torched as she lay asleep in the old couple's shack. Scoundrels had come out of the jungly gloom where Swamptown ended at the bordering swamp forest of palm groves and pine. Behind the man with flammable in a can came another with a rifle. Junn had come awake in the spare McFee room, his own rifle close by. The marsh was deep in season now. One could hide bodies in it until winter found them carried south by the slough tide. The law would never be able to trace them here. But much as he yearned to kill those two, he could not risk harming Swamptown people in a shootout.

"Besides," he added, "they was nothing but poor whites paid to do for richer ones. Someone ain't about to rest till we dead or gone." In moments his shack, just dry planks holding up a roof of old doors, was a heap of sparking embers in the night.

The terror had receded, but it reared again with this burning. It had cramped Majosee with stomach pains most of the time, and was returning after the blaze. So were the ferocious waking dreams that sucked her away till she jerked herself free as she did from nightly dreams of her five beastly enemies. Junn's goodness comforted her, but puzzled her too.

The day she helped him transfer valuables to the neighboring shack of the sisters, Majosee had asked why he accepted this trouble as his own, and the answer he gave was to amuse her.

"More interesting than most stuff. What else a Swamptown

man got to pass the time of day?" Then in the dawn of acrid smoke his reply to the same question was humorless. "A black man's time narrow down no matter what. We can't stay on here, Majosee."

She made ready with him. All his neighbors helped, old Ramsey providing an inflatable army surplus life raft to haul their main supplies. Junn was most grateful, though, for Majosee's equipment: without her canoe they might not have had a way to penetrate Big Cypress Swamp in depth enough for a camp that was reasonably safe from pursuers. But the fear of treacherous whites, all conspiring to murder them, pierced her like a thin cane spear, and she fell cramped with bowel pains that kept recurring. So not until dawn could they leave their frightened friends.

From old Seminole training Junn knew how to brew the snakeroot cure for stomach pain. He needed no instruction to build an Indian log frame for the cooking grate he had salvaged from the ashes of his home. Though hoyacini was easily available at the nearest willow head, he put little stock in it as provider of good luck in hunting. But he did paddle to a bayhead for sweet toli to brew, just in case the source of Majosee's pain was fear of the unseen and the unknown.

Junn wove them a surface of sabal thatch to lay like a whitefolks table of fancy fare, and soothed with rambling dinner talk so much of her aching cramps as the bay leaf and snakeroot failed to relieve. Even more entertaining than a Mikasuki storyteller, this black man was like a picture-show performer. Nor did he need any hoyacini leaves for luck at the hunt, bringing in not only cranes' eggs but a crane itself to cook with a young water turkey and swamp cabbage and coconut milk in what he called a stewzie.

The frogs he trapped, however, Junn would not prepare for consumption, leaving no question, finally, of his Indian streak when he stored the legs away to sell in town. Vending them to restaurants was traditional with her people. He even looked Seminole, explaining the need of money that was sure to arise if the trial took place as she wished and they had to spend time in Keyport. And just like blood kin he refused to venture forth

until she might feel abdominally well enough to go along. He could neither chance entering Hammerhead without his rifle nor get himself to leave her behind without its protection.

Maybe it was the devil's eye he sipped, but he did amuse as well as comfort her. One moon-dappled evening by the fire his reply to a simple question about the years behind him made her laugh out loud. "Well, little friend," he said, mimicking the self-importance of white men, "early on I thought I might study law and seek public office. Then I considered becoming a brain surgeon. But I don't know, stuff come up to distract me, and next thing I knew I was old."

It was sometimes hard to remember she did think him old. He was like the self-replenishing forest that sheltered them. Later it stormed. He always stayed by the fire until she was asleep in the tent he had pitched like a chickee, and even that night he went out to leave her snug, reassured against her inbred fear of storms by the ease with which he bathed himself in the downpour. Yet fear lay coiled within her, a pigmy rattlesnake that reared to strike sharp fangs at her bowels.

Majosee longed to be home with family, to see the games and dances of the busk, to rest her shame in the hearts of grandmother and aunts. But that other serpent, her bitter vengefulness, stubbornly demanded retribution though the prospects for that in Keyport were dim. She was of the Snake Clan, sure enough, to harbor such reptiles within. It seemed clear that she must regard them as totemic signs, and wait for the third snake sign to rear with its instructions.

In the morning Junn took over her cooking chores to busy himself while she bathed in a newly risen pond. He had seen her naked twice in derangement, yet respected her modesty now that she was well in mind. Majosee felt well in body too, he was that much a comfort, the man. So, camp made fast, he poled her back to the Swamptown fringe and stowed their canoe with the McFees. Stopping off briefly at the Pratt shack, he then walked her directly to the inner streets, carrying the frogs' legs sack and his rifle.

Junn was scared. He made no effort to conceal that, where

Hammerhead Depot poured its freight yards deep into central Swamptown. He had to be there for Bowie Pratt's return from his run between a freight hopper and the new spur to Ochopee. That good friend had leased a pickup truck to haul gravel for the railroad out to gandy dancers who were laying the roadbed, and Junn was assured he could borrow the rig at sundown to route his frogs' legs to restaurants around the county.

Majosee shared his fear. But worse than that it made her ill to smell the age-old stench of congestion that pervaded the huddled inner district of shanties. She was reluctant to bother Junn about it, but her discomfort was plain. In the crowded, sunny thoroughfare he set his sack down and pulled out of it his bottle of devil's eye, saying, "Onliest way to outdo this smell, if you ain't used to it."

The offer offended her. Depot louts, walking sticks their latest affectation, swaggered everywhere casting flirtatious remarks, and she was already conspicuous enough in her Seminole dress. "How you expect me drink any of that, all these folks looking?"

"Nobody out here care what we do, long's it ain't at them we does it." True, no male or female black paused to watch him swig some unashamed. Powdered women turned up their noses at loud quips from the dandies, but not at the odor of putrescence, as far as Majosee could notice.

One bad smell to turn away by any reasonable means. Yet anger stimulated her to say, "The way them evil boys made me swaller some?"

"Nobody make you. I'd never will you no harm, Majosee."

It was strange to hear him say her name amid the storefronts and telegraph poles and people glistening with heat in the noise. Somebody smelled sweet in passing, a portly woman likely as black as Junn beneath the yellow face powder. But it would take more than one sweet smell for relief from the Swamptown stink.

Junn's fearful eyes, roving in search of danger, fixed gravely on Majosee. "Little friend, we gits down them freight yards, smell be gone. But we go run into worse. Mostly white folks work this railroad. Bad-ass, some, maybe Bayfront trash. Who knows? I use this rifle, you go have to git on back in that swamp all by your own self."

He held out the drink to brace her. She had not noticed the gold in his eyes before. His shack was aflame in them. Her shame burned there too. So calm he was in this rancid sun, prepared to kill if he must and die for it rather than for nothing. Her mind showed her other brave men purging with bitter Black Drink at the busk, both her grandfathers turning to look at her in sorrow.

Junn consoled her with a friendly whisper. She liked to hear the black man say her name. He was the sole comfort left in the disaster that had seized her life. She wondered if a swig might not strengthen her with the power of having endured the test of a savage flavor she remembered only as the taste of death. It might come to taste of life, since it was Junn's in this instance.

Majosee held her breath, and took devil's eye against the terrifying danger of the freight yards below, and the overwhelming odor of Swamptown.

The Cultural Center Endowment Dance was held, like most local celebrations of quality, amid the sea-scented laurel and dogwood of Buenaventura, Loker Brisburn's estate out on Wildcat Point. To get there, Prewitt had to drive through the Bayfront district. Its ramshackle hovels and open drunkenness along brawling Front Street put Fenneran off; his wife and the Christians worsened it with sentimentality.

They were sure prosperity was all it took to eliminate human tendencies of depravity. Fenneran, conversely, believed that degenerate inclinations were inborn and not necessarily the results of poverty. Improved physical surroundings merely fostered pride enough in possession to induce the outward show of dignity, which to his mind was the entire moral condition of the more fortunate classes. He loathed the unsightly decrepitude of the slum, and preferred to work diligently for its improvement rather than take easy comfort in moralizing about the poor.

In that regard he spoke continually with Carl Meyerberger, who owned this embankment of limestone wastes (and the marly bogs of Swamptown), about relocating these Bayfront people in order to develop the approaches to Wildcat Point and

so link all of Key County in an ongoing evolution of its precious environal resources.

But it got Fenneran nowhere. "Maybe they like better the bay," the patriarchal philanthropist had lilted just last week in his deathless foreign accent. "Maybe they ain't used to, afraid to stay inland."

Of course the choice was theirs, Fenneran had conceded, meanwhile reasoning that means perhaps existed to narrow that choice and thus do business at last with the stubborn old Jew. Barry caught sight of an altercation in the street and guessed it must be over money, their wives nodding sympathetically and no one mentioning all the structural decay the limousine slid past in mud-flat slime. They were like children, with no sense of the realities in Fenneran's determination to replace this entire eyesore with a great new divided six-lane highway.

It cheered him up to reach the town that shared its name with Wildcat Point. Prewitt, as always happy in his chauffeur's cap, whispered them smoothly through streets colonnaded by tall old poplars and lit not unpleasantly by screened porches alive in rows with the festive chatter that was all diversion amounted to in these parts. Fenneran hoped that gracious life in the county would soon be more various than mere social gatherings every Saturday night. To that end he had contributed diligence and financing to the Cultural Center conception. Now at its acceptance he felt aglow in the lilac sweetness of his wife.

Telling about the crocodile and swamp girl made all five boys feel like liars. Price Fenton's way of diverting anyone who kept after them was to embroider a tale about the disappointment of a lustful black man when a willing alligator turned out to be more sizably male than he. Price used the same wheeze on his father's tomato-picking sidekick when scrawny Mr. Hoyt pressed that curiosity, strolling down a dark street toward the bay, and it got them all laughing amid the shuttered fish stands, even Guy and Chuck, who had heard it before. All but his brother Wayne.

Big and barrel-chested, he threw a sullen glance when their father tried to humor him with jesting whispers. But Wayne

came alive at the abandoned warehouse full of men and frightened dogs that Mr. Hoyt led them to. The din of barking stirred them all, echoing in dreary battery-powered light, the frantic lunging, the growls of leashed mongrels with lips already curled back though no contest was mounted yet on the tarpaulin flung out across the rubbled concrete floor.

Men were offering bets to quickly match their dogs. Someone had a bucket of canned beer to sell, with thirsty buyers crowding close in the banter. And women were on hand to sell themselves once the excitement heightened. Hoyt pointed out some experienced pit fighters by their heavy studded collars and their scars.

"The rest is learners," he said. "Doubt any of them ready yet to fight. Ole Jessup brang this nigger down, learned us a lot I didn't know. I knows I'mo charge folks money to set and watch, git these good ole boys organized with their curs. Another thing I knows," he said at a distant wail of sirens, "is we got to git." He pulled his hat down tight by the brim, spinning off to depart at a guilty crouch. "Let's go. Git holt of Wayne. Ain't supposed to let nobody leave, once they inside. Else the law show up. Don't ask me why, all's I know Jessup's little nigger say so."

Price found his brother too excited to listen in the noise and high sweat. Wayne said, "Some of these dogfights last for hours." His eyes danced and his breath came short. "Crack their bones and kill each other. And you see the poon? Look at them tits go swing-swang, Bubber. Hoo-ee!"

Breathless with more to say, he fell silent and heard the approaching sirens when the battery spotlights went out one by one. Price had to laugh at the confused faces of men who kept looking at each other for guidance as he dragged his brother around them, hurrying out. He laughed, but Wayne turned in on himself, growing sour and unresponsive again as they hastened away in the exploding laughter of others.

That surly preoccupation lingered at the Wildcat Rest, all through the horse laughing out back in the big open beer garden of crowded tables. Their father set up beer for Wayne, trying to engage him in the fun, but he would not respond. It bewildered Price until Lam Cordhall showed up with his cousin,

Rider Newgate, who seemed as perplexed by Wayne as Price was, and said, "Ain't you told them yet?"

"No," Wayne replied, shifting restlessly on the table bench. "I been thinking not to."

"Yas, I notice you to do a mess of thinking since we seen ole Jessup's coon in the yards."

Chuck said, "Which coon? Coon with pit dogs?"

"Huh? Coon with Injun gal," Rider told him, taking one of the beer bottles for a swig.

Chuck got up on his feet. "Ole Black Junn?"

"That's him. We was running a bad order to the roundhouse." Rider paused for another swig, all bulk like his cousin Lam. He worked with Wayne in the Hammerhead rail yards, had burnt Junn out with him too. "And right there by a gondola full of gravel we seen that swamp couple passing time with some black trucker. Rifle in hand right by that hopper, smart-ass coon."

"Knew them by her Seminole dress," Lam said before anyone could ask. "Ain't likely more than one such couple around here."

"You seen and never said nothing?" In a furious sweat the old man leaped up to confront his elder son. "You knew they ain't been scared off and you keeps it quiet?"

All of them were glistening in the breezeless heat. Price got up; his brother said, "You set back down or I'll knock you down!"

The noise of surrounding voices battered Price down. Few things so frightened him as Wayne's anger. At the harsh sound of barking he said, "Looky, Wayne, here come some of them pit dogs," and his brother rose, apparently welcoming the distraction as Hoyt conferred with two men whose pit terriers were quarreling.

But Lam said, "Junn selling frogs' legs like an Injun. Ride seen that just now in Gulf Glade."

Guy stood up saying, "We best see Mr. Christian."

Chuck said, "No time for lawyers, if Ride seen that."

"And you," Price's father stormed, burly chest to chest with Wayne. "No mind to tell and save your little brother?"

Wayne looked sorely troubled, muttering to himself as Rider

went on to say, "Seen that headcloth and stopped off to make sure. Cook at the Dewdrop Inn said yes, some coon been in selling frogs' legs. Yes, pickup was drove by a bitty colored gal, could be Injun if I put that to him. Told the nigger try Wildcat Point, the swells eat like horses and likely he sell out his catch."

Chuck shook his head in a rage. "Take me home for my rifle. Guy, git yourn and your daddy's jeep, don't take no shit from him. Up to us shut that nigger mouth for good. Where's Brady?" Price got to his feet again, but Wayne was quick to crack him backhanded across the mouth and knocked him half over the table. "You son of a bitch, you mind me! I burnt that coon out for you, that poor swamp gal he took in!"

"You burnt down that shack," their father contradicted him, sputtering, "for twenty dollars apiece."

Wayne glanced around desperately. "Yeah, you still so proud I near committed murder, and now you wants him to. Niggers and Injuns human too. You all save your ass and git out quick!"

"We can't git out," Chuck barked. "Be jumping Mr. Jessup's bail, and nobody better run out on Mr. Fenneran's man."

"Fuck his bail," Wayne shot back, "and fuck his Mr. Fenneran. That big shit, his sowbelly kind feed off of our sweat, keep us down to serve them. He never miss that kind of money."

"Ain't the money," Chuck warned ominously, "it's his arm. Longer'n the law's. Jessup told us so, powerful connections this whole state, and the minute we let him bail us, we owed him."

"We owes him hungry nights and busted backs," Wayne persisted. "Go git him in his blame big house instead of that sad-ass nigger, or be picking tomatoes all your foot-weary life like these ole swamp croppers."

"White folks," Hoyt spoke up, "we all owes Mr. Fenneran." All gangly bare but for his worn overalls, he eyed the indifferent crowd for eavesdroppers. "That's his nigger ole Jessup brang to teach us pit fighting the right way. There's big money in them dogs." A belch made him blink his smarting eyes. He scratched his crotch. "You all hear Huxton say they just paid off some Glade cops? We all going back to that there warehouse. Dog game only chance we ever gits to pay our way out of this dirty piss hole, so you all stop fussing over niggers."

Price's father could neither follow the man nor be pacified. "Low-down Commonist trash," he assailed Wayne, irate and ashamed. "What's mine is mine and what's yourn is mine," he mocked with baiting gap-toothed laughter, and Wayne punched him right out. Wayne struck his father's chin a clean fast blow that spanked the old man down all stunned and awkward on the paving.

Wayne next caught Chuck a good one in the face but got struck right back and it was a brawl, the crowd parting to make room and goad them on. Women screamed with laughter, the pit dogs snarled. Blood smeared both men's faces before Hoyt and the cousins piled on to pin Wayne's arms back, unable to hold him until Guy leaped in to help. Chuck crouched forth with fists to punish, but Wayne's father got up and interceded.

"Stand back, boy. Let white folks whup their own."

Panting and flushed, spitting blood, Wayne said, "Call me a Commonist. You gangle-ass ole turdhead, you mess me, I'll bust your bones back home."

"I'mo mess you good," the old man huffed, close to tears but drawing back his hairy fist, "and you ain't likely git home no home of mine again, by God."

The sound of smashing glass stopped him short. He turned to see Price, licking his bloody lip, approach with a beer bottle he had shattered. The sight froze them all in amazement. Even the onlooking crowd fell silent, even the dogs. Alarm glinted in all the eyes but Wayne's, which hung not on Price but on their father.

"You call yourself a pa, but you plain shit. You all git off of me or I swear I'll kill the mess of you."

He spoke evenly, without regard for the razor glass of the bottle passing before him. The weapon stopped by the face of Hoyt, who let out a horrified bleat when Price plucked him back by the throat with glass cold and lethal against his jaw. "Git off of Wayne," Price said, "or I'mo cut this manjack's face off."

Nobody bothered to protest. It was clear Price meant what he said. His father gave an injured nod and Guy, unhanding Wayne, went to stand by Chuck. That was enough for Wayne to shake himself loose of the husky cousins. He swiftly shattered

the end off a bottle of his own and lunged over near Price, who shoved Hoyt forward. The dogs barked. Laughing people turned away. The brothers backed off side by side, Wayne saying, "You little shit, you getting out. I'mo bust your ass. I'mo see you gits a job upstate or beyond."

"Damn Commie pinko yard bum," Chuck shouted after him, a handkerchief at his nose as they cut and ran and the crowd closed them off. "Guy, make sure your rifle's loaded. That nigger be the death of us, we don't shut him up."

COLLAGE 5

Oversized Japanese lanterns bloomed on the Brisburn veranda, all orange and pink above friendly people dancing to music that drifted tranquil from the ballroom. A merry dissonance charged the atmosphere with vivacity, and had the flushed old planter beaming in his dated white finery.

Fenneran elected him chairman of his secret board. His first bourbon inspired the idea. Hillary's father had refused to let the loss of his son keep him from hiring bands and doing up his parties in grand old-fashioned style. He was adamant, even ruthless, when business or his responsibility as a county selectman demanded, but one had to admire him for the simple goodness of his motives.

With his second bourbon Fenneran resolved that this Endowment Dance was really an unconscious meeting of his secret board, in plenary attendance by members unaware of its existence. His plan embraced them all. That included County Prosecutor Wilmont, just arriving hawk-eyed grave as ever with his

smiling wife, who did all his scintillating for him. All his flirting, waggish adversaries called it, and she would carry it even
further, some around the courthouse implied, if it took that to
advance her husband.

Fenneran dismissed it as cheap, envious gossip, if not down-
right political smear. He greeted the Wilmonts and other members of that hypothetical board of directors, who stood only
to gain from his conduct of it. There would be reward for all
in the county who worked hard for the trappings of decency
—as Miss Honey Baines worked hard to suspend hers with
breast and thigh at the moment, dancing for his influence. Remarkably coherent for once, the young newswoman had promised him a dance and returned for it, flirting unintelligibly
in the habitual way that made her journalistic gifts so con-
founding.

Clint Bocaleon stopped him for a fishing date and got Honey
to dance with instead. This rising executive in the County
Power and Light Company might fit usefully into the plan if
he'd only outgrow his tedious practice of boasting about marital
infidelities.

It amused Fenneran to think of Carl Meyerberger too as a
member of the board, if not an invited one tonight.

Tate was in good spirits and loved the dreamy elegance of
music, even the complacent people dressed so well as to seem
without blemish, like Hillary's immaculate mother, who enjoyed being enigmatic and whose older daughter, Jennifer,
kissed him as her bony husband asked if he could find a branch
site for their Palm Beach department store. Strangers congratulated Fenneran on the progress of Ceremony Bridge while
the Sheriff, turning from the bar with a highball, met him with
the flattest gaze.

Dexter was still glum, still not satisfied there had been no
bribing of his deputies or other collusion to permit incendiaries
on the Swamptown Road. Fenneran could not convince him
that no reason existed to believe it was anything but a private
Negro dispute that caused the blaze and drove the black tenant
away with his swamp girl. The Sheriff's expression seemed
guarded. In his dark dress suit he appeared more top-heavy than

he did in uniform, but his eyes were as cold and cutting.

Fenneran touched his glass to Polsen's, and next thing he knew he was handcuffed. With chilling invisible motion Dexter had locked a cuff on his best friend's wrist. People were turning to look. "You're coming with me." The Sheriff cuffed his own wrist too in the laughter of guests. "My baby sister Nola's brought her kid and husband all the way from Nevada, asking after you."

Fenneran was angry, but reminded himself to disregard this inconsequence and play it out in Polsen's detached manner. It seized onlookers with hilarity to see the two squeeze by, mirthlessly handcuffed together. Then somewhere the Sheriff's wife called his name and, unchaining Fenneran with haste, Dexter said, "Get your wrist out, fool, she'll call it symbolic and there goes our snook fishing."

Deejay came threading her way around people, flushed by the night air and looking disturbed. "Officer Fairboro wants you, Dex. Came driving right up to tell you there's been an awful car crash and the Indian girl's there with her black friend." Dead or alive, Fenneran almost asked as he followed Polsen out with Deejay saying, "Good Lord, just when the buffet is out of the kitchen all smoky."

The party exhilaration ran out of Barry Christian when Fenneran took him in the limousine with their wives to follow swiftly behind the Sheriff's sirening car. The trip seemed interminable, though it was little more than ten miles from Wildcat Point to the accident site near Hammerhead.

Arriving, they learned all the rescue work was already done. Hillary and Marge chose to stay in the car. State Highway Patrol spotlights on broken glass revealed the point of collision, though the smashed sedan, around which officers were busily guiding traffic, lay a distance away where impact had flung it over on its back, all sprung out like something dropped from a height.

There was considerable blood. In the commotion of noise and spinning toplights the ranking sergeant explained that a Negro couple, though shaken up, was all right in the other vehicle involved. But there were two seriously injured young men who

had no one to blame but themselves. They were lucky to be alive.

As County Attorney Wilmont hurried across the highway to a dented old pickup truck, Fenneran said, "Did you say Negroes? I thought the girl's Indian."

The sergeant said, "We did radio that, because the young fellers thought Injun gal and Injun nigra. But it ain't's so. Those boys were just delirious."

They all crossed the highway after Wilmont, meshing through traffic and a wreckage crew in its luminescent vests. Officers with lanterns had no doubt a crime had been committed. Comatose, the boys had confessed as much in their agony of broken bones. Bayfront drunkards had gone on sprees of racial assault before, and the State Patrol was glad to give the case over to County.

But the Sheriff would have no part of it, not even when shown bullet holes in the pickup and a recently fired rifle discovered in the demolished old Nash. "If you all discovered a crime," Polsen told the surprised patrolmen, "you're the authorities to properly make any arrests. Too late to keep the peace here, which is all our job calls for, my office."

"Your office," the sergeant said, "radioed back that one of the smashups, the Stowell boy, is a rape suspect of yours."

"That's right," the Sheriff said, nearing the pickup truck. "You can see we have our hands full, guarding these coloreds against reprisals from that lot."

It left the sergeant confused, but got Dexter Polsen out of a sticky spot between two adversary friends, Tate Fenneran coldly eyeing Harmon Wilmont, who returned a gaze impervious as glass. The County Attorney, unable to hide his disappointment at not finding the rape witnesses he expected, blocked the pickup door to prevent Fenneran from taxing the black couple inside for the whereabouts of those witnesses.

Christian admired the Sheriff's deftness and the Prosecutor's tough independence. But he wondered if Tate Fenneran was not being unduly challenged—to apply his considerable local power against Prosecutor Wilmont, and to question the extent of Sheriff Polsen's dependability as a well-placed ally.

*　　*　　*

Ramsey came to take Junn's place in the dark, the Pratt children quietly asleep. Bad omens had awakened Majosee, the old man said. "She scaring for you like a child. I'll set up with the kids till Bowie and Dora gits back."

It was good of the couple to take his frogs' legs run for Junn when, at his phone call, the Prosecutor insisted he avoid any possible encounter with Bayfront people. In carbide light just inside the Ramsey door the old woman whispered, "She preglin."

"Might have thought so," Junn muttered. "Never rains but what it pours." Kneeling by Majosee's pallet, he said, "You hurting any, little friend?"

"It's biting sharp, but that ain't all." She laid his hand on her belly. "Snake sign coming, like time to go home and tell."

"You wanted me to git that Prosecutor all set again."

"I know. But my two grandpas come to my dream, and they was angry. Had a bear with them gave me date sticks. So I know they wasn't really my grandpas but the two souls of my father, he over the Milky Way. Say Green Corn Dance to me."

He never did have the ear to fully make her out. Gently he stroked her belly in the thin cotton shift, saying, "Well, ain't the busk a good sign to dream?"

"Not when angry look at you. Bear say busk in its third day. Them date sticks was to tell me I'm late."

"Go on, sleep some now. We be leaving, come daylight." She pressed his hand down on her abdomen, and that instant of her pain seemed the right time to tell her. "You late according to the moon, gal, not the Green Corn Dance."

The old woman knelt then to help hold her down, but the girl lay still, shifting glances anxiously in growing comprehension. Without going high strung, she shaped the fact and climbed all the branches of its meaning to her. Then all she said was, "How you know that? My stomachache?"

"Sure enough," Mrs. Ramsey replied. "And how it make your knee go sometimes, you sweep this floor. Thems and how you been yiping in your sleep. Had a daughter once done all that, long ago. You just turn off to sleep, child. Me and Junn go talk about a cure."

"A what? You say cure? Oh, God, you get this beast child outen me? Ain't me my gone father angry at, it's them nasty boys. I can't bear they child."

"If I can call back how." The old woman told them she once knew a means of aborting the unwanted, and turned down the lamp to let Majosee recover sleep. In the darkness at the door she told Junn, "Been too long. Maybe it come back, though, if I set a spell with some womens."

On that she took to the night. Majosee was restless. Junn knelt by her, stroking her poor young head until, with Ramsey's return, she found the innocence to sleep again.

Outside, stars crowded the sky. Crickets scraped in the spikerush. The pickup truck stood black against the moon. Bowie came out of his shack with the devil's eye jug for Junn, who needed a deep swig before he heard all Bowie had to tell about the highway chase and the gunshots and the accident.

Junn said, "You will wear that headcloth like us Injuns," and they laughed. "Truck been shot up and dented, you got fifty percent coming now. You all sell much?"

"Sold it all. But we still ain't taking but our two bits on the dollar. Well okay, thirty cents."

"Make it forty and we got a deal."

They laughed again, and Junn gave Bowie the devil's eye to drink while they divided sixty-five dollars. Bowie said, "Prosecutor," and Junn saw the pallid little man wearing horns. "He say tell you something," and Junn decided to drink no more when he saw Wilmont eating little black children with a spoon. "Say tell you there's a hundred ways folks can interfere with justice, but not if you stick it out."

"I stick it out," Junn said, "and they go cut it off."

When Bowie was through reeling in laughter, Junn handed over some money to buy him cartridges and coffee he would come back to pick up when he could. "That might be some time, though. Could be I ferry the gal home."

He sent Bowie in to get his book studying done with Dora. This couple had high hopes he wished he could believe in. A light was burning in the McFee shack, so Junn knocked. It was Mrs. Ramsey that came to the door. She touched his elbow for him to follow as she hobbled to the dark moonless back of the

place. "You ain't say nothing my old man, is you?" she demanded in a whisper. About no cure I knows?"

"Ain't been told none."

"You ain't about to be. Sisters heard tell about some such, but wasn't sure what. Still it put me better in mind. But no decent body can say it out, such, so I expect some one of them go write it down. Be under your pallet, maybe, you wakes up come dawn. To hear it told, they like to die."

"That evil, hey?"

"Say that again, son."

He kept from laughing till she was gone home. Those sisters were something. Or some one of them was anyway. Junn washed up at the pump. Inside, he knew better than to intrude on the sewing they were concentrated on with spectacles aglint over beautiful gossamer wings spread out on the table all ready for some angel's flight. All three pear-bottomed lank angels stood there busying themselves that way in order to avoid even the least mention of a problem so biological as the abortion of pregnancy. They would leave him an instructive note, and he was not to know which one of the three had turned from her psalms to write it.

Their dainty murmurings were not over angel wings, however, he noticed on the way past. Ordinary window curtains lay sheer and white upon the table. The drink had tricked his eyes with those of the devil. Still he allowed himself a nightcap on retiring, and the moon took him away.

The moon floated him out across the Gulf on curtain wings until a sister called him back over the shoal sands and jungly hammocks. To her sweet sound he descended at a glide on naked silk. Thunder rumbled in the moonglow. She was up on her hands and knees, her breathing pitched high, facing the window as if to bay at the moon. He woke to her hand searching him out. With a moan she jerked to get him up behind her.

"Oh, Lordy," he whispered with a shudder.

"Shhhhh."

She tucked him and softly whooped. He made the same surprised sound, too quickly excited in her heat. Up on his knees, her mighty hips in his hands, he was already set to fly but

willed himself back, slowed their glide to linger in the bliss. Suddenly his own hips were seized, someone else was there. Intimate hot hands, someone was hammering him at her sister, who gave a hoot that sounded like pain at each thrust. Frightened, he heard a tinkling voice gibber behind him and thought the woman had gone moon mad to rise at them that way in the dead of night. Then all at once it came to him.

This was the process to help Majosee. This was the note slipped under his pallet to teach him, the only kind a shy McFee could permit herself to compose. Two had shown themselves, a sacrifice to help Majosee.

She too must sacrifice. To dislodge the fertilized egg. To free herself. No rape child bastard to bear. He must guide her to hands and knees. He was being told to punish her so. Without joy to himself. A young slip of a girl. Hips half so ample for this hammering. How could he drive at her so? Or even bend her to such peril, the child?

"Hoo-ee," he whispered to contain himself.

This rapture of sisters, one smashing him at the other while another slept, in it he heard the child scream with hammock birds. Slight hips, frail ribs, she had taken five without breaking. Slender miracle of youth. Some forest afternoon. He heard her hoot there like this McFee with cruel pain at each thrust, yet likewise with pleasure in the devil's eye.

Taking her turn, Majosee poled in silence across the slough tide with their heavy tow. But only till noon, when the stomachaches cramped her severely. Junn had to labor alone from then on.

The pain made it impossible for her to remain silent long. "Junn, you must be crazy," she wept, "to be so scared of some cure. Tell me how, and I do it myself. To get a baby we all go hate, I rather die."

It felt bad to shrew him so. Back in Swamptown, his big hand at her belly had soothed her to sleep until the Ramseys woke her at dawn discussing the gun attack on the Pratts and she felt the third snake sign coming without seeing its shape. It drove her off to help Junn prepare for escape at once despite the pain. She

asked outright, but he was afraid to admit the old woman had taught him her cure. He stammered. He tripped in the marsh. Finally he said it was just too dangerous to try.

When she begged him to let her decide that for herself, he sidestepped to tell her the gunfire was actually meant for them. Those who ravaged her had gone out last night to kill them. But in their absence the Pratts sufficed. It mattered little which dark people they slaughtered. It mattered little to officials with the power to protect them but no kind of will to do more than talk up a storm for election.

All morning they forged east. Breezeless, the air lay parched on the open wash, sun flaming overhead without mercy. She kept asking what the cure might be, and he kept working the jug just to plug up his mouth. Finally he advised her to get drunk too if she wished the cure defined, it was that nasty and bound to disgust.

That silenced her at last. She had loathed the devil's eye in deep Swamptown, and recalled the neighborhood reek with the revulsion he now conveyed. In brooding resentment she helped him pole them away from danger, until the stomach pain cramped her so badly that she called him foul names and doubled over begging for the cure no matter how vile it might be.

"Go make you scream and hate me if I tells you," he said.

She shoved the jug away, all huddled over her knees in the dugout. "I hates you now, you want me drink like them evil boys made me do."

"Make you hate me louder," he shouted, quivering at the lips, "if I does you like them boys done! But that's the cure!"

She heard, but could not grasp it. "What you saying, Junn?"

"Saying I got to hit you harder any them boys done!" Poling, he drank one-handed, gleaming wet in the swelter. "To make you bleed! To knock they baby clean outen you!"

The pain stifled her, so that her voice came up hoarsely wailing. "Oh, my stomach, my stomach!"

"Ole woman Ramsey say so, not me!"

"Oh, stop off here! Oh, boil me some snakeroot and bay!"

With hasty industry ashore, he used her army pump stove for the brewing while desperation bent her to the horrid devil's eye

against her pain. He hacked palmetto logs for their better stove while she warmed to the stomach brew and asked why he had chosen to make camp so long before dusk. He was drunk enough to say his mind had its better reason to foresee the afternoon as best time for her cure, if she insisted on having it administered.

Majosee wept to hear such talk from him, even drunk. She shared his jug just to deafen herself and to keep him drinking into a haze that might turn such degenerate thoughts aside. And soon she could only laugh to see him even drunker. He was so drunk, she had to make his shade by bending palm fronds over and catching them in a bough above him. He fell to hazy speech in his dozing, coins of sunshine finding him through the overhead.

The whisky and the stomach brew had dulled her pain. Junn talked and talked and, drunk herself, she dozed along in her listening, a dapple of crafty sun baking her down as well.

"How I go make somebody understand?" he said to the trees. "So worrisome, I like to perish. The danger to the gal. Just nature, I tells myself, she woman up to it. Yeah, nature, some nature things just selfish, some plain and simple ugly."

In her own sleepy cradle of fern she thought of telling him she understood the weaving ways of nature well enough, but fear of his motives gave her pause, and watching him doze, she dozed herself until he woke her, maundering anew.

"Oh, shit, here I goes dreaming white folks again." (And she, Majosee realized, had dreamt crocodile in a wink.) "Worry follow me to sleep, keep coming off in wearisome dream of white folks pinning me to whole lot of sorry talk. They do go on. No stop to it, so pasty in the face, like death himself. Try my very soul. Drive me to drink." He laughed to hear himself say that, his long hand groping for the jug, but only to rest on it. "She go think me plain natural bad. Unnatural, my age."

"I think you son of a bitch, Junn." It poured from her and, crouching there, she leaned behind a joewood tree to hide from his bleary search. Still, her resentment goaded. "You sure unnatural say you do me them damn boys' way and worse."

Too drunk to lift his head, he kept sliding glances around to find her, but soon gave it up and said, "What they done to you

ain't no nature thing. More like murder, what they done you."

"What you say cure is? That a nature thing?"

"Ain't my cure. Old woman. Them nice sister ladies too. Like to die, they hear it told." He drew the jug near, struggled with the cork. "I think they all crazy, myself, hurt you up so, scare you to Jesus and all."

"Ain't scare me. Just so low down, I'm ashamed of you."

"Low down? I tell you low down." He told her nothing, though, dozing instead with one eye not quite shut. A laughing gull woke him brashly winging by, and he picked up the thread as if it were needled to his brain. "Low down, no natural way no way, I'mo tell you. That be man go hard to woman morning urine. That's low plain ugly down."

"Junn, you hush now. You one ole son of a bitch, Junn." She crept over in a sudden welling up of tenderness for him, and softly covered his mouth. "You sleep some now, hear?"

He took her hand aside and drank from the jug, gasped, said, "I ain't down for that ugly, no woman. Nor so selfish I wait for night to lust me, go poon in mind to youngster she in trouble."

Drowsy beside him in the relentless hot eyes of the sun, she teetered on the scales of her concern between desperation for the cure and revulsion at the sense of it. "Junn, I wish I knew what you on about, ole son of a bitch."

"Simple." He sighed. He yawned a long time, fluttering off to a groan of extreme relaxation. "Importance of a sizzly, droney hammock sun. That's why my brain tell me afternoon for it, you wants that cure. No love bone, that be greedy. No piss whistle neither, that be low-down ugly shame. But at least the plain ole honesty of a good ole lazy hardon."

Her head quaked in reaction. Her teeth chattered for an instant. She believed no greater shock was possible, until the thing bulging out before him in one hand stunned her, and the halo of sun on its head made her laugh. Majosee laughed in a dawning indifference to nightmare, the balancing of her rancor and anxiety at last where animals stirred. The rank bristling forest of the sun was alive with beasts looming primevally. She laughed to hear the black man moan her name. She watched great reptiles gather to copulate in frolic and aggression. She wept with shame and screamed with pain as she watched.

And she laughed with the pole in her hands, having vividly beheld a prehistoric mating amid the shrieking fowl, to awaken next from feverish sleep with a vague memory of being one of those grotesque beasts against a sky of egrets storming over. Poling the canoe in her turn, she could not meet Junn's eye in her confusion of embarrassment and relief, yet she laughed, causing the dugout to falter in direction.

Junn sprang forth to take over the pole and thwart the tide; she fell down laughing at his astonished face, at her recollection of his lazy mouth casually drawling those indecencies with his eyes stupefied in detached witness. Her laughter was beyond control. Like devil's eye it took her mind off in sun haze, until the open slough surrounded them. The immensity of space horrified her. She shrank from it at the canoe bottom, without laughter any longer, dizzy and appalled.

His cure had bled her. The spill was heavy, and after her long intoxicated slumber the stomach pains were done. But not Junn's fear for her or Majosee's fears for her people. He was afraid that the remedy might have damaged her, and she that the blood flow that had released her from anguish also foretokened war. Her own blood was the third snake sign and she had to go home, but to the downfall of her people, who could not survive armed conflict against the whites.

She tried to find in Junn's eye the only help she could hope for in this wilderness of her life. With bitter tremors she said, "That whisky change me or turn me crazy, one. That was big ugly 'gator you climbed up on, not me."

"More like brontosaurus, seem to me. Shiny scales and great big teeth and all."

It cut her to the heart that he could have seen dinosaurs too. Choking back a taste of bile, she said, "Same dream, us both?" She began to swoon. "How could that be?"

"Devil's eye. Devil's eye. Make everybody stand back and watch his own self. Make everybody see the same, somebody say it out, like, or maybe holler something."

She trembled there in nausea. The blue cavern of daylight dwarfed and estranged them, leaving them lost in the world like insects on its vast and lonely surface.

Pink flamingos winged over. White men small as insects had

raped her in the vastness of the world. The same vermin wanted to kill her now and she was carrying it over the flooded prairie to her people, to bring them war with her hopeless, helpless savior. "Junn," she said faintly, searching for reason, "we married now."

He stared, dumfounded. Alone and insignificant they floated. The dreary vista of tree islands lay dispersed before them like derelict ships, far out to the bleak horizon. Their heavy tow of war meant suicide. How could they go to the reservation so? But where else could they bring the injustice?

The flamingos swept overhead like blood running on the sky. She felt unable to bear much longer this infinity of open slough.

When she whispered his name again Junn knew she was going to add, "We got to turn back and face them white mens. Just got to see them bad boys put away."

"You scared to go home, little friend?"

Suddenly out of control, she shouted, "I told you don't mix in this!" A fury he could not comprehend drove her on: "I got this to do, not you! Get out my boat, we gets back! Rape me like them boys done to save me? Seed me and skin me like them! Make me low down lizard just like they done!"

Junn poled back to let the slough tide reverse the canoe as she screamed words so foul he never knew she had them. As she stormed he said, "We sure enough married now."

Because she had bled so, his fear for her safety outlasted the deed. Soon he had the canoe turned full around and they were heading back to confront the white people again, her rage gone with her fear of suicidal war as rapidly as the seed of her enemies had run out with her bleeding. Devil's eye had saved and maddened her, both for only a while.

He saw no justice ahead for her in Keyport.

Devil's eye. He had known she would condescend to drink it for the necessity even while two McFees were blurring him into one with them. Not likely the third sister had slept through, but he was not to know. He need wonder no longer if more than one of the three came to slake with him in the night. But he must still allow that at least one of the three perhaps never

did, and always show each of them the reserve due that one. Because of the McFees he did not mind going back. His true wife existed among them. More welcome to have two (if not three) that behaved as one than one that behaved as two, like this poor child of sweetness and wrath.

The big clapboard house he grew up in was paradise to Barry Christian. The many rooms were balmy with memories. But much more, the people dearest to him still gathered there in Tarkey every Sunday after church. Each weekly homecoming felt like a return from the revulsions of war, a reward to compensate for all the grief and despair that war had cost his sensibilities.

His mother was in the congenial fluster of her kitchen, supervising his two sisters when she was not governing their five children and his brother's three in the rumpus room downstairs. His father, newspaper sheets hanging in disarray from his burly hands, went inside and out looking awed by the swift proliferation of descendants. Barry's brother sat drinking beer and ridiculing the political disputes of their brothers-in-law while Chester's wife did her best to engage Marge in local gossip under the shade trees that canopied the big round garden table. The grounds were large. The children could range far and yet stay safely in view.

Only they would not come outside—not until the Sheriff appeared, replete with the fame he had won this week as a real old frontier-style gunfighter. The sight of Polsen leaving his police cruiser out front breached a family ambience so serene it had enabled Christian to put all the tensions of his employment by Fenneran behind him. Now his first thought was that something had happened to the Fennerans. But he rejected that fearful idea as merely the result of his wife's interest being stirred at last by a vague aspersion his sister-in-law had just made on Hillary Fenneran's girlhood.

Christian's nightcap visit with Marge to the grand old Hammerhead house, following the car crash, had been unexceptional beyond the charm of the hosts and the distress Fenneran caused, pressing him to phone Jessup. It was unlikely the Sheriff sus-

pected that communication as the source of Chuck Stowell's allegation, in a *Key Journal* article, that *return* fire had caused bullet holes in the Negro truck. Nor could this surprising visit by Polsen be connected sensibly with Price Fenton, whose bail-jumping disappearance had impaired the case with so pat a betrayal of guilt.

Noticing Dexter Polsen at the gate, Marge said, "Now here comes someone who's known Hillary for ages."

Nothing about the mystery of his presence here in Tarkey (and in uniform on a Sunday) not forty-eight hours after his spectacular arrest—which the same *Key Journal* blazoned—of so many connected to the growing rural vice circuit. Christian crossed the lawn with his fruit wine cocktail in hand and, trading smiles with the Sheriff, said, "This another raid?"

"In a manner of speaking. To separate you all from some money. New stunt of Wilmont's, his idea for the Christmas Fund."

"Struck a mother lode here." Christian swung open the gate. "You sure saw us coming."

"Well, that's the whole idea. Catch folks at their Sunday best, fresh from church and spoiling to pay for their sins."

A flat gaze attended that, lacing the remark with innuendo. But Christian chose to take it as no more than banter. Friday's lightning raid on those illegal dens had caused a sensation. Sheriff Dexter Polsen had encountered gunfire at one of them and bull-horned a challenge that he was walking in to put everyone there in jail, whether for vice or for murder being left to their own immediate reactions. "Those raids must have been child's play," Christian warranted, "compared to the adulation you probably had to endure today."

To that the Sheriff reacted with a grateful nod. "You're one man who appreciates the merciless obligations of this badge."

Again it seemed his choice of words implied more than jest, this time even suggesting the possibility of a warning about Fenneran's excesses. To meet it as badinage, Christian contrived a smile and asked about the reactions in this neighborhood of old-timers. Polsen told him that Hackling, the office supply man, was curious to know if peace officers took training in the

quick draw, while Lucci, the stonemason, had asked touchingly if it didn't break a Sheriff's heart to think he might one day have to kill a man. Then they were in the midst of Christian's family and he was able to relax.

Only the Sheriff, right on their home ground in person, had more attraction for the children than the innovative television now in the rumpus room, and that permitted their grandmother to come out with them for a while. So did Christian's sisters, until dinner preparations had to be completed. Even his roving father, aflutter with newspaper sheets, drew close to drawl a greeting.

The whole family was rapt. This idea promised to be a marvelous one for the poor at holiday time. With beer pressed on him, Polsen had to beg off because he was driving, but he warmed to the hospitality with a pleased grin. Until Winetta asked immodestly how much truth there was to the rumors about Hillary.

The Sheriff seemed to blanch (Christian himself wincing), but recovered quickly to say, "What rumors do you mean?"

"About her being fast as a girl."

Christian saw his sister-in-law's innocence weighed and accepted by the Sheriff's cool, appraising eye. Polsen broadened his smile. "Fast as greased lightning," he allowed. "Glad I wasn't Sheriff back then—I'd had to jail her or see her driver's license revoked, one."

The wine in him lent Christian the audacity to say, "You could always have turned the problem over to the Highway Patrol."

The Sheriff swung his grin on him and chuckled. "You liked that, didn't you? I could tell."

"Lawyer's weakness for finesse."

Around the table this blossoming conviviality alerted the men as if to something momentous, but Winetta and Marge in their deep garden chairs could not let the gossip alone. "Just cars?" his sister-in-law pressed, and his wife (provider of the silver lining for all matters disquieting) said, "Horses too, I suspect. But that would be all, just knowing the lady she is."

That icy gaze of Polsen's judged Marge and, deciding she was

without sarcasm, he confronted what he must know and they might learn in time. "Cars, horses, and beaux. She ran them ragged. Never let a car stall, a horse balk, or a suitor have his way. Though it's likely that some pretended they did. The insecure ones." He grinned at Christian for approbation and, getting it in a nod, said, "Hope Tate takes kindly to Prosecutor calling on him for Christmas Fund." In the high Gulf breezes he counted five-dollar bills all the men had handed over. "This one heck of a good idea. Wilmont's one good man."

"Seems like four good men," Chester said, toasting with his beer can, "go make one heck of a county out of Key. Adding you, Mr. Fenneran, and my baby brother."

Though smiling, Polsen was drumming his fingers. He stood up as Luanne's husband, Renny, said, "Know what the Injuns hold. Two great chiefs, one be slower. Three great chiefs, one be fit to deceive. Four great chiefs, one be devil son of a beast."

Christian and the Sheriff regarded each other with squints of mock suspicion till Polsen shook his head and said, "Must be Tate or Harmon."

"Harmon Wilmont's right from this town," Chester put in, "so he's out. That leaves Tate Fenneran your devil beast, I'm afraid. Understand he's from away up in Georgia somewheres."

"So am I, you cotton picker," Marge protested, holding down her straw hat brim. "Though I can't recall it."

"We all go back to Georgia," Etoille's husband, Scott, said, "except some of the Injuns and all the Jews." He glanced around, sensing disapproval, yet could not resist adding, "Even the darkies do."

That was when all of them laughed, tempering their scorn for un-Christian bigotries with mercy for such marginal ones. The tolerant levity helped them surmount that most awkward turn, and praise of the Sheriff brought them past it with Christian remarking that Fenneran had telephoned yesterday to boast about the success of Polsen's strike-force raids.

Disparaging in his modesty, the Sheriff said, "They'll be back in business before too long. Organized crime behind them. That's Tate's judgment and mine too. Makes that kind brazen."

The women expressed shock. Scott muttered something

about foreigners, but Renny silenced him with a weary glance, and everyone was quick to agree with the Sheriff's view that stronger vice laws were needed for enforcement. Then he congenially took his leave and Christian walked him to the gate, thinking Fenneran had to be at the bottom of Polsen's visit here.

But whether he had come in concern over Tate or prompted by him, Christian was not ready to guess until the Sheriff, abruptly rather grave, said, "Hope it doesn't appear I'm trying to prejudice your case or like that, but the Indian girl means business this time, and I mean it too. So I feel duty bound to warn you I'mo bust those young fuckers of yours down to toe jam next time they attempt any intimidation of the witnesses."

Heatedly Christian said, "They're no fuckers of mine. Beats me why you even mention them on Sunday."

Raising dark glasses to put them on, Polsen stopped with a look of surprise. "Guess you haven't gone through the Sunday papers yet. Miz Honey Baines speculating on this case with sudden interest since she picked up Stowell's lying contention. Today she twisted Fenton's jumping bail into something maybe the Prosecutor's done, like spirited him away to make them all look guilty. Now *somebody's* put that in her empty head."

The reason at last for Polsen's visit: to leave a message he could not personally deliver to Fenneran. Though annoyed by the antic of handcuffing him at an open gathering, Tate had left no doubt about the affection and high hopes he had for the Sheriff. Christian himself felt an easy respect that bordered on fondness for this whimsical, flinty officer. But his hard gaze, now, Christian could only interpret as accusing, and resented it.

"We all appreciate that trash kept to their own neighborhoods, Sheriff, away from our women and children. Whole county admires the quiet strength of your office, but not nearly as much as Tate does. Sure hope you don't think he or I have put the newslady up to anything like that."

Their eyes dipped and recovered. Polsen said, "You telling me straight?"

"Straight as I can."

The dark glasses hung in midair a moment longer before the Sheriff put them on, his doubt conveyed though he said, "Can't

tell you how much it pleases me to hear that. Tate's my old buddy. See you don't let him lean back so far for Key County that he bump his cracker head."

Then he was gone. Barry Christian lingered at the gate a while, pondering what must surely have been Polsen's declaration that he meant business where it concerned not only the Bayfront hoodlums but all nemeses of the law, even if that included his own best friends. Christian hoped he could find reasonably functional areas between his conscience and a client whose ethics might prove disproportionate to his ultimate good intentions. It had indeed been Fenneran's idea, transmitted by Jessup, to have Stowell say he was fired on from the pickup truck before he opened fire himself.

In Fenneran's view, telephoning such instructions to the trucker was inapt for him, but not for the lawyer whose charge Stowell was, and Christian's compliance dogged him with a guilt that grew suddenly acute at the shouted sound of his name.

"Barry," like a reprimand, "Barry!" He spun around to see his father coming at him in a blown trail of newsprint—and loping right on past, yelling, "Barry" again, "Barry!"

The sunken cheek of dread rushing by, the bulging eye—he believed his father seized by a mental convulsion. Then he saw Chester's twelve-year-old Jim hurdling the brook behind the house, and laughed. His father had often chased after him that very way, intolerant of unnecessary hazard, and was only confusing the names of a son and grandson (and maybe time as well) in his excitement.

The boy's grandpa had hold of him. Christian's nephew was safe, if he himself was not. Marge had observed that Fenneran looked dangerous. She enjoyed that notion of him without any sense of risk, much like noncombatants who were thrilled by war. Christian had risked the jeopardy of war for far less than anything like the promise of wealth and power that Fenneran represented.

The man's machinations were so complicated, they kept returning in his deep voice to haunt Christian and make him feel precarious. So did going to trial against Harmon Wilmont. But Christian was confident he had the resources to meet any chal-

lenge. Maybe because of a lifelong faith in his taciturn father's devotion, he could anticipate the future with the same enthusiasm he enjoyed at the moment, walking into a discussion of tag sales and children that blended his dissimilar loved ones around the shaded garden table. They were all so decent, basically, and all so safe in their debonair Sunday casuals.

"Barry, Barry!" and a crash.

He thought his mind had echoed back his father's earlier cry, but a second heart-wrenching sound of collision drove him at a gallop to the old man's pointing finger. Jim was pointing too, and all the others were racing with Christian to the brook, where Polsen's cruiser lay sinking in smoke, COUNTY POLICE inverted on its upturned side, one wheel spinning free against a backdrop of splintered guard rails on the old Spanish arched bridge above.

Eerily the car resembled that wrecked auto of Stowell and Newgate, which impact alone had flung over on its back. Even the women were hurrying. By their flutter of woeful cries he knew Polsen was trapped in there. Yet something drove him past the wreck—one sound, a screech of escape on the roadway above.

Others would see to the Sheriff. Lunging, Christian scurried up the embankment, Scott overtaking him with furious curses. Someone had done this. It had Scott raging, short of breath. "The bastards hit him and ran! A panel truck, I saw it bounce off!"

In a blur of shoving, Christian got past people who stood around the avenue in paralyzed bewilderment. He was next driving a powerful sedan with his brother-in-law beside him pulling the opposite door shut, barely managing in his breathless outrage to cry, "Collier Road, they've got to head north out of Key County! The palm grove marl roads!"

Christian banged the horn incessantly to get around slow Sunday drivers, and kept it going with Fenneran's imperious voice echoing back to trivialize any resistance to his borderline miscarriages of justice: "In all my ruthless assaults on the prim skirts of convention, I assure you no harm will come to anybody."

In the commercial center of town Christian overtook a green panel truck. Feeling absurd, he thumped the horn indignantly to halt the truck, but of course it was not about to stop. Its increasing speed proved it guilty. Christian pressed after it, afraid to look at the speeds he was reaching, the old car they had commandeered rattling as in a gale wind at the last suburban edge of town where billboards trailed off to scrub pine and the highway ribboned through open farmland straight for the palm groves that meant hidden escape routes for the criminal truck.

"This shore of ours," Fenneran drummed on in memory, "an arid shell-beach wasteland now, is on solid oolite, Barry, and begging to be transformed into real property of incalculable value, social and cultural as well as financial. I'm exposing you to a process of expedience, not a transgression. Jessup's mission would not be stretching things too much. Maybe cause a standoff, is all. Child's play, considering the larger purpose."

A wet mirage, shimmying beneath the truck far ahead, eased to stillness and vanished. They seemed to be gaining on the vehicle too rapidly, yet Scott cried, "Don't slow down," in a voice keen with fright, "keep at them!"

Someone slid out on the right side: the truck had evidently stopped in the distance. But not to surrender. That was clear when the man faced them at an aggressive crouch with both hands at his face and a tremor shook him. "Get down," Christian shouted just as the report reached them, "he's shooting at us!"

"Ram them, ram them," Scott shrieked, ducking down. "Go right at them and smack the bastards!" The driver got out too, a black man who came forth shooting at a run, and Christian jammed the brakes, skidding left, with Scott down low but raging, "Plow into them—what's the matter with you?"

Pistol shots, not likely to find their marks at far range, would be more telling the closer they got, and the criminals could easily leap aside to let them go crashing into the truck and be killed. With pistols cracking, the pair charged nearer to shoot strangers dead, a black man and a white in summer sportshirts, dressed that way to murder. Christian wheeled full around south on screeching wheels to escape, Scott screaming, "Drive at them, hit them! Don't let the bastards get away!"

With a glance at his florid cheek, his mindless fury, Christian said, "Up close, Scott, those pistols'll kill us."

He wondered if Jessup's thugs could be behind this. Whoever they were, those men had smashed into Polsen intentionally, the panel truck probably stolen for abandonment later in the palm groves. They had no doubt followed the Sheriff all morning, patient for their best chance to kill him. Jessup could have brought people in, or his poaching connections might have.

Christian raced back to see if the Sheriff was alive. Tate Fenneran was surely above having any part in a crime like this. Christian could tell himself that much. But not with absolute conviction.

Incredulous, he said, "What kind of people can they be, who deliberately set out to kill like that?" He remembered setting out just that way in combat, and grew so sick he had to add, "In peacetime not people at all, but beasts. Beasts."

COLLAGE 6

Dexter Polsen could not live. All of Christian's family were sure from the devastation they had seen. All wore the same mortal look of consternation. Christian searched every face around the hospital, but in none was he able to detect a sign of any capacity whatever to commit premeditated violence on another human being. There was a cosmic difference between those who could and ordinary people. Fenneran was not like ordinary people.

He equated the advantages of a major new highway with defending a rabble against just charges of rape and attempted murder. When Christian questioned the attitude, that night on their way to the car crash, Tate had said, "It would be less than convincing if I pulled out all the threads for your inspection. One inevitable day you'll see the importance of that rabble to more than just a highway—to jobs for the formerly shiftless, to housing, parks of industry and leisure, in a fabulous metropolis."

Tate Fenneran was an extraordinary man, who could put an

exact value on every facet of life large and small. That, a formidable power in itself, seemed to be the core of his nature.

Christian saw Hillary just arriving in the crowded hospital lounge, looking around in ghostly white bereavement. Her beauty never failed to stop his breath. Even now, and here, her flawless grace entranced him. He advanced to lament with her, but an uneasy conscience turned him away as if from their fidelity to Tate, as if the Sheriff lay dying of that. Stricken, Barry Christian left the place with a handkerchief to his mouth, and went out back amid the lonely shrubs of the grounds.

An air of uncertain morality prevailed wherever people with growing children gathered socially. So it always struck Tate Fenneran, and most especially at the Key Country Club. Now he sensed an air of uncertain mourning where the membership had congregated to socialize with Dexter Polsen at his death.

Polished gentlemen of the trophy room, who scored many a commercial trade while flirting, did a brisk muffled business here in praise of the Sheriff's accomplishments. Powdered ladies of the dance floor, who brushed one's lapels in rosy suggestiveness, blushed now with awkward sympathy.

People from every town had gathered in sorrow, all laundered and groomed to respectfully await the end. County leaders came to grieve and pray, common citizens too, who had just that day enjoyed the Sheriff's visits to solicit their alms for the poor.

Dexter had suffered positive skull fracture along with broken limbs and probably mortal harm to his spine, if not the brain as well. Honey Baines asked Fenneran if there was anything she could do. There was nothing she would not do. He had won the reporter girl's gratitude by sending her early to this selfsame hospital for an exclusive on the racial car fight. Now they stood together with Dexter killed and everything was mist.

Everything was myth, except the physical promise of Key County. Now blood was needed for Dexter and Honey grew faint. The newslady fainted, a tool for anything but blood. People spirited her away, their brittle cries fading in the mists and myths. Down old corridors Fenneran accompanied members of the board he had secretly formed while Dexter lived, bright and

acrimonious, saying "People we know maybe killed" from his deputy's car, and now it was Dexter crushed beyond all the citrated blood the board of donors gave.

How different this was from the wreckage of Stowell and Newgate, who lay now in beds upstairs, how grudging pity was. But how keen the instinct that had him employ Honey to save that pair of simpletons from their witless blunder. Now there was work for brutes like them if Dexter lived or died. For law was grudging too in its protection of the just. How prosperous the corrupt grew on that. There was no way in reality to restrain them. They must absolutely be destroyed.

Fenneran believed that in the depth of his grief over Dexter. More than a friend's life mattered here. The entire future of Key County teetered on one's reaction to this atrocity, every bridge and park and dream. Every museum blessed with handicrafts like the adz he had brought home from Tallahassee.

He weighed the heft of its shaft in mind while donating blood to Dexter. Hundreds of years ago some Creek or Cherokee had fashioned the adz to trim wood surfaces. The blade of dolomite or calcite serpentine was ground smooth and tied fast and forever to the hardwood with animal sinew. Plant fiber would long since have given way to rot or weariness. But the sinew wound tight while wet had dried as firm and permanent as tough steel wire. How sad that Hillary had no feeling for utilitarian art. Nor had Marge shown interest in the colonial pewter tankard he displayed to occupy her while Barry telephoned Jessup on request, a short while ago it seemed as Tate lay bleeding and dreaming.

Over and over Christian asked himself, What kind of beasts could they be who set out to commit such deliberate cruelty? It became a rote in his mind, like waves falling on a shore.

Fenneran offered a simple answer. The criminals who had set out to murder Sheriff Polsen were outsiders bent on establishing a vice enclave along the fertile Gulf Coast. Christian, carefully watching Tate's face, had just related the events of the afternoon step by step in a scrubbed area of metal chairs full of people. Though Fenneran betrayed no sign of emotion beyond a gray

pallor, that was enough to project his bottomless desolation. But there appeared to be no rankling bitterness, a fact to which Barry Christian's suspicion clung.

Tate Fenneran discerned as much, meeting Barry's gaze flat-eyed grave to add, "Would any Negro but an outsider dare participate so openly? Calm thought would have made it obvious to you that underworld people engineered this brutality."

Christian felt shame—and fear. It was obvious too that Fenneran would tolerate no such threat to the whole legal structure of Key County. In the mere concealment of his sorrow the prospect of measures he might take was chilling.

Laboring without rest, the surgeons did all they could for Dexter Polsen. By evening his life was hanging by a thread. So said Marge Christian in the operating room vestibule. Soon Loker Brisburn arrived with Chief Judge Peter Arlington Dow; in Fenneran's gloom their very presence reduced eminence to the commonplace, and was the proof of implacable mortality. He sank to the bleakest pessimism concerning Dexter.

Hillary's father was the most important marketer of commercial sponge from Tarpon Springs to Key West, aside from his vast lumber holdings, lime groves, and produce farming. If his headquarters ever moved out of Keyport, the economy of all the surrounding region would falter. Key County was not only the arena of his life but also its reflection: he viewed anything inimical to local institutions as a personal abuse. No one was more outraged than Loker by this wanton attack on the Sheriff. He met Fenneran grim with suppressed emotions, as on the day word came that his son was dead in the Pacific.

Bald and blinking in the reception room, he seemed not even to be sweating normally. How pathetic the three of them were, standing mired in helplessness with all their power reduced to fluff, an irony that so affected the Chief Judge that he cast Loker an almost beseeching glance, then awkwardly congratulated Fenneran on the progress of Ceremony Bridge.

"Yes," Loker murmured, "yes," with one hand lightly on his son-in-law's shoulder. "We'd never have been able to budget in that brainchild of yours if labor costs proved higher."

Fenneran nodded to that elementary remark, contrived to break the cumbersome silence in this well of tragedy. He was counting on Loker, flint hard when it came to business or politics, for the support he needed in the urgent business at hand.

Already taking steps, he had assigned Christian a chore outside, where Prewitt sat weeping in the limousine. Both to comfort the Negro and to equip himself for making use of Jessup (possibly others too in the pit-fighting enterprise), he had asked Barry to take Prewitt's account of his scary Bayfront visit with the trucker recently, and to remember every detail so as to miss no name or element that might prove useful. Fenneran had not let his end purpose become evident, but Christian was aware it entailed finding Polsen's assailants, and was bright enough to anticipate the implicit dangers.

"Jobs are good," Loker went on, "but too many of them attract unionism. The day we get unionized down here is the day progress ends. Because that's when the black man gets parity and stops representing a reasonable check on the working man's appetite. That'll be when labor costs get prohibitive. Life will change."

Even at a time like this Loker could not help worrying about all that a new highway to Wildcat Point might bring to the future. Fenneran nodded with a look of thoughtful attention. "Be bearing that in mind after all this." He turned to Dow. "But we won't be past this till I can find the attorney they sent from Miami to counsel that scum Dexter apprehended in their sinkholes."

The judge was puzzled. "Wilmont's office," he asserted in a whisper of seemly condolence, "can provide that."

"Those locals are just guinea pigs, Your Honor. The attack on Polsen was a warning to us by powerful interests that they'll brook no interference with their exploitation of our growth."

Fenneran's father-in-law regarded him contemplatively. There was no hope in legal procedure of rooting out the criminal incursion that was costing them Dexter Polsen's life just as a start, and they silently communicated their perfect concord on that. Loker gave a brisk nod to confirm it. "Lawyer's not from Miami, but from away over in New Orleans. Isn't that so, Pete?"

The Chief Judge looked down, hair falling white across the overheated skin of his forehead. He glanced to one side and the other, then said with a heavy expression of discomfort, "He's staying at the Ponce de Leon. His name is Pierpont."

"Not to say he told you," Loker undertoned, Barry Christian reaching them with his wife just then through the crowd.

Marge was in tears. Extensive brain surgery had been necessary, she reported. Deejay was being allowed to stay by Dexter in the Intensive Care Unit with their minister. It meant that hope was dim.

Seated beside the chauffeur, Christian had scrawled his notes comprehensively, but they conveyed little more than Prewitt's fears and tears. Fenneran listened to the details on an isolated hospital balcony high over a vista of the bays.

The Negro could recall no names. It had horrified him to set foot barely in the outskirts of the Bayfront where southern fringes of Gulf Glade tapered off amid abandoned warehouses. Talking into a handkerchief with his voice caught short by sobs, he took Christian back to a cavernous old structure that echoed with the barks of three nervous mongrels the men hoped to train as pit fighters. They had rounded up two kittens on his instructions to Jessup for half a dozen, and nobody had remembered to bring some kind of spring, or even a rope.

Prewitt had to make do. In a greasy cold sweat of fear, he dumped both kittens into an onion bag and asked a cadaverous tall man to bounce it gently at arm's length, then had the others unleash their slavering dogs to attack the bobbing, squealing kittens and parry their defensive claws, his voice echoing dreamlike with the snarling barks and the cries of excited men.

Christian quoted abominable data about kittens mauled to provide the dogs a taste of the kill, then finished his report with Prewitt priming himself, in case anything should anger those coarse white men, for desperate escape to nearby Gulf Glade, where they were no more welcome than he, and no kind of violence would be tolerated by the law except the harmless kind like pit fighting, once a cop or two received payment.

With a shrug Christian met the level gaze of Fenneran, who said, "The punch line yours or Prewitt's?"

"His assumption, based on the ease of paying off Hammerhead cops to allow dog violence in Swamptown."

Fenneran considered that worth pondering, and it was not long before something came to him. "Didn't you think it rather odd that there was no sign of the police till you and your brother-in-law returned from chasing those gunmen in the van?"

"You mean the Tarkey police may be corrupt too?"

"They could all be. And where corruption is entrenched, it probably flows to or from the top." Fenneran had pretty much all he needed. "I'd like you to telephone Jessup and have him come down here for a visit with his boy Stowell. Your client, you visit him at the same time, say to take his deposition since he can't leave the hospital to give it in court."

He saw Christian stiffen, go on guard.

"Barry, Wilmont thinks he can make a case against people who cover their tracks in anticipation of every legal action against them. They'll kill him as well as Dexter if he gets convictions before somebody uncovers the ringleaders. That damned fool can't rid us of those atrocious outsiders. We, however, can."

He paused to let that sink in, then gave Christian the New Orleans lawyer's name and hotel address for Jessup, explaining that the trucker was to contact this Pierpont and pretend to be an emissary of police interests grateful to have Polsen put out of the way. They had sent him, Jessup was to say, after the considerable financial backing they required to expand Gulf Coast pit fighting into big business with its concomitants of gambling, prostitution, and usury.

In the breezy night shadows Christian seemed resentful, as if unfairly put upon by this. "For all the cruel leavening of war," Fenneran said, restraining his own resentment, "you still have sentiment and moral pretensions to surmount. The hollow elements of life, to which some people cling forever. But I doubt you're infantile or defective, as they are. Disease attacks, the surgeon defends. The Nazis attacked, men like you defended. This, Barry, is where we separate the men from the boys."

Susceptible like all veterans to army cant, Christian stood

there digesting Fenneran's use of it to challenge him with the implication of power and opulence for the courageous. He looked out over the bays, conscious, Fenneran perceived, that there was no turning back if he hoped to prosper in Key County, but not yet won over and not to be, altogether, for some time. The lights on Seashell Key twinkled like feeble mortality. "Is Jessup," the young old soldier said at last, "a man who is likely to succeed?"

"I think he may die trying. If instead he establishes with Pierpont, have him telephone me about a landscaping delivery of swamp humus and peat. I'm banking on your comprehension."

Fenneran knew he would have to convince more old pragmatists than Loker Brisburn that progress posed no social threat to Key County, and more young idealists than Barry Christian that every blow must have its counterblow to maintain a civilized society.

Bringing prosperous equanimity to the region was going to be difficult. The best people opposed it.

The night was mostly sleepless for the Sheriff's wife, who spent it dying away with him in his isolated hospital room. He lay inert as wood, encased in white, and splinted and strapped to every ponderous sort of apparatus. She reviled the animals who had violated his body, and the doctors who had raped his brain and left the remains to expire by degrees before her, his humorous good nature betrayed, his manhood insulted, all his fortitude evaporating like water. She cursed the evil that had lurked in their optimistic world to ambush them.

Her sons and daughters were a blessing from his careful strength. She begged him to survive for them. She prayed to her husband more than God to send Dexter back somehow replenished. And with all that was mighty about him, he was the frailest of her children in the eternity she sat losing her mind by his bed.

By dawn his life had ebbed. Nurses awakened her to be ready should contingency medical procedures fail. Everyone close remained to keep the vigil except County Attorney Wilmont.

Looking vindictive, as if he knew just where to place the blame for all this, he said he had work to do because the rape hearing was scheduled for that day. Abruptly he departed with his frosty gaze, leaving the crowded visitors' lounge funereal in a sunlit haze of faint aseptic odors.

Christian was inclined to hasten the proceedings, feeling anxious about the state of his wife and unborn child in those heavy hours of emotion as Marge and Hillary stayed attentively close to Deejay. But over their coffee-counter breakfast Tate Fenneran advised a careful unfolding that would induce the prosecution to withdraw and avoid trial. Livid with grief, he said, "Wilmont's determination to bring those rapists to justice is politically a needless test. But he's got them dead to rights. If this reaches trial by jury, it'll mean real trouble, a serious and maybe violent racial confrontation in this county."

"I'll elicit that crocodile testimony."

Fenneran gave an approving nod. "Once vanquished, the Prosecutor's bound to be grateful for any good gesture from the victors. That's us, Barry. Call it domination by magnanimity."

Christian despaired to find himself the beneficiary of Polsen's death, which would make the contest with Wilmont that much easier. Yesterday in his father's yard a thousand tortured years ago, he had imagined Fenneran standing like some unseen god over his chosen lawyer and chosen lawman, amused that each had to dispel the other's fears about Tate in order to dispel his own—that neither would ever show disloyalty to him in front of the other. Having chosen them for such assured integrity, he could use it to subjugate them both, along with Wilmont, in the abundance of his promise—his magnanimity.

This picture of Tate Fenneran was awesome—a personification of power forever consolidating itself by its very nature. To Christian it made the man seem mechanical in his genius, unable to temper the forces in him with even the best of his instincts. It made him seem dedicated to every good, yet capable of any evil.

Up in the swamp from the highway, Chitto Jumper prayed at busk. No word of Majosee had ever reached him, and he believed from visions that the enemy had harmed her. Only her

safe return could pacify him. This he vowed to the Breathmaker, swearing himself to vengeance in the language of his heavy heart.

Boos-ke-tau was ending here, but not on the reservation. Emathla had told him in the telephone that the Green Corn Dance was date-sticked later by some days this year. Chitto had time to canoe there before busk ended with general amnesty for all the guilty of the waning year. When the sun sank toward the tall tree domes, Thlotlo Ulgee, called Fish William nowadays, carried the paired-feather cane to the edge of the hammock with everybody following. He lifted his voice in the death whoop, and Chitto saw a swift cloud, one white mist on the eternity of blue, a vision of power soon to reach him.

The tide ran clear as river water. Chitto waited with war in his heart for Fish William's signal. The old medicine man planted his white-feather cane to bless the earth, and every man leaped headlong into the slough. Dripping, they rose with death whoops. Chitto's were mighty storms of the heart, and all eyes lit on him with the fire of the sinking sun. All knew he was going for his deer rifle without washing off the clay and ash as they would do in ritual. Even his grandson (with fresh leg scars and a man's name now) realized he must find Majosee, or grief, or war, before he could be restored by *Boos-ke-tau*, as each of the others already was, to himself, his family, and his nation.

An emergency surgical gamble raised Dexter again to the brink, on the knife edge of which he was expected to survive at least another day in the sorrow of his family and friends. Short of sleep, Christian arrived in chambers early; the Prosecutor, making the most of his day in court, denounced Fenton for his surrender of bail by abscondence and Stowell for wrecking himself in a car crash that resulted from criminal behavior. Christian was not averse to the rest of his clients seeing in Judge Cheatham's gelid eye the retribution yet in store for them if ever they strayed from Fenneran's restraints again.

The depositions were taken. The Indian swore the whites had all five brutally forced themselves on her in the swamp; the Negro identified them one by one, attesting to their command that he conceal her bodily remains on pain of death, and to her

mental as well as physical condition when he rescued her from the lettuce lake; the culprits took their prepared position that she had submitted to them willingly as far as they could determine.

Wilmont chose to stop at their word against his witnesses' rather than refute with the Sheriff's exhibit even though it displayed clear evidence of assault and battery on the girl. That left Christian with little doubt that testimonial allusion to the crocodile accompanied Polsen's report, an issue the prosecution realized it had to evade at all costs.

In this austere gathering, Christian spoke the Sheriff's name, and rose from the long polished table around which all were seated before the bench. By the bank of domed windows towering amid their heavy velvet drapes, he said with reverential brevity, "We all know why Sheriff Polsen was unable to attend. It seems elemental that his deposition should be entered by his devoted friend, Prosecutor Wilmont, as trustee."

So Judge Cheatham directed, with Wilmont in helpless accord. Apprehension shadowed the Prosecutor's facade. Obliged to read Sheriff Polsen's certification of evidence, he provided all the defense needed to contend with the Indian girl. But Christian, quailing in the pathos of her stricken eyes, eerily suffered a disheartening sudden recall of his worst wartime fear.

His gaze faltered and fled from her to meet the Negro's for an instant across the table. Junn Cavalo's fear was drawn down tight into a coil of pure animosity. Christian admired his courage in the circumstance of security that depended solely on two sidearmed court officers as hostile to him as the scrubbed young thugs, whose clean-shaven faces resembled stage masks.

The uneasy crosscurrents of enmity had become just another absurdity in the comic opera of dialects and status disparities. Yet nobody laughed, nobody was anything but tense in the moment that Christian experienced the identical sense of incongruous doom that had multiplied the jeopardy he lived with as a platoon commander in the war.

Children had terrified him in combat. He had lived in fear that a German child would kill him. In final desperation the Nazis had armed eight-year-olds with burp guns to spray death at the unsuspecting. Christian had endured the last months of

battle in dread of being stunned by sudden confrontation with an armed blond tot, of losing to hesitation the crucial split second that meant survival for the quick. He had often fallen dead that way in his nightmare-riddled sleep, and could not understand why the same helpless sense of perdition should return to disturb him now.

The Sheriff's report did mention sexual congress with a crocodile, but only as a hysterical phantasm the girl had experienced during the rape. Looking out the imposing windows as Wilmont's recital ended, Christian turned and said, "Underhanded concealment of the facts is unlawful in sworn testimony. Subreption, it's called, and committing it may lead to imprisonment for perjury. If that is not clear to anyone, please speak up."

No hand was raised. Everybody understood. Wilmont knew his case had fallen through and sat by glum as Christian questioned first the girl, then the man, and next the stolid defendants. Employing crude euphemisms, Majosee described her intercourse with the crocodile as either a dream, in her best judgment, or a visit by the Devil, to whom she had prayed for vengeance. Her eyes shifted insanely from side to side at that. The Negro appeared to comprehend its effect, almost mimicking her reaction, but could only say it had happened just so according to the five boys.

One by one the three who were present testified as instructed that none had ever told him any tale of the sort at their campfire in the swamp, where he drank devil's eye instead of eating.

He called them liars to their faces and they bristled, Wiley nearly pitching over his chair, springing up. Judge Cheatham himself, demanding order, looked astonished at the phenomenon of so unequivocating a Negro as Christian shoved his beastly client down.

Junn Cavalo had gained an advantage, but sadly too late. This extraordinary black man evidently sensed what was happening and made a last valiant effort to salvage the prosecution of these brutes by describing his frightful contest for the girl with a crocodile that strangely kept her from drowning while unconscious. But it would not avail. On the basis of such testimony he had to be construed as superstitious or unreasonably supportive of the girl at her hysterical worst.

Yet in a sudden clammy sweat, Christian believed it, frail girl and gigantic crocodile in copula.

But the critical issue was in the depositions. It would tax any trial court's credulity and impugn both prosecution witnesses as mystical, hallucinating primitives. Wilmont would never bring anything to trial that could discredit him so, and had to agree with the judge's view that a discontinuance of proceedings seemed in order. So did a consultation at this time, Christian concurred, and Wilmont invited him to his office for that.

For a moment Christian had believed the illogical lore of these primitives (no doubt out of sympathy for the colored pair) though he had dismissed it as drunken nonsense at first mention by his obnoxious clients. In the corridor he quickly had them leave to avert a confrontation with the Negro. They had no idea what had happened, and he was impelled not to exhilarate them with clarification. Instead he sent them off to brood in miserable suspense until further notice.

As for himself, the sweet flavor of triumph did not blossom. He had a few refreshing sips of a cold drink at the vending machine. Then he left some colleagues in midconversation to go have it done with, the tool of a complex man he found opinionated, pedantic, even frightening. But the future lay with Fenneran. That was undeniable.

Christian had tasted that in full flavor as, walking away from Stowell's smashup, Tate said he considered the Prosecutor no problem, for all the strength of the upcounty group that sponsored him in the election. "His rigid integrity makes him vulnerable. Being sincere about it, he believes they admire that integrity, whereas they just rely on the popularity of it as coin for their own political use. I can win a political beast like Wilmont to myself by the same means of playing up to that integrity —and win his Tarkey backers too in the process."

There was no ploy Tate shrank from to enhance the prospect of wealth and power for the intrepid. But the chauffeur stood smiling on the highway, the limousine sat waiting with their vivacious wives, and the whole wild-eyed world of lights was surging with the portent and the challenge of Fenneran's implications.

Now Christian still felt galvanized, despite concern about his pregnant wife and his bereavement over Polsen. With all his will he had to resist the instincts that urged him to refuse Fenneran hereafter, just as Wilmont would be loath to refuse him when the time came.

Entering the County Attorney's office, Christian found both defeated complainants seated by the desk in plain discomposure, and could not help seeing himself as a conscious participant in their oppression. Wilmont looked just as rueful—pale and grave, nodding to encourage Cavalo, who was saying, "She ain't expected no justice here no more than me. Just scared made her come here, me scared the same, her folks to learn how you all done her."

Wilmont seized on that to drill Christian with flashing eyes and jab a thumb to target him while stating acidly, "Not we all, John. They all. They're his boys, not mine."

Christian stammered in angry protest, but before he could shape his remark the girl emitted a shriek that electrified him with awe, and from her chair she sprang fiercely bucking, hopping in a circle around the big desk without ever taking her frenzied stare off him. He recoiled from this spectacle of insanity as Wilmont rushed to help the Negro restrain her.

But her shrieking descended to shrill whoops and squeals, her prancing to a measured dance, and Cavalo drew back to leave her room. The Prosecutor also deferred to that compulsive gallop around the office in a gibberish of toneless language, her violent eyes fixed on Christian.

He had never felt such sharp and sweating fright except in the war. Her eyes following him like a curse, she leaped in apparent torment, grimacing, bending, gesticulating, and crying out between her incoherent declamations. It was preposterous, but far from laughable. And in the midst of this perplexing sight came a sudden diatribe from Wilmont that shocked Christian all the more.

"What you see here," the Prosecutor said with cutting eyes, "is the start of an uprising. Make no mistake about it, Barry Christian." The girl danced in lunacy, her yelps attracting personnel, who entered to stand transfixed in a captive audience for

Wilmont to sermonize. "This is the result of our profane hypocrisies before God. Our sacrilegious failure to provide equal justice can only drive people to take it for themselves over our dead bodies." The girl was tireless, the Negro trancelike in a watchful crouch, the Prosecutor shamelessly orating his doubtful prophecy. "They are bound to burn us down. They must inevitably organize to militate against us. Separate equality will no longer suffice, and I will remind you all I told you so. All of you who are so willful as to bargain away integrity, honor, and dignity for small advantages."

Christian was aghast. The girl, still fastened to him with her fierce eyes, swept up the stars and stripes on its shining staff in the corner, the Negro quick to restrain her, taking her wrist. "Put down the flag, Majosee. It ain't ours."

Obeying, she stood there stiff, her dance over but the madness imprinted on her face: teeth bared, a glare of hatred stark in her eyes. All at once Christian was afraid he understood the strange recurrence of his bleak wartime fear of children. Some defense mechanism had likely crawled out of the past to warn that he was being pulled into a game played imperiously with the lives of small people by those with power, and warn too that he must beware the pawns as well as the masters to escape destruction.

Now a new sense of Wilmont alarmed him more than a man so steeped in power as Fenneran. The use of power could be tempered, the will to it was usually ferocious. Hoping his own drives did not prove ruthless, Christian indignantly said, "I'm here for a stipulation of discontinuance of proceedings, or a trial date."

A slowly rising wail of agony escaped the girl, and she sank down doubled over on a chair. Wilmont said, "It's being drawn up right now. I anticipated the possible subversion of this case by a mere whim of hallucination. I just hope we live to recover from this fall of rectitude. May God grant that Dexter does."

Clerks and secretaries began to withdraw. The Negro was trying to comfort the Indian girl, but she said, "Ole son of a bitch Junn, pain biting sharp again. Ain't what you think, though." Her sliding eyes held on Christian with flat contempt. "Can't back up no more to save nobody. Them snake signs

showed me blood on the sky, war go bite everybody's life out now."

"Sometimes ole stupid take us," the Negro moved closer to tell the white men obscurely, "and we mostly wants to die."

Christian left the office, Junn's meaning clear to him as a perception of the idiotic racial war that was all Majosee had left to seek, and remarkably war had just started again, far away in Korea. People in the courthouse corridors were talking about it, a full-scale United Nations action. Even so, most of the combat troops were American, committed by the President.

It hazed Christian with impending doom, like his World War horror of children so recently. Child's play, Fenneran had termed his machinations, considering his larger purpose. Child's play was all the deadly burp guns were to those German kids. Did one have to rescue the murderous likes of them for social progress?

Not in war. The Nazis attacked and Lieutenant Christian defended. It was as simply true as Tate had put it with his uncanny sense of just the right nerve to touch. Even when those Nazis were mindless children. Christian had rounded up several discovered to be armed and sent them along to rehabilitation. But as long as he lived he would remember one April morning at the River Elbe, when pale boys ten years old and younger came out of the woods firing burp guns in a line like infantry.

He had cut them down. That was the most unforgettable fact of his life. He had hammered away with the machine gun mounted on his jeep because he was responsible for the lives of his men.

Someone called his name. He turned to see Harmon Wilmont overtaking him with a smile, as if he had not really expected to win his action against those boys. A phone call had come, he announced. Dexter Polsen was going to live through.

Through what, Christian thought, this continuing war in the world? "The necrotic tissue removed from his brain was only minimal," Wilmont exulted. "His spine is intact, his broken bones will mend. It seems miraculous."

But the Sheriff was never going to be the same, Christian knew somehow. The world was never going to be the same.

He had deliberately killed the mindless German children.

COLLAGE 7

Okaloacoochee Slough poured the boundless summer drain sixty miles south to Shark River, flooding all the brooding reaches of Big Cypress Swamp. Tree heads marked the depths. The shallows eddied in tall sedge. Silent and somber, this risen wash reflected the sky like blue glass around numberless dense hammocks and acres of slash pine flatwoods.

The swamp fires of winter had left their tall ruins ghostly on limestone outcrops. Beyond those charred sentries, deep in shrouded stealths of the surviving verdure, fauna teemed in secret. Where swamp buggies could function no longer, only traversing airboats introduced any sound of consequence through the desolate expanses; the loud aeronautic engines, howling here and there beneath the monumental cloud banks, were themselves contained, muted, isolated by massive sun-cooked space.

Army engineers on transverse road site inspection, three gloomy officers in coveralls and campaign hats, fought mos-

quitoes and cursed the endless tracts of shadow and luxuriance. They vented foul obscenities, so sure of solitude in all the dismal miles west from the sweeping sawgrass plains of the Everglades.

Piloting the boat, a captain shouted in the engine roar, "Some hold that it's a shame to molest these godforsaken waters. Why do people say that?"

"Because they lack good sense," a flushed major behind him replied at a high pitch. "And taste. To me, everything not man-made is a fucking eyesore."

Not far off a larger airboat skimmed the misty waterways. It carried six men just as plagued by insects, just as deafened to nearby travelers by the propeller-driving engine mounted high above them, but disheartened not at all by the apparent absence of life in all the region. Amid the superstructure pipes Elwin Hoyt held a pale, stumpy cur by its studded collar and fanned his hat to keep the bugs off while Guy Helker steered at the helm and Brady Wiley stood watch between them with a rifle. Below, Nat Jessup stood with his back to the prow rail, shouting to be heard by the lawyer Pierpont, who was seated with a nameless aide in the bucket seats.

"They be down from Jerome and Ochopee to look that hammock over. Ranchers, construction operators, not just no ole laborers and farm hands. Maybe from Hendry County too. I'mo make out like the N'Orleans folks sent you all special to see about backing our Swamp Stadium idea. They be right impressed to hear that."

The paunchy lawyer, suave in a bleached hat and riverfront clothes as white, beckoned him to lean closer. "What," he called into the noise, "is the big one with the rifle so riled up evil for? Nothing to it, putting up some benches and pit sides for a dogfight, is there?"

"Oh, ole Brady just can't git off of studying 'gator skin money is all. We can't chance poaching for a spell, and he's that smart he blaming it on carpentry."

"More like nigger skin's on his mind. I heard he's got this grudge, some coon in this here swamp."

"Yeah, well he ain't likely find no nigger in this haystack."

Pierpont turned for a look at Brady, fighting insects up in the

superstructure. Then, arching his heavy black eyebrows, the lawyer said, "Got law sailing these runs in airboats, now water's high. Please make very sure he mixes us up in no coon hunt."

Jessup gave him a wink. "I done let them boys ruin my 'gator poach. But I'll turn Elwin's killer dog loose on Wiley before I lets the fool stop us building our arena, Mr. Pierpont. Your help, we even pay off the wardens here, and sail clear."

Miles westward, another airboat forged the winding slough runs. Straight up from the coast it went in a course for Gulf Glade with Tate Fenneran piloting. Beside him sat Bo Traggan, the oversized, splenetic U.S. Congressman from Key County. Some years ago he had labored with Loker Brisburn in the struggle to establish Everglades National Park below Shark River. People of the low coast, who had solicited their sponsorship for the park, were now stubbornly resisting the development of an international airport in Big Cypress Swamp, and on behalf of his father-in-law Fenneran shared Traggan's resentment of this wasted visit down the coast.

The Congressman sweated and squirmed, depressed by that opposition, disturbed by the uninviting wilderness, and glad only to be leaving the mosquitoes behind. On a back seat, however, Carl Meyerberger sat coolly poised inside the netting that hung from his Panama hat. The frail little merchant was recuperating from a blood circulation disorder, and Fenneran had invited him along ostensibly for the balmy excursion, but both tacitly understood their actual purpose concerned the Bayfront slum.

"Aside from the big Keys," Traggan roared over the engine drone, "all there is to Monroe County is the National Park, and we gave them that. You'd think they were conscience bound to reciprocate and line up with us in Key and Collier."

"They're just Audubon folks," Fenneran howled back. "Audubon Society, Bo. Worried a major airport'll hinder the drainage to that park and destroy the wildlife." Over his shoulder he called out, "What would you suggest we do, Carl?"

A wispy smile rested on the old man's lips. He made no response whatever, disks of light on his glasses lending him a blind aspect of inertia. He seemed most unconcerned, sitting

there in the propeller wash. After all, he was seventy-nine and ailing. But the moment Fenneran shut off the engine, Meyerberger raised one hand and said in the descending silence, "People, you push them, they push back, bend them a little, they bend back. Best thing, far as concerned, let them have it their way."

He could not have heard them in the noise, yet grasped the situation, apparently comprehending the exchange by synthesis. His high, brittle voice made Traggan uneasy. The Congressman blinked and panted, uncomfortable always, but more so in the participating presence of a Jew. "Carl is suggesting," Fenneran interpreted for him, "that we strike an intelligent balance between progress and conservation."

It left Traggan foundering like the boat. "That's just fine," he said impatiently. "Ask him how."

"Tell him drain off," Meyerberger said, "and drain back."

"That means get an accommodation from the army," Fenneran hastened to say before Traggan might perceive the defiant whimsy in Meyerberger's mimicry of his rudeness. "He means get the army engineers to dredge out around the airport site. Drainage canals to deflect the wash and return it to the park."

"Sweet Jesus, that's a mighty tall order. This chap's talking about a fifty-mile canal, maybe longer."

"He's talking about taller," the old man retorted. "An airport, you gonna need to blot up the whole swamp anyway, no?"

"Guarantee the park for them," Fenneran murmured. "Can't you sell Loker that kind of intelligent balance?"

"I can sell him seed and farm tools, not a bayside highway. Progress, it's no way but toward the Big Cypress for him."

Roseate spoonbills flew over, now that the airboat sat quiet. "Can't we move on?"

"Just a minute, Bo. It's really your Bayfront poor folks in his pine brake he opposes, Carl."

"Not true. He's proud of you. Told me hisself you gonna build for them nicer homes like they never seen in their whole life. So I says old packing crates could give them that."

"He says too that I'm tampering with class distinctions. If we blur those disparities, we destroy the entire social structure of

this country, and with it all prospects of self-improvement. Now what do you say to that?"

"Nothing. Far be it from me to harm class differences." The old man chuckled, poking a thumb to point at Traggan, who blanched in choking silence (aware the Jew could buy and sell him a hundred times over—and provide him with campaign funds too, should he ever find good reason to). "Self-improvement, that's the ticket. Nobody could be a person in this country if somebody else makes it soft for them. Poor whites got to do for themself. Blacks got to. Indians. Just like us Americans done."

It left the Congressman gasping. An eagle soared from a domed head of bald cypresses, streaking north. "This lonesome wasteland," Traggan bawled, "make civilized man sick to his soul."

"Civilized?" Meyerberger tapped Fenneran's shoulder to forestall him as he turned to kick off the engine. "It's Passover by the Indians. Green Corn Dance, why not?" The old man was purposely slighting disdainful Traggan. "Historians last century, they thought it's a Hebrew rite. Guess what year, us Indian chaps." He sighed as Fenneran gunned off in the eagle's direction. "Before you can turn around, it's 5710."

Ahead of the hunting eagle, far over the trackless cypress strand, beyond the willow heads and lush hammocks towering with palm, a simpler people celebrated the fertile earth and their hard lives on it. In the piney flatwoods of their reservation, friends and relatives had gathered, young and old together all festive at busk, all to be shriven of a fading year's venial sins. An ember of new fire burned in every kitchen hearth. The new year was blessed with young corn and ritual.

But upon arriving with his daughter and her son, Chitto Jumper found no celebration among the Wolf Clan of Craig Emathla. Yet neither was the camp in despair. Majosee had returned from the place without breath only the day before, and Chitto wept with happiness at the sight of her, expressing his gratitude to her black savior. So had her other grandfather and her uncles. Thankful to see her alive, her aunts had dressed her afresh in colors of calico, and decked her with many strings of

the beads customarily bestowed as virtue gifts even as she recounted her woeful experience for the sympathy of her grandmother.

Her mother held her close. Chitto pulled his tunic off to bathe away the clay and ash of mourning he had voyaged with for two days. But then the disgrace of Majosee's agony reached his understanding. Bare but for his breech clout amid the fierce mosquitoes, he fell to a *hadjo* war dance loud with death whoops.

The white jaws were monstrous, the black jaws were knives. A massive head to crush bone, a long muzzle to slice life away in swift passes, they belonged to animals silent and stalking, sinewy and scarred and driven together by conditioned hate.

One was a squat mongrel of strong pit-bull strain, bead-eyed pale as a demon not of this world. The other was a full-blooded Doberman pinscher, rearing slow and deadly like a threat of darkness eternal.

Only the leashed onlooking mongrels growled, goaded to sympathetic truculence by aspiring managers burly and unshaven in the crowd of enthusiasts gathered. The sun blazed. Birds screamed in hiding. Insects flocked to cower in the air plants. Currents of emotion animated the local men, but the two visitors from New Orleans sat glum with apprehension in the midst of too many rifles where beer and wine passed freely about.

The lawyer Pierpont asked if these men could become troublesome in their excitement, and Jessup said, "Not if they don't git too drunk. I knows most of them good. Just stay close by me, and you all be just fine."

On the tarp the fighters, lunging to break free and kill, made no sound but that of scraping claws. Their masters held fast to the heavy studded collars, down on their knees to cajole in grunts of endearment until, at a signal from one to the other, they let go. With lips curled the dogs flew to collide in a bony crack of bared fangs.

Inside the new plyboard apron with them, Elwin Hoyt sang, "One turn," to the crowd. "Just one, folks, you been invited free. Ain't counting it a scratch here." The dogs tumbled, sparred,

their masters crawling along to egg them on in hoarse rumbles. "Can't chance a break, these dogs fed red meat daily, cost a heap. Ain't starved, it's exercise keeps them scrawny. Watch that black work the stifle. But the white's at her ears and paying no mind. Watch that terrier, ear dogs is murder!"

"It's a turn!" someone shouted when the bull knocked down its foe, and all the crowd yelled, the seated men and those who stood where benches were yet to be constructed.

The Doberman had whirled away, trailing bloody saliva. But back it came full of fight—only to be withdrawn by its master, and men complained in excited shouts. Hoyt came over to say that some were offering payment to have the match continue. "Talk to Huxton," Jessup advised, though his eye was on the lawyer. "See if he'll referee."

Pierpont's spirits were brightening and Jessup's were high. He took his New Orleans guests beyond the clearing, where three whores were setting up their army surplus pup tents. In that same bower Lam Cordhall served the beer and wine to men loud with self-conscious jocularity while Chuck Stowell accepted payment, nimble on his crutches. Guy Helker prepared sandwiches for sale on a table, Brady Wiley standing by with his rifle to keep order.

Roving with Jessup, the two visitors were pleased. The prospects for extended vice—prostitution, bootlegging, gambling, loan sharking—were obvious to Pierpont. He produced a hundred-dollar bill for Jessup to split between the presentation dog owners if they agreed to fight the match to a finish.

And soon amid the bird cries, lethal jaws were tearing at the bodies and faces of both dogs. The terrier and pinscher strove to kill each other for the love of their masters on that secluded hammock of Big Cypress Swamp. Pure ferocity powered them, and the impassioned goading of men on all fours like the dogs, drenched with sweat like the dogs, only not bleeding like them, or living to be destroyed like the dogs.

Claws scraped desperately. Blood spattered the tarp, sprayed the young board walls. Potbellied men in the pit urged their dogs to slaughter. Men roared from the benches with money to bet on the silent fighters. Leashed dogs, watching, growled with

fierce blood lust. The Doberman caught the pit bull by its muscular throat and they tumbled, clawing like cats, grappling like men, tearing with jaws like the alligators that lurked in the fens.

Buzzards circled high above the blood in the pit. Opossums hid. Stalking panthers waited for prey in the shadows. Scents of flesh and orchid baked in the sun. Pelt matted with its blood, the bullterrier struck heavy-pawed to go free, and lunged to pitch the Doberman over with teeth clamped on its foreleg, its cut eyelid bleeding. The leg bone cracked, a sound that echoed in the forest, and all who heard it cried out, slavering. They paid for beer and wine and began calling to the whores with bursting sensation for the balm of their vulgar replies.

The silent dogs parted, and clashed again. Jaws locked fang on fang, they scraped the tarp, each sinewy thrust measured and crucial. The terrier danced back into a stance that transformed it into a sledgehammer force in massive drive at its nemesis. The black sword of the pinscher slipped sidewise across the assault and opened the heavier dog's chest.

The pit bull fell. Its master, calling it Spike, begged it to rise. The Doberman's master, calling it Nightshade, commanded it to kill. The beasts leaped to obey and collided. In a geyser of blood and saliva, bone cracked again. A tooth fell on the tarp in the din of men and birds. Huxton salvaged the tooth in his dance around the dogs, sweating like the dogs, an eternity at this conflict like the dogs.

The pit bull turned away. Calling out, somebody named that a scratch and claimed a side bet. The owner caught his terrier hurdling a pit wall and kicked the hurt dog back inside the apron, demanding a return stand. Jessup explained that rule to Pierpont as the other master, holding his dog by the collar, laughed at the bullterrier's failure to attack when released. The lawyer laughed too. Flushed and happy, he allowed his bodyguard to slip away with a soliciting whore.

The crowd bawled obscenities. Birds crashed away overhead, exploding mice and insects down from the airplants. The referee called for a courtesy scratch, and Jessup explained the term patiently as men tipped wine bottles in the baking fragrance, drank beer, claimed their money victories.

"That ole terrier cur is done in," Jessup told the lawyer.

"Doberman seems bad off herself," Pierpont observed, winded with excitement. He glanced up at the circling vultures.

"Yeah, her leg's busted. She hurting real bad. Ain't necessary to kill the bull, but she got to show heart enough for a go, or there's no decision."

In went Nightshade, a black arrow in flight. But before reaching the woebegone Spike, the pinscher fell on its broken leg. Up at once, it continued at its prey, lips curled and teeth pink with blood. The crowd, fallen dead silent like the dogs, exploded in visceral cheers that awarded the victory to Nightshade's master and all who had bet the graceful black to win. The opposing master struck his dog a blow that knocked it flat. He cursed the terrier for never winning a match though fed constantly on expensive red meat.

Exuberant victors tore down a pup tent. A naked whore took the exposure in good spirits, and accepted exhibitionistic clients without rising, five dollars each into Chuck's waiting hand. Men joked in loud choking voices amid rank flesh, the disarray of pup tents, and curt replies by Jessup's surly assistants to those who asked slyly if they planned any display of alligator wrestling, swamp-girl style, by the prostitutes.

The mention of alligators inspired in Spike's master a way to conveniently dispose of a pit fighter not worth its feed costs. As Nightshade's master applied medication and treated friends to wine and women, Spike's dragged it, dehydrated and exhausted, away to the marshy shore. There he threw the whining, yelping mongrel into slough water, where alligators came swiftly to thrash in the blood, and the circling buzzards hung thwarted.

Jessup slapped at mosquitoes, watched the grumbling vultures wheel away, and winked when Pierpont, all rosy and breathless, beckoned to a whore who stuck her head out of a tent that bucked and thrashed like the feasting alligators. She leaped out naked, a pulpy woman bleached half blond and lumpy with fresh insect bites. Soliciting the lawyer with a coarse wisecrack, she stank of sweat and rut. Yet in the surrounding noise her voice had a birdlike fragility that he yearned to plunder.

His breath came hard. Returning Jessup's sleazy wink, he

seized his woman by the buttocks and, one knee driving blunt between her legs, marched her backward, gasping at her neck. But she cautioned him that men were fighting in her tent, so he followed her off to some cartons full of garbage that she proceeded to fashion into a private bower while he plucked at his clothes to remove them.

The men in the whore's tent were Guy, Lam, and Pierpont's own armed protector, on whom the two had pounced while the crowd swarmed to watch churning alligators consume the white pit bull. Chuck already had his pistol when they finally dragged the man out, still struggling, half undressed, and Jessup arrived in time to see Brady club him to the ground with the rifle butt.

Upland men laughed and drank, asking halfhearted questions that Bayfronters answered vaguely, some dragging the New Orleans man bloody and unconscious behind others who followed Jessup's crowd to another assault. They plucked the lawyer from the cradle of his whore's limbs, and punched him when he screamed.

They held the whore down, and someone in the crowd got on her while the others cheered. They kicked the lawyer nearly senseless, then stood him up and let him fall back seated on the garbage cartons dazed and bleeding and limply fending off the insects. It made them laugh to see his hairy belly heave for breath, his dark darting eyes search for reason, his wet penis shrivel up in a cauliflower shape.

"You all in N'Orleans," Jessup said as men stood the bodyguard up to flop him back beside Pierpont. "You come to take us over. Poaching, gin mills and whores, pit fighting, every blame good thing down this coast."

The lawyer tried to disabuse him of such thoughts with a weak wave of his hand, but could say nothing in the drunken sudden uproar of laughter around the whore and her newest client. When it subsided the lawyer labored to say through his swollen lips, "We all," and gasped with pain, still fluttering his hands at the insects. "We aim," he tried again, "to pay off the law for you all. Millions to be made. Think."

"Made by you'uns," Jessup came back, "and peanuts for us. Somebody explained that to us, ain't nothing he don't know."

"This man," Chuck Stowell said, pointing a crutch at the bodyguard, "he the one smacked the Sheriff's car, sure enough?"

With a bleary grin the man nodded. The crutch shot forth at his eye and he fell over with a howl of the extremest agony as Pierpont cursed him for a fool. "I said tell them nothing," he shouted in the laughter all around. "Didn't I tell you stone it?"

The man writhed shrieking in the grass, and Chuck struck him with the crutch as Jessup said, "Sheriff ole buddy to this boy. Found him a powerful good lawyer, and you all come along busting him off a bridge to kill him."

"That's right," Chuck addressed Pierpont. "Now you tell us where we find the nigger helped this white shit, he look more like a nigger hisself."

The lawyer stood up regarding him with contempt, and faced Jessup with a dignity he managed despite his awkward nakedness. "By now the nigger in question has sent your name and address to N'Orleans. Understand. You're trifling with an institution you can't escape. I can let all this go, up to this point."

"Fake name," Jessup said. "House you picked us up at belongs to bail-jumping turd we don't mind seeing dead. I wants some real names and addresses from you in N'Orleans, the people who sent you here. And don't shit me."

"Understand this," the lawyer persisted, slapping at bugs. "Our society covers the world and never lets up. There's big money for you. Big. Understand what I'm telling you."

"Someone a sight bigger'n your society wants them names."

The lawyer looked up with Jessup at the returning buzzards, then down with Jessup at the bodyguard squirming painfully, blood on the fingers crossed over his eyes. Chuck jabbed with the crutch, but Pierpont evaded the thrust and cursed him in a foreign tongue. Laughing, Jessup got between them, and at his signal men dragged both the outsiders along behind him.

At a word from Jessup, Bayfront men threw the bodyguard splashing into the slough run. The lawyer maintained his rocky stance, but only till the alligators surfaced, racing to blood. "Get him out!" he screamed. "What kind of people are you all?"

On Jessup's instructions Guy Helker came through the brush with a grapple and went right to work. He hooked the man and

with Lam Cordhall's help hauled him thrashing and gibbering from the alligators' jaws. The lacerated thug fell unconscious. The lawyer wailed with horror, yet shook his head in refusal when Jessup again demanded the Negro's location. Jessup told Brady to kill the hooked man, and at the shot Pierpont fell sobbing to his knees.

Somewhere a panther roared, and birds shrieked, but the sole human sound was distant cheering, stirred by the contending dogs. The buzzards swept low. Pierpont braced himself for a glance at the shattered face of his aide, then looked up at Jessup and fiercely spat. That clear acceptance of death awed the Bay-front crowd. Jessup looked around, no longer smiling. He whispered something to Brady, who, just as drawn and flushed, handed him the rifle and got Lam's serrated knife.

Unable to believe it, Pierpont watched him kneel and take hold of the murdered man's penis to skin him like a reptile. The lawyer exploded a strident gabble of all the information Jessup had demanded, but there was no way to stop Brady Wiley. In hysteria Pierpont, incoherent on his knees in the attending jests and laughter, in the wild sound-killing vastness, fainted dead away.

That was a mercy, because Jessup wanted his skin rolled up too and tubed, with the Negro thug's as well, for the message a friend and benefactor must send to New Orleans. Men drew cards for the privilege of shooting the outsider dead. Birds clamored everywhere. Insects swarmed in the sun of the swamp. Soon the cloying fragrance seasoned the carrion that buzzards tried to pick from the jaws of armored reptiles in the slough. Mosquitoes feasted too, on living flesh and the dead.

Gulf Glade, grown only in recent years out of dock heads for the railroad sidings of Keyport, was already a sizable town of bright dwellings clustered beyond the levee, which bustled loud with workmen when Fenneran brought the airboat in. A rental man stood waiting to take it back up the canal.

Waiting too was Prewitt in his chauffeur's cap. Obligingly he hastened to drive the Congressman away through ranks of tall palm toward the remote smokestacks of Keyport. Fenneran sat

with Carl Meyerberger in the pleasant Main Slip Rest among oldsters like him who lounged until the Seashell ferry arrived to wend them home in luxury. A waitress served mint coolers as Fenneran said half playfully, "If you give me that Bayfront easement, Carl, I'll give you a causeway to replace this slow old ferry line."

"You give me a causeway, and I'll give you a hernia."

Fenneran laughed. "Carl, our pine-brake housing is under way. That's going to force your hand."

"Is that so? Listen, my poor folks so lazy, they wouldn't move out the Bayfront even you gave them rent free the pines."

Fenneran had a final ploy in this chess game of land and lives: to let the old man offer Swamptown blacks as well as Bayfront poor whites a share of the opportunities in the new development. That mix could be a temptation too devilish to resist for a Jew with so long a lifetime of battered ethnic sensibilities. But he resolved to hold the idea off for optimum timing, and tried a little more banter instead. "Decisions should not be left to the lazy," he said in saline breezes of the slip, where ferry attendants waited to help the feeble board. "The choice is yours. But you may have just one."

The old man stopped to weigh that caution. The pallid sight of him, silent amid the shrill gull cries, put Fenneran off like the presence of death. Until, serene with years and smiling sweetly in his rock-bound cynicism, Meyerberger piped, "Don't make me laugh. It could kill me."

Fenneran's limousine stood waiting again under giant clouds. He wondered if his remark had left Carl feeling endangered. If so, it was just as well: fear might move him out of the way, or to his timely rest. The smiling handyman-chauffeur held open the door. Getting in, Fenneran said, "I have a special chore for you, Prew, and black folks go have you to thank for the housing we get them in our peaceful county."

In ritual, a deadly water moccasin lay coiled in the shallows of a run, eyeing Chitto Jumper's heel. He had journeyed here for a war judgment by Tribal Council, but instead was being judged himself, for his very life. And if he survived, he must judge his loved ones for their lives.

Seated on the moss bank, he kept his rifle pointed at the snake, eponym of his clan. All the tribal lines that constituted Seminole burned in his Mikasuki blood, his ancestors all witnessing his willing submission to death judgment.

He had shed tears of joy to find Majosee alive on his arrival, but learned next of the vile injustice done her, and tasted bitter hate. Then by nightfall everything turned even worse. In the kitchen chickee that Emathla had provided for his Snake Clan relatives to spend the night, there was no sleep for Chitto. He lay awake in agonies of shame and fury, once his daughter Cose brought him her confession. At dawn he took the Negro and awakened Olata Micco for war against the whites.

The Snake Clan chief was very old. It confused him to hear about the outrage committed against a granddaughter by Americans, and against Chitto by both the girl and her mother. The Micco roused two clan elders half his age but dead with sleep. He shocked them awake by seizing a chicken that clucked across the melon patch and wrenching off its head to splatter everyone with its warm life blood.

Then in the dining chickee, selected for Chitto's hearing, Olata Micco gave him the slain fowl, still animate with energetic death spasms, and spoke words that struck Chitto's heart only now.

"Here is the bird of life. It has no head."

The horror of that meaning stared from the bead eyes of the snake of death. Behind Chitto the three clan elders sat as he sat waiting for the arrival of his kin to stir the reptile into action. Before those men he had bared his chest to rub chicken blood in the clay and ash, saying in American, "Shame in my heart, blood on my spirit, as an honor sign I tell you things. My kids been brought up Mikasuki, to say yes or no but bullshit never. Do their duty last night and tell me things I like to die."

The black man, he explained, had saved Majosee's life and cured her of a disgraceful pregnancy resulting from the rape. But Chitto hated him for curing her by marital act, as he hated the white authorities for failing to punish the criminals after troubling to pretend a trial.

And he was angriest with his daughter Cose. Her own daughter had taken her aside to detail more than she dared for aunts

and grandmother. Neither the pregnancy nor Junn's outlandish cure brought tears to Cose despite her grief. But the girl's dream made Cose weep. Both restless souls of Majosee's dead father had angrily brought a bear to her dream. So conscience drove Cose to Chitto, revealing in confession both her own sin with Sint Itcho of the Bear Clan and her daughter's immorality with Junn.

In their reluctance to call for tribal war verdict, Olata Micco, Yuchi Tom, and Julius Green Hawk let nothing Chitto said arouse them, except Cose's shocking breach of widowhood. And they soon got over that, to wheedle him with praise of his bloodline and flatter the uncomfortable Negro by asking his name and his derivation while each of them shook his extended hand.

"Cavalo," he said. "Old name, south Florida. My people Injun blacks. Cowaya in the wars, Injun way to say Cavalo."

"Cowaya," Olata said. "Yes, I seem to remember such a name in stories of the Negroes who fought by our side. Senegal, Ibo, Ashanti, Egba. A fine-looking people. As a child I heard good meanings about such Africans."

"Fine-looking, my ass," Chitto shouted in protest. "He no more'n a common drunkard."

His voice shaking, Olata said, "I see no need, such fire you burning to tell a shame on your camp." Then, in Hitchiti, to keep it from Cowaya's understanding, he said he had learned something in his ninety years, that when a man volunteered amazing candor, it was usually to hide the worst of his wrong, to obscure the fire in its own smoke.

It struck true like an arrow. Chitto's fear of them learning Majosee had lain with the devil beast made him shout, still in American as if to hide nothing, "I told you all they is!"

"No, you left something out," the Negro said, mortifying Chitto—and relieving him next by saying, "cure ain't work." But he was crushed again to hear Junn add, "She still preglin."

Hastily, Olata said, "Go, Cowaya, prepare your canoe. Forbidden, a man not Seminole to stay on the reservation, Green Corn Dance. Grandfather tell you how we all decide. Next time you see him, he be Chitto Fixico Jumper, sure enough. I, as Micco, have the power to name him so."

Chitto tensed with excitement, but with suspicion too. And

when Cowaya withdrew, the ancient said, "There are more granddaughters than yours to remember. Sheath your knife for the sake of sons and daughters here and yet unborn. A new age demands a new fixico leader. Do not drive us to suicidal war over one mere rape, we who have been driven by worse into the enemy's power."

Rising, his head quaking with compulsion, Chitto drew his knife and plunged it into the dead chicken, irately crying, "For what will you name me Fixico? To squat when I piss?"

Olata Micco studied him across the impaled chicken, then gazed out at the slough run, silver in the morning haze. "You have stabbed this bird," he said, "as Asi Yaholo drove his knife into a treaty just as headless to refuse it. Great chief though he was, he destroyed our people thereby, and himself. Let us, though lesser chiefs, do better for the Seminole." His old eyes found Chitto again. "In every generation, Mikasuki like you are born to revive the wars. I can see that life will not decide you between our doom and our survival. Then let death. I send you as Chitto Fixico, if you are truly fearless, to trial by pit viper. Any *hadjo* can take a scalp, but only one absolutely fearless in conduct can brave death to discover his righteous soul. If you live to make judgment on your camp, I promise you war judgment by Tribal Council."

Chitto could not refuse. Nor would he, Fixico, choose to. How this cottonmouth snake was beckoned by an old chief's will, he would have to live as long as Olata to learn. The other elders had told him so with cozening proverbs, and here the poisonous reptile, pit-headed, leaf green in bars around its thick scaly sinews, waited to meet him at doom time, this ordinary moment falling on this sunny day of crisis in his life. How sweet were the birdsongs and aromas and the green light of the woods.

It seemed no more than right that his loved ones, who had forced him to this test, should become the threat to force the action of the snake. Yet it might strike even before they arrived, his souls asunder in a moment. One soul already welcomed death, an end to this ordeal. He felt the other coiling like the water moccasin, a fierce power to swiftly aim the rifle and kill.

*   *   *

On every previous occasion that Prewitt drove the Fenneran limousine, any clean shirt and his visored cap had sufficed to invest him with the station of chauffeur. But this balmy Sunday was an exception. Black orderlies smiled when he arrived at the hospital all liveried and eager. They were proud to greet a fellow menial so favored by important people as to be allowed free access to the Sheriff's private room, and moreover saluted by the white policeman standing guard outside the door.

The reason Prewitt was in full uniform, on this particular day, posed a responsibility and a danger that filled him with awe. But the assignment was in behalf of Dexter Polsen, for whom he would willingly die. Or so he thought, until death threatened suddenly at the Sheriff's bedside.

Amid the pulleys and plaster casts of traction, Prewitt saw the yawning hole of death look at him from the revolver in Sheriff Polsen's rising hand, and saw the face of death beyond, three round holes in a masking helmet of plastered white bandages. Afraid to move and barely able to speak, he managed to rasp, "Don't shoot, it's me, ole Prew!"

The gun descended. He fanned himself with his stiff cap. The service revolver slid out of sight in the sea of white sheets, but the Sheriff gave no other sign of comprehension. Prewitt sobbed, and caught back his tears.

"Oh, Sheriff, you gonna be all right. They promised me that. Oh, Sheriff, who gave you that gun?"

The pause that followed seemed just long enough for the life crouching behind those three dark apertures to gather thought and say, "My friend Tate."

He spoke with a voice like sand, even more abrasive than Prewitt's. "Yessa, Mr. Fenneran he doing for you, Sheriff. Ain't let nobody get at you no more. He think of everything, even maybe bad-ass cops, to give you that gun." He heaved a sigh. "I must of turned white as you just now."

A pause, and the painful scrape of a voice again. "Knew it was you. Thought you maybe sent by black son of a bitch hit me."

"Yessa, he ain't go hit no one no more. Nor his kind, this here county no more. Mr. Fenneran tell me so."

No further word came from the mask. Prewitt waited, then

touched the Sheriff's hand. Soon he left with burning eyes. They had told him not to stay long. They had told him of brain matter gone, and even if it proved as hard to notice as everybody hoped to expect, something was already different for Mr. Polsen to think anyone who loved his goodness so could be sent against him.

At Tarkey Road Prewitt turned the silent limousine north out of Keyport with Sweetpea beside him. She sat contentedly wagging her tongue. But Prewitt's eyes were flooded, his throat burned with fear and vengeful bitterness. All the sunny ride east to Armistead, the air conditioning was a necessity to help him compose himself for the important job ahead.

This college town, famed as the liberal center of the state, boasted a colored hotel of high quality, replete with a history of guests as distinguished as Jack Johnson, Sojourner Truth, Matthew Henson, and Ethel Waters. A rambling wooden mansion of three stories, it reposed in a palm grove off Hammerhead Road, with convenient access to Swamptown some distance below. By the time he pulled up outside, Prewitt had attained the necessary calm.

He knew how to strut and he knew how to glow, and reached the front desk radiating good cheer in his tan uniform and leather puttees, his snappy cap, with Sweetpea well composed on her leash. Prewitt's bearing so impressed the manager that he personally telephoned upstairs to tell Mr. Caultree his car had arrived. And soon the professional assassin, who had coldly rammed the Sheriff's car with intent to kill, came down.

It was frightening to confront the man, yet Prewitt smiled. Big and muscular, this Louisiana black had the wary eyes of a swamp lion. But beyond that Prewitt saw no sign of suspicion that negotiations might not be progressing well for the lawyer, that this limousine, chauffeur, and chafing dog might not be Pierpont's lavish message of prosperity but the ploy of enemies. Still, Caultree wore his stylish sportshirt loose over the hips; Mr. Fenneran had anticipated even that as a possibility, warning it would likely mean a gun hidden in the killer's belt.

Sweetpea sniffed his leg. Prewitt lodged his suitcase in the

trunk. Scraping and beaming, he swept the car door open for the man. Remembering to carefully use the name Fenton in place of Jessup, he said with a tremor he hoped would pass for servile shyness, "Mr. Pierpont say be sure I remind you call N'Orleans, say how nice Mr. Fenton's hospitality."

"It's done," Caultree said close up. Bending to get in the car, he added, "Don't say no names, man."

"Sorry, man. Just we got no phones, out where we bound."

"Don't man me, nigger."

Prewitt stiffened, and held tight to Sweetpea's leash. He shut the door gently, but had the good sense not to apologize, not to grovel, not to give himself away by continuing to toady in the face of affront by another black man.

Down Armistead Road to Hammerhead he drove in silence, but for his replies to measured questions from behind. Yes, he said hoarsely, an airboat would be waiting in Swamptown to carry them deep into Big Cypress Swamp for their rendezvous with Pierpont, his bodyguard Soretta, and "Fenton." Yes, this was one of the dogs that would perform for them in the pit fights today. No, there would be no redneck objections to the presence of a Negro in the audience.

Prewitt had already said most of this earlier during his phone call to make contact (supposedly for lawyer Pierpont), and feared he was being lulled into a trap, that his lack of some prearranged watchword between criminals had given him away. But he kept from turning to see if the gun of this murderer was aimed at the back of his head, as likely as it seemed. The silence that fell increased that fear almost unbearably. He felt the oozing sweat grow chilly in his armpits, but hate and vengefulness kept him steady in the air-conditioned drive.

Soon Hammerhead Depot came sliding past and they were in Swamptown, heading for the marsh amid folks in their Sunday best, who somehow made the evil visitor laugh. He kept chortling at every raggedy child and waddling woman and Prewitt dreaded that as evidence of lethal mockery, expecting the hot wallop of death in his brain all the way to Marsh End Road where the airboat sat waiting beyond the hackberry trees. The sweat poured from him when he stepped out in the high morning sun.

His cousin Alf was there, looking scared, to stand watch over the limousine until Prewitt returned. Caultree looked wary too, spying white skin in the boat, and that inspired Prewitt to vent the unbearable tension through his bursting voice.

"HEYahhhhh!" he shouted to set Sweetpea growling in a lunge at the boatmen, and restraining her, he laughed in extreme relief. "Pay no mind them dock whites, sah. They bad-ass, sure, but ain't go mess with this pit bitch of mine awatching over."

No rifles were in sight, but he knew two existed, secluded in the pipe structure by the boys who stood up there to pilot the airboat. Jessup came forward smiling, not as "Fenton" in this role as a common boat owner for hire. So was the pair of boys to go nameless, though he knew them as the thugs Sheriff Polsen once brought to the house. Prewitt would never have been capable of accepting them as allies against the Sheriff's enemies if not assured they were by Mr. Fenneran. He would not have gone one step into this throat-knotting danger by any incentive but that assurance, and kept alerting himself to use all his wits.

He easily subdued Sweetpea, who knew Jessup well enough, and they got under way with Caultree in the bucket seat next to the trucker's. Prewitt stood his back to the prow rail, as if serving the killer in a tacit black man's concord by keeping an eye on the two boys above. The howling propeller engine made speech impractical. The mastiff sensed antipathy here, and strained at the leash, ready to attack at the earliest provocation. And that came soon, with the dimming of the forest cries.

Caultree, not expected to, discerned their westerly tack along a canal route Bayfront people often poled in the opposite direction to take small game from the swamp. He reared at the sight of open sky and, aware they were heading for the coast, reached under his shirt before demanding an explanation. But he never got out the gun or a word. Though Prewitt fell mute, Jessup threw Sweetpea into action with a loud "HEYahhhhh!"

The outsider's bleat of helpless terror made Jessup laugh. He had Caultree's gun. Sweetpea's teeth were in the man's hand. Prewitt found voice enough to command the dog back, and Jessup showed their prisoner Brady Wiley's rifle pointed at his head.

"I just saved your life, nigger," the old man shouted over the engine yowl. Then he gently smiled, pretending not to hear Caultree's questions or even notice the torn bleeding hand he protested. Prewitt kept the man guarded by Sweetpea's restrained lunges as they passed into a Gulf creek for open water.

This time those gathered in the abandoned Bayfront warehouse had followed instructions. They stood waiting with a heavy dock net and a big wagon spring lashed to an overhead beam, half a dozen ragtag white men with as many hungry canines restlessly looking for trouble. Through Jessup, a gang as vicious as Caultree had ever seen was at Mr. Fenneran's disposal in the revenge he was after. These men threw the thick rope skeins of their loading net over Caultree, and strung him up on the spring like a kitten in an onion bag.

In the growling of dogs, human voices echoed around the warehouse, this cavern of just retribution, and Prewitt thrilled to hear his own voice explode with relish, crying, "HEYahhhhh!"

Sweetpea leaped without a sound. The lean leashed mongrels barked, echoing. Caultree echoed, his outcries thudding against the distant walls, the high windows blinding with glare.

Blood trailed in the wake of Sweetpea's turn for another silent lunge. Her jaws caught a flailing black hand and tore it open. All the curs snarled with envy. She opened the leg of the New Orleans man who had rammed the Sheriff without feeling. He screamed with plenty of feeling now, bobbing up and down on the big wagon spring in the echoes.

Nearly drunk in the sheer lust of it, Prewitt welcomed Jessup's command to pull Sweetpea off. He rubbed the dog fondly to calm her as the old man demanded names from Caultree with a smile. He wanted the identities of those who had assigned killers to the destruction of Sheriff Polsen, he wanted an address in New Orleans where messages would be sure to reach such kingpins. From his damaged face, Caultree spat blood at Jessup defiantly. Tell or not, he knew he was a dead man either way.

The shrieks were too much for Prewitt to bear when a signal

turned mongrels loose and white men laughed to see the black assassin bounce among the savage jaws. Prewitt was one with white men, but he alone of them all grew sick. Over Caultree's echoing pleas, Jessup echoed back, and at last he got what he demanded. Prewitt recoiled from the wails of Caultree naming his criminal superiors and begging for sweet mercy, this merciless villain who had cut the Sheriff down to death mask and plastered misery.

In the noise Jessup handed him Caultree's stubby automatic, and smiled. Afraid he understood, Prewitt knew he did when other white men also smiled to bestow on him the honor of destroying his benefactor's mortal enemy. He aimed the gun, but lacked the nerve to pull the trigger.

Bloodthirsty curs were straining their leashes tight for the kill, but Sweetpea sat watching Prewitt raise both trembling hands to point the gun again in echoes of dooming laughter. Again he was unable to kill, even as a mercy to the tortured murderer. Prewitt sobbed, and dropped the gun. Dismally he surrendered his chance to kill the deadly black beast for Mr. Fenneran and the Sheriff.

A single shot by someone else shattered the terrible day.

There in the distance came the canoes with a vivid yellow raft in tow, and Chitto Fixico Jumper felt death enclose him in the swamp heat, the odor of greenery turning fetid all at once. In mind he saw death's face, whiter than the gruesome enemy's. He tasted mildew dry in his mouth. With darting tongue the cottonmouth promised its sting. The man knew he was a fool to die, but must or kill the innocent reptile.

Life came closer up the slough run, his family to stir the guiltless viper. Life and death were locked in this moment at his throat. Chickens clucked in the camp. Air plants hung fragrant in the day. Like echoes, faint laughter of the busk sounded in the silence of this war he was losing to death. Suddenly Chitto Jumper saw without seeing, felt without feeling, knew without knowing all that war meant. He could not battle white strangers in place of others who had raped his child.

He lowered the rifle. "Go, pit viper," his heart had him say

in the pale language of the enemy. "Go, cottonmouth. Git along, now, moccasin snake."

And the creature, sensing the approach of new danger, uncoiled in a swing toward the depths, where pond apple grew. Called by all its names, it spared him in order to escape the looming vessels. Chitto sat up at rest, with time now, with breath, and agony. In the small canoe he had dug out of a cypress log for her, Majosee approached, poled by the brave black man his heart would not let him love as her husband. He had loved her father for the sake of Cose, and their son for the sake of their line, this new-named man standing over his mother, poling Chitto's canoe.

He had loved them all, but none so much as Majosee, who shared with him a vision beyond language. Her cause was just, but it meant the shooting of innocent strangers, the blood of innocent friends, and the dying of the tribe. He thanked his perceptive ancestors for sending the death viper to show him light. But there was no heart to this gratitude, no relief from sorrow. Her cause was just, but life was not.

Chitto raised his hand to stop the family downstream. In Hitchiti, to exclude the Negro from the deliberations at hand, he reminded them that he had come here in clay and ash, bringing a new man named in his mother's widowhood, and they understood he had meanings to speak for them. He declared that no food had passed his lips yet all this day, reciting leaf names next, and it was clear to them that ritual judgment was in process.

The old men chanted behind him. At his signal the two canoes advanced to the shallows where death had coiled to strike short minutes past. He explained that they had entered into Snake Clan Council, the blue dome of sky their temple, the tall trees of their heritage in witness. Ancestors were around them in the air. The Breathmaker wanted a verdict, the Great Spirit had alien speech for Chitto's miserable hungry mouth to decipher.

Then he said, "A bear has come to my eye," and Cose turned away in shame, her son squatting in the canoe to face her solemnly.

The sun had cut sullen shadows in Majosee's face where she

sat hunched over her knees, biting back her stomach pain to regard him evenly. Behind her the black man sat in their canoe as motionless as an Indian, alertly watching though deaf to the language Chitto's spirit directed at Cose, his daughter.

"I paid beads to your virtues all your life, necklace by necklace each year. Only to see them removed in bereavement, leaving their weight still on your heart. That burden I would have carried in your place if I could. This I asked as a boon from Fishaki Omechi when they washed you and tied your widow's braid and dressed you in dark color. I thought your mourning solemn as the fire at his grave, I thought your heart was broken like his pipe and spear and knife prepared for burial with him, father of your babes."

He scratched for dirt to rub in the chicken blood on his breast, his hand to press against the pain, which sang out on an escaping bleat when he asked for some snakeroot to be brought from his canoe. Like a deer the boy Luke fresh with his man's name, Chopka, flew to serve him, then waded back faithfully to his mother. Chitto took some leaf of the buttonwood snakeroot and chewed it until bitterness infused his spirit. Then he spat it out, retching. He swallowed bile, and spoke.

"Dry winter burnt far off, the day we laid his logs on him. Pine sent big smoke to tell us, we thought the world on fire. Like peat my children's hearts smoldered before me to ash. The boy will be a man, I thought, the girl will marry. I thought perhaps another from the Wolf Clan might be found to lawfully reduce the mourning years by half. But no, to the Bear Clan you went instead, to Sint Itcho, attracted by the lean jaw and strong muscles like a white woman, in no more than one year's mourning."

The three elders chanted a deep lament. Tears glistened on the cheeks of Cose, but only sun shadows rigid as stone lay on Majosee's. The black man's face was just a shadow behind her, not even the eyes apparent. But Chopka's young face glowed, all ancestry in blossom to the sun of time yet to come.

"Tribal law and tradition, the last strengths left for our survival, you taught your daughter to disdain. By your example she did as she pleased. And I, grown foolish with years of no mettle, abided. Protesting, scolding, yet carving her canoe for the wil-

derness, equipping it with supplies. Armless, warless all my years, I am punished for a fool by the heartless judgments my mouth is forced to make today."

He chewed snakeroot, swallowed his vile saliva, and retched. The elders chanted. "Majosee," Chitto said. "Though your grandfather be fool, it was your duty to heed his dissuasion and not go alone in the swamp. Though crisis was upon you, it was your duty to leave husband choice to your elders. What good is that black man? Does he not get drunk? He could not even eliminate the monster your error has left to grow inside you."

"It is destroyed," she cried, a shriek on the enormous sky, a madness like lightning in the sunlight. And no elder's hand, raised to warn that such interruption was taboo, could stop her. "Only fear for me makes my husband think the bastard child lives," she screamed, shadows insane on her face. "It has bled to death!"

Her mother and brother watched with alarm. But the black man, who comprehended only the anger in her cries, remained unmoved. From a vaporous slow swoon Chitto recovered with acids of rancor in his throat to say, "You, Majosee, went to the whites for justice before seeking it in clan."

Behind him Julius Green Hawk intonated, "So to break a precious stone of Seminole law."

And Yuchi Tom pronounced with equal flint, "We saw here a daughter of seventeen banished to the swamp for copulating with pale faces. To rut with white is no worse than with black."

The two elders were jaws crushing her to glut the crocodile of war she had brought. The girl leaned over her knees with face shadows dancing in pain, the canoe listing beneath her like a thing alive—a breathing alligator, Chitto saw, or crocodile, the beast that had cleaved her. In place of her boat he saw the crocodile of a dream her rapists too had dreamt to tell the black man. Log of cypress, dug out by one's own hand, if it could stir into life for this instant of his eerie eye, so could an Alachua legend of war for one instant of spawning into reality a vengeance of the ages. Drunk with hunger, he dreamt his thoughts. He raised his rifle overhead to make pronouncement.

"Cose, daughter, who breaks faith with ancestors and cares

not for their protection, who calls her father's unrighteous soul to command him, be away from my camp to Imokalee or Sears, where the white ways are like tangled vines and giant fern of the hammock to hide your sins."

The woman was stone shadows like her daughter, who breached law again, lunacy seizing her to cry out, "Grandfather, if you banish your daughter, what for me?" Her mother cautioned Majosee to be silent, but she called out, "Will you shoot me, as the Mikasuki punish murderers?"

Silence thundered like a storm. There was no comprehension the young could receive from counsel. Chitto swung his rifle down. The black man pointed his own rifle on a tense instinct to make war if pushed to it in this stark sun, and Chitto suffered the cruelest envy. In that moment, which could crack the world apart with a single gunshot, he loved the man at last as Majosee's husband, and offered the Breathmaker his own life in place of theirs, which he must condemn, surely to perish in the swamp.

Hoarse with emotion, Chitto spoke in American to include Cowaya in what pertained to him. "You went up in the swamp alone, Majosee, no respect for elders who told you no. Now you talk in judgment time, no respect for law say you be quiet. You ask what about us to judge the pale faces who took onto you. You who went first to their own kind, expect they punish for rape. They who been raping us, our land, our spirit, our power, for centuries."

His righteous soul, blinding him with tears, firmed him for final verdict. He raised his voice to the furious height of his anguish, crying, "One like you she lay herself down for them pale faces, like to lay with death, she been doomed to hide in the wilderness from swamp fire and hurricane. She—"

"Old man, you hide from war," she interrupted in a rage unfamiliar to his years of Majosee, screaming, "your fear of pale faces you call wisdom now!"

"Be lost in the swamp then," he bellowed in a wretched wail of sandstorms, "after her to hide from the beasts for judgment!"

"I'll survive to show you war! Old men, if I live the world will die!"

"Majosee!" His voice shattered. "For justice you went to the white. For baby riddance you went to the black. Majosee," he wept, "Majosee, for judgment . . . " his voice collapsing, Chitto threw it as high as he could to force out " . . . go now to the crocodiles!"

COLLAGE 8

The Gulf Glade Playhouse opening was celebrated, following its maiden performance, at palatial, antebellum Buenaventura. Loker Brisburn's guests were exclusively people of eminence in Key County and beyond. The theatrical event itself, however, was patronized by ordinary citizens, whose numbers made that Cultural Center inception a proud and extraordinary success.

In this first social engagement of Dexter Polsen's since the criminal attack on his life, Tate Fenneran spirited him and their wives out a side exit to avoid the crush of public well-wishers. The limousine headed for Wildcat Point with Hillary and Deejay discussing the program as if it had offered more than just an amateur presentation, while Fenneran, who had helped all he could to launch the Cultural Center, said he hoped professional road shows would come from New York to play here one day soon.

Dexter remained inexpressive, as he had all evening long, and Prewitt was just as morose at the wheel. His crucial mission had

proven too much for the simple handyman-chauffeur, and the shock had lingered all summer to keep him in deep gloom. He required broader counseling than Fenneran sometimes attempted. But not this night. The state of the Polsens was more acute. No shock or horror could quite match theirs. Deejay at least tried to bring life back around them, but Dexter seemed adrift in morbid apathy, with scarce interest in personal revival or even the prospects ahead for his family.

She had spoken to Fenneran about it one afternoon as Dexter napped upstairs. A short while earlier, Polsen had sat on the porch impassive to news of the County Board's assurance that the Sheriff's Office would remain intact for his return. Medical advice had everyone alert for signs of personality change, but there was nothing Deejay or Tate could be sure of except the disregard with which Dexter would suddenly turn blunt and biting. All in the limousine had experienced that.

Careful not to overdo the effort, Fenneran had endeavored to stimulate Polsen with an account of Meyerberger's continual rebuffs. But the Sheriff had stared past him in abstraction, as he did when Fenneran confided that the underworld power thrown against them had been cut off at its roots in New Orleans. Trying again as the car swept them through the Bayfront slum, Fenneran leaned forward on his jump seat and tapped Polsen's knee, saying, "Old boy laughed at me when I said the choice was his, but quit that when I said he might not have but one."

Polsen spoke not a word. But, seated between the women, he nodded as if in sympathy with their patter about the incentives of need and desire in the evening's play by Tennessee Williams.

In the shadow of the limousine, Prewitt tried to urinate, but his humiliation restricted even that. He sobbed in melodic music faint across the parking field of tranquil Buenaventura. Other chauffeurs chatted in the distant chirping of insects and birds. Cars glistened. Placid light shone dimly in the windows of the house. But that Sunday of endless nightmare had never left him. Nothing could free him from the miserable shame of not having been man enough to more than watch them skin the

other black for Mr. Fenneran, or man enough for Sissy any night thereafter.

"Now you can't even piss," he wept, "you dumb ole cock."

"Keep it out," somebody said, "and hold it in the door."

Frightened, Prewitt saw Sheriff Polsen without relief, sensing no humor but only more trouble than he already had. "Oh, Sheriff, you sure gave me a start."

The man had come up behind him making not a sound. "Get it on out again, I'mo mash it in this door."

He was different, sure enough. Something had turned him spooky as a ghost. Prewitt said, "I think I died and went to hell."

"Dead or alive, I'mo mash that snake of yours. Right here and now. Unless you tell me answers I sure mean to have."

Hog plum sailed the breezes. Under the big veranda lanterns, dancers smiled pink and orange in music from the ballroom. With Loker introducing repertory actors to some guests, the instant seemed ripe to approach him about influencing stubborn Meyerberger. But someone intercepted Fenneran on his way through the crowd.

"Dance with me, Tate."

Lantern light painted Deejay young. She looked so composed in her freckled prettiness, but sounded much too plaintive. It could not be the trying weeks past—she had borne them so well.

Deejay said nothing for a moment, smiling at others who danced by. Then she murmured, "He's not the same, he's not the same."

Fenneran had avoided verbalizing that very thought. "Well, his first night out, Deejay."

"Oh, I hoped going out would make the difference, but it hasn't. He just asked Congressman Traggan to produce his invitation or the skeletons in his Bayside warehouses."

A bolt of alarm left Fenneran so stunned that he continued dancing a little after the music stopped. Traggan's warehouses were too close to the killing of Caultree for comfort. "That's too funny," Tate managed, "to be called a personality change."

"You might call it one," she said with a hopeless quaver, "if you heard what else . . . " Deejay trailed off, then covered her

embarrassment saying, "He loses his temper whenever I say Officer Fairboro instead of Deputy Fairboro."

That demure evasion troubled him. In conveying to Polsen that the strongest possible message had been sent to New Orleans, Fenneran had implied an acknowledgment of violence, but not murder, his purpose being to assure the Sheriff he was avenged, and even more, to vindicate the use Fenneran once said he might have to make of Bayfront delinquents for the county's good.

He had taken pains to remain general, and Prewitt had sworn himself to secrecy. The possibility was insubstantial that Polsen had learned the horrific details elsewhere, yet Fenneran felt the currents of panic. "Deejay," he said gently, "whatever could Dexter have said to upset you so?"

"Things I could never repeat, and he recited them with no more emotion than reading a grocery list. He's become so literal and detached, it's frightening. Look. Is that Dexter Polsen?"

Inside, through the ballroom congestion, they had come in view of her husband standing with some people near the bar. Unlike the others, Polsen had no drink in hand, which was good, for he must resist alcohol on Dr. Tartara's most urgent orders. But he stood inexpressive in the midst of laughter, and that was anything but good. Once usually florid with responsive color, the Sheriff now hung sickly pale; once the very center of good-natured humor, he now seemed a stranger to it and apart.

When they came near the convivial group, Gulf Glade Mayor Hepwaithe was boasting about the Playhouse with shameless self-gratulation, and had Mayor Stydervant of Tarkey wearing a waxen smile of envy—until Dexter said, "Hep, you contributed no more to developing the Cultural Center than I did undergoing surgery."

Stydervant's laughter dominated the ringing chorus of it. Deejay's eyes fled to Fenneran, and his to the Sheriff with a hard gaze to deter him as Dexter said without a smile or any note of ambiguity, "Hope you can still laugh hearty, Mr. Stydervant, when your police force is indicted right up to the chief."

As if all this was in jest, the laughter escalated, but Fenneran exchanged a glance with Deejay in the knowledge they shared

that Dexter was not joking. Harmon Wilmont had all his evidence documented for the grand jury convening in a week, but that was supposed to be confidential. Deejay tried to dance Dexter off as the music resumed, but he sidestepped behind Fenneran and then around others to evade his wife, when Hepwaithe seized the opportunity for his own escape by dancing away with her on a galling popular tune from the band.

More men and women had joined the laughing group. "You all can now see," Fenneran told them, "the secret of Key County's successful anticrime program. We have an intrepid Sheriff who laughs organized crime to perdition."

With a grip on Polsen's arm he left them gingerly applauding. But on the veranda there was no opportunity to confront the Sheriff about his brash and indiscreet new boldness. First Barry Christian arrived by the grace, as he put it, of his wife and their month-old daughter, who was in fine voice. Then Judge Dow stopped them to say how pleased Loker was with the extensive marsh fill for Fenneran's new milk plant, and Polsen's sister was upon him next with kisses of gratitude for his survival.

Visiting from Nevada with her husband, Hillary's cousin Burl, Nola brushed Fenneran's face with kisses too, and said, "You ever see anyone so handsome? Now it can be told. We were engaged to be married when I was eight."

With a pensive smile Burl danced her away, and there came Deputy Fairboro, who had run the Sheriff's Office these months, to report that the mayor of Tarkey had just driven off without his wife. Polsen said, "Stydervant's go give himself away when he gets home. Harmon's got a wiretap on him tonight."

It struck Fenneran that his own dubious conversations might have been subject to surveillance in the carelessness of these stressful months. By a column where flowering dogwood was in view he said, "Dexter, the Tarkey people are Harmon Wilmont's political base. He'd sell you to the Devil for them."

"That's why I trust his word," Polsen said with lantern light bloody in his eyes. "Even with my head corked and plastered, I knew his moral drive in the rape case was to impress you with his integrity for a judgeship. Congressional run next, if he roots out corruption countywide. Can't do that without my office,

yet I stay only Sheriff forever. Providing you last forever."

Some of Dexter's brain had been cut away. Not anything critical to his intelligence or wit, evidently, just the part that once stirred him to smile. That was frightening enough. "I expect to last," Fenneran said, "as long as you're Sheriff." He ventured the jest of adding, "That's the only reason I brought your gun to the hospital for you."

Dexter held him in a probing gaze, and nobody passed a word their way, dancing by. As if all the jubilant guests of Loker Brisburn could sense the impasse in this trance of rosy lights and music, nobody interfered. Not until Loker himself came along with Hillary on his arm and whispered something to Polsen. But as always Fenneran was taken first with his wife.

She smiled in the glow. How fragile her beauty often seemed. How very fine she was at heart. Ever since the miserable flight she took from herself upon her brother's death, old friends often met Hillary with poorly concealed indulgence that stung her like scorn. It startled Fenneran to see the Sheriff lay his arm around her bare shoulders while saying right into Loker's teeth, "Can't pretend I mind Bo Traggan's hostility, Mr. Brisburn. His friendship could drag an honest man to jail."

With that he abandoned Hillary for her valorous mother, revered by all and thus a prime political ally to have in Key County. Burl stood in attentive conversation with her. Fenneran traded an uneasy smile with Loker and took Hillary to dance in her faint lilac aura. He loved the silken intimacy of her hair at his cheek. Romance deeply stirred her. It was usually after seeing a movie that she came to bed with desire.

"Fire," somebody said, and people started heading away. Everybody seemed to be hurrying into the ballroom, Fenneran leading Hillary by the arm. "Fire," a shrill voice echoed in the music. "Something's burning across the bay."

There was an exodus to the portico, from which the shore could be seen blazing across Wildcat Bay. An epicene voice rose above the gibberish of murmurs to cry, "Gulf Glade is on fire!"

Barry Christian, his face grim with anxiety, fled by and ran down the stairs to race away through lancewood trees toward the car park, where already automobiles could be heard growling off.

Hillary said, "Hadn't we best get over there with Barry?"

"No reason to worry, Hill. It's probably just some deserted old warehouses county pays rent on as patronage. Marge'll be okay."

Breathlessly she said, "Save Barry from this Korean war, Tate. You know he's in the reserves. They'll take him back."

"Well, if I can't manage that, your father surely can."

"Father will send him back to war," she said in the noise. The crowding confused her. "He sent Todd. Will you send Billy and Donny?" Their eyes met, and hers wavered in an unstable gaze that scattered. "All fathers sentence their sons to war. It's impossible to forgive any of you for that."

Not since her pregnancy with Cassandra had Hillary slipped back so to such hostile fringes of delirium. Pitying her father, Fenneran gathered her in and swayed with her in the fragrant night. Loker Brisburn's faith in national principles was so strong that he had refused to keep his son from enlisting, but he could never forgive himself for preventing his wife from dissuading Todd.

"I mixed things up," Hillary said at the weakest height of her voice, and faintly sighed. "But I meant that about Barry. And Dexter's audacity with Father didn't escape me."

"Yes, that was a veiled warning. Loker was almost angry." That quickly she was over the threat of dementia. One moment he held a morbid casualty of war, the next a devoted wife of breathtaking beauty. "Deejay's more worried about Dex than we are."

Her smile continued troubled as she nodded to guests who passed by remarking on the fire. With an excited flush she said, "And speak of the Devil."

Dexter came threading his way over through the crowd with people who were trying to engage him. That included his sister, her husband, and Deejay, who looked distressed even before she was audible, imploring him not to go wherever it was he intended.

"Nobody imagined Bayfront," the Sheriff said. "Everybody thought Gulf Glade till I made some phone calls. Tate, will you hold these people off me so I can learn how all that fire could start all that fast?"

"The entire shore's ablaze," Burl said as others drew closer to see. "That whole slum's on fire."

Deejay said, "He should be getting home by now, not to a big fire all out of control."

"We can take him in the car," Hillary suggested to reassure her. "You can't stop Dexter."

"No stopping what somebody just has to do," Polsen said with people following him away. "Who knows that better than Hillary?"

She glanced sharply at Fenneran just as a drum sounded fanfare for an announcement. "Glad it's not Gulf Glade," someone declared, and another voice cried, "But people are in trouble."

Descending with Hillary past guests on the portico stairs, Fenneran caught Honey Baines by the arm to say, "Gather the Theater Committee. Please tell them I want the Playhouse made ready for evacuees. Opera House too for additional problems."

Hurrying, they caught up with the others at the lancewood grove where Dexter, pointing out across the bay at a sweep of shoreline flames, said, "Beats any swamp fire I ever saw. Tate Fenneran's go get his highway to Wildcat Point now, sure enough."

Nola Brisburn said, "Oh, Dexter!"

But her unsmiling husband seized on it, his voice drawn thin with awe. "The choice is ole Meyerberger's, but he's got only one. That how Tate phrased it, Dexter?"

A gigantic flash caught them in the blossoming light of an explosion that sent no sound across before it illuminated the same stark abstraction as Polsen's in everyone facing Fenneran in those spectral woods, the same narrowed mind of condemnation. Even in Deejay. Even in Hillary, who said, "Tate Fenneran," her voice trickling winded and fey as darkness came sweeping back, "you never did entertain a single idea that was not utilitarian."

The detonation reached them that late from over the bay, a blast that shattered him with Hillary's attack, though Nola said, "You can't possibly believe Tate had any part in this."

Laurel flavored the sea scent. People were dying in the slum. Indignantly Fenneran turned back toward the house, Nola run-

ning alongside with her gossamer skirts held up girlishly. "Aren't you coming with us, Tate?"

"Hillary seems to need some distance from me now."

"Not the distance I can use from Burl."

Fenneran stopped in the dark of the woods facing Nola, her head cocked in pathetic silhouette as people strode between them rushing to the car park. He wondered what could be troubling her marriage to lean Burl Brisburn who, severe of eye and voice, shrewd and private in his turns of thought, had been severely beaten by his father as a child. Her sleek hair dangling, the impulse was to embrace Nola protectively, but a fire big enough to blow the storage tank over there could be catastrophic, and the county had no emergency plan he knew of except for hurricane evacuation.

"Wait," she said as he turned to go. Strains of piano music flowed with the breeze, a recital Loker apparently meant to present, disaster or not. "It's a fugue by Saint-Saëns." Nola whispered, though no one was near any longer in the woods. "I can tell by the peculiar sweetness of times past in it. Puts me in mind of Hillary."

"I have to telephone the army base for demolition means and maybe troops. I want to set up some kind of staging area."

She silenced him with a cool finger on his lips. "Others can. Why must you?"

Distant sirens wailed. "Wildcat Point fire units," he said over her slender hand. "They've called for assistance clear around the bays—it's just too serious to be left to others."

"Others divide us."

Her mouth came warm to his lips—young, generous, and tasting inoffensively of whisky. But this romantic abandon at such a time, like the piano recital inside, seemed desperate and hysterical rather than merely amiss.

All inevitability came screaming nearer with the sirens, yet no one was out on the portico. Clouds flamed over the burning shore, yet all were indoors attending Loker Brisburn's recital. Dexter's sister seemed depraved, yet Fenneran took her close.

And Hillary would blame the man-eating world forever on her husband and father. While kin like Nola forgave her with

envy for the use she had made of herself that fugitive year. In cities of the far-off war. Which was never to end, never to end for Hillary.

"No, Garth, inside! You have calls to make."

"Who's Garth?"

"I mean Tate. You can phone from my suite."

The curious flocked from all over to see the Bayfront burn. They came by foot, on bicycles, in every shape of motor vehicle, which flickered red with the faces of the pressing crowd. Fire trucks from more distant points could not get through to help the engine companies of Gulf Glade and Keyport fight the spreading blaze. Officers of the State Highway Patrol told Polsen so at the edge of the traffic snarl, and the shooting flames confirmed it.

Nobody knew what to do until the Sheriff, unable to get the Fenneran limousine through, strode over to a county squad car in his party clothes and took some gear. He got himself a Stetson to wear, a bullhorn over which to order vehicles off into the marl roads even in reverse if necessary, and a shotgun to threaten any driver slow to heed his directive.

Strangers were alarmed. Those aware of his injury and surgery were terrified. But he herded them away. He opened a lane for the Highway Patrol to route cars ahead with its lanterns. "A hat is everything," he told deputies. "They'll obey a hat, and a shotgun for sure."

It heartened his men to see him sufficiently recovered for his old ironical ways. But when he sent the limousine on with his wife broken down in Hillary Fenneran's arms, it began to seem doubtful that pungency had any part in what threatened to be arrogation of power beyond his authority. Dexter Polsen was a damaged man, possibly more than anyone realized. Though deputies conferred about that, at his command they assisted the Highway Patrol in establishing roadblocks where traffic pressed into Front Street full of passengers craning their necks to see.

The Sheriff himself tried to drive a squad car in but found his way blocked by spectators ganging out of the honky-tonks from which coarse music still emanated over the burning streets of

the slum. Engines clanged, begging to get through. Distant sirens approached the obstruction, ambulances from Keyport General that stood meager chance of finding a way to the injured.

That condition the Sheriff learned over the squad car radio he used for control communication with headquarters. Right up on the sidewalk Polsen drove, forcing onlookers back with protests about his dangerous tactics. Then he wheeled around and raced to meet the aid he heard clanging to a halt on the south end.

He got out waving his shotgun where fire trucks from Wildcat Point shuddered in delay behind Highway Patrol cars attempting to cut through the traffic jam. Fire Chief Kronecker readily agreed in the spinning red flashes of his toplight to let loose a hose into the crowd to disperse it. That was when County Attorney Wilmont showed up on his way to Loker Brisburn's party and questioned the legality of hosing citizens down.

But it worked so well that Kronecker got Polsen's sanction to water-hose the congestion of cars as well, the Sheriff escorting Wilmont back into his sedan, greeting his wife as the Prosecutor said, "I told you it wasn't over with the Indians, with that angry black what's-his-name. I told you they'd burn us down."

Moments later, just as Fairboro reached him to report the Sheriff's use of naked force, Wilmont saw Polsen smash a windshield with his shotgun butt, sending the car to shriek off in a bounce of sharp turns that let the impatiently clanging Wildcat Point ladder company get through. Fire trucks from Hammerhead thundered across, but had ample labor right there on Front Street where the saloons had ignited, and the pool halls and other storefronts, practically all the property of estimable value in the district.

Luminous hose water poured high at the tiers of hopeless buildings angrily ablaze down all the inner streets. People were shouting in the clangor. Wherever Polsen braked up, occupants remained in their flaming homes hypnotized by disbelief, immobilized by fear of loss. A man accused police of trying to evacuate him in order to steal his television. An old woman had to be dragged, clinging to belongings wrapped in a bed sheet, off her capsized porch. Others leaned out of lower windows to watch the flames lick out above them. Rescuers lunged from

houses empty-handed. Shadow figures gathered casualties on makeshift litters in the smoke. He saw charred children scramble out of alleys into the arms of police, and fatigue came on him all at once.

The ambulances were finally getting through, but there would never be enough in the flickering crimson night. The awful curious had to be recognized as lunatics. Crary at headquarters reported that Tate Fenneran had hurricane evacuation systems in service and receiving stations established at the theater complex, with Red Cross and Civil Defense units already in liaison. That meant the hospitals would not be jammed up and rendered ineffective.

Fenneran was something, all right, yet might have to be arrested by the friend he had avenged, if Prewitt proved believable. And just when Tate got his right-of-way with Meyerberger's wooden hovels burning to rubble all around, the silver nozzles gushing, the scorched wet odors like death, the multiplying sirens louder.

People seldom spoke their minds, and when they did it was most often to justify themselves by claiming more than the facts supported. Cant and subterfuge seemed to be everybody's language, and Polsen had no patience for that. It was hard to remember if he ever had any, or exactly how he was before his injury. Bells gonged. Windows vomited flame. Firemen ran hose to gutted structures. Friends and relatives told him he was the same, but their eyes confessed they thought otherwise.

Everybody seemed to have a whisky bottle. He considered rounding people up for interrogation to discover the actual cause of this inferno, but felt like sleeping as the heat crept closer to his cheeks. His brain was repaired, less some minor inhibitory tissue perhaps, but with no indication of mental lag or lapse. Skull fully refurbished with tantalum plate, even his hair was presentably grown in by now. But weariness collapsed him from time to time, attended by a haste to complete any task at hand. He had almost finished Prewitt off that Sunday at the hospital, and had scared him too harshly tonight.

Polsen felt his injuries, amazed by all he saw or pondered. He felt unequal to the responsibilities upon him in this sudden

dream he seemed to be having of revelers tippling in the flames, drinkers in a yard full of tables who were watching the Wildcat Rest burn away, the historic old way station inn. People screamed in the windows as others laughed in the beer garden, cheering each swell of flames on the roof while fire trucks clanged to a halt behind a bus abandoned sidewise as if intentionally to bar the way. The Sheriff radioed for assistance.

All he saw or dreamt appalled him as he drove up on the tavern sidewalk. So many cheered the fire. He saw or dreamt they had looted the place for its whisky knowing others were trapped in the chambers of fornication above. Fenneran's friends believed he had the Bayfront torched and his adversary blamed Indians for roasting these dregs in their bawdyhouse to the glee of other wantons. They screamed to see the roof cave in with a shower of erupting sparks. Dream or not, he knew he had to kill them.

He expected them to disobey, yet got out raising the bullhorn rather than the shotgun and ordered them all to remove the stalled bus with their shoulders and hands. Gaunt men and women turned their hollow eyes on him, screaming pleas for the lives of the imprisoned ones. He had merely dreamt their mockery of doom.

He felt impaired. Through the horn he boomed, "I'll get them out. You all go help those firemen. Move the bus, move the bus!"

Like a school of fish they swarmed away. Polsen ran, though unfit for the exertion. Still smokeless, the interior of the inn looked ghostly where the back bar shelves were empty. Tumbled furniture blocked the stairway solid. Their own looting had shut the wretches off upstairs. He saw their choking faces in smoke just starting to descend. They jabbered and coughed but did nothing he could see to dislodge the barriers. It seemed as if hopelessness, their sense of life since birth, gripped them in catatonic resignation to the inevitable. That, more than sloth or iniquity, must surely be what transfixed people like these while their lives burned down around them all over these bay shores.

Hating them for it, he ran to wake himself from the nightmare of their fatalism. Out back the night grille was locked

across the door, and a press of coughing people lay against it, incompletely dressed, spattered with soot, in their indecent faces too defeated to obey his warning bullhorn and vanish up the back stairs.

Smoke from the roof fell at last into this dream of a doom that mocked itself. Coughing in its foul stench, he leveled the shotgun and fired a mercy to be done with such people once and for all. Dolly Jane was home, his children secure. His house was full of appliances. Squad wagons were everywhere with sirens wailing, Harmon Wilmont in it all with Fairboro. People were weeping. Firemen were hosing. The roof was exploding sparks to inflame the impoverished world beyond and then the very improvements that allowed life to work better in hopeful Gulf Glade.

Yet the pretty new town was safe. The Prosecutor said so, looking incongruously distraught. Could the shotgunning of hopelessness really matter? "Army's here to blow up the old warehouses and stem the spread north. Deejay's right worried, Dexter. She wants you home."

The Sheriff climbed into Wilmont's car, sapped of energy and awake only to deputies evacuating half-naked refugees who coughed in red lights that spun on the tops of cars. "How'd these people get out?" he said. "I gunned them down."

"What? You blasted off the padlock. Bullhorn's what saved them, though. Without it you'd never have got them out the way, back upstairs into smoke. You gave them precious little time."

"Deejay has her Mixmaster."

"What? Your hat too, that helped. Any sign of authority, they rush to it for orders in a crisis."

"No shit. Is that Clint Bocaleon half out of his clothes?"

"What? He's a scandal, he was in there. How do you feel?"

"Mind's not all there yet." Nauseated, leaning back with dreams of the dead, Polsen tasted the abject fatalism of the poor. It seemed a depravity shared by all in the surrounding affluence that permitted it. The pretensions of Christianity resided in every slum of the world. "Let's get on," Polsen said. "Smells like I just woke up with my nose in somebody's mouth."

* * *

The Bayfront burned out of control until a dawn rain doused it to simmer and reek. During the night, engine and ladder companies sirened in from every town in the county, but with limited effect. The curious, thwarting access too long, had surrendered time to the sparks and murdered people in the dry tinder of their homes. Key County's worst fire in memory had choked or scorched a quarter of the slum community to death.

Statistics accumulated by the time Sheriff Polsen got to his office in the morning revealed that some four hundred souls had been trapped by sleep or drink or panic, never to escape the serried porch flats and shanties alive. More than that many had suffered burns and smoke inhalation, or were missing. For the survivors, the merest portion of housing remained habitable.

And those devastating facts shocked the Sheriff no more than the number of rapes he found accumulated on his blotter over the period he had been away. In about nine weeks there were forty-one complaints, a virtual epidemic apart from the unreported incidents, with only six arrests on record. Then, before he could get settled at his desk, another complaint came from the Cultural Center.

Acting Gulf Glade Police Chief Tolstadt was still a deputy Sheriff reporting in as such to say it was a very serious case this time. "Aren't they all?" Polsen said.

"This violation's on a prominent person, Dex. Can't much make out what she's saying. Think you can get over here?"

All the telephones were ringing, the switchboard overloaded, the day shift busy predominantly with curious inquiries. But the Sheriff felt refreshed, though dismay over Hillary Fenneran clouded his mind with Tolstadt's expression of particular concern.

Polsen had arrived home from the fire too exhausted to notice the redolence of lilac on his pillow until morning light woke him to the scent, which troubled him even after his wife explained its presence in their bed. With Hillary overwrought by Tate's possible role in the fire, Deejay had bundled her away like a child to tend, easing the wait for her psychiatrist to come take her off.

Where she went from the doctor, Polsen did not dare guess. He pictured her racing through the night in desperation, afraid to confront Tate at home, and finally going to be of some use when she learned how he was serving. Only to encounter at the Center that worst of all abuses. The Sheriff asked Tolstadt who the victim was, steeling himself with a forlorn premonition that it would turn out to be Hillary Brisburn Fenneran.

"Gave my word I wouldn't say on an open line. Lady's right here by me in the Art Cinema office. Says Indian who did it was no Indian. Too upset of course to be very clear."

In the squad room Polsen noticed Fairboro signing out with other men on overtime, and asked about the action taken with the rape suspects so far. Up all night and half asleep, the lanky senior deputy yawned. "Ask Wilmont, he's got the cases."

"What's holding up the rest of these complaints?"

Fairboro shrugged. "They're colored. Mostly black. A few Seminole maids, maybe, up toward Imokalee."

Feeling impatient perhaps too hastily with Fairboro, Polsen took him along and sat down in his office to telephone the County Attorney. Wilmont's office reported him out inspecting the razed Bayfront with other authorities. Telephones rang on the Sheriff's nerves. "How come you didn't press these rape cases, Walt?"

"Dex, I told you." Fairboro sat slumped, his face haggard and open-pored. "New priorities, piled onto routine cases. All this new construction. Zoning to enforce, patrol expansion to Ceremony Key since the bridge opened."

"What you told me was that those violated people were colored. That's all you told me."

Fairboro dismissed him with a chuckle, putting on his hat as he rose. "Ain't slept since church, Dex, be a pal."

Polsen also got up, to head for the Art Cinema office. This deputy had alerted teams from the utilities to neutralize dangling live wires and set up gas lines. All night long he had public works crews searching with power shovels and cranes for entrapped survivors, meanwhile alerting various police and fire units to investigate all possible causes of the conflagration. Word

was that he had conducted the county police as efficiently, these past months, but Polsen had grave doubts about that.

The County Attorney's chauffeured car turned into Buttonwood Levee, once just a creek embankment dense with black peat and brackish marsh, until fill derricks joined it to the coastal plain over which Gulf Glade had grown. Now the new Cultural Center blossomed there in pink concrete and white cupolas hazy with rain amid the plane trees.

Explosions in the middle of the night had excited Wilmont with all the impact of Fenneran's power. The man could so handily bring army demolition personnel to arrest the fire in its spread toward property of value. He had induced radio stations to appeal for emergency volunteers, and admirable people had responded from every community to go among the screaming and the dead for Tate Fenneran. In their trucks and buses they had transported the dead with the injured and the homeless to this shining Center where cultural space as yet unused was adapted for housing and first aid.

Earlier, Wilmont had toured with selectmen and found the three hospitals overcrowded but functioning. He had praised Fenneran for effectuating that, the board members agreeing to proclaim him a public hero of Key County as a means of allaying vicious attempts in some quarters to impute the tragedy to the man, ironically, who had saved so many lives.

When the county police chauffeur stopped in the downpour, the Sheriff's sister was waiting to show Wilmont around the Art Cinema before she left to get some sleep. Young Mrs. Brisburn had given Fenneran her volunteer work there all night. So had Barry Christian, asked in to supervise the processing of casualties with other sleepless volunteers. Wilmont had intentionally let him win the rape case on a device one could doubtless have battered down at trial. But as a consequence Fenneran was being very gracious lately, dropping broad compliments behind the Prosecutor's back.

There was, as his wife always said, no friend like a propitiated antagonist; anticipating Fenneran's warm political support, Wilmont listened attentively as Christian explained how Tate

had made the Playhouse over into a coordinating headquarters.

By running in extra phone lines, he established communications sections for the military, medical, civil defense, police, and public works units operating in the disaster area below. Red Cross workers supplied coffee and sandwiches there through the night, a diversion of sorts from the dead, who were laid out onstage and beyond over the huge backstage deck to the rear doors, where volunteers carried them in, then out to the morgues once relatives confirmed identification. But the sensitive acoustical design, according to Christian, had projected the wails of grief to somber the busy aisles.

The emergency had of course demanded this extremity of turning the Cultural Center into a crossroads of death and misery. And with that inauspicious beginning Fenneran also worked out a disaster plan for the future, sorely lacking in Key County before. Another necessity was immediate new housing, and Fenneran met that too by requisitioning Quonset huts from Fort Copeland for hundreds of families burnt out with single individuals by the score.

The tension of sleepless long hours was heavy on Tate, Christian said. But he discouraged Wilmont from going over there to urge the man home. "That's the witness," he then indicated as Polsen descended the Art Cinema's broad marble staircase with a slight girl bandaged on both arms. "Just a child, but up late enough on a porch to see those Indians toss their Molotov Cocktail. I held her here for Dex."

Wilmont resisted saying he had warned of retaliation by Indians. Others would remind people of that. This hour belonged to him. He could feel it in his bones as Barry, getting his trench coat from behind an office door, said word was circulating that Polsen had become careless about the limits of police authority.

The Sheriff threw on his slicker coming across the lobby to them past refugees and helpers. The County Attorney said, "Dex, can a kid that young be reliable?"

"Reliable as star reporter got her tail split snooping around the old ice house where so-called Indian was hiding out for his getaway. I've sent her to the hospital." Sallow and vexed, the Sheriff was even more incomprehensible next. "Same assault

been a hornet's nest on colored women since your rapist scum got away with it."

Christian's perplexed look enlightened Wilmont enough to say, "Can you be alluding to rape in connection with Miz Honey Baines?"

"Promised not to mention her name."

Wilmont followed Polsen outside, Christian coming along to say, "Harmon, I can attest to your prophecy that the Indians would torch us one day. But you never warned us they would plant Honey Bee's stinger for her in an ice house."

His attempt to lighten the situation fell flat. "Indian girl," the Sheriff said as they walked in the nagging rain, "looked no different than this victim the day Black Junn brought her to me. Eyes looked just the same."

"Same Indians," Christian pounced on the word digressively, "threw the flaming bottle that burned the Bayfront down."

"Colored have their good and bad and don't know which is which, just like us." Polsen led them through an imposing statue garden. "Ole Prewitt thinks he's unmanly for not being up to murdering somebody in gratitude to his benefactors."

"I'm tired," Christian said. "I'm not making you out, Dex."

Entering the Playhouse behind Polsen, Wilmont exchanged a concerned glance with Christian and sadly shook his head.

The magnificent new lobby lay deserted, and inside, the auditorium presented a scene of eerie gloom. On the distant stage, bodies still unidentified rested under shrouds in macabre bright light, one lonely figure picking among them, likely for missing kin. Fenneran sat alone in his deep theater seat as if caved in beneath a terrible weight of exhaustion.

He looked around at the sound of people. Intuitively, Wilmont suppressed an impulse to extoll Tate's exemplary humanitarian accomplishments this dreadful night past, and Fenneran turned his back, sinking lower in his seat. Then he rose to face them again, paling with an anger Wilmont had never before seen him betray.

Fenneran went straight up to Polsen saying, "Does she think I'd kill hundreds of people and leave a thousand more with no place to go? No armory, no convention hall within the county.

Calamity like this could have happened any time in that heap of sticks. Only luck delayed it till this Cultural Center was completed to accommodate refugees. But it didn't need luck to keep those people safe. Nobody would have died last night, and nobody would be suffering maimed excruciation today, and little Bayfront rats would long since have been on the way to becoming normal kids if I only got the simple cooperation I asked from that nose-picking old son of a bitch!"

In that echoing tirade Wilmont shivered with excitement. His courthouse prognostications about racial vengeance must be ringing through all their heads, and all around Key County he was sure to be the prophet who foretold the Bayfront fire. But the moment seemed too ripe, with Fenneran so emotionally vulnerable, for the restraint intuition urged. "The Seminoles," he asserted crisply, surprised by the amplification of his thread-like voice in this morgue of an empty theater. "Tate, I'm afraid it was the Indians who torched the Bayfront."

Fenneran regarded him. "Have no fear. That is not so."

More accustomed vision showed others in the house. A couple of men stood apart with rifles by the wall. "Sheriff," Wilmont ventured unconfidently, "don't we have testimony to that effect?"

"The arsonists were just dressed up like Seminoles."

"Are you saying it could have been . . . someone like the Negro Cavalo, known as Old Black John, who wears a headcloth?"

"No, it wasn't Junn," a remote voice said, tumbling forward young and hurt. Someone was addressing them from the stage, alone with the dead in a poncho. "I been by him in the swamp every minute. Till news came of this fire."

Fenneran turned to face the stage, then stared off to one side. As if that gaze were a direct question, an old man's voice said, "That's Price Fenton, Mr. Fenneran."

Wilmont felt tension ripple through the silent hall like shock waves. Suddenly back from oblivion, this boy could do no less than confess his part in the swamp girl's rape. Polsen said, "Go on and speak, boy."

His face obscured by the poncho hood, Price shuffled monk-like to the front of the stage and peered out on those few present. "Please don't shoot me, Mr. Jessup," he said. His frail young

voice rode its echoes. "Our sin was drove by the Devil. We done the Injun gal like Junn say. Crocodile and all. And sent him off to hide the evidence. Junn told it true."

Fenneran collapsed into a seat. Wilmont took one next to Christian. It had looked bad for a moment, but now further political entrenchment seemed at hand. Tinny rain drummed on the ventilation ducts. Young Fenton peered around to make out faces, and Wilmont seized the pause to eliminate any possible extenuation of this hard testimony before witnesses. "Did anyone coerce you to confess, or is this of your own free will?"

Christian spoke up in sonorous assurance. "You're not under oath, Price. Reply only as you wish. What did you want to say about the crocodile?"

"Nice going," the Prosecutor whispered. "Hang onto that lizard's tail. The kid may be your client, but he's my witness."

"No man drove me here," the boy said. "No one drove us to spoil the gal and throw her to the devil beast." Rain lashed the sidings on wind gusts. "We all sent Junn to bury the remains. But the Great Spirit went ahead of him to save her hide alive. Junn drove the buzzards off, and the devil beast. But it already spawned in the gal with us. So went the Wheel of Life. The Maker and Taker of Breath over us all."

"Did I understand you to say," the Sheriff resonated from behind, "that you heard tell of that crocodile spawning—"

"I seen it fuck the gal. Aimed my rifle to save her, but my other soul drove it down."

"You were drinking devil's eye?" Christian called out.

"Yes. And been drinking it since in the presence of God. It never made me see Him like I seen the crocodile big as a plow horse between her legs. Would pale the dead sight of my pa."

The boy fell silent, his face just a dark hole in the hood. He hung there as if waiting for a message from above. Christian whispered, "Your witness forgot his lines."

"My witness," Wilmont rejoindered, "has completed his testimony. He's just your client now."

"Sounds mostly nuts. I'm satisfied with your witness."

"Three holy sisters told me to confess," Price Fenton said, "so I'm confessing. They told me fire and brimstone on the Bayfront, and lo it's true. They found me stark in the marshes,

screaming at the birds. I seen Injun scalp my brother Wayne. Junn my salvation. And me part of Brady say he murder Junn if Ole Black shirk at burying Injun gal's remains. Three sisters come canawling up from Swamptown to tend her most days. Devil spawn biting hard inside her, like to bust her brain. But Junn save her like he save me. Potions he boil. Braveness he hold in his patient hand. Brave is to be careful for other folks, he say. I always liked the man. Let me come and hunt to cotton up in penitence. Say please her some, maybe she forgive me one day. But her pain so keen, it drive her stark. Some nights she live that rape all over again, her hate so bad she like to murder me in my sleep. Junn see her through. He Joseph to her Mary, that come to me. Them three more like kings come to Bethlehem, we been told so long. Sisters pray on my head the Lord forgive me. Gal pray Fishaki Omechi, ask why He let five no-account boys spawn in her. It come to me wasn't us no more'n crocodile, and I say devil beast. That like to turn her into one before my eyes. She show lion teeth, to hear me say that. She go flying like there's bat wings on her. She come down sick with fever. Sick a lot worse myself, that way. Three sisters spend the night in swamp to tend us. One taken onto me in the night. So holy in the day, she pray my forgiveness. Night come, she steal away to take my badness into her own self, I thought it was the fever. Her face go like rubber in the moon. Bat face. Melon face. Maybe fever make me scream, but it was sister wipe me down and hush me. She swim all over me, birds all screaming on us, it come to me her own badness in that. Maybe two from heaven, one from hell, to hear that sister grunt. Maybe all three from heaven and hell, maybe all of us is. Pray and lust, two-headed all our days, but never confess it like the Seminole see their two souls plain. The strong and just. The weak and evil."

Half dazed, Wilmont looked around to see how the others were reacting. Christian sat limp alongside in total absorption. A few rows down across the aisle, Fenneran sat low in his chair, perhaps asleep. Wilmont sank back to listen as, with some people crowding close backstage among the dead, Price Fenton removed his hood and went on in the clatter of storm rain.

"She prayed to the Breathmaker and cursed Him, off and on. God and the Devil all in one, like her own two souls. Fishaki

Omechi most likely the true God, this world, I seen Him play out nativity on the Injun Wheel of Life. Lightning flashing like today, thunder clapping too. Ain't like the peaceful snow come drifting down on Bethlehem. Three kings come in split-tail black disguise. No camels under them, just a canoe. No fancy gifts of gold or smelly stuff. Just coffee grind, and soap, and cartridges for Junn's deer rifle."

Women had arrived backstage to hurry the volunteers along in evacuating the dead. Wilmont saw men in white and other uniforms. Fenneran's wife came to mind, the debauch rumor once displayed her in, and he pitied her somehow as he did the Indian girl and Honey Baines. The world was not safe for women.

"Rain hit down hard around Junn's chickee. Mine not half thatched yet, still them sisters drove me out to it for her sake. She screaming at me to see a baby come could be my own. Bird life screaming in the thunder. Lightning come to sizzle through right where we're at. Great Spirit remind us all our breath right in His palm. I seen them boil and do whatever. All the smoke and running. Heard them cry out behind the rain they delivered her. But I heard no baby cry. Just screaming more from Majosee, like from her hate, not pain no more."

Christian startled Wilmont with a query snapping sharp beside him. "Baby in three months or so? How could you entertain such an impossibility at your age?"

Price Fenton stood speechless on the stage as men removing corpses laughed at him. He walked off to one end of the stage and then the other in his baggy poncho. Unable to locate a stair, he dropped light as a bird into the orchestra pit, to rise as nimbly and go drifting up the aisle. Glancing around, the boy stopped just past Fenneran and swept sandy hair away from his eyes. "Crocodilians," he said, "don't take but thirty-nine days to deliver they eggs. She took longer, hatching inside."

Only the rain on tin ducts sounded. Nobody knew what to say. Until a shirtless tall man in overalls said over his cradled rifle, "Price, ain't no trace of your daddy."

"Guess he died for his sins," the boy said. "God rest his souls. Poor bugger, I've seen worse, these parts. Sorry I went at you that night, Mr. Hoyt. Nothing personal."

"Some Injun go and scalp ole Wayne sure enough?"

"Ole Injun man. Stay out there near they camp awatching like a swamp lion. Shoot any white gits too close. All's Wayne wanted was some help for me down with fever. We was lost."

"What happened in the swamp?"

That came from Fenneran, turned half around in his seat. The boy stood unresponsive. Christian said, "Did she give birth to a crocodile?" and laughter came from the old man who had identified Price for Fenneran.

"Nosir. She gave birth to a litter. Can't rightly call them man or beast. Monsters I seen born. Six I seen him carry down the slough, her screaming at him to kill them. None of them bigger'n your hand. Babies, only they was green and spotted. Half tail. Squirming. Animals, but with little faces, round heads like us. Junn showed me before he sunk them in the slough to drown. Rain bashing his face. Said he wanted me to see what we done that gal. The real picture shape of what we done in the world. He always did talk Injun kind of meanings. Rain bashing my face. Like a whip in his careful hand. Compared to the sight of monsters born, the scalping of my brother Wayne run pale."

"Jesus God," a woman cried in echoing frail voice onstage amid the dead. "Oh, my God!"

Removing his hat, the lank man said, "Heard tell of a scare doing like that to woman's child. But six?"

"Did he drown them?" Fenneran said.

"Nosir. Nor chased after them when they swum off. To see them wriggle newborn in the storm, you like to die."

Wilmont suffered a chill of pure horror. Rain lashed and echoed, rattling in the ducts. He felt absurd in his fright.

"Lightning shine Junn's face. Him looking through the storm to other things he knew. While sisters screamed. They all wants him catch them babies man or beast. I can't believe they wants him murdering in daytime. But that ain't it. They tells him protect the little infants from the beasts of prey. He looking through the storm till he see something make him take up lettuce flags in his two hands. He brush the babies along. He walk among them brushing. Spawn of God the Devil, I seen them

wriggle away go hide in hyacinths at the bank. I see they little claws."

Christian chose that moment to stand up and get out of it. But he could not seem to do so without a pitch of breath that sounded like the casting off of heavily restrictive emotions. "That's about all I can tolerate of this bayou witchcraft. Tate, we really ought to get some sleep."

"Been getting some. Right scary to hear all this satanism half in and out of sleep."

"Don't you all believe me?"

Price Fenton stood there amazed. Christian said, "You're obviously in narcosis. Devil's eye it's called?"

"Yeah, devil's eye. But sisters ain't drink none and they seen the same six monsters. Right up near to the borning too. Ain't devil's eye made them save monsters. That was Breathmaker. You calls Him God. Same Fishaki Omechi bent Junn to ole Injun legend spell your doom." He was getting very worked up, heaves of resentment shuddering through his weird cries. "You don't believe me who been sent to warn you all be careful for yourself. Or your houses to destruction, your children to slaughter. Your days all being numbered in the swamp."

Advancing toward him, the Sheriff said, "Take it easy, boy."

"You all believe in the same Jesus as me, him born immaculate. Believe all them miracles in ole-time book called Bible, and you don't believe what my own two eyes seen?"

"Come on, boy." The Sheriff was inching closer. "Let's go see if we can't find your daddy."

"He been damned long since. You all think I half expected to find him? Knowed him dead when three sisters come in the middle of the night. Tell of jubilation in Swamptown, happy down the dirt streets. Praying thanks to God sent down big fire to punish evil Bayfront to death."

Deftly Polsen swept the boy's poncho aside and snapped his wrists behind him in handcuffs. "You're under arrest on a rape charge. Anything you say may be held against you."

Christian was there. Wilmont arrived in time to hear him say in angry undertone, "Did you think this kid might be armed?"

"You bet your sweet ass," the Sheriff replied.

Oblivious in his indignation, the boy went right on. "So ashamed of niggers hating us all that much, they come to canoe me here in the night. I knowed my pa was dead. Still I felt myself drove here. Turn out sure enough it's right in our house Breathmaker set the fire to burn sin down on them shores. And here's you all not believing. Like the Pharisees and Scribes and Sodom and Gomorrah."

"Wasn't your Breathmaker," Polsen said, turning the boy over to deputies. "Was hired locals dressed up to resemble Seminoles. Got your name from New Orleans."

Wilmont realized the colored retaliation issue had just died. Yet disappointment was least of the desolation to which he sank in this rainy gloom. The Prosecutor, a religious man, felt paganized, diminished into some haphazard ingredient of a large scheme played out around a rapist turned idolatrous proselytizer.

"Grand jury go have to seek indictments for organized pit fighting," Polsen said as deputies left with Price Fenton. "And murder, which is what provoked this fire by outsiders."

"Is there evidence of that?" Fenneran wheezed with fatigue.

"I have an eyewitness," the Sheriff responded flatly.

He seemed unstable, menacing. Wilmont touched his arm. "Dexter. We're your friends."

"I always expected truth from my friends. I can believe that drunken hoodoo kid easier than any of you three actors."

His gaze looked insane on Fenneran, who nodded sleepily and, heading for the lobby, said, "I believe in monsters. A breed unwilling to permit any civilization to function in ethical accord." Tate crossed the lobby stiff and shaky, with everyone coming behind him. "There's no civilized defense from the brainless drive in monsters to pillage the fruits of our best-laid plans." He eyed the windy rain outside. "There's no act too savage, in my book, to eliminate them from society."

"My sentiments exactly," Polsen said, shoving open the door. He ducked into the rain. Fenneran went through, but paused with Christian and Wilmont under the sheltering marquee.

"Dexter," he shouted to stop his old friend in the downpour. "In a week's time I'll have all that old Shylock's poor folks

housed in the pine brake up over Hammerhead. Good many of them been finding employment with my contractors around the county. Others who want work can put up dwellings for their own families on my property at scale labor wages. Quonset huts make better houses than any of them have ever set foot in."

Deputies were squeezing the Fenton boy into a patrol car. Turning, the Sheriff walked past them sullen and aloof, rain splashing on his hat. Fenneran heaved a sigh so wracked with languor it fluttered. A like feebleness came next from Christian.

"I think he's in a bad way. He may be dangerous."

Wilmont took a long breath to say, "I may have to prosecute any prima facie case he may have for the grand jury."

"Only if you remain County Attorney," Fenneran said, and Wilmont felt himself color. Then he grew even warmer upon Fenneran saying, "Not if you resign to accept a seat on the bench."

Rain splashed on the patrol car as it churned away. Other cars floated off and left dry parking spaces steaming. Wilmont met Christian's waiting gaze, then Fenneran's. They were all practical men of dedication to the public good.

He nodded his acceptance.

PANORAMA TWO

DEVIL'S EYE

WITNESS BEHOLDS MONSTER YET CAN MAINTAIN NO BELIEF IN ITS EXISTENCE. You, Storyteller? You, who collage human grotesques by profession? If you have two souls, is it the good one or the bad that cannot accept this half-man beast you saw as the ancestor of monsters far worse in human form? Storyteller, they appear in our media every day of the week, as they have preyed in our midst for generations.

You can read and believe there are men who live to slaughter women without number? Could your human hand do that, even if you tried to force it to? You can believe because the newspapers say an ordinary optician laced his own child's Halloween candy with cyanide to collect on an insurance policy? Is there even a human being you personally despise who could possibly do that?

Today the media report an entire Ohio family has been stabbed to death in its sleep. Your heart knows that was done by a monster, and yet, just because the discovery of your own eyes was visibly half beast, you can't believe a monster has risen from the other side of the water to propagate its genes in mankind?

Try, Storyteller. Try to believe.

COLLAGE 9

We set out at dawn to fish for snook, Barry Christian and I. Salt mists braced us in the pass. To judge by his glances, he seemed to suspect I had invited him out for more than just the sport. My manner betrayed a troubled mind, I guess. But also, the puzzles that dominated his work as Metropolitan Attorney, those days, had him wishful about relevant information from people in his confidence.

Something terrible had happened in Pinebrake. That much Barry knew. But his grasp of it was limited to the gruesome evidence police investigation had documented for his office. No one thought there might be witnesses. Everyone believed that slaughter was the full extent of the atrocity. Though I lived right by the tragic site, I had pretended to be familiar only with as much as the newspapers had spread or Barry himself brought out when considering the matter aloud.

The assault was so horrendous that the surviving victim could not conceive of it as reality even in his comatose ranting. Few

at the hospital accepted the details that came from him as anything more than terrified hallucinations. But I knew better. I had seen it. And more. I was there in lucid sight of something literally incredible.

Of that the bereaved and brutalized man was unable or unwilling to speak. The Indian housemaid never would about any of it, given her weird personal involvement (and a speech impediment to boot). As for me, to tell meant admitting the nature of my presence across the canal that ribboned through our suburb. I might have to expose myself as adulterous, if not sexually aberrant as well, and for all his worldly intelligence, Barry Christian was a man of principles as traditional as his name implied.

Moreover, any scandal would redound on my children. My wife concerned me too, of course, in that regard. And I was a natural target for vilification, having some prominence that gave me standing in the community, though an outsider among its home-grown artists. Still, what I had witnessed threatened the security of all Gulf Glade. The city had to be alerted. People's lives were at stake. Sick with the dilemma, I floated us out of Wildcat Bay.

I had heard the screaming, but others had reported it. Police cars and an ambulance, sirening banshees in the night, had converged to find the young family mutilated, torn mostly out of its clothes between the house and the canal. A small girl and her mother were dead. Her father lay half alive in a tangle of shrubs. Stunned by what I had seen happen to him, I stood rooted in horror till the keening sirens drove me to swim back across the canal, dreading the unearthly apparition of a beast that had plunged in only a while before.

I had learned from Barry that for days the man, clawed open in places like his lost loved ones, both arms broken and his ribs cracked, kept repeating in semiconscious amazement his recall of a huge lizard dragging his child out of the house and attacking her parents when they followed in hysterical pursuit. Some took him to mean an alligator had risen out of the watercourse to maraud. Others thought crocodile, not merely because alligators were seldom known to be homicidal: those who remembered the

rape of an Indian girl, some years before my time there, thought crocodile for reasons beyond my comprehension then.

They were terrorstricken by the prospects of such a predator having found its way into the network of canals the county had dug clear out to Hammerhead. But a crocodile was tame compared with the monstrosity I had seen performing its unimaginable act.

Barry and other city authorities were hard put to believe that a single assailant of any kind could have wreaked so much devastation. They sensed some hidden ingredient in the victim's use of a general term like lizard for so bloodthirsty a reptile, as if he had cause, even in coma, to balk at asserting alligator or crocodile outright. When doctors at Todd Brisburn Memorial decided at last to allow it, Barry interrogated the distraught man specifically about any features of the attack he might not yet have reviewed. But they soon stopped that as a dangerous mistake on account of their patient's reaction.

After responding only so far as to describe a crocodilian miscreation with elongated legs on which it could rear back like a primate, he began to quake severely and lapsed into a feverish dementia that required sedation.

Everybody was bewildered by this pall of dread. But Barry realized it hinted at something more, not medically obvious, too unspeakable to so much as contemplate. That was exactly how I felt about the details I could give to substantiate his surmise. It was all too unspeakable for even the Metropolitan Attorney to be told. Even the public danger left me reluctant.

But I had brought him out on the Gulf of Mexico knowing I really had no choice. And who could I trust if not my old buddy? He had introduced me to my exhibitor, beautiful Hillary Fenneran (and to her illustrious husband, Tate). His associates bought my work. In fact Barry had attracted me south to begin with, several years after a German sniper separated us with my second wound of the war. He always forgave my excesses, genially blaming them on my head. That was how he liked to put it, alluding to the injury that kept me from painting, all those years.

Optic nerve damage frustrated the resumption of that part of

my life. A grievously reduced field of vision robbed me of that. I searched for a discipline that would permit me to structure a composition piece by piece without boring me like geometrics, and discovered a visually narrative way to metaphor. I work in collage, in images and artifacts that I join together to convey the ironical complexity that life has always seemed to me.

As Barry sat cutting bait, I asked how his daughter Gretchen liked school. Each of us had a second child beginning and a third too young, and marveled at the curiosity of having become fathers at almost identical times though apart since our life of mutual dependence in the war. Rediscovering me in an art news feature, about seven years after the great Bayfront fire, Barry had wondered if the county Sheriff and I might be of help to one another in coping with the problems of brain damage that we had in common.

Neither of our head injuries was recent, but the suggestion could not have come at a better time. I seized on the opportunity of settling in the subtropics as a gamble to cure my eldest of croup. And it worked. Relations with the sardonic Sheriff were difficult to achieve (for others as well as me), but my daughter was never sick again.

I mentioned her, vaguely hoping to insinuate in Barry the urgency of keeping as much as possible from disclosure for my family's sake. I said at nine Lissa could already be trusted with the care of her two kid brothers while they all fished off our wharf block. They were always in my view from the studio wing of the house, but she knew nothing of that. I was likely to be watching the house directly across anyway, for a glimpse of the woman who resided there. It was a compulsion, I said, and Barry's frank blue eyes alerted to a sense of something afoot that might prove important to the Pinebrake case.

The victims had lived in a house out of sight behind dense pines and drooping palms across the narrow blade of water. Before the tragedy I had not even known such a place to exist. Barry understood as much but had no idea I was over on that side when I first became conscious of the house nestling there in a grove. He was about to learn that and more. The sun was up, warm on my back as I throttled the outboard down. I felt

composed. I had eased into a pertinent line of discourse without meandering—or having any notion how far I dared go.

The house I habitually watched was pink as dawn. It reposed long and low at the heart of its lush garden, usually in a sunny haze, with a small jungle of palms leaning over to canopy the screened patio and hide most of it from my view. The occupants were a childless middle-aged couple. (Barry had questioned them.) Sometimes the bald and gangly husband was out tending his roses and hibiscus, or taking awkward thrusts at the canal with a bamboo spear on a string, which never seemed to bring in game. On occasion the woman came out to browse amid the flowers. But customarily she just rested in an armchair with her back to the canal, colored green by the patio screening.

I could see little of her from my drafting table due to the obscuring palms. But the window of my studio toilet lent a perfect vista of that patio, and whenever I peeked between the frosted jalousies she was sure to be there with a tall glass to sip from and a book or magazine to read. Barry asked if I meant to tell him I stared at her from the toilet. It gave him a start to hear I went out of my way to be there and stare. I said considerably worse remained to be told. I hoped it would not disconcert him. He smiled and said he would blame it on my head.

My head was such as to soon take affront. I was soon to mistake his disgust as a reaction to the thing I did and the three unbecoming women I described to obscure the one of them I did it with. Army doctors had assured me that my brain would compensate with broader rational perception for the narrowed visual field I had endured, yet I seemed to be as limited and obtuse as the next wise guy. I surely was the day I took Barry fishing to confess a sin for the sake of public safety. Raw with self-engrossment, I misconceived his revulsion in that vast solitude.

At the scorched height of afternoon, when sunny bright glare hovered unstirring and the mind lazed, I'd feel a communion with the woman nestled on her patio across the canal. Something, the hot garden colors, or inanimate things like pink stucco walls and palm trunks, seemed to quiver in a way that

touched the deepest wellsprings of life, and I'd sense a debt I owed her. She was older than me, and ungainly, with an evident fatigue of the flesh, so the essence of her humanity seemed all there was to explain my obsession with her. I paid only glancing attention to her husband. I felt no disloyalty to my wife. Not even when I crossed to the other side at last.

The worst times were at night. I frequently saw her sit for hours in her gentle lamplight. Marissa thought I had taken to working on the impulse of sudden ideas, and left me to myself. That was fortunate, because one of those nights I undressed in the heat of the compact toilet. Standing there naked, I tried to communicate myself telepathically. The woman showed no receptive sign. I slipped outside to try—it was compulsive—and failed of course to reach her there as well.

I was ready to say it had just come over me to drop in for a swim, in case my wife caught me naked there in the dark. We had just attended a parent-teacher meeting. The tedious garrulity of self-aggrandizing little pedagogues was insufferable, yet Marissa had refused to leave. So it was natural for me to withdraw to my workshop, once she sent the baby-sitter off. I hoped she would not come in to forgive me or apologize in whatever propitiating turn her thoughts took, because powerful forces were compelling me. I was indeed going into the canal for a closer look.

The woman sat like an effigy when I dropped from the wharf and swam. But there was no sight of her when I crawled ashore on her side. I felt a disappointment bordering on anger, like a paranoid lover who suspects deceit. Recklessly I made my way through the shrubs. I crept slowly around the house until I saw them in a window. They were carrying the oldest individual I had ever beheld. Gangling husband and languid wife, they had formed a seat with their arms and were removing a shrunken woman that way, a withered, wizened, dessicated mummy of a woman who rapidly chattered in a dress like dust.

I must have been insane. As if in that classic of all ridiculous nightmares, I stood there naked away from home. Yet I thrilled to the wistful face of a stranger's aging wife. I was obsessed. It felt like a mission of rescue. Deep in my work at the gilded top

of every afternoon, I would faintly think I smelt the moldy armpits of decay.

Barry turned to me from boatside, where he had just cast his line. He displayed concern that my distraction (as he called it) outlasted the hours of stupefying southern sun. Then he asked if I suffered insomnia as he sometimes did. I said I suffered worse. In my sleep I often felt myself trickling down the walls of my life; it woke me in a sweat of groundless despair. He nodded with recognition, and asked why this came over us. We were only in our latter thirties, easy about the future like Gulf Glade itself in its phenomenal growth. I said it must be the eternal crises of the world, like Russia aiming Cuba at us now.

Waking up in that state one night, I made a second crossing. This time I wore swim trunks, a token of precaution should Marissa awake and come searching for me. Not the woman, I noticed over on the opposite shore, but an Indian maidservant occupied the patio chair. She too sat with her back to me, but neither drinking nor reading. The couple was out. The servant had apparently been put on to look after the time-plundered crone, who was nowhere in view.

I missed the spongy housewife, and rankled with disappointment again. Still, I sat on the wharf block watching the gaunt, angular person sit immobile with a neck full of beads and an old-fashioned Seminole hairstyle. When she suddenly reached up and shut off the light, I hastened away before she might see me under the moon.

The sun seemed hotter every day I watched the passive woman. The moon seemed brighter the next time compulsion goaded me from my bed to the beckoning canal. My fear of detection also intensified, almost enough to make me foul my swim trunks. Barry laughed nervously to hear me say so, and recollected that I had not seemed quite that fearful crossing another canal, not even when an enemy ambush trapped us on the other side. His gravity returned when I told him I had enjoyed those German gunners more than I did my experience over the Pinebrake canal.

The patio lights were out across the water. I envisioned the man cavorting sexually with his wife, inept as in his spearfish-

ing, and went plunging in resentfully to intervene. Swimming over, I got the shock of my life on the shore. Nothing in the war ever struck such terror into me. Right before me at wharf's end I saw the most horrible face. It leered in my face. A woman crouched there in an old mattress cover or something. She cajoled incomprehensibly in a drunken twattle from which I assumed she had been waiting there for me. A bottle glinted on the cinder ground. Her ghastly smile cushioned the edge of my fright. She prattled forebearingly, as scared as I.

Then she exposed herself in the moonlight.

I baited my line. It took Barry a minute of my silence to ask what happened next. I wondered if I could deny the rest by omission and just say that was when the screaming began. But doing so might confuse me into leaving out details of possible significance. If one more person died as a result, that would amount to murder at my hands. How strange it was that one could machine-gun an entire enemy platoon without remorse, as I did once in the war, and yet quail so at the mere possibility of allowing human harm to come.

I told Barry she looked so unreal it seemed consistent when she spun around and bent over to invite me. I said I did what men do in such dreams. Only it was not a dream.

He eyed me aghast, aware it had to be one of the three un-prepossessing women of the house. I admitted she had later asked me to conceal her identity among them when I reported what we saw as she knew I must. It was during our base rapture that the shrieks broke out across the night.

I knew they were cries of agony. I realized more people than one were in torment. Yet I could not let her go though she kept gibbering and struggling to break free.

Barry covered his mouth with a handkerchief, nauseated without even knowing how really sordid it was—her speech defect, the moonlight glowing on scar tissue where the tip of her nose was missing, the monster she had mistaken me for and turned her rump to like an animal. To forestall any statement of his repugnance, I said sex was an overpowering drive. He agreed, and expressed surprise that this sly means of eclipsing a woman's identity, with its origin in some sophisticated Euro-

pean story, should be conceived by a primitive Indian house-maid.

His profession, I supposed, had given him the ability to pick her out of the clues I had unwittingly dropped. But she was not my concern at the moment; it irritated me to see that concupiscent encounter so easily distract him from an eye-witness account of the episode so critical to him and all the community. I asked if he thought I had hauled him out there to boast about my depravity. He apologized, growing sicker, it seemed, as he gestured for me to go on.

I was able at last to let her disengage in the screaming. When she sped away I pursued to help the people, whatever the trouble they had come home to might be. The screams, however, came not from the house she was hired to care for but from the one I had never detected before. One glance that way stopped me short. In the light from windows I saw death there and I saw the impossible. I prayed it was delusion afflicting me, but saw the housemaid and knew this was real. She ran like a bobcat with that bamboo fish spear raised in her hand, her face a disfigured agony in the moonglow. People lay dead at the clawed feet of the beast. It was ferocious, with teeth like daggers bared, yet there she raced straight on to thrash it with her spindly spear.

When I said it resembled a dinosaur, Barry asked me to hold on, he was losing me. I said tyrannosaurus, legs too extended for an alligator or crocodile, head too blunt. I had looked it up, tyrannosaurus, only it was no larger than a man.

Though the survivor's raving testimony coincided, Barry clung to reasoning skepticism and appealed to my intelligence. Pale as the handkerchief at his mouth, he said, "Not like you to watch those dimwit TV movies, Gabe. Dinosaurs come back to haunt the wicked earth?"

"It wasn't haunting, Barry, it was humping. Same ugly crouch as mine moments earlier. But an anomaly of some kind. Longer forelegs too—or arms, I don't know. Face like a human fetus, except for the savage teeth when she thrashed it with the spear to make it quit and run."

On that, he really got sick over the rail. It made me feel like hell. I hauled anchor and headed back toward Ceremony Pass.

The fishing was over. I thought the dialogue was too, but Barry knew there was more to be revealed and came around to speak testily through his handkerchief. "Killed the poor woman with love. Kogen, I'mo punch you out in a minute. You know that?"

I was getting sick myself. But I had seen it. House windows lighting it. Two female bodies twisted into the grass. And that fantastic beast up on its two hind legs, fornicating. "I didn't say it had the woman that way, Christian, or the little girl. It was him, damn it, the guy in the hospital."

Barry's hand was trembling. He asked if I had taken any devil's eye, and I was alarmed as much by a dim familiarity with the term as by the weirdness of its use. I asked what he meant. "A narcotic booze some colored people drink down here," he said. "Devil's eye. That's what she may have been drinking. If you were too, you could have imagined all this."

That was just a rational grasping at last straws. He knew better from the trauma his questions had caused the surviving victim. I said I had not drunk any. Not before the savaging, at any rate. But I did remember words she spoke, just before stooping over for the illusion I was to her.

The heat of her hand on my dripping chest had surprised me as she said, "I made you man in devil's eye."

I barely made that out in her defective patter, and had found it senseless. Barry stared at me, handkerchief in both hands at his mouth. I thought he was going to vomit again. In difficult, forced speech he asked me when it was I did drink devil's eye. I said right after. She brought some over to shake me free of my horrified trance and move me out of there.

But I didn't go until the police sirened near. The moon shone pale. I was a madman staring at the carnage in its glow, bolting gulps of her whisky to shock myself back to reality. At the start her encouraging had come in tones of fear more than lust, as if I were someone dangerous to be humored. Urging me to leave, telling me how to disguise her identity when I gave witness of this, she reached an abyss of desolation I had never heard in any human voice before.

In that woebegone garble I gathered at last that the tip of her tongue as well as her nose had been snipped off somehow, and that it was the monster she had huddled there waiting for, a

rapacious killer she had the capacity to drive off like a child.
She had some relation to the beast. Recognizing that, I stood
there in a rat's nest of emotions as she said, agonized and only
half coherent, "He just an animal. What can he know but a body
to fall on when he got to?"

The Metropolitan Attorney was unable to bear it. His cheeks
were drawn, his eyes lost in hollow shadows. He looked like
death, and soaked the handkerchief to bathe his chalky face. My
best friend washed me away with some evasive remark about the
case really being in the county jurisdiction of the Sheriff, which
I could not see as anything but a sign of disgust with me.

Few regarded Sheriff Polsen as more than a figurehead any
longer, and I had never been able to get close to him, much as
mutual friends wished I might. Though I had enough of Barry's
reflections in my three years down there to discern he was
harried by compromises ambition had forced on him, I was too
concentrated on myself to wonder if the bestiality I had detailed
might not mean more to him than I could perceive in his history
with Key County. I had no idea a similar abomination was
supposed to have occurred ten years back with a notorious inter-
racial rape he mentioned before we docked. He said nothing
about bestiality as we droned through that enormous void of sea
and sky.

Swamp people told me another day over devil's eye. But after
betraying myself to Barry's moral judgment so, I was overwhelmed by a feeling that I could no longer count on his respect,
and avoided him thereafter.

Brain-injured people are urged to resist alcohol. We risk the
danger of epileptiform seizures and maybe worse. Yet I let Deputy Sheriff Price Fenton take me drinking with swamp natives
in auras of hostility and violence.

For all my art and high ideals, I was no less an animal than
that homicidal beast in the obscenity of its mindless lust. The
Indian housemaid's parting words convinced me of that. What
could I know but a body to fall on when I must? The foulness
was mine. It woke me in the night, loathsome and abject, shrink-
ing back from contaminating my wife's easy sighs of innocence.
I was just an animal. And divulging that to Barry Christian

had not elevated my sense of self in the slightest degree.

Desolate, I thought of returning north in spite of a leg wound that suffered in winter. But even a measure that desperate was impossible. The family I had come home to from war was just as fondly solid as Barry's, but unlike him I had come back changed. I was everybody's damaged source of pain, no longer the son and brother who had gone away to save them all from fascism. So went the consequences of war. I couldn't go home anymore.

And there was nowhere else to remove my family without confessing to Marissa the abominable use I had put myself to, over the water line between city and county jurisdiction. Fenton's county visit was evidence that Barry had not permitted his own city doubts to dismiss me as absurd. But Dexter Polsen apparently did, responding to my testimony about the monster with a sarcastic comment that the Metropolitan Attorney's office should have sent its report to the game warden's instead of to the Sheriff's.

His deputy told me so. For all my efforts to befriend him, Polsen had remained too caustic for any hope of sociability. I understood he was a good Sheriff until his head injury got him using excessive force in upholding law and order. But while his impairment had left his vision intact, my own had rendered me incapable of enjoying even the sports of my exuberant boyhood, yet he had the insensitivity to ridicule me for playing golf though aware my halved scope of eyesight could manage no more. Still, I had to admit Polsen's damaged brain never made a degenerate of him, so I couldn't even blame brain damage for my degradation. Nor could I lay it to combat psychosis—that would only mean I had hallucinated the monster I had definitely observed.

So much for seeking a way to excuse myself, or finding comfort in my guilt, or escaping from the insecurity that felt like duty when Deputy Fenton called. He was a soft-spoken man under thirty. He stammered with my wife. Even my children made him shy, drawing up close to stare as Barry's nephews and nieces did at television when it was new. Price would not sit down, and declined my offer of a drink—yet later drank on with the rest of us in the swamp.

The inconsistency left me wary of his mild manner, as if it concealed the striking impulse of a snake. That ominous quality made his gun fearsome when I found myself possessed by the narcotic liquor and primitive insights of men who, teaching me how the swamp girl was violated long ago, suddenly seemed sure to kill me in a moment for violating someone kindred enough to maybe be her mother.

Fenton had given no indication that he knew the extent of my relations with the housemaid, so in a submissive spirit of shame I consented to go describe her for a clansman anxious to locate the woman she might be. We imbibed devil's eye into nightfall with an old Seminole chief near the Tamiami Trail, a highway that crosses Florida through the Everglades. When we ran dry, they canoed me deeper into Big Cypress Swamp for more of the spooky brew from a Negro who was also intent on contacting the Indian woman, and rambled back in time about her as all of us sat drinking.

I had already communed with that period in the ruminations of friends like Barry Christian, but never so vividly. The narcotic content of their whisky produced visions lively with sensation. I imagined actually seeing Price Fenton participate as a boy in the Indian girl's rape. If that scared me, it absolutely curdled my mind to discover myself amid immediate relatives of the woman they were seeking. She had to be Ole Black Junn's wife, Josie, or Chitto Jumper's daughter Cose—swamp dialect drowned in devil's eye obscured that—and the way I had known her was carnally. I was drunk with her husband or father and a family intimate wearing the most dangerous-looking gun on his hip. The home of that gaunt Negro was a Seminole chickee, just a roofed platform without walls to block out the spiced night air, but it was enclosed for me nonetheless, in breathless menace.

Muddled though I was, I managed not to betray my fornication with their kinswoman while recalling the bestial assault we had witnessed together. I managed to contain my fear. I managed to get home alive, but the brutal slaughter plagued my dreams to wake me in fevers of morbid agitation.

I kept staring over the canal for my hollow glimpses of the housewife on her patio. Unwitting, she had beckoned me over the water to know her servant carnally. Or the mesmerizing

temper of the swamp had. And again it did, one day of hypnotiz-
ing sun. I drove around there, compelled by illusory feeling for
a stranger, and knocked on her door in bashful perversion.

My hostess was congenial, with painted little lips that made
me stammer like an itchy schoolboy. As if I didn't know the
Indian had disappeared to avoid police interrogation, I pretended an interest in hiring her for day work. I pretended a
decency like the lady's, and soon left with an address in Armistead Hammock of two sisters who might be able to help me find
the servant.

The McFees struck me as nice black ladies glad to be of assistance, until they directed me to a hovel in Swamptown. Most of
the Negroes were moving out into nearby boroughs in the flush
of Tate Fenneran's prosperity. Those who still tenanted that old
wasteland of abandoned shacks were either shiftless or equally
embittered ineffectual people. Virtually no criminals existed
any longer in the city of Gulf Glade but Swamptown blacks.

I was obliged to tell Junn or Chitto where to pick up their
search, but had no way of knowing how to find them in the
swamp. I could not ask Deputy Fenton, being disinclined to lead
the county police to her. In my right mind I would never have
ventured into Swamptown, but my burden of self-loathing left
me no choice.

The scarred Indian woman recognized me. Her impeded lo-
cutions were no easier to decipher than drunken dialect. But she
had reduced me to an animal with the words she spoke to exten-
uate the murderous lust of her beast, and though she made her
contempt for me plain, I stayed to purge myself in it. Across a
makeshift table of fruit crates, we faced each other in the decrepit shack. I shared her devil's eye (which curiously lowered
the barriers to comprehension between us), and tried to make
sense of her dire predictions of adversity to befall my people in
a while.

I asked her what she had against the Jews. Americans, she said
she meant, as factual as her poor ravaged face. Oh, how she hated
us. I listened to her family history of abuse, concluding from the
dialectual blur of names and incidents that she was both Junn's
wife and Chitto's daughter, mother of the Majosee raped by man
and beast. And abruptly in they came, the Negro with the In-

dian and my death, I was positive, despite their apparent indiff-erence to me. It seemed to be Josie they had tracked here, or Cose, which sounded just like it in the old chief's throat.

As far as I could determine, they felt driven to keep her from somehow bringing calamity on the Indians as well as the whites. Without understanding half the reproaches I heard, I saw peo-ple eaten alive by monstrosities of her vindictive raging.

In the devil's eye I saw her father and husband willing to kill the woman and let tidewaters of the slough carry every trace of her away. It frightened me so that I drank more than I should have dared. Junn and Chitto had Josie by the arms when Deputy Fenton barged into the stinking, stifling heat to say he had followed me there. I did not object. I was even glad when he drew that fearful gun of his, which forced them all to sit down and reason better.

I was drugged in that excitement. But I kept drinking with the four of them quarreling into dusk, and into dark, and all I heard I saw. I stared with them at echoes of their minds in that subtropic hearth. I watched narcosis spin Ole Junn back beyond discretion to expose a strange morality of sisters McFee that showed how Josie had learned to hide one furtive person among an innocent three. (The sisters were two now: the twin of one had died in recent years.)

I swam through collages of their mutilated lives, then swam back at last to the insulated world their subjugation served.

My sanity felt threatened, but nobody seemed to notice. I laughed with buddies at the Artists Bar. I went out with my wife. My children climbed all over me to my delight. Friends visited with pieces of junk for me to incorporate in my work, and also with biases as random as the fragments I clipped from various periodicals to catalogue in bin drawers.

I took pains to tell associates about the patience of blacks and Indians, but found white people to be without interest in cus-toms other than their own. Josie, however, had considered us all without discrimination, hallucinating a prediction of devil hordes rampant from the swamp to devour people of every kind, whose customs hardly mattered, who hardly differed, one from the other, in their common doom.

COLLAGE 10

I was the friendly neighbor who smiled at everybody in my street of sizable houses. I was the congenial shopper in the Pinebrake Avenue mall. Nobody noticed my constant abstractions, nobody knew I was crazy with guilt over Josie, or that I had purchased a shotgun and warned my kids to stay away from the canal.

On the beach my friends engaged me with hilarity, their wives with amiable flirting in the presence of children. Patrons, whose homes I visited with new elements I thought of adding to collages already bought and hung, indulged in discussing the concord of inconsistencies I expounded as my thematic search. Nobody suspected anything strange about me, not even my wife. Not even when I departed some mornings without her for the luxurious Fenneran spread down the beach.

I supposed that was because Marissa deplored real opulence. A seasoned Greenwich Village culture vulture, she worshiped poverty, in concept at least, and as long as I kept it from our

door. My collages stimulated her only when bought. Every sale inflamed her sexually that night. What rewards lay in store for me if Tate Fenneran was sincere about a profitable assignment he had telephoned to say he might have for my talents.

Much of what Tate was like, before his marriage reached the alienated state I found it in, was passed into my cognizance by Barry Christian. A little more came from my exhibitor, Hillary, who was principled enough to be more discreet about her husband than herself. Shuttered evenings at the gallery, as we planned a show or hung my work, I often listened to her soul till I was sick.

Her partner, Deejay Polsen, provided aspects of Tate Fenneran unawares in eulogies about her own husband that sometimes gave me the creepy feeling he was dead. She was the Sheriff's closest confidante before and after his job demolished him.

But the clearest pictures flowed from Fenneran himself in the entertainment it afforded him to bait what he called my "liberalistic" posture, while expressing (presumably to sting me even more) his preference for prime accomplishments of craft over anything regarded as fine art. At times he spoke of Great Gulf Glade as such a masterwork of his own in progress, the most prodigious personal statement ever to be expressed.

Tate obviously believed that, despite his careful modesty of tone, the day I was his uncomfortable luncheon guest at the Harvester. I was uncomfortable everywhere, after betraying myself to Barry as the only means of alerting him to the Pinebrake horror. But Fenneran wanted to discuss the possibility of my designing a new wing for that pet restaurant of his, and I needed the money. I could not afford to shy back even though I distrusted him as Barry Christian used to say he did when I first arrived and we naturally kept filling each other in on our postwar years apart.

Early in their relations, Tate frequently had Barry to the Harvester with something specific to consider as they dined, and invariably it proved to be a façade over more sensitive matters on his mind. I had never built anything before but my own Pinebrake house, and in my thin-skinned fear of Barry maybe

informing everyone that I was depraved, I had a squeamish sense that Tate had come to fetch me not for so important an architectural project but with the deeper motivation of punishing me somehow.

Knowing I was infatuated with his wife (everyone was, including Barry—even Polsen in all his moral fundamentalism), Tate loved to confide the most intimate things about her, aware it inversely got me as jealous as a husband deceived. He could be droll at that, in his cordiality at her gatherings, but it had turned almost spiteful since she decided to live apart from him in their beach house on Banana Key. For all his depth and brilliance, he had come to suspect every artist in Hillary's gallery of enjoying casual intimacies with her.

That began to develop when their three children were all beyond grade school, years after the fatal Bayfront fire she laid to him. Marriages take that long to decay. Both their boys were already in college when the same insecure suspicion goaded Tate to pretend he detected her scent of lilac on me in his limousine. He was joking, but it left me sad. Barry often recalled similar rides with his wife and the Fennerans back when that elegant couple's time of mutual sympathy seemed to be eternal. But the ashes of tragedy were soon to settle between them. Tate had a society to advance, Hillary was strangely haunted by her brother's death, and flames were soon to sweep the noisy Bayfront, the seafood hutches and shanties full of people in the back streets, the tattoo parlors and pool halls and roisterous saloons down the old Front Street route to Wildcat Point. Hillary was never able to quit blaming Tate for that awful conflagration, which made possible the six-lane highway we now had to the Point through scenic Bayfront Park, where the ugly slum once festered.

There was a difference too between that young Christian and this older Kogen: I lived amid the proof that Fenneran's plans for the advancement of Key County had always been sincere. His limousine swept us past all he had made and was making of Gulf Glade turned into a megalopolis—the industrial park above Keyport borough, the racially integrated section on the hammock joined to Armistead, the developing marinas and lux-

urious hotels that attracted big winter spenders. Fenneran had initiated them all and more, but he took visible pleasure only in telling me he had won the highway from a tough old member of my tribe.

Whether he was harassing me as a Jew or just boasting, his canny look of amusement did not reveal. His civilized eyes made it hard to perceive him as capable of genocide, yet Hillary believed the ripeness of his industry had driven him to incinerate an entire suburb to realize that divided highway. Though no one ever denied he sought the broadest social good, there seemed to be no ethic that could restrain Tate from his determinations. Of course the exact shape of good was a perpetual matter of opinion, thus of political conflict, and there we disagreed from the start.

I came to Gulf Glade dedicated to the civil rights thrust of the period, while Fenneran lived on the other side of the issue. That too had helped his marriage along to the brink. Standing up for black rights, Hillary had strongly influenced the powerful class of her parents. Tate took our successes with grace, even with pride in Hillary. But their ties appeared to finally unravel in the rhetoric of her fund-raising parties full of sardonic wit—her Russian-fiction salon life, he called them.

Fenneran always left me feeling guilty of a part in that. But pinching my conscience over Hillary seemed his least preoccupation as we lunched, once he started to justify his use of the Bayfront rapists, years back, and Barry's complicity in their defense. I couldn't see why he troubled himself to perplex me so with such an admission, until he confessed a brief enticement of his own in swamp heat with a matronly secretary named Mrs. Needles, and I surmised he was trying to mollycoddle me into a fellowship of lechery.

But I felt temperature flood my face when he added, "I was able to contain it, however. Those vile offenders could not."

That put me in my decadent place. Shaken, I barely managed to catch myself back from asking if our friend the Met Attorney had betrayed my incontinence to him. Fenneran eyed me autocratically across the leafy centerpiece. I had only resented Barry for reacting so intensely to misbehavior sheer responsibility had

forced me to admit; I was furious to think he might have told Fenneran. It would hardly take more to alienate me from both of them forever. We were dining on Maine lobster too flavored with my stress for me to enjoy its excellence. I was fit to storm right out of there, but Fenneran chose that instant to endow me with his rich architectural assignment, and effectively punctured my wrath.

I always needed money, and there was twenty thousand dollars in an acceptable plan, with a generous 20 percent guarantee if my design failed to work out. That four thousand alone was enough to make me swallow my resentment of his role in the betrayal of Majosee, and to ponder hiring not her mother but the girl herself to keep house for us, if I could find the woman she was by then.

Moreover, the aim of Tate's new wing was to try out an impressive idea he had for the Harvester: high cuisine at modest prices based on the low cost of massive wholesale purchasing. And he demanded the purest creative effort, which to me was no less than an invitation to the total freedom few artists can work without. Inspired, I ate my dessert in excited silence—then nearly gagged on it when Fenneran blandly told me that my neighbor over the canal was his own Mrs. Needles.

I knew he owned most of Pinebrake. As Hillary had made my parcel available to me, Tate had installed his secretary. It was that simple. But I was startled again, next, to hear him confess having surrendered with her to that jungled hour of their lives after all, once the great fire eroded his bond with Hillary. She shrank from him. He could not endure the chill of her withdrawal. She ghosted burnt Bayfront bodies all around the house. Knee deep in her blame, he sometimes let the swamp sun bake him into his palm grove with a flushed and flustered Mrs. Needles. In a year or two he retired her in comfort with her husband.

His baffling candor frightened me. Those furtive moments he had snatched seemed as desperate as mine across the Pinebrake canal. I wanted to believe that this admission of his own susceptibility was to put me at psychological ease. But his purpose was rather to deliver small shocks of surprise about far worse than

goatish impulses. He openly admitted to inciting conspiracies, years ago, that ruthlessly endangered life. An amused confessional, it came at me like an insult, as if he were challenging me to have him charged and be fool enough to expect legal action against someone with his constructive programs, his reputation for integrity, and above all, his raw political power.

He had enjoyed two martinis. I told myself he was drunk. But Fenneran refuted that with his most affable smile, advising me to go home and design and forget about Seminoles like Josie as just another fragment of Gulf Glade's pragmatic history. I felt myself color in his smile, and said I was looking for Majosee, not Josie any longer, for some housework.

"Josie," he said, "is short for Majosee."

It sank my soul to hear her turned so suddenly into her mutilated mother. She was once a tender girl, so lovely and hopeful with youth. I thought the shock of it was meant to finally discourage me from pursuing that pathetic Indian, but Fenneran was really manipulating me to engage her even more.

I was simply not equipped to recognize the art of real power he was subtly exercising. His elaborate hints of intent, his sly interposing of Mrs. Needles as the probable key to his knowing my movements, all his jolts and temptations, were just a wizard's smokescreen over his main objective of this meeting, an intention too deadly for anyone like me to conceive.

The limousine sat waiting in breezes to carry me home while Fenneran remained for another conference at the Harvester Bar. He would not object if I brought Josie over to housekeep for my family. So he said, making it seem merely conversational, though using me to draw her into his control. I might have guessed as much when he said, "If you believe wars are fought exclusively by soldier boys, you'll remain a kid all your life."

In my sportshirt I sweated like a horse, but Fenneran could wear a suit and necktie in the summer sun without discomfort. He whispered briefly to his chauffeur, Alf, who sized me up with a glance and nodded, then got right in behind the wheel. I was too stuffed with food to weigh that exchange, and piled in beside him.

Driving off, the chauffeur laughed. "Mister say you be doing just that. Told me you democratic. That's why I ain't stand there pull open the back door for you."

The remarkable Fenneran never wasted a word. Deejay Polsen once dropped that to me, and I had never found a reason to doubt it. He was one of those insufferable people whose every remark sounds calculated to hint a greater intelligence than yours. Why he should anticipate my "liberalistic" posture for his chauffeur was beyond my patience to wonder. Nor did I have to.

There was apparently more that Fenneran had reason to have me learn about before my time there, and he meant Alf to be his means of instructing me. The strapping Negro said he was cousin to a missing servant that Sheriff Polsen had driven to the crocodiles, and I said the term left me in the dark.

"That's just a saying we got down here," the driver explained. "Like to mean the swamp took ole Prewitt away."

I didn't want to hear about it, I wasn't that democratic and already knew the power of the swamp to seduce people, at least those like me that life made susceptible. But Alf told me anyway, about the awesome murder of a black man from New Orleans during an extraordinary service for the Sheriff and Mr. Fenneran that cousin Prewitt undertook to his grief.

All this was weird. Even the infinite relatedness of the Fennerans and Polsens seemed bizarre to an urban northerner like me. The Sheriff's kid sister was the wife of a close cousin to Hillary. Dexter knew, before Deejay married him, that she had dated Tate at college. And Fenneran had shrugged off their marriage without acrimony, convinced he would find a wife as pretty and adjusted. That was how Barry put it to me, without smiling, in his straitlaced regionality.

But the wife Fenneran did find was more than pretty and anything but adjusted, and to me his aplomb in the matter was the same cold ability to plan the burnings and executions he had just revealed. I had always sensed his possible hostility toward the esteem his wife held me in as an artist, but never dreamt he could be capable of deliberate homicide.

*　　*　　*

204

Drowning in self-contempt over Josie every night, I gasped for air to save my life but woke up wanting to die. Yet when Fenneran invited me up in the air to glide with him, I declined. I would not even risk horseback riding when he asked me to join him. Even meeting at his restaurant again felt dangerous, but that appointment I had to accept. I had preliminary Harvester wing designs to show him.

Nothing could erase the aftertaste of my experience across the canal. My wife's glances abraded me with imagined accusations and fears of venereal disease. I could no longer face the eyes of Christian. Fenneran was forbidding. He absolutely appalled me. And worst of all he had me wearing a necktie out in that sub-tropical heat. Then I felt obscene in the air-conditioned world he never left for long in such clothes.

The bland lighting of the Harvester Bar seemed so coolly balanced that one accidental intrusion of sun might shatter its moodless tone. Though I was dressed like all the men of reserve in their fine suits, I could have stepped on their faces. Someone murmurous said, "Glanced at Will's think piece in the *Sat Eve Post.*" We had a fatuous kind of literati coming into Glade. Another sepulchral voice said, "Is he air-conditioned up there?"

Fortunately I wasn't drinking. I was praying that all the un-metabolized devil's eye in my system would not catch up with my head. But that qualmy afternoon I did enjoy Fenneran's approval of my first sketches for the restaurant wing. I distrusted him no less, though, and reacted with affront when he suggested putting me up for membership in the Key Country Club.

Fenneran admitted the measure would serve an end of his own. His son Don occasionally made a disdainful point of writing out the club's name with KKK initials, and Tate wanted to put the wise guy in his place. I tried to laugh, but the prospect of being anybody's token Jew prevented it. Until he added that the climate seemed just right for me—and artist friends as well —to tap the club as a rich vein of prospective collectors.

He had me by my need, or greed; my sheepish snigger betrayed me. Quick to assess my self-consciousness exactly, Tate invoked the same member-of-my-tribe ploy he had before, say-

ing, "Old Carl Meyerberger never let anything embarrass your mutual persuasion. Although I doubt he could kill people as methodically as you did."

It stung like a slap. "But that was war."

"And Hitler's Nazis felt as divinely justified as you. So did a certain persuasion of outsiders who once saw fat pickings in Gulf Glade's growth, and believed they had a sacred duty to plunder it. There's never been but one war. It's between cultures, and it never ends. Only the enemy changes. I'll take your kind of Jew over Meyerberger's to face that deadly constant."

"Sure, I'm alive. How long's he been gone?"

"That Methusaleh?" Fenneran looked ageless himself in the athletic fitness he maintained. "Must be ninety, and still shrewdly playing the game."

"The deadly game of Nazis, thugs, and soldiers?"

"Call it Jews and Indians." Tate flashed a smile at the very moment he was stirring the dreadful undercurrents between us and maneuvering to enlist my service in his enmity for Josie. "Everything's just a game after all."

The surf was the same on all three of our keys, and so of course were the breezes. They smelled of salt and sky, and of honeysuckle nectar from the woods when bay winds shifted. But the sand on Banana Key was different from sand perhaps anywhere else in the world. So fine, it never chafed. People could wear their swimsuits all day, dining and dancing in the cabana clubs, without any need to change.

We always swam all day, the entire family. We ate and danced at Key Mañana, a rickety surf lounge that went by the isle's uncorrupted original name. At four my Sam was a twist star, a tireless dance inspiration to strangers, and those hours of sunny splashing revived my spirits somewhat.

I usually telephoned from the Mañana before strolling over to see Hillary, but one Sunday Deputy Price Fenton drove me there unannounced. The offshore was still in county jurisdiction, and I encountered him patrolling in his beach rover, the only vehicle allowed on the public end of Banana Beach past the causeway mall. He was so congenial that I broached reaching Josie through him.

Though neither of us said as much, heavy burdens of guilt had us both feeling responsible for her safety. It disturbed me when he asked if Fenneran had put me up to luring her inside metropolitan limits. Who would ever have feared that even the most ruthless of men could mean to further harm that poor woman?

Majosee, Josie. She was still a Seminole hunted by whites.

I just rode with Price, afraid to ask why the Sheriff's Department would be shielding her from Tate. Such resistance by county seemed at odds with the ongoing friendship of Dexter and Tate. I had not yet learned about Price witnessing the birth of monsters, or how that related to just about all the towns of Key County consolidating into one dynamic megalopolis called Great Gulf Glade. Nor did I comprehend how this rapist ever came to the legitimate side of society. And where were the rest of the brutes Barry had defended?

Posing such riddles would have taken more temerity than I could muster with an armed man. But before Price dropped me off, I got one answer that was likely more intentional than it looked. I reached Hillary's patio apprised that old Chitto had escaped prosecution for the murder of Wayne Fenton because Price, the only witness, had refused to press the charge. He deemed that the discharge of his indebtedness in the rape of Majosee, and I wondered if such penitence might lend him sympathy with my plight of not knowing whether Josie had confessed our chance coitus to her husband and grandfather. But that was another question I lacked the nerve to venture.

I knew I would be forgiven for not telephoning. Hillary had no capacity to maintain a grudge. She only sounded like bells, and met passing time like the sunrise she resembled, and drifted through tenuous scents of lilac with the grace of white egrets. She had even borne the horror of genocide exquisitely, without subjecting Tate to scorn. One had to pity him for losing her, as I did whenever he asked after Hillary in the perfunctory manner of some impartial acquaintance.

Asking, over my wing designs at the Harvester Bar, he was forbearant enough about her increasing use of their servants at this beach house to have told me the Sheriff's widowed sister would soon be coming to keep house for him in place of Sissy —who answered when I rang amid the trellised vine leaves.

Mrs. Fenneran was upstairs with Mrs. Polsen, she told me, but when I headed there she held me back to entreat my interest in Prewitt. I had not even known she was his wife. Her plump face twitching, the honey skin suddenly paling to gray above her uniform whites, she said, "You friendly them Injuns, Mr. Coogan. He in they swamp with them, my Prewitt."

No one else was present in the spacious rooms. It was ghostly in the silence. "Who told you I know swamp Indians? Who said they know Prewitt?"

"Mr. Fenneran. He say okay I ask you when you comes here. Sheriff, he turn on Prew, disgrace him into swamp."

That was what I had tried not to hear from Alf. I let her take me to the kitchen, where amid the russet tiles and bright appliances she told me how the recuperated Polsen, altered by his injury, had intimidated the man who idolized him into divulging some sworn secret, so that Prewitt retreated in shame—somehow to Josie. "Go to crocodile for her. You please ask her send him back to me? Say I don't care if it be true about croc womens."

My cheeks flamed as if slapped by what I knew about Josie that fit with all Sissy was implying in her dense swamp dialect. My ears rang with frightened confusion. "What's that really mean, go to crocodile?"

"Swamp folks say she make mens lay with monster she spawn."

"Croc woman? Now, you don't believe that, Sissy."

"Swamp gal myself. We believes nothing and believes all."

It made me as sick as Barry on the Gulf. Feeling insincere, I promised to speak for Prewitt if I could find the Indian Josie, and asked to be excused. I was no longer in any condition to socialize, but Sissy called my name upstairs to Hillary, and I could not very well just leave.

My exhibitor waited at the top of the stairs in a white beach robe, and a blush I mistook for sunburn when I reached her asking for Deejay. There were two solariums. Hillary guided me to the one she used as her file gallery. She wanted my help in choosing collages to represent me at her Windgate Museum exhibit up in Riopunta next fall, but I had an idea she was

stalling me to cover the retreat of a lover my arrival had surprised.

I suspected Sissy had stalled me for the same reason. As Hillary rhapsodized over each of my works on the wall among others, I could only gaze at the alluring cleavage her loose robe disclosed, and say, "Must we sublimate?"

Hillary could laugh. Often when I felt like sobbing. "Fool. Every last thing is half a joke with you. Help out."

A new idea for the Harvester wing had just come to me below with Sissy, as an afterthought to whom I asked if the Sheriff never visited, living so close by. Her flushed laughter left me even more suspicious as she said, "Dexter? Why, all he needs is a cork in his neck."

She was saying monster now, like Sissy. Her flush vanished, her humor gone in an instant. That quick pallor was not unusual, still it scared me. I had brought this on myself by digressing though aware digression was an art with Hillary. I didn't even see it coming as she murmured, "How could I? Ridiculing poor Dex. I wanted to die in his place."

She trailed off, and once again had me captive to her soul, recalling on a high abstracted note the guilt she felt as Polsen lay dying long ago, the obituary faces of his friends accusing her in every corridor. As if her dislike had crushed him in his car, she fled to her therapist anxious to tell at last of the contempt she always sensed in Dexter's excessive kindness.

The sun was too hot on me for this in solarium glare. It was uncanny how she constantly managed to snare me. I never liked her taking me too intimately into her past, and tried to get out of there. But Hillary's subjective nature was second only to mine, so I fancied desire to be in the hands she played at my beach-shirt thong. Her wistful green eyes beamed me down to sit beside her on a sunning mat. Under my own collages of the dangerous world I was the agreeable client listening to Hillary digress from Dexter's dying hours to the night the Bayfront burned.

The presence of other artists' work gave me an uneasy sense of people eavesdropping on the sunny cooking of my brain in old plaints. So I fell back with the beach hat over my eyes and

no perspective on the larger role of Deejay in this repetition, or the significance of that variation. Old friends, dear friends, they needed one another that night like the wives of fishermen lost at sea. Hillary could not understand a husband who would set fire to a population. Deejay was beside herself over Dexter. Hillary yearned to have her brother back or join him finally, and she was losing me, but I didn't care.

Maybe she was losing her mind, but I half dozed through her saying Deejay's sleepy children came down to the parlor looking like Dexter, looking like Deejay, to greet Hillary with kisses while the Bayfront burnt to death. Suddenly I sat up alarmed, because she was crying, "Oh, I can almost remember!" She was wet with perspiration and looking faint. "Oh, I need my doctor!"

"I'll call him! I'll call him!"

"No. No. I meant back then, Deejay had to hold the whisky glass to my lips. I was so distraught I might have screamed."

"I might scream now. Let's get out of this sun."

"No, wait." She caught my shirt, but I was too determined and she had to rise with me. "Deejay tried to help me and I saw something, saw, something time had set on fire. Gabe! I could almost see time, and I can almost see it now!"

That stopped me at the back stairs in a sickly mix of sun and fright. "Hillary, don't give me a seizure!" She pressed me to the wooden wall with her hips, her eyes misted over with reflection. "Hillary, don't make it hard for me!"

"Deejay said Dexter suffered auras just like mine of incomplete apprehension since his injury. Pretty Deejay called up my doctor but I longed to comfort her and told him later, later."

"Later," I said, and leaped to the stairs for salvation.

"I never felt that way till Tate set our lives on fire."

Uncomprehending but sympathetic, I turned in the stairwell lusting for her more than Tate ever got me to with his unblushing confidences. "You've driven me to another woman," I said to shame her. "One so older than me I humped her maid by mistake."

"I'm older than you," was all it stirred out of Hillary.

"A year, so what? You could pass for my daughter."

She smiled at that. "I've passed myself as Tate's. So you see, we're all given to deceptions, only his are worthwhile."

Testily I said, "Then why aren't you home with him?"

"Well, the bodyguards." She reached the step above mine. "Not just the danger they prove, their constant presence."

"What bodyguards? I never saw bodyguards."

"You did too. They're everywhere he goes. Headwaiters. His chauffeur Alf. And others you just don't notice."

"Alf?" The cutting glances of the man came back like warnings to heed Fenneran better. "What the hell does anyone need bodyguards for in Great Gulf Glade?"

"It started right after the fire. So did war again." She whispered then to add, "So did I."

For a second I forgot what that meant. Remembering, I sat down on the steps, exasperated. More often than I could stand, she had taken me to city upon city of her wartime compulsion. Wearily I said, "I never really believed that obsession of yours for obscurity as your only respite from sorrow." She sat down beside me. "For self-abasement as a penance for some private sin you imagine killed your brother in combat. That stuff with young soldiers, Hillary. It's old in literature, you know."

"Still, it's true. I suckled them like babies. I stood them up into me stiff with life before they went off to die. Soldiers like Todd. With doting fathers like mine."

"I'm a soldier," I said. "I'm dying right in front of you. How come you never suckle me?"

"Marissa. That's how come."

"Marissa didn't stop you from driving me to trim some squaw in a shelter-half. A scarred face like marble, for Christ's sake."

I saw tortured Majosee hiding in the forest of her life, and must have looked entombed in grief because Hillary, without a notion of what I was talking about, swept close to my face and asked earnestly what was the matter.

I said, "Six kids between us to guide, and we sit here chattering like kids ourselves."

"Donny wants to paint, Gabe," she digressed, showing two pearly teeth like a chipmunk, and I had to kiss them. I was

kissing Mrs. Fenneran lightly between the lips as she said, "Can't he hang around your studio? He likes you."

"Yeah, I guess there's no danger in art for a rich kid."

She let me kiss her eyes, but not her breasts, murmuring, "I love you, Gabe," and I almost fainted before I heard the rest. "Please be my brother. Todd was exactly your age."

It broke me out in a sweat of the keenest tedium. "People," I moaned, "are forever making me the file bin of their anguishes. Why me? What is it about me? The tantalum plate in my skull? This lush red mustache? My exotic ethnic difference? *Something* keeps opening everybody's floodgates of restraint on me."

Hillary didn't laugh. She stunned me instead, saying, "Don't resort to feeling abused. That's just an evasion of guilt. Like a masochist's whipping. Soldiers were my whipping, the sense of abuse I needed to evade my guilt."

"Bullshit," I said spitefully though she was in morbid abstraction. "Horny girls were always coming from other towns."

She wanted that kept covered more than her breasts, and pulled me there. She let me kiss them bare. I had never seen them before. I had never seen anything like them budding anywhere so rosy and miraculous. They could save me. Hillary could save me from the scarred face of my misery.

But her glazed eyes reminded me that without brain injury she was as paramnesic—given to spasms of memory disorder— as Polsen and I. Rising over her, I tried to ask if she felt all right. But Hillary shuddered, drawing me back, and I lost the heart to break a spell so divine. Still, I realized she was off, responsible no longer to my wife, or her husband, or the six children among us. But oh her beach robe had melted aside, oh, our thighs were warm on warm and it felt proper, it felt just. Was it harm I was going to do her? So tender. I was only going to love her after all.

The sheer temperature of Hillary Fenneran overwhelmed me. I cautioned myself to stay calm in her sweet scent. But she slid away, her whisper fluttering, "Wouldn't do if Sissy saw."

"Hillary." My heart leaked out.

Her hand flew me by mine down the stairs. "I have to send her back to Tate. Billy says the house is a shambles."

"No," I said in the library where she locked us in. "He's

okay," I said where the mildest sun reposed and the plush velvet couch beckoned with snowy arms. "Your cousin, he's hired her to housekeep for him."

"Cousin?" she said with tremors just like mine, pointless talk between us nervously at last. She was out of her white robe. "We have no female cousin."

Pale Hillary was all gold and strawberry. Her hips were at me, her style in that an endearment unique to her. But oh she had never applied it unclad before, oh I was kissing Mrs. Fenneran stiff with life while whispering, "Sure, the Sheriff's sister, Nola Brisburn, in New Mexico."

"Burl, his widow." I thought I heard Hillary dispute me insanely, calling me Burl in my arms, but she wasn't even in them. She eluded my groping hands, a flapping white blur of beach robe retreating all over the rug. "She's coming to Hammerhead? Excuse me. I must take Sissy there."

She was out of the library. I was alone. It was no joke. Something was creeping up on me, maybe a seizure. I got out of there with my beach wear in hand and the wall of small leaded windows clinging too long to my mind. That bastard Fenneran had programmed me with a relative's name to send his wife home among the rest of his utilitarian art objects.

Downstairs I passed Marge Christian pulling off her swim cap all wet on the patio and throwing me a kiss. I threw her my shirt and ran to dive in the water for my life, almost losing my beach hat. Too warm a surf to shock, the gentle Gulf was reviving. I came up salty blind but recognized Barry Christian in my face. "Blabbermouth! Okay, you had to tell the Sheriff's Department, but did the whole world have to know?"

"Tate would have known anyway from the newspapers."

I yielded to that with a nod, and kept right on nodding, right on submitting. "I guess you had to reveal me as your witness, no way around that."

"To the Sheriff to get search parties scraping the canals. To Tate to get it in the newspapers my way, not theirs. Imagine the hysteria if they told the readers we were searching for a monster of some kind."

"Right. Calling it a big-assed crocodile is enough to alert ev-

erybody. Paternalistic, sure, but the sensible way for public equanimity and order."

He stared, facing me down. "All right, for political advantages too, but only secondarily." Barry thought I was waxing sarcastic in the Gulf where I once made him puke. He probably knew what I had just been trying to do to unstable Mrs. Fenneran. He never would no matter how deep into her infatuating power she got him. I felt like a loathsome reptile in his level gravity. "Tate," he continued, "had the press influence for it. I didn't."

"Sure, I can see that."

"He knows what he's doing, Gabe."

"I know, I know." No one knew better. I was so awed I couldn't stop sounding sarcastic, so I started swimming away.

Christian's shout after me was no help. "The shitheads we took orders from in the war! Look what it got you! This general is smarter than us, Gabe!"

Marvelous Barry. How rare to be capable of acknowledging an intelligence superior to one's own—and without even being stopped at the portals of that smarter man's wife. Stopped so, exploited by remote control as his instrument to send her home, I kept swimming out to sea, overcome by the fear of Fenneran's genius and unwilling to go on living with it. But Barry turned me around by yelling loud enough to be heard on shore. "It took courage to come forward with such self-exposing admissions, Gabe Kogen!"

If his wife heard, that paragon of enlightened decency, I would die. Swimming back, I cried, "Did you tell Marge?"

Still at the top of his voice, he shouted, "No relevant purpose to that, any more than to giving the newspapers a field day with items about lurid testimony coming unsolicited from one of the city's most distinguished artists."

"Or giving the lurid testimony itself," I shouted for all to hear, lunging past him toward the shore. "Imagine the hysteria —a man sodomized by that so-called crocodile!"

"You're going to look abnormal if anyone hears that. Even a bit suspect with regard to the murders."

"You mean you're not disposed to believe my every detail?"

"Suffice it to say no one else will." He came along toweling himself. "We gave out no more than credulity would support. Only that one killer reptile was swimming those canals for county and metropolitan to hunt down. Paternalistic, okay. But there's reason to believe we've driven it off, we've seen the last of it and nobody has gone bananas."

"No? How about me? There's a whole freaky thing going on. The Indians. Blacks too—Sissy just told me her old man's in the swamp fucking monsters or something. That was her word. Monster. Doesn't that bother you?"

We had reached the patio so he was unable to reply. Deejay Polsen was there, mixing drinks with her usual look of cordial resignation, A maid was bringing hors d'oeuvres. Marge was delighted to report that Hillary had sped home to Tate with Sissy and wanted me to go bring Marissa.

I got my beach shirt. Barry offered to come help round up my family, which meant he wanted to keep talking, so I didn't say I intended not to return. Up the beach I was about to ask how come he never told me the Brisburn married to Polsen's sister had died, when Barry said, "Let it alone, Gabe," startling me till he added, "haven't you suffered enough self-revelation?"

"It won't let me alone. Swamp natives won't, my head won't, and Fenneran won't. Why does he require bodyguards?"

"Keeping the criminal element out, you make enemies. Wars never end. No one knows that better than you."

He was alluding to my wounds as a permanent torment. It was sensitive of him to reason they were. Few people did. Still, I thought he was evading and said so—that he appeared to have learned Fenneran's trick of fascinating me with distractions.

Barry denied it. With that irritating lofty kindliness of his he said, "I'm trying to put you out of the danger of misconceiving Tate. The future is as vivid to him as the past is to the rest of us. Can you grasp that?"

"I'd be the last one to underestimate Fenneran."

"Be serious, Gabe." He ruminated a while, then said, "You left me to fight little children when you quit the war."

"Well I'm sorry. I had to go on jury duty."

"Tate knows we're still at war with children. He knows they may have a deadly weapon in our very disbelief."

"I have no disbelief. I don't know what to disbelieve in."

"Something too grotesque a quirk of nature for even you who saw it to believe. He may be using you as the bait to foil it."

My scalp crawled in that clear warning of the peril I already sensed. But I found it hard to believe he held his loyalty to Fenneran second to his concern for me. "Who should I consider more dangerous, the swamp monster or Tate?"

"The Indians," someone said behind me, and I felt my scrotum shrink. Turning, I thought I saw Vice-President Johnson wet from the Gulf in swim trunks. But it was Dexter Polsen. He always looked strange without his Stetson, and seemed more so in his pink bareness, saying, "The Seminole war never ended, you know."

"Yeah, they refused the treaty." Shifting glances between him and Barry, I chose the Sheriff to ask, "How come Tate needs armed protection but his wife and children don't?"

Polsen looked at Barry, then at me to say, "No person who owes Mr. Fenneran a debt of violence would dare the consequences of harming his family while he's alive."

Then he looked at Barry again until the Met Attorney withdrew. Obviously the Sheriff meant to hold me for more indoctrination, yet I felt honored to be his guest. I followed him to his patio, where, pouring for us at a table, he said, "Price Fenton brought me this devil's eye. Won't harm a head case like ordinary whisky can. Now you know why Indian hoodoo is called medicine."

Devil's eye was not Indian, it had originated in Swamptown. To resist drinking it I reverted my distrust to the use of his sister against me by sorcerous Fenneran, rashly saying, "How'd your brother-in-law die?"

"Heart attack," Polsen replied directly. "Visiting Buenaventura, a few years ago." He showed me a small news clipping from out of state. It reported a rumor of monsters amok in Great Gulf Glade, and described the Pinebrake slaughter as correctly as it quoted the survivor. I told Polsen as much with a glance.

"And I thought," he said, "I had our Swamptown cutthroats under control."

He was watching my eyes. Watching his, I said, "They mean swamp monsters, the kind Sissy thinks her Prewitt went to and his cousin thinks you scared him away to."

"Price heard that you go swamp humping like some of the Bayfronters Tate put up in Pinebrake."

"That sounds terrible! Whatever it is!"

"It's what some say about Prewitt. Doesn't necessarily mean it's so about either of you. Or about me driving him out. Always wondered how Sissy could believe I'd ever harm Prew. Now I wonder who'd leak this sort of thing to newspapers."

"Or why." I poured devil's eye down over the mortification stopping up my throat. "It'll draw the inquisitive down here in droves. Won't that make protecting Tate harder for you and city?"

He faced me like a block of ice, then chilled me even more with a smile. "Jews really all that smart?"

I knew too much about his postsurgery impudence to be intimidated by it as Deejay once was, and gave him a frosty eye of my own. "That may seem smart to some gentiles, but it's obvious he'd need more than a few bodyguards to screen out any dangerous elements slipping in among the new arrivals."

The Sheriff weighed a reaction, the smile lying flat on his face like something left behind. He had quit smiling altogether consequent to his injury, leaving all who knew him awkward with dismay. Barry told me so, remembering his own misgivings. And Fenneran once said he was galled by the specter of that withdrawn and humorless Polsen, but not so grimly as he was by the stored animosity Dexter projected when he began to smile again.

I felt the same unyielding, authoritarian, maybe even lethal, cheerlessness of that smile as it faded out. "County Clerk's Office the center of Tate's protection. Anyone settles here long enough for a plan on him go have to register domicile, business, school application, or like that." He poured, I drank. "In addition, Fenneran's got FBI charts on every crime organization in the world. His enemies know he's got influence in Washington, and

more ole Bayfronters in places like Miami and New Orleans than in Pinebrake to hit anyone he buttons them to."

"In Pinebrake!"

"I just told you. Your neighbors are mostly Tate's people."

"An army of bodyguards he made those people?"

"Only those fit to shake off the slum. The kind that don't mind blacks down their end. Your civil rights, you all helped him get them placed among other clowns and crooks. No one knows how many, but Tate Fenneran is invulnerable. Except to some-one that might be placed real close to him by the circumstances of life. Like me." He sipped his drink. "Or you."

COLLAGE 11

All I had to remember at the Key Country Club was to forget about judicious murders in the past, and I would not have to fear extreme measures against me by Fenneran. He allowed violence only on those who blocked social progress. Assuring me of that over his patio drinks, the Sheriff had indicated he shared Price Fenton's view that Tate might be dangerous to Josie. If I could remember to forget about her too, and the voodoo witch Sissy had made out of her with fornicating monsters like the one I myself had seen, it looked as if good times were coming.

My relations with Tate's wife felt like cotton in my mouth, but I had, after all, served as his dumb implement to incite the jealousy that restored her to a married state so accustomed that her aversion to visiting the club with us seemed to please him as much as my wife's reluctance pleased me.

In the glow of the elegant bar, Tate introduced me to all the groomed mercantile egocentrics who flocked to greet him brightly with expectant smiles, and to their precariously decor-

ous wives, who, dressed with the formal daring of movie stars, vented all their forbidden urges in flushed ballroom dancing. Many racy members were familiar with my art in Hillary's gallery, and acknowledged me with patronizing comments. As a degenerate individual, I really felt in my element.

Dr. Stu Larrup rumored a new flu epidemic with the jocularity of a toastmaster. Judge Harmon Wilmont invited me to a round of golf with the stern, cutting eye of a statesman. His striking wife asked my permission to dance Fenneran off, and thanked me with breasts she brushed across my arm. Other women coquettishly tampered with my necktie while reciting chaste platitudes of welcome. Some even kissed my cheek to forgive me for being Jewish. The perfume and chatter highly entertained me, until Marge Christian asked why my wife was not with us.

Coming from sweet, blameless Marge, to thin-skinned me, it struck me as an insinuation that my depravity had alienated Marissa. So I said defensively it was marital boredom that had, and moved on to brood over the state of my mind, which brought Majosee to it, of course, and I had forgotten not to remember her.

What Fenneran meant to do with Josie, the Sheriff had refused to presume. "But whatever it is," he had allowed, "Tate Fenneran knows better than to do it in my jurisdiction."

I knew better than to press for explanations from these hard-nosed patricians of strange ambivalence. Yet when Tate finished dancing with Stephanie Wilmont, I thought it droll to outflank his guarded resolves by asking if he had sexual designs on Josie. "To exhibit," I added, "such subtle disinterest."

I used to drink well, but my head wound changed that. We get drunk cheap. A couple of drinks will take the brain-damaged all the way. When Fenneran asked why that idea should cross my thoughts, I said, "Well, since Barry went into such unnecessary detail, he must have told you the exciting position she struck to invite my pleasure. It happens to be one of my favorites. Maybe because my wife takes being turned around that way as an insult."

"I thought it was only a slightly voyeuristic curiosity that

placed you in sight of those murders. Barry didn't tell me there was sex with Josie. You just volunteered that."

It felt as if I had drunk not Scotch but devil's eye, which passed one right into delirium without any awareness that intoxication had set in. All I could say in the flush of my self-loathing was, "I suppose membership is out of the question now."

His laugh came late, as if he had just prompted himself to let comedy salvage my poise. I hoped I was not going mad in his indulgent smile. "Everybody likes that position," Fenneran said. "Except Marissa, I guess."

"Heyyyyy, leave my wife's name out of this."

"Except Honey Baines, then."

"Who's Honey Baines?"

"That question would surprise her. Feature editor of the *Gulf Glade Times*. Thinks everyone knows she was once raped. And thinks she's the only woman it ever happened to. And thinks it's on all these smutty little minds forever. You'll find her as sexually withdrawn as Hillary. But Nola liked that position." He seemed to sway. "I'm sorry. How tacky of me." I warmed to him for that clue of human frailty. But warily—even drunker than me, he'd never have blurted that without a reason. Leaving the noisy bar crowd, he said, "Let's get some air."

His humility hardly shook off his preoccupation, which reverted him to the Bayfront fire, already vivid for me from Polsen's recounting in devil's eye. On the terrace of the club, where people smiled, Fenneran said he hoped the Sheriff's widowed sister would not return, now that Hillary was back, and confided a sudden passionate entanglement with Nola, that night over ten years ago. He had made emergency phone calls in her Buenaventura suite, then hasty love, convinced Hillary's departure with Polsen and the others meant the return of a sorrow that would feed her to soldiers in training for the new war a world away.

This disturbing trust in me, continuing as Fenneran led me through the rose garden, was plainly a display, like his apology before. It seemed as tactical as the generosity of his sponsoring me among these leading lights of Great Gulf Glade. As he rumi-

nated aloud, I reminded myself to remember that Fenneran rarely uttered a word of no specific purpose.

Rash with youth, Nola had inflamed him again in firelight that reflected all the way to his new offices in Gulf Glade, where they stopped off to telephone further appeals. Then yet again she consumed him at the Art Cinema, where the injured had to be staged for removal to hospitals. All through their grisly labors at the Cultural Center they cleaved in a passion as unbidden as the conflagration doing his work for him in the slum. They wallowed in the Opera House, where she measured upstairs offices for sheltering the homeless. They lusted on in the sight of the dead at the Playhouse converted to communications hub and temporary morgue. All night long, while succoring the helpless, they gave in to the luscious, relentless spell.

"The Bayfront became our crucible, a test by fire, melting everything away. Everybody's illusions, everybody's faith. Everybody's morality. Lust seemed to be rampant. I'll bet Hillary told you, in the sentimental egoism she calls honesty."

"If she did, I guess I wasn't really listening."

"It's very hard to really listen."

"Hillary tells me intimate things because she's unresolved. Why do you volunteer them?"

"She's willing to resume our marriage. But not to give up her lover."

I had never known that flattery could terrify. His moonlit gravity made me cringe. I sucked in my breath. "We're not lovers and never were."

"It's Deejay she won't give up."

I let out my breath in disorder. We had walked over a lawn, and faced each other near beach cabanas stark beneath the moon. It came to me my wife must know, that was why she trusted me with Hillary. Maybe Marissa alone on all this seaboard of evangelical naïveté was sophisticated enough to see beyond the provincial local modes that viewed Deejay and Hillary as no more than close old friends. "Come on, Tate," I was barely able to say, "you couldn't be this unresolved if you practiced twice a day. Why are you telling me all this?"

"To distinguish value from trivia for you. Infatuated people

tend to make fatuous decisions. It's very hard to do, but I want you to really listen now. The sentimental notion that all people are the same will be the death of us."

I tried my best, and heard him say in apparent contradiction that all people were the same. Only, he clarified, some people were not really people. We harbored animals, I heard from him, and spoke up to say, "Monsters. Did you know someone's leaking that about us to newspapers out of town?"

"The Nazis were not people. We should never have accepted them as human beings. Millions of human lives would have been saved."

I could not disagree—or avoid feeling humored as a Jew.

"That Indian girl can't be restrained," I heard, and saw Majosee scarred in the paradise of her youth while Tate bummed around in the fraternity house of his. I should not have drunk. I fumbled in my pocket for a phenobarbital pill to swallow as he said, "Animals, monsters, they're your fight and mine. If we don't restrain them, we'll be destroyed."

It was all right with him for me to get my head smashed in his war and mine while he shot pool. "Not our generals. They fight from safe distances."

I had to throw that, but it missed. His purpose could not be clearer when he said, "She'll destroy us all unless you get her over on the metropolitan side of Pinebrake for me."

An ultimatum at last, delivered in his circuitous urbane manner. I noticed Alf under trees a short way off, the tough black chauffeur I had not paid any mind until learning he wore a gun in his armpit. But the threat to me was not of violence. It was worse. The general had just issued an order that I lure Josie to his power or lose the Harvester assignment.

I was sure of that when Fenneran's smile became leaden and he said, "I wish you weren't Jewish. Just so I could ridicule you for believing in Christ but not in the revolt of nature your own eyes saw. Price Fenton once witnessed an eerie nativity. But the resurrection it promised meant catastrophe to come, not salvation. So nobody believed, nobody repented. He could not get over the disbelief of Christians. See if you can believe him, and repent."

*   *   *

I didn't sleep nights anymore. I tossed in bed for hours, trying to believe the assurances Fenneran ended up giving me that he merely wanted to encourage Josie's permanent removal from Florida with financial compensation and anything more she might require. As to why, he would only say I'd learn soon enough if I didn't yet comprehend. That made me uneasy, and sensitized me all the more to the girl that Josie once was.

The woman Majosee had become I traced through Bowie Pratt. I simply looked him up in the phone book when his name leaped to mind in connection with Junn, who haunted me my next visit to the McFee sisters. My intentions were pure but, having learned from his indiscreet rambling the sexual deception they had conducted on him when they were three, I felt lewd in my willingness to see the remaining two for Fenneran.

They were as hospitable as the first time, but told me nothing. When I asked if they could bring Josie to see me at their tidy cottage, they denied knowing where she might be any longer, trading a glance that told me they were lying. One smelled of fresh soap, the other of something that took me a while to recognize as vitamin emulsion. Respectable odors both, they nonetheless reduced me to a queasy itch for the sport the sisters once fostered, women even older than the one I had taken Josie to be when I imagined I had trysted with her mother.

I took the McFees' evasion personally, as if they sensed my lurid urge. Repeating the halfhearted offer of housework for Josie, I left feeling as sleazy as a pimp.

Bowie Pratt welcomed me in his law office with a cordial expression of pleasure at seeing me again that left me ashamed. He was the black activist who had rendered every contest academic by producing the precise legal means of opening Banana Beach to multiracial use, and I didn't even place him that way until he asked after Hillary. For all our long hours of dedication beside him at the Hammerhead Baptist Church, my "liberalistic" memory evidently remained lily-white.

I was ashamed when he explained that the McFees knew Josie was back in Big Cypress Swamp with her husband but had

become suspicious of my reasons for wanting her. I was ashamed to learn that I had misunderstood Junn and Chitto, who were inclined to kill not Josie but the beast she was protecting. I was ashamed of everything white in me and the world until he said the McFees now feared I might be searching Josie out for Fenneran.

All my shame evaporated in resentment, which deepened when he coldly shook his head to dismiss my contradicting offer of work for her. He misinterpreted my insincerity. I wanted to propitiate Josie, not Fenneran. I wanted to help her escape from Tate and Barry and every other wellborn hardballer of Great Gulf Glade.

"Tell your Mr. Fenneran," Bowie said across his desk of pickled pine, "that she's gone to stay at the reservation by now."

"I'm nobody's agent but my own."

He seemed inclined to believe me, but constrained to reserve the judgment. "I expect you'll have some word from her soon, for whomever it may concern."

I felt full strength the racial breach between us, yet did not blame him for distrusting whites on principle. I even wondered if he was not in fact seeing through a defensive rationalization that allowed me to serve Fenneran. These people had my sympathy. The gentiles had my need. I was the Jew between, feeling like neither, attracted by each, and resistant to both. I could feel the tow and countertow on my wary sensitivities, like the tow and countertow that played me in my work.

In my workshop I sought the harmony of complements, and wormed my dismal way between them in and out of consciousness each night as fevers of distrust pervaded my sleepless misery. My wife sometimes heard me getting up and asked what was wrong. I'd admit I was in nasty shape, tapping my forehead with a finger.

"Headache?" she'd say, recovering her sleep. "Take a pill."

I had plenty of pills from the Veterans Administration. APC was for headache, seldom my problem those nights. There was also Dexedrine from a manic VA doctor to stimulate me and phenobarbital from a depressive one to sedate me, the one physi-

cian thinking my work lags were as bad for American culture as the other thought my threats of seizure were for me. I was the head case between, swallowing uppers and downers down the long nights and up all the roads to Fenneran.

I coveted his wife more than ever, now that I knew he regarded Deejay as his sole competition. I wanted my Harvester wing executed, now that I was confident I had come up with a superlative plan. I wanted his son to steal my wife, now that Donny was hanging around in obvious infatuation with her. I wanted the Key Country Club to make me rich, now that Tate was prepared to formally put me up for membership. There was just the one price to pay of hiring Josie over here where he could reach her. Then, if he really meant her no harm, I might be able to sleep, which I wanted most of all.

Marissa interpreted my desire to join the club as a sellout. But that diluted none of her zest when the judge phoned to include her in our golf date there. Donny Fenneran thought my interest in joining was for expanded sexual opportunity like everything else people did. That was how he could talk at seventeen.

That was how he could stir me with such fantasies about his mother that I took my wife instead of a pill. And even in fantasy I was limited to the basic position with Hillary, because the surrogate help of Marissa was necessary and she would countenance nothing more imaginative as moral—or "beautiful," as it comforted her to style the carnal experience.

She tried that term on Donny one twilight, and he disputed it in favor of "funny" as a truer sense of coitus. Right at the dinner table he exposed a picture of Catherine the Great in congress with a horse, which he intended to reproduce for his Christmas cards. Marissa, upset to see that massive erection invoked for an exercise so patently impossible, protested that it was cruel to horses. "Why?" Donny asked with all the ingenuousness he could feign. "They never show pictures like this to horses."

I loved that boy. I wished I could love my sultry wife as consistently. Her reaction to his joke was a mordant smirk that accused me of impairing his morals. Then she somehow as-

sociated my sellout to the country club with a view, which she based on a Sunday supplement article about the stars, that Hollywood reduced the world to frustrating disappointment with its false values of romantic love and avarice. When I begged her to spare me her bland contradictions, she raised her flawless nose and swept out of the dining room with regal contempt, enunciating, "Philistine!"

Donny hated most movies and all stars, but resisted taking this occasion to ingratiate Marissa by saying so, even though he was always glancing up her skirt romantically. He just lamented a while the difficulty of rebelling against a father who appreciated one's wit, and left me to the owls.

Owls were my company, the long wakeful nights, cooing their messages to distant relatives under the cruel stars. But that evening, as I desponded alone in avaricious fear of Don's father and romantic lust for his mother, I saw a McFee signal me from the Needles side of the canal.

Never Josie again but one of the McFees stayed with the decrepit old lady when the couple was out. A midnight interlude with that horny choir matron seemed a better prospect than fighting for sleep against the disdain of Marissa. But now that I was designing well, I no longer suffered the sick temptation to start playing the game of McFee, if it had indeed survived the deceased third sister.

I shook my head, smiling in coy refusal. Deputy Price Fenton stepped out of the bushes, beckoning. Though I was curious to hear about that "nativity" he once saw, his ominous armed mildness was too repelling. My gesture of reluctance brought Chitto out of a shrub, and another old chief in a Seminole dress of colored strips that looked so comical it diminished my apprehension of danger, enough at least for that to be superseded by a sudden eagerness to satisfy Fenneran. I had seen such ceremonial finery so often at the alligator-wrestling stalls along the Tamiami Trail that its familiar quaintness felt like safety.

Wistful dreams of reward overtook me from the exhaustion of my wakeful nights: for doing my master's work on Josie he would build my ingenious wing, and confer club membership on me, and give me leave to his wife, and have Donny abscond

with mine. Already in my shorts, I swallowed my heart as I used to heading into battle, and swam over to the other side of the water.

Sooner or later I had to learn if Josie's people knew or cared how intimate we had been. But the presence of Junn kept me from inquiring. A deer rifle lay across his knees right in the pleasant parlor of the house. Relaxed in his swamp clothes, he poured congenially from his jug and introduced me to Yuchi Tom, whom he seemed to anger by addressing him as Uncle.

This old man said as I sipped that he had come from the reservation to reassure the white authorities. That, Deputy Fenton conveyed, meant the Sheriff's Department and Fenneran. I was there, Yuchi Tom went on, to tell Fenneran that the Snake Clan had punished Majosee for the murders her misconduct had caused. "Tell him too," Junn said, "her clan ain't go let her over there where the city limits start. No way."

"She step her first foot there," Chitto Jumper put in, "Mr. Fenneran bound to see her wiped out."

"He mean to murder Josie," Yuchi Tom concurred.

These people stunned my sensibilities. Price Fenton's flat denial made it worse. Yet I laughed with the others when he said, "Mr. Fenneran only means to help her out. But according to the Sheriff, she could easily die of that."

It seemed a property of devil's eye that one could laugh on the fringes of alarm and be irritated by laughter meanwhile.

"Why," I said with tremors, "would Mr. Fenneran ever want to harm a helpless woman?"

"She ain't helpless," Junn responded candidly. "And he like me somewhat. Ain't believe what he can't see, but ain't disbelieve it neither."

His reference was doubtless to the monster. "I saw it," I said, "and can't believe it."

"That about says it," Junn reacted.

He gestured a toast and drank. So did I before saying, "What's that beast to Josie?"

"Ain't go believe it if I tells you. So you best ask ole Uncle that, he know so blame much to please white folks."

Miss McFee was serving cookies. I laughed at Junn calling

Yuchi Tom Uncle until I realized it was to mock the old man as an Uncle Tom for hesitating to confront the whites at a critical time years ago. I drank as Junn blamed Chitto too in his discursive reminiscent fashion and Yuchi Tom kept justifying himself by invoking the name of an ancestor called Olata Micco and I thought I saw Olata's fleeting ghost.

In the fright that overcame me, Chitto contended it was not Majosee but that late chief who had stood the Clan against her when she demanded resumption of the war against America. An old sage from the beyond sat on Miss McFee's lap in mellow lamplight. She had turned the hoary crone into Olata Micco right on the Needles couch, a great marvel of devil's eye that made me delirious in a keen sense of some horrifying magic taking hold here.

No odor of soap or vitamins reached me. I asked Junn if this McFee could be the sister who had died. He sat by unresponsive, awed by the ghost that came alive, retching, to declare that the happy New Year celebration depressed him, the festive busk. For he had seen his children turn gray, and old friends go, all to the Milky Way, yet still had to purge with foul decoctions.

"In my time I have seen the rattles turn from terrapin shells to tin cans filled with pebbles—"

"And you still bullshitting," Chitto interrupted, "you up the Milky Way your own self. Made me smell death back then too."

"No," Olata piped, "your brother grandpa laid a sadness on my heart. A girl was lost, a flowering Seminole. He drank black tea with me to say you be coming soon with your rifle. A poor swamp grazer, Emathla purged with me in harsh sun to defend your thirst for revenge. But I understood him better than he did. Concern for Majosee was all he could read in his heart, but deep in its cloud shadows he wanted no hostility set off in the whites."

"You mean you didn't," Chitto retorted. "You wasn't scared of war, you was scared of riling university medicine people, they promised reservation beef yield go from ten pound per acre to maybe eight hundred with breed improvement."

What was this? A meeting of the Seminole Chamber of Commerce? I had to get out of there. But I couldn't move. I was

trapped in the wiry mesh of their talk about Spanish scrub cattle crossed with Brahman more tolerant of scrubby native pasture mostly under water, and bogs drained for improved grasses like Bahia, Pensacola, Pangola with clover, tremendously increased calving percentages—statistics as galling as the ghost that said, "You can see what such gain meant to our suffering people."

"I can see," Chitto shot back, "same bog and sand ten, fifteen years later, same lousy cattle breeds. You went and trusted white men's lying and corruption, made me drive my children out instead of stand and fight."

The spookish ancient nodded thoughtfully. "It is easier to bear anger than grief, for small men. History is written in blood by such *hadjo* blunderers as you, Chitto. The headless bird of life flew like a turkey vulture into Emathla's camp, and before me I saw a man's two souls in conflict. Was it the strong and just, or the weak and unrighteous, that yearned to avenge a child at the cost of tribal blood, rather than see the whole tribe maybe prosper?"

I felt both my souls giving way, the wry, the dull, as Chitto turned to another sudden ghost, unscarred Majosee shadowing forth to say, "Micco, the fear of pale faces you called wisdom despaired you to your death. We all come to sadness. We all sit at last with heads fallen sidewise. Unless we die in the mouth of war."

The indignation demonstrated why they never signed a treaty. The stolidity showed why we persecuted them. My palpitating heart threatened to give out, but whether from frenzy or this dreadful comedy of hallucination I might never know. I drank enough to see the mummy in a dress of dust say Majosee saw true that he had died of shame. I drank too much to understand his admonition to Chitto that no man may both forbid and permit. I kept drinking as Chitto reviled Yuchi Tom for being the instrument of her punishment, and found myself laughing at such quick shifts of concentration.

But the joke faltered when I divined from their solemn quarreling that Yuchi had ordered Majosee's tongue snipped for causing monster birth, then her nose for causing a white scalp taken in vengeance, and finally her ears for causing murders by her beast right here at the Pinebrake canal.

Afraid to look at her ghost in this clear acknowledgement of the monstrosity as an adjunct of Majosee, I dreaded even more my envisaging of the clan impairment she had endured for years with Chitto her grandfather protesting only his revulsion and her husband Junn doing no more about it than to bait her persecutor while cordially imbibing hooch with him. And most terrifying of all was the sudden impact on me of man's inhumanity to man down the ages with victim and violator confused into a single identity.

I sat up to exult in that as revelation, which expanded when Olata Micco said he had not deemed Chitto or Emathla false for hiding fire in its own smoke. This, in the dim drunken mists of incandescence, seemed to perfectly explain the mysteries of Hillary disclosing to me all her wanton drives but the homosexual, and Tate audaciously boasting his lawless schemes but only their penultimate goals, and all the smoke that people spewed to obscure the flames that tortured them. The Micco had returned to life with expurgative, transporting revelation.

Bright in that magical sunshine, he warned us all that danger must be withstood, even in the young. "With pain and sorrow, to be sure, but also with the strength to see that our blood survives forever."

All at once, without understanding how, I understood what the first words of Josie had meant at the canal: she simply believed the hallucinogenic devil's eye had transformed the animal into a man in her vision. But why had she summoned such a deadly monster? How could she have been expecting it? "You been told," Junn said, "but you ain't believe. Ain't go believe the next time neither. You too smart. That's right."

I had no idea I had asked the questions out loud. Yuchi Tom said, "Tell your mister the devil beast been killed to punish her by Seminole law. You can have the head of her son."

"Her son!"

He pointed behind me. Turning, I screamed—not at the severed monstrous head I expected but at one more grotesque, the bony mutilation of Josie where unscathed dewy Majosee just stood, the girl of grace by heinous men undone. A hundred voices rose to call her a living legend of vengeance against man's inhumanity. I was in that talk with an altered voice. I thought

the bomb was in her threat, and Cuba coming down on us. In a frantic sweat I described *Counting Down*, the collage I was working on, and Donny's inspired way of dispelling his mother's fear of the bomb.

I had just that day asked Donny if he supposed his father could be dangerous, and he told me he had advised his mother to see Tate as an act of God, like the crisis weighing on us. Hillary was terrified by the confrontation we were having with the Soviets over nearby Cuba. She was sure the bomb would fall, we'd be atomized, until he told her it was out of our.hands. Washington and Moscow were in the hands of God. There was nothing anyone could do about Kennedy or Khrushchev or God. Lightning would strike or not strike. The bomb would fall or not fall. The divine fatalism of it had actually set Hillary Fenneran free of fear.

Free to suckle Deejay, free to scramble them up in each other quivering with life. The eternally surprising Fenneran didn't mind, and had laughed to prove it in the rose garden of the club, saying, "By now I've come to believe that all women are predisposed to homosexuality. I'd never say that to Hillary, though. Not because she might accuse me of male arrogance, but because she might think I regard her as less than unique."

I was laughing at all that alone, so I thought I must be telling it inside my head. Until Josie, changing before my eyes into Majosee again, said, "Come, Storyteller, I give you head."

But she gave me only the solace of that honor name to absolve me of the lust Josie's will had lured me to. Her fading away informed me so in the magic, numbing devil's eye. There was no head to see but that old relic of a woman's gazing from her shroud of dust to teach me through the night, in the bird's voice of Olata Micco, all the illusions of history.

With vivid sequences of Majosee banished in slough run and forest, devil's eye impressed on me the birth of monsters. Yet next day I could not believe in it any longer once Harmon Wilmont's version of political history unfolded the "nativity" for me on the golf links, centuries, it seemed, after the pasty dawn flowed me home to bed.

Dripping, I moved Marissa to sensual curiosity without wak-

ing the dark nude by Modigliani that my narcotic eye repainted blond, Brigitte Bardot tasting her fingers wet with me. One by one all the stars of those cheap movie values licked their fingers to arouse me. Magic breasts were mine to choose from, the moistest secrets of Hollywood in the devil's dawn. Fenneran said the choice of his wife was mine, but gave me all our wives merged into one limp Mrs. Needles raising her knees while ghosts laughed in the swamp.

"Haw . . . haw . . . haw . . . haw-cue!"

And there we were, all enjoying golf at the Key Country Club, two natty couples around seven years apart, with one lunatic glad to have his infantile mind off sex for a while. I had my smoky Modigliani painting of a wife, Harmon's was a Renoir with power in her buxom loveliness, and nobody could tell I was perverted—due maybe to the women making each other self-conscious to a level of extreme loquacity, and to the judge going hatless in the southern sun though bald as a glans.

Chatting away on the fairway, Wilmont seemed unconscious of the sanctimonious impression he made, trying to portray himself as only mortal, yet committed, subject to all the cynicism time inflicted on good men, yet earnestly believing that politics need not be accepted as a spoils system subsidized by the taxpayers. Somehow he caused all my proud civil rights activity to feel more like civil self-righteousness when he praised it during our rounds.

Listening to him confess his envies and ambitions, I recognized what Polsen had meant when he said on his patio that some people imagined they were impressing Fenneran with their honesty when in fact they were merely losing his respect by betraying squalid impulses. Still, I sympathized with the judge, less because I had betrayed some squalid impulses of my own to Fenneran than becauseHarmon's complicated wife toadied to his private sense of himself in cunning ways as if that were all he required of her.

Quick to assess the objectives of other people too, Stephanie Wilmont seemed ulterior, intent on putting everybody to her use. On the terrace as we lunched, she asked about my studio

workshop, saying Hillary had told her my deepest comprehensions hung there in images of life contesting space and time.

With sly ambiguity she said, "I'd like a really intimate look at art in action. Just once before I die."

"You don't look moribund to me," I said to leave it tentative. Not because I had grown all that sick of being depraved, but because the night just past had left me crazy enough to sort of like Judge Harmon Wilmont. At least up to that point of the day.

But then he read his record into the devil's eye that adulterated my bloodstream, a recital so tedious there was no relief even from Price Fenton's annunciation of monsters born, the way Harmon recalled it in our marches over the fairway green.

Considering how primitive Fenton was, some eleven years back, I thought it phenomenal that he could have fabricated so inventive a macabre gestation, even by hallucinating it as I must have in the devil's-eye telling last night. But his performance was the least event for Wilmont in that Playhouse repertory of death and unrest. The judge practically dismissed it to concentrate on the Sheriff's erratic behavior that day and the political guile it forced realistic public officials like Wilmont to employ thereafter.

To illustrate the breakdown of Polsen's credibility as a peace officer, Wilmont resolutely told me, "Dexter brought Chuck Stowell in so violently beaten up that he readily named the cop who set the Bayfront fire as a paid agent of Tarkey police elements. By plea-bargaining the charges from mass murder down to the rape of Honey Baines, I got the perpetrator's testimony to successfully prosecute Tarkey Mayor Stydervant."

This judge, who could brush off mass murder that lightly, I could not look in the eye without laughing. The intenseness of his morality made one distrustful of one's own.

"Realizing," he went on, "that his resignation would reflect adversely on those close to Dexter politically, Tate suggested leaving it to the people, who ousted former Sheriff Peacham for the same brutality that made Dex a threat to democratic institutions. So we engineered a recall referendum to unseat him. But a sentimental electorate refused to vote down an official so damaged in the line of duty. Only one way remained to disempower an unstable Sheriff Polsen, and that was to redistrict his county

jurisdiction into a reduced rural area where little could occur to incite him."

You're a judge? I thought, daring to look him in the eye, and laughed. I laughed at these enormities of reprehensible pragmatism an uncompromising world demanded of his goodliness, and thought I must be imagining all this in the lingering stupefaction of devil's eye. I laughed at my own neurotic expectations of virtue in everyone but myself. I even laughed at this Chuck Stowell guy getting punched around in every account I ever heard about him, and an odd experience surprised me. I remembered the sensation of remembering, like a vapor with salt in my nose, like a drifting slow undersea run, and saw Wilmont looking so feverish and worried I thought the Cubans had bombed us and World War III was on.

In the decelerated blur I took out a phenobarbital and swallowed it as he said, "I was even the one who advised Tate on how to silence Dexter's murder witness by telling him nobody was missing, no dead bodies were ever uncovered."

So that was what scared Prewitt into the swamp. Petulant Wilmont never dreamt that being goodly but human, with no alternative but duplicity in this hardhearted life, exactly fit my definition of every common schemer in the world. That included Fenneran, comfortable in the psychopathic self-justification of every manipulative planner in the world. The man could scare me from any distance, and here he had a judge in his service to do it with all that subterfuge of the past.

I watched our wives putt. Nobody seemed to realize how disoriented I felt in the sun. Euphemistically, not to offend, I said, "What did Tate send you to advise me, Judge?"

His scalp turned raddish red. The judge sat straight down right there on the fairway and went rolling down the slope to a border of the rough. Down, down, I was already down there helping him up when our wives came running from the hole behind. He seemed to have fainted. His wife scolded him for golfing with no hat. My wife scolded me for letting him. So I put my hat on him, thinking, This guy's a judge? He was just a little fellow who had trained his eyes to pierce, feebly saying, "Where was I?"

"Don't you mean where am I?" his wife revised.

People without head injuries seemed worse off than Polsen and me. Hillary needed more pills than we did. I said, "You were trying to put me in the picture, Judge. For or against Fenneran."

Wilmont had a sweet smile for me under my hat until our wives retreated. Then he glared portentously to say, "Yes, I was trying to make you intimate with the reality of Tate's power. If you choose to resist it, don't claim I didn't warn you."

I drove, then Wilmont selected a club and drove. As we marched ahead of our caddies, I hoped that was really his errand. I hoped it was not to lodge in my mind a connection between Josie's monster and the apparitions Price had conjured up from the swamp. The evidence imposed on me by then was overwhelming, but I was just too sick to stomach such an idea.

My day with Wilmont shoved me to the edge, but nothing distressed me more than Fenneran's satisfaction with my report that Josie's monster had undergone an Indian beheading and the proof was available to him. His voice came over the phone mellifluous with triumph, but the implication of no further concern with Josie provided me little relief.

I went to his wife for that, her touch and fragrance, the music of her wistful voice. It took her tender face to wipe the ruin of Majosee's from my conscience. Hillary's kiss was heavenly, our deceit exquisite in her locked and lamplit gallery. In my arms she asked me not to tell Deejay of our advancing intimacy, and promptly abused it by holding me off though we were alone.

"You and she are lovers," I blurted heatedly. "Admit it."

"I already have," she insisted with surprise. "I thought you resigned yourself to that maturely, as Tate has."

"Has he resigned himself to the strangers you surrender your virginity to from time to time? Has Deejay? No, I'm the one you treat to those details." As she turned away I remembered that ghostly lesson from Indians about the flames people obscured in the smoke of a candor they professed, and I asked straight out, "What's the real iniquity you mask with those demoralizing confessions of yours?"

"My therapist?" She intoned it like an offer, which I refused,

making for the door. Hillary caught my arm close to her breast. "My therapist. He had me the night of the fire. To open my mind to another fire hidden there." She made me physically ill; intense nausea imbued me so suddenly I almost vomited. "And so much came back" she continued. "In visions not quite discernible. Almost seen, Dr. Ryerson had a French term for it . . . "

"*Presque vu,*" I finished for her, and rushed to leave her ranting there about vile family compulsions from violence to incest. *Presque vu*—almost seen—that terrible paramnesic phenomenon often attacked me in seizures, and even discussing it sometimes brought on the threatening auras. Her latest disclosure didn't help. I was sick to my soul from the unrelieved burden her mind was to Hillary, and ran to evade the mercy that begged me to strangle her.

Wherever I went I found monsters. Like one of the worst, war had pounced on her as it continued to on me with seizure, which ambushed me once more when her husband approved my final sketches for his restaurant expansion. Following my guilt-saturated mortification by his wife, his enthusiasm was enough to trigger the spasms. Or my reaction was, to his pronouncement that my wing plan was the single most brilliant idea he had ever seen.

There was all that devil's eye in my brain, and in my heart a self-disgust at the liberties I was soon to take with the wraith of promiscuous Hillary in the cradle of my trusting wife. Marissa was so aroused by the rewards now to come from Fenneran that she began to cosmetize for bed while the children were still awake.

Along with *presque vu,* there are also *déjà vu* and *jamais vu* in the clinical lexicon of anguishes that befall epileptiform people. I experienced them all in my seizure, a ghastly one, though only a petit mal, a "small bad," as the clinicians call it. I never did learn why French is used in that discipline instead of Latin or Greek, as in the rest of medicine.

Hillary used to live at the fringes of those abnormalities in her precarious time before the Bayfront fire. Small doses of *déjà vu*

are normal: everyone has gone somewhere that felt *already seen.* Hillary's *presque vu* was of the same mild degree, at least when compared to the harrowing form of it in actual seizure. But her *jamais vu* was extraordinary. She had *never seen* again the violent force she once discovered in her saintly mother, or the incest of her sister and their late cousin Burl, until her obscene quack ravished her on his office couch to rescue those traumas from oblivion. She was trying to make them mine when I ran out of the gallery, too sickened to dare seeing through all that smoke to the fire at last of her hell.

It was hard to grasp the real shape of Fenneran's relation to the decadent people who were family to him permanently through his children. I could not look at my own kids without wondering how awful it must be to discover in kin the degeneracy one took with such detachment in newspaper items about strangers. But thanks to Tate's approval, with the conviction to order his contractors right out building my wing, I could pay my children's bills.

I was getting the little rebels out of my boat, where they had disobediently gone to play after supper, when Needles came out to flutter his inept fish spear at the water, and its awkward flight set off a vascular spasm in my brain. That was what the doctors called it, in English for some reason. The consequence was an iridescence in the sightless half of my visual field and a blinking in pulsebeat rhythm across the remainder.

I had Sam in my hands, and his freckled grimy face was changing. So was Toby's as he climbed up on the wharf in front of Lissa, who also looked like someone else in the blinking. That was *jamais vu.* I had *never seen* those little faces before, though the smallest kid laughed at me, still too young for conscience, the middle one simpered in his ripeness for it, and the big one smirked as usual, having matured enough at nine to see right through my pithless angers and challenge me always, with a thrust of her chin, to punch it or shut up.

Oh, how I loved that diamond mind of hers. Slowly I revolved with Lissa in my arms. I helped Toby climb up too in the pulsebeat of twilight, and caught Sam up in one arm. The boys were laughing. Lissa was kissing my eyes, behind them the fish

spear hovering familiar, *already seen* the first time I saw it thrown this day, a *déjà vu* recalling man inept in his own behalf and Josie's beast in Fenneran like a sickness.

That smelled like a clue to paste up on the theme *already seen* by my blinking brain as I carried my children home. We could not go on forever lamenting man's inhumanity to man. A violator and a victim existed discretely in that concept, not mutually evil.

I asked Marissa for a metaphor to isolate the eternal violator. Or thought I did. She wasn't even there. She was getting the boys off to bed. I heard them laugh with Lissa in the sad, pulsating darkness of my bedroom. I was hiding there from dread *presque vu*, yet pursued its phantoms, compelled by the fascination of almost, almost, almost catching sight of them in this worst of the three paramnesia forms I won in the war.

Oh, don't send your kid to war. Somebody please listen. I raced despair through the palpitating iridescence of my sinking brain. Marissa, I said. I can see through walls, I said. Marissa, I'm on a trip through time to the ultimate secret of the universe.

"You blacked out. What did you see, what did you see?"

"Aaaah, a whole bunch of nonsense. Do the kids know?"

"No." She assisted me up off the floor. "Lissa's reading the boys *Peter Pan*. How do you feel?"

"Like a pickled herring. How do you think I feel?"

"You always see everything and wake up with nothing. Expanded consciousness, like those LSD freaks. They even picked up the language you've always used in seizures. It's fucking spooky."

"The only difference between us," I said on the bed, "is that the freaks enjoy a fit and I hate it."

She could have blamed this on my drinking, but would not so aggravate my state, I knew. She just bathed my ears and face with alcohol to quickly cool the skin surfaces. She knew what to do. I felt the love in her sympathetic kiss and returned it, thinking I was a madman to have forgotten the flavor of our beginnings in Greenwich Village. What easy lovers we were while other couples were taking their hangups to innovative psychotherapists, climbing into boxes for "orgones" from the

sky, even getting themselves slapped around the clinic to invigorate their gonads.

I used to love to see my baby come around. When she showed up at a bar to meet me after work, I used to tell them here comes my orgone box. She was a hostess at Longchamps and often arrived with a sixty-dollar doll some rich clown had bought her there for a smile. She would present it to the first kid we saw in Little Italy when we strolled over for the homemade ices. I loved her for that as much as for her magic body. I loved her faith in me as much as her gamin face.

I caught her flame in the night of that seizure, and woke up next morning with Hillary meaning little more to me than a *presque vu* image whose tail I almost, almost, but never caught.

How lucky I felt, not to have let true love fall under the shadow of my wife's small defects. Like obtuseness. And rigidity. And a lousy sense of proportion.

Even the Cuban crisis was over.

COLLAGE 12

The new wing I designed for the Harvester was not a walled enclosure but an open platform, influenced by the Seminole chickee. With the roof flanged wide for any downpour, and wall panels of glass to be slid closed at once in storms, it had so enthused Fenneran that he added an adjacent promenade park to create Harvester Mall for the further growth of Gulf Glade.

The simplicity of design allowed for construction in a matter of weeks, during which the Fennerans toured much of Italy. They were enjoying a formal reconciliation amid the classics of architecture, Hillary in her enchantment with all manifestations of art, Tate in his addiction to every utilitarian form of it. My fears were beginning to subside. I had fulfillment and station. People greeted me with cordial joviality everywhere from the theaters of Buttonwood Levee to the bank at Peacock Square. Life was as fine as I had ever hoped to see it again, after the war. And with the return of the Fennerans came the inception rites at Harvester Mall.

Important citizens attended to honor me in the presence of the press. The Mayor was there, even five selectmen I could count, and the Country Club Membership Committee in its flattering entirety. Proud smiles beamed at me from personal friends I dined with at the Artists Bar. And I saw Hillary among the numerous guests, diaphanous white silk trailing her shoulders like wings. Deejay was lovely too in her composure, the Sheriff not on hand in the assemblage of happy, successful people. But Hillary's Palm Beach sister was, with her suggestive smile and her flirtatious husband.

I found old Carl Meyerberger seated between Metropolitan Attorney Christian and me at our long table on the dais. They had brought him at ninety to sit among the dignitaries, my own token Jew in a wheelchair. "Zader is Jewish," he sang in a frail, deferential tone, "but 'gator is gentile." I was surprised, having heard so much about his wisdom. In that dainty voice of age he added, "Kogen is Jewish, but Hogan is gentile."

I had heard of his waggishness too, and patted his hand with a smile, hoping he would not laugh and start coughing and maybe die there. Shawn Hogan, dean of the Sociology School at Armistead, was climbing a podium at table center to join the Mayor and Fenneran for some speech making, when Barry coaxed me out to the promenade. We walked in silence for a while beneath the trees.

"Don't wallow in guilt," he presently said, sliding me that cold gull-eyed glance of his. "It's too much like self-pity."

I thought I was displaying the best of spirits for a man with so much buried fear, and felt myself burn to think it showed in that jubilating crowd. You, I thought but didn't say, never fucked a gargoyle. I did say, "You never saw something that shook your faith in your own brain. As not even a bullet could."

He nodded slowly as we strolled toward bay water glittering in the sun. "Tate believes we've seen the last of your killer beast. That concern is over, leaving other concerns ahead."

"He stopped worrying on the word of swamp natives?"

"He took nobody's word. He took the head. The monster's head. It is a monster's, Gabe. And Josie chopped it off on pain of death. They say it was her son."

"No." I still had no stomach to absorb such an enormity, and turned away in revulsion. "No, Barry, that can't be."

"Says you. And I. But if we're wrong, she could have other such sons. And daughters. And they could have more."

So Sissy had implied. We headed around into a twilight that mellowed the trees and blue benches. Harvester Mall was charmed with incredible beauty. Hillary drifted in that serenity of light and shade, Deejay reeling in laughter beside her. Baked moments of the afternoon were floating behind my eyeballs with all the secrets Mrs. Fenneran had invested in the collages of my mind no gallery would ever hang. Compulsions darker than anything that drove me over the Pinebrake canal had seized her in two wars. Between them she was faithful to her husband. In the crackle of loudspeakers I heard him declare that financing was complete for his proposed sports complex in Tarkey Meadow, and all my painful sympathy for the Brisburns seemed to collide with sick images of Majosee gang-raped amid charred Bayfront bodies to turn my day hideous on waves of raw emotion. Yet it didn't occur to me that I was on my way to another seizure, a massively graver one, in French.

Grand mal was brewing like a storm. At sight of me poor Hillary smiled like a thief. Her teeth gleamed in my heart. Her skin could make me sob. But I no longer coveted her with manic passion. I had found the power to love my wife as devotedly as Barry loved his. Everyone was cheering Fenneran. Hillary's eyes met mine and danced with trust. "My darling Gabe," she said. "Why have we no black guests here, after all our hard work?"

I caught Barry's placid sea of a gaze, and told him, "Tell Tate no. I'm not dealing with Josie for him anymore."

Before the blow fell, I spent productive days in my workshop and pleasant evenings sporting my wife on the town among friends, with plenty of family fun in between. But all that changed. The blow was not my grand mal (which resulted), it was a letter of rejection from the Key Kountry Klub.

I was sure Tate Fenneran had set me up for this humiliation with the dominion he held over all those mercantile elitists who

rode their careers like parade horses down their pompous little lives. I'd have preferred being thrown from a horse or dropped from a glider at his whim.

I felt so bad I couldn't work. I just stared across the canal from my workshop toilet, weighing sullen retributions so demented as to include kidnaping Mr. or Mrs. Needles' grandmother or great-grandmother and holding her for ransom. There was nothing I needed less than Marissa calling me Jewboy with all the amusement of her great sense of proportion.

The club was going to make me rich. My artist friends held private shares in that delusion. Speed Byrd, a tranquil sculptor woolly as a sheep from head to chest, was in training for the patronage of heiresses. Baldy Haverstraw, a madman with all his hair on his face, presumed their husbands owed him thousands of dollars for paintings yet to be made. But we were blackballed. My kids were not excited by news items about my Harvester gazebo. So was Donny too young to bother comforting me. Just a callow prodigy painting with my collages as his themes, he was too immature to believe how mean even a mental ace like his father could be. All I had left was his mother. But I was in no shape to endure Hillary's ignominious confidences. So I telephoned her mother instead when my wife opened her heart to tell me I had sold out to the Philistines for nothing.

I drove out on the pretext of some amendments I had for a big collage Buenaventura had bought. Faith Brisburn entertained me by blaming the Mayor of Gulf Glade for her absence at my Harvester celebration. She never went anywhere he might be, ever since a dinner party back when he was just the mayor of Keyport. "He said something hilarious at table, and when I laughed, rice came out of my nose. I left at once, never to look upon Vern Barnegat again."

I saw no trace of the violent impulses Hillary once suggested. It was easier to believe her envious view that gossip simply would not attach itself to anyone of Faith's dignity and fortitude, even though she was perhaps too doting a patron of the ruddy sculptor Ron Quillen, who wandered with us by the high columns of Hillary's father's house. Yet, hard as I tried to be consoled by this gracious company, I was not, and went to

phone old Meyerberger as he had invited me to at the Harvester. "Shleesel is Jewish," he had sung at my side, "but Seashell is gentile, even they both keys. Come be mine guest."

Loker Brisburn sat in to ride with me and visit his friend, assuring Faith that one of Carl's people would drive him back. Down the shore we spun past empires he ruled, Loker musing that Fenneran was inspired, incorruptible, and farsighted, but not yet leavened with restraint. "Why is it not obvious to Tate that a small society will carry us in its orderly progress, but a great society will only trap and demean us with countless frustrations?"

What a simple conception of the world from a man who owned so much of it. Didn't he know that Tate shaped integrity to fit expedience, or guess that both his daughters were as wanton as mice? Didn't he remember sentencing his son and me to war?

I watched Loker wheel the old man's chair around his estate on Seashell Key and chuckle at his jests about Bo Traggan. A hazy sun boiled me down the long years of their recollections. Now the times had passed Traggan by, they agreed, and Fenneran was grooming a candidate to unseat him: Judge Wilmont.

Harmon had made it a point to come up and congratulate me at the Harvester. I said, "The son of a bitch blackballed me for Tate."

They didn't hear or didn't care. Old Carl just guessed my parents must be thrilled with my new fame down here. I confessed that my entire family was without pride in me. When I telephoned, my father always wanted me to hang right up and save money, my mother wanted to know who was sick, and my grandmother thought I was my uncle. My brothers addressed me with the condescensions kind people offered lunatics. My sisters made excuses to end the calls because I bored them with digressions from their topics of house furnishings and vacation trips.

The old men didn't care or didn't hear. In their graceful white clothes they were waving to a procession of cars that had driven up to the tall manor, and we soon arrived there. The saddest

smile I ever saw was Meyerberger's when he glanced from face to face and a Seminole housekeeper restored to his memory the names of smiling children, grandchildren, and great-grandchildren under shade trees across the lawns. He sent her in for something. She brought out a large octagonal tray of gilded silver with a center bearing the enameled imperial crest of Napoleon as king of Italy.

"See what Tate got me?" the old man said, and in a fleeting mist I saw the servant carrying my head between the outspread handles like an offering from Fenneran to accept or reject.

The choice was mine. Meyerberger's progeny congratulated me on my Harvester gazebo, sounding as if that were their sole purpose in coming, though constant family visits were without occasion for this polyethnic Meyerberger clan. There must have been fifty people in the reassuring brood. An almost redeemed feeling came over me from their sincere, affectionate faces, but the consolation was not lasting.

I drove away down surreal streets bleak with sun and stark shadow, brooding on the prosperous who despised me. Passing their houses, I could see through walls as in seizure, to rooms festooned with hollow faddistic art that betrayed their class as tawdry. Primped and pampered minds, they were always looking for bargains in our galleries. Now they had ostracized me with a blackball.

Preoccupied, I forgot to look—a taxi leaped out of my blind periphery like a bronco. On a shriek of brakes we swerved just in time, and before my heart came back I found myself drinking in Ruby's Causeway Lounge, a bar frequented by menials who served the rich of Seashell Key.

There in the shadowy rock of twist music, Guy Helker said something intolerable about Faith Brisburn. Until we were nursing our injuries later in jail, I didn't know Helker from a medicine man, and if I did, I would not have recognized him in that sunless murk. I just heard Hillary's mother come out of his prattling about "the millionaire gold star mother" who was "giving head to the Sheriff for years."

"Why don't you clam up?" I said from Fenneran's golden empire tray, as amazed to hear that escape my head as were Guy and his audience of three.

"You mean me?" He drank down his beer.

Something sick was creeping up my spine. I mistook it for the pungent charge of excitement such events used to lend me in army towns full of surprises. I drank up my whisky and said, "You've got a rotten core."

I had Guy and his cronies figured to take a moment for that to sink in, but he let me have his beer glass right across the face to shatter on my eye. Men gathered around. I could see Guy through the fingers of both my hands over the blood, his face distorted in apprehension of the consequences, so I positioned him for the first of them as the bartender complained obscenely.

Guy was taller than me but not as beefy. I let him have it from my heels up my leg and torso, shoulder, arm, and fist. I knocked him cold on his back across the sawdust floor. I coal-hauled him, as he later put it in the county jail, telling me, as they doctored us, about Chuck Stowell doing Brady that way once.

Grand mal was stealing in by degrees all the while, until it overtook me in the old Keyport jail downtown. I remembered the bartender thanking God I had punched Guy out and so saved his place from the wrath of Deputy Fenton. As if it were long ago I remembered Price laughing at my threats while handcuffing me behind my back. "I'll shove these cuffs up your ass," I swore as he drove us off with manacled Helker cowering. Every word echoed back as I woke up drawing an escape route on my cell wall in the laughter of my neighbor behind our separating bars.

On a rattling thunderclap the storm broke in his babble. In the beating of iridescent light at the edge of my vision I learned how Guy became an institution at Ruby's as the besotted gossip of Gulf Glade. He told me the rain poured down on the country, and it was *already seen,* as Chuck struck Brady in the Sheriff's car while Polsen sat inside with Fenneran. Chuck said a heavy shower struck the windows of the rich man's house as epilepsy seized me.

I was wrapped in a blanket, riding a jeep, and so thought war was on again until I saw the Sheriff driving. I had crossed the water somewhere to monstrosity and only half returned, not sure where the rest of me was.

The Sheriff didn't notice that, taking me home from the hospital. Probably his own tactlessness convinced him I had recovered from the violent seizure when I said, "How'd an admitted rapist ever make deputy with you? And that other shit, Helker, do you realize what he rumors about you and Faith Brisburn?"

"Nothing to get your face stitched up over. You sure fry in rumor, don't you? He just confused her with Mrs. Lionmouth and me with Price is all. Mrs. Brisburn comes by sometimes to demand I lock up courthouse crooks like former Sheriff Peacham, who demands the same with respect to every Negro. You must've heard ole Bull shoot his shit on the radio and TV."

"I never pay that hate any mind."

"Well, nobody pays Guy any. He just keeps putting one and one together to make three. Price, he's successfully rehabilitated. Best deputy I've got anymore." It seemed just a smokescreen to absolve Mrs. Brisburn. "You want to come?"

I didn't know what the Sheriff meant. Or was it Guy Helker slurring that? Half of me was still in jail where Chuck was coal-hauling Brady and laughing amid the bars to say in Guy's voice, "Brady cussing put me in mind of my stepmama's cuss she teach me. So we go spinning around in the rain till Brady bite off the head of a frog to put our spell on the Sheriff."

"Where's Chuck now?" I said in a rainbow pulsating on the storm fence of my perception where eels snaked through the loops.

"Why, he's up in Naples running ole Jessup's army surplus. He'll tell you it was him on that airboat we taken them N'Orleans customers, but that was me and Brady."

Even in my dwindling grasp of time and place I could tell the man was unbalanced. Even locked into seizure, I was ashamed to have punched so sick a man. So, to stem his prating of names I knew or never heard before, I reached between the bars and strangled him to death.

"No you didn't," the Sheriff said behind his wheel. "You just dreamt that while he told his senseless tales."

Like a freak on LSD or devil's eye, I was dreaming my thoughts out loud. Had I asked Dexter if he knew about his wife and Fenneran's while Guy went his rabid way? I almost saw the

women loving. I thought I saw dogs fighting alligators in the marsh while Price laughed, losing shape in the three paramnesia spasms attacking all at once. I thought I was losing the world, but it was just a collage about crocodilian children gunning soldiers down or gold star mothers sucking Sheriffs off and other trophies of war in a sardonic trip around my brain. I was in my own collage, dancing to my drives like Majosee with war whoops. I thrashed around like her in Helker's gossip. He spoke names I almost knew in that grand mal. I glued them to the past. I almost remembered the future. That was how seizures went in a dream of order to synthesize with casein paint. That was how collage was pasted up with nostrils full of salt.

My doctor attributed the severe pain in all four limbs to thrashing out in epileptic exertion. I heard him call it charley horse in the other world that lingered for days. Guy Helker met Todd Brisburn there in my war dance, Al Jolson yodeled with Walter Winchell in War One. Everybody blustered through his nose in 1930, that was the style. It gave me a pain in the ass when I was a little kid with a flag, my own picture on a collage with *Dance of Death* from which Donny was painting with the genius of Paul Klee, and Bill came over too, imagining my reason had revived. Seeing both brothers at once poured sorrow on my heart for their war-crossed clan, with soul-shrinking reveries of the whole Brisburn tragedy funneling into the insatiable hole of Miss American Myth. I saw her rutting in the grass. Huddled in my blanket, I awakened listening to secrets Hillary had to reveal in the sun, enchanting me with skin of milk under a broad straw hat she kept fingering by my lawn chair. At a time like this she had to reflect on her girlhood obsession of confiding in her brother all her sexual adventures. I was speechless with disgust. All I had said to bring it on was half a joke about having wanted club membership only for income tax evasion.

"Don't you know," I had to force my speech, "how much your divulgations hurt me?"

My winsome exhibitor blushed, glowing on the lawn. "I was only trying to divert you from your foolish self-concern. You accused me of hiding the truth. I'm admitting I promiscuated

even as a girl. And I told my brother, to interest him in girls."

The woman had two grown sons and a daughter practically nubile. And a gallant husband with Marissa at a lawn table in smiling resolve not to apologize for names that nettled my dozing, the Membership Committee he made me fall for. But I was too sick to confront him about the blackball. So instead I told Hillary, "Being rejected by those gentiles felt like a pogrom."

"We nearly never go to the club," she said as reassurance. "But, boresome or not, you should go till they get to know you."

"Okay," I promised. "The way I used to go with Barry on prisoner patrols. I'll drop in on your psychotherapist too."

Her flush deepened, but she smiled, aware like Lissa that I would never consciously harm her. "Come here, Cassie dear, Gabe Kogen is awake."

We had to bring back a man from behind German lines with bones mashed to jelly by our gun butts, with limbs and ribs all pulped to make him voluble for the interrogating officers. That was how I planned to socialize with her quack behind enemy lines.

My daughter hitched up her jeans and solemnly brought Hillary's kid over to kiss my cheek self-consciously. At fourteen the girl was a beauty in full flower, but solemn as a convict in her austere white knee socks and ribboned straw hat. When Lissa took her off in search of Sam and Toby, I asked Hillary if Dexter understood her and his wife as maturely as her husband did.

"My goodness, don't tell him! He'd kill us both!" In the same breath, though it seemed impossible, she said Todd used to wait up for her to come home and tell him about the latest desirable stranger she had driven out of the county to find. "We always spoke for hours. I left nothing out, never realizing till it was too late that I was affecting him differently than I meant to. I never knew if that or Father sent him to war and made me sick."

"What a pity. You were so healthy before."

Lime green eyes were fixed on me to kill. "That was why I told you every kind of thing I used to tell my brother."

"Because you were so healthy before?"

"No, to see if you were. I just had to see if confiding such secrets would make you escape like Todd to suicidal danger." With a sigh she added, "I'm so very glad it didn't." "

"It didn't?" I picked myself up and went to my car, unwilling to sleep and dream until my wife brought others to visit me to death. Hillary felt this was an appropriate time to reveal my worth to her as an expendable. Marissa felt it was coarse of me to avoid people just because of personal suffering. I felt there was no better time to escape that symptom of childhood schizophrenia peculiar to many women, the inability to distinguish where they ended and we began.

Everybody watched me drive away. I imagined my disability rating, which entitled me to PX shopping at any military base, also gave me access to just about everything else but restricted areas. I was deranged enough to believe that, and it worked.

At Fort Copeland they put me up for the night.

In officers' mess I met some engineers who had heard of my wartime outfit. They knew Barry Christian and were so delighted to meet his platoon sergeant that they assigned me to their drainage inspection detail through the Everglades.

They didn't know I once shot up an entire squad of engineers who forgot to phone in before setting out to repair the barbed concertina wire up front. They didn't know Fenneran had used his influence to keep Barry the young father safe from Korea. They surely didn't know where the rest of me could be as someone said, "You want to come or not?"

It seemed the Sheriff had said exactly that, inviting me to Sunset Bayou while driving me home from the hospital. "You can go with Price and come with Gulf Glade Gas and Light."

Finding me too discomposed to respond, Polsen had explained that the utility president's wife gave head there because Lionmouth was their name in Spanish or something. The whole joke started for Dexter with factional competition for his authority back when he was injured. Something like that in my fractured memory. Now the poor Sheriff's staff was reduced, yet he preserved an equable intrepidity, unlike these peevish garrison soldiers. They were all staring at me across the mess table like alligators basking on a distant shore. But I didn't care. I didn't want to see anybody, and army personnel was about as close as one could get to that.

I had my pale eyes, my mustache, my hat, so I just looked at

them without speaking, as I sometimes behaved to get Lissa laughing and by her lead the boys as well. It didn't make the officers laugh, or the Sheriff. I stared the same way after he asked how it would strike me to learn he believed what Price said about Josie and her monster. I had even resisted saying I'd blame it on his head. Nor had I said anything when he attempted to draw me out with the names of other credulous people, including Fenneran, Christian, and Wilmont. I knew how to keep my mouth shut, which was all it ever took to get along with cops or soldiers.

Even when the major decided, once we got under way, that he knew me well enough to ask about the fresh catgut stitches above and below my eye, I didn't reply. No one seemed to mind. They just engineered around the plans for a vast international airport, complaining about the insects in profane shouts above the engine roar. I just kept to myself and let the insects bite. I needed that respite from people who, believing in Jesus, could believe the monster I saw was Josie's son. Some of my best friends believed in demons, yet considered me the crazy one.

Fenneran's limousine sat waiting with his armed chauffeur among other cars when I got back. I had telephoned earlier, so I guessed that Marissa was throwing a sudden party to lift my spirits with people I liked or hated or knew by name only. But I was too hungry to run away again. My day with the U.S. Army Engineers had been all ham sandwich and beer.

In a scanty hostess gown Marissa was attending a less self-consciously adorned Metropolitan Attorney Christian and wife, also Hillary and Deejay with their husbands, all dressed as casually, and Feature Editor Honey Baines of the *Gulf Glade Times*, somewhat more in partying attire. But, despite the Sheriff's sportshirt, his presence told me this was not just a party.

No other guests were there. I thought I was a missing person so reported, to have the chief county peace officer's attention as well as Barry's for city. My deadly exhibitor came right over with my wife: I was still everybody's personal maniac with a bullet hole in the head and so to be indulged. But Marissa did

exercise her privilege to solicit me with wifely concern, whispering, "Where the hell have you been?"

She was marvelous, carrying a whole tray of barbecued spare ribs, sauced and steaming. I said, "To the swamp."

Hillary's poise astounded me. Also her heartfelt, "How are you, Gabe?" after tempting my doom so systematically for so long.

"Oh, I haven't been too well, lately. I was blackballed by the country club. Then I got in a fight at a bar and had a seizure in jail. These stitches don't come out till Monday."

Hillary, gambler of my life, could as always laugh, while Marissa said with weary patience, "It *is* Monday. The evening Honey had an appointment to interview you."

At the moment so could everyone else laugh but Dexter, who after all had a reputation for unimpressibility. I asked if he would put in a word to have the jailhouse doctor forgive me, and he said, "Don't give it a thought. He knows you're not right in the head."

He had a reputation for insolence too, of course. It embarrassed the others, even Barry, who usually laughed at head jokes. The spare ribs were great, none but Dexter partaking with me. Not altogether because of his damaged head, I liked him more than anyone else in the big screened parlor, though I knew it had to be a heavy matter that brought him under my roof.

I knew my Marissa. She had told no one I was missing, but could have told them all it was my streak of violence, not my being bashed with a glass, that made me punch Helker out. But I loved her for her spare ribs, and supposed Polsen did too. He certainly wasn't hanging around to hear Miss Baines interview me. Dexter maintained a stony reserve, eating his saucy ribs, as Marge helped Marissa serve coolers and Honey posed her enthusiastic questions and I asked her what she meant.

I could not make her out. It was like talking to Josie, who at least asked no questions. After a while I quit seeking clarification and just answered as I pleased, chewing my barbecued ribs. When Honey seemed to ask if I conceived all the ideas in my collages before I painted them, I replied that Hillary was arranging a one-man show for me after her Windgate museumwide

exhibit. Deejay reminded Honey there was a minimum of painting in my kind of art. Marissa said it was basically all cutouts but I did wonderful work. When I said my efforts were to adumbrate life in metaphor rather than just reflect it, Honey distinctly asked if any of my reflections were favorites. I named collages that never existed and, jotting down their titles, she pretended a solid familiarity with each.

Hillary and Deejay looked uneasy when I said, "Banana, My Banana," because they knew there was no such collage. Then Marissa squirmed when I said, "Missionary Love," because it identified a position that found its way into our sexology dialogues on certain nights. But I got only a smile out of Fenneran when I said, "Jewboy in Paradise." He could set me up for that humiliating rejection by the Key Country Club and still come to my home repeatedly, smiling in my face. His arrogance was boundless. I was unwilling to be put in my place by him any more than by Hitler without reacting. I finally made Tate Fenneran stop smiling with an apt little discord I invented: "The Night the Playhouse Hit the Fan."

It literally wiped the smile off his face. Hillary glowed pink in the lamplight. Deejay, dropping ice in a glass at the bar, turned her back to pour the wine. Her husband alone had no reaction. The Christians looked simultaneously depressed. Even Marissa showed a fidgety awareness that something had just rattled the evening, though she had no idea the Fennerans had come apart the night the Gulf Glade Playhouse opened.

Unanimous pallor I had never seen before. But no one seemed quite as stricken by my reckless vindictive sally as Miss Honey Baines. She swept back the long, lustrous hair that gave her name its color. Her tinted eyelids dropped. She touched both cheeks with her fingertips, the painted nails like blood my leg once bled on German snow, and her windy voice quavered as she said, "Have you a collage as yet called Honey Bee?"

I didn't know what that meant. Then I did know. I had somehow struck Honey across the face with the fish of her once-upon-a-time rape, and guessed it might be time perhaps to leave home again because I was in danger of laughing. She thought it had happened for all of us, like the Crucifixion, and laughter was

bullying up out of my craw full of barbecue. She thought rape the cruelest atrocity, ghastlier than brain plunder, more sinister than nostrils full of death. She thought she was what life was all about, and I was going to laugh and laugh, but the Sheriff got me out of there, saying, "Let's go wash our hands."

A brilliant tactic, but it was in the bathroom that he really quelled me. There the laugh escaped in a curdled scream that would have reached the parlor but for his hands choking it back down my throat. Cold eye to bulging eye, he was strangling me and I was laughing, glad he had washed some first, my elbow already had sauce on it from him. When my hysterics subsided in desperate gasps for breath, he said, "She was raped the night everything hit the fan."

"I know, I figured," I said, coughing and washing.

"Fatmouths went calling her Honey Bee, once it got around."

"I figured, I know. That jerk, she should have seen Caglower get his scalp rolled up like a window shade at San Lo. She should have smelled McAllister burn at Remagen. You should have gone off the bridge on *her* head, that insipid cunt. What brought you here anyway, the barbecued ribs?"

"Good damn ribs. But no. I came here to tell you Josie the Indian's pregnant."

"Yeah, how thin was Honey's skin over that girl's rape?"

"That's enough washing. Let's go."

He took me out the back way to dark night air that was most welcome. Because that was where Josie's being pregnant caught up to my heart and stabbed it. "You don't say," I said with a stammer. "Well, why tell me she's pregnant?"

"I don't know. Those two buddies of yours, inside, thought it material to the Pinebrake slaughter case that I should."

Why didn't they just tell him what I had volunteered to Barry and let slip to Tate? They wanted me to personally? Southern chivalry? There sat Mrs. Needles like a big green toad behind her patio screen, pensioned off by Fenneran. He pensioned people off. The starlit night was full of their ghosts. He, not the Sheriff, had frightened Prewitt into the swamp. He had pensioned Dexter's widowed sister off to New Mexico. I knew, if Dexter didn't.

Polsen said, "There's some details they thought you might want me to know, if I told you that about Josie."

"I'll tell Barry to give you all I gave him."

"No need. He'll take my word you said okay."

I felt like rapping him one. I was sure he, as well as Tate and Barry, tolerated the absurdity of an animal as the offspring of a human being only because Josie was colored. I felt like stomping them all for dumping this eerie bullshit on me. Inside through the window I saw Polsen in animated conversation with Fenneran and Christian at the bar, while our wives sat on the couch all facing Honey. I could not imagine Dexter killing Deejay or her partner in love and art as Hillary feared he might. But the window, like a lens of time, showed me the raped shape of alienation weaving its symptoms around everyone.

I pitied us all. I sorrowed for the irretrievable past. My future was in tears.

COLLAGE 13

Tate Fenneran touched my arm. I had not even seen them leave the parlor, and all three were looking in with me at our wives, the four of whom sat shoulder to shoulder, trying to fathom Honey's plaint. Barry asked what I was staring at, and Polsen, slowed down not at all by brain damage, said, "Mount Rushmore."

The reacting laughter, my own included, reached me as mockery of my feelings. Of my life, my work, the integrity I was clinging to. I could never face my children again. Beckoned along to the workshop, I followed honest Polsen, pragmatic Fenneran, the upright Met Attorney whom I had warned of communal danger at a sacrifice of my self-respect and our friendship.

Confronting me in the floodlights, they looked like a collage, three disparate worlds of conscience brought together on the single theme of Josie, mother of my shame. Through pangs of hopelessness I asked why they were putting the finger on me if

the Indian was knocked up. Anybody, I equivocated, could have done it.

"No," according to the Sheriff, "she told Price she never does that with anybody. Not even her husband. She won't talk to any white man but Price. Except you, now, I guess."

"Why should you three confront me if she doesn't?"

"To apprise you," Christian said. "She might confront your wife, Gabe."

I missed my wife, what she once was to me. "And that's why you sicced the Sheriff on me?"

"No," Fenneran said, "to provide him with the fact that she mistook you for the animal she was expecting."

"You're saying she was waiting there to commit incest?"

Fenneran said, "What would that matter to anyone with a son like that? Cared so much about him as kin that she agreed to behead him."

"To cling to her miserable life," I insisted on specifying.

"To make her war of retribution," Fenneran narrowed it further. "To produce more monsters, a tribe of them against us."

Nobody said anything. They just looked at me like hillbillies. With considerable heat I said, "I regard this as a wanton insult to my intelligence."

Christian asked Fenneran if he ever saw the monster rape a young father. "No," he replied, watching me so levelly that he seemed unfeeling. So was Barry's eye cold on me as he asked the Sheriff if he saw Josie discipline the animal to make it desist. Polsen moved his head in negative reply, studying me. Barry said, "I never laid eyes on the beast either. Did you, Gabe?"

I had to confess I did. Then I was obliged to agree I had taken no hallucinogenic devil's eye beforehand. I had to repeat for him Josie's mistaken idea that drinking it had enabled her to hallucinate the monster into a man. With his final question Christian asked why I supposed she had waited so for the monster. To relieve it of its mating lust, I suggested. To keep it from harming people like the family it attacked.

They watched me simmer. I had just admitted the likelihood of having caused that family's destruction by intercepting a lure

meant for the animal. I was facing what looked like a lynch mob. But the slaughtered family was far from their concern, and farther still a Seminole maid's impregnation by an outsider.

"We don't share your guesses," Barry said.

"We believe," Fenneran put in, "that her intention was to mate and conceive. But not with you."

"And that she may have managed to," the Sheriff said. "And not with you."

Like Barry grasping for last shreds of logic that day on the Gulf, I was too mortified to speak. It took no more than imagination to tolerate mystery, but one needed religion to believe in the impossible, and I was bereft of that.

My wife was suddenly there, scolding. Startled, I thought she was throwing Josie up to me, but soon found her castigating us all. Marissa wanted someone to explain the male urge for separation from the presence of females except when that keener urge drove us back to them simpering like baboons. What a diatribe. It was funny, but nobody laughed. Personally, I vomited. I made it to the little studio toilet just in time and threw up all that barbecue in wretched heaves, while stealing glances at Mrs. Needles seated green behind her screen, asleep like all Gulf Glade to monsters gestating in the swamp of the city's history and future.

Restored to even breathing, I washed and gargled and staggered out to find myself alone with Tate and Dexter. Barry was apparently jollying Marissa back to the parlor. I said, "You submitted me to that humiliation by the Key Country Club. To show what happens to those who don't listen hard enough."

Fenneran faced me without descending to evade or deny. "Yes. I had to make you feel as vulnerable as the man in the hospital. To strike you, as no logical argument ever could, with the intensity of Josie's hatred. You gave me reason to fear that even Jews want to forget the full taste of such hatred and such mortal vulnerability."

How dangerous he seemed in his disarming candor. He was playing me like an instrument in his collection. On guard, I said, "What do you want from me if you don't think it's my kid?"

"That would mean nothing to me," he responded. "I respect

you for coming forward at personal risk to lay everything before Barry. I don't know what we would have done without it, and without Dexter alerting him too, as soon as he learned of this pregnancy from Deputy Fenton."

"By her son the beast." I sat down on my leather couch. "To bear another monster, a line of them. That's what you expect me to believe. A raped Indian woman, impregnated by a crocodile, who wants to pollute us with the crossbreed."

Barry returned with steaming coffee for me as Fenneran said, "The possibility exists that we're witnessing—and not for the first time in evolution—a genetic aberration. That's only our considered judgment. But if we're right, just think."

My heart froze over. If they were wrong, it was my baby. I savored the hot coffee with relish.

Barry stood impassive. Pacing, Fenneran drifted out of sight behind my file bins, as if hiding his own strained credulity in the darkness to preserve his flawless reasoning. His voice flowed as if from the bottomless depths of time.

"We incline to believe in salvation, and to disbelieve in calamity. Disbelieving will free us of the problem—but not necessarily later. To give it credence would pose a dire responsibility—and maybe save the future from disaster."

Polsen said, "If we choose for the moment to believe, what do you propose to do?"

Barry Christian drew a breath for the practical strength to say, "The housemaid would have to be reoriented, deported, or otherwise disposed of."

Every Seminole in south Florida knew Josie was not about to put up with rehabilitation or banishment. "By otherwise," the Sheriff said, "you mean exterminated. Don't set foot in my jurisdiction to carry out anything like that."

There was a bridling silence, until Fenneran said, "Dex," from the shadows, "I didn't have to ask you in on this."

"Sure you did. And you still have to lay it out flat."

Emerging in the floodlights, Fenneran looked as grave as I had ever seen him. "This is a time that demands all the fortitude we can summon. We have to make a decision."

"And our choice is but one?" The Sheriff spoke with icy

significance, wryly wagging his head. "You had people murdered to spare this county from criminal corruption. I exceeded the limits of my authority to save lives. So you redistricted ten towns into one metropolis to suck near all my jurisdiction away."

"The damage to you," Fenneran said as coldly, "was another reason I took those strong measures, my personal reason."

"Let's not recriminate," Christian intruded. "I can vouch for Tate's sincerity in that."

"You did back then, fox. And you were just as solid for telling Wiley his friend Stowell framed him as Honey's rapist and seeing Wilmont lock them in solitary together."

The Met Attorney flashed me a glance. I had never heard him called "fox" before. So Polsen had not brutalized Stowell, as Wilmont had let me infer. Lieutenant Christian had turned Brady Wiley into a combat prisoner patrol to make an easy witness out of Stowell with broken bones. "You were dangerous," Barry said. "As much to yourself and family as—"

"Horseshit. I was dangerous to Tate's circumventions of law on the large scale. So you went over the heads of the voting public to set me aside, and I've abided by the letter of the lawbook ever since. I told your people to get in the jungle where they belong if they can't abide by civilized law. I tell you the same right now. Take your dogfights to your city. Don't cross over that canal where I'm responsible for county."

They had me set up like the sucker in an old gangster movie, in danger of being rubbed out for knowing too much. "Leave me out of this. Why'd you come here to play it all out for me?"

Fenneran and Christian consulted, pacing the cavern of my workshop, so Polsen took the moment. "I needed a witness. And you did cross over and stick it into county."

Then Barry faced me solemnly to say, "Tate wants you to arrange a meeting with someone responsible for Josie. Here, on this side of the canal. Will you agree to that?"

"The choice is yours," Polsen said, strolling around to inspect collages large and small on the walls.

These men terrified me. I said, "I can phone Bowie Pratt."

"You're a man of civic responsibility," Fenneran reacted.

"And a soldier capable of facing a mortal commitment. I hope he trusts you enough to bring a Snake Clan chief along. I can guarantee their safety. Give him my word on that."

Polsen chuckled at this weakness of Fenneran's to indulge people in so obvious a patronizing manner. "He'd need Fairboro's word on that. Like Prewitt should have had."

Fenneran's smile was impossible to reconcile with the Sheriff's remark until I realized, by his rejoinder, that they were in a game, one of Fenneran's deadly games. "Walter never confronted Prewitt with a threat. You know that, Dex."

"But I doubt Prew did. When I let Walt go see him for the facts, I should have realized he was your deputy, not mine. I'm sure no metropolitan cop can keep his job if he's dumb enough to openly threaten anybody, but I doubt that any black or Indian feels no danger of racial persecution in Great Gulf Glade."

Fenneran's teeth flashed in the light. "Police Commissioner Fairboro stands behind civil rights just as all of us have come to. He also understands the medicinal value of drugs, but deplores drug abuse like all rational people. So does he oppose civil rights abuse. By which I mean the extremely dangerous coddling of vicious people who happen to be black or Indian. Our streets are safe as a result. Gabe?"

I had taken a phenobarbital, and not a moment too soon. His smile, no mere feature of his customary sparring, had the purpose of implanting in me for communication to Bowie the very threat Polsen had just enunciated. The choice was mine. I could play Fenneran's game, or lose.

I swam in fever. Polsen hovered in it, saying, "How come there's firearms in so many of those pasteups of yours?"

I said, "The head cases I attract. I could start a country club of my own and call it the Head Club."

"Dandy mascot for that right in Miz Needles' freezer," and Polsen's expressionless look at the others sickened their smiles.

That freezer, Barry explained, was where Tate kept the severed head of the beast. "For anyone to see," Fenneran added, "who still fails to grasp the danger we're in, calling it social or racial, as you please."

*   *   *

Asleep on my workshop couch, some days later, I was reply-ing to my wife in a dream of her asking why there were always guns in my art, when gunfire exploded outside.

Even in dream it seemed weird to question a phenomenon as prevalent in our time as guns, like asking why my work should show ears on people and shoes on their feet. So I felt entitled to apply sarcasm, and told Marissa the reason I used guns as sym-bols of power could not be what her clinical mentality pre-sumed, because my dummy was always in my hand when I worked, and that kept it from sneaking into my mind.

I was saying guns were the symbols of man's inhumanity to Kogen because wars refused to end. I was saying we could not just lament man's inhumanity forever without identifying the violator, or we would never stem the deterioration of civilized life.

Everybody was getting uncivilized. Sharks had lulled me to sleep, oozing across my TV screen in human disguise. Over-dressed jowly merchants invaded my unguarded dreams, cut-ting their inflated markups. Meat packers with impish German accents ate their own weenies in public. Famous men vamped me to open bilking bank accounts. Everybody was pandering in Tate's Gulf Glade. No wonder I blamed the Sheriff's curiosity and my own self-doubts on my wife before gunfire shattered the dream amid her screams.

Waking, I thought those shots were part of the joke on her. I went out to laugh at Marissa, and gathered from her screaming that someone had just shot Tate Fenneran dead.

The shock hammered my heart. It stung my face. I shrank with guilt over Hillary. I prayed for it not to be Tate staring at the moon right there in my floodlit driveway. Then I realized with disappointment that it couldn't be. The corpse was old, and wore a ritual Seminole dress. I had misunderstood my wife's shrieks in the scurrying. Someone had just killed Chitto Jumper. A rifle still lay by his side.

He had come to kill Fenneran, that was what her hysterics were about until someone got Marissa inside. "Oh, my God, he's dead! Why'd anyone want to murder Tate?"

That was why I thought life had caught up with Tate at last,

and I must have said something of such a nature, still stupefied on the dragging skirts of sleep, because Harmon Wilmont called that a curious way to put it. His eyes flashed in reflection of police lights spinning. One lid flamed with the pustule of a sty.

It was amazing how fast the cops got there. I could not imagine why Judge Wilmont had, or the others in the crowd. Bowie Pratt had told me he was able to bring Chitto tonight to confer with Fenneran, Christian, and Polsen, not Professor Hogan, Police Commissioner Fairboro, a writer name Pritchard, and President W. Horace Dildress of the Great Gulf Glade Chamber of Commerce.

I came more awake to Dexter consulting with Fairboro among officers around the body. I saw the cavity of blood on poor Chitto's chest as Wilmont filled me in. Just about everybody Fenneran invited had arrived within five minutes of one another and parked all around the cul-de-sac. When Alf drove Tate into my yard, Chitto came ceremoniously around the house from his canoe to take deliberate aim with a deer rifle he uncovered from the folds of his color-stripped Seminole cape.

I rubbed my face hard in the oncoming ambulance wail, the decelerating siren that recalled another removal of the dead, across the water. I hoped the children were being kept to their beds. "He came by canal?" I said. "He took aim in this light, all dressed up like that for ceremony?"

"He never got off a shot. Four bodyguards fired."

Wilmont followed me over to Fenneran, who was just turning away from Hogan and Dildress to accompany Fairboro somewhere as cops backed newsmen off. "I didn't invite all these people," I protested. "What are they doing here?"

"You agreed," Fenneran paused to say, "to the meeting here with a Snake Clan chief. These men are directly concerned. Or were. Harmon, I've told Bill and Neil they needn't stay now."

"Now that Chitto came and set himself up to be killed," I completed it for him. "You do understand that, Harmon, don't you?" Fenneran and Fairboro walked away. "For the protection of Josie," I said, pursuing them, feeling ridiculous, yet compulsively going on. "He swore his life to . . . listen, he agreed to meet with you just to . . . now you can't go after Josie. The newspa-

pers would read it too much like"—I stopped short of saying *another*—"a genocide."

Wilmont took me off by the arm as Bowie approached. Lighting his beacon gaze on me, the judge said, "I've had to face the reality that righteousness is no longer heroic but stupid in its loneliness." Photographers flashed, startling him. "Isn't it time you faced that too?"

The only thing I had to face was the suppurating fester on his eyelid, and that was bad enough. I said, "Says who?"

"Gabe, in the long run dissent becomes sophomoric, tiresome, and gauche."

"Says you."

"In an ordered society," he concluded, and looked confused in a sudden change of expression that signaled me to glance down where I often failed to see objects proffered right under my nose. I had just been blind to the hand he was extending. I guessed he was asking me to pardon him for the blackball, and all at once he seemed guilty of my blindness because he never went to war, of my seizures and occasional inconfidence in the durability of my mind.

I walked off to Bowie, who was explaining that Chitto had given no signal of his intentions when he agreed to the meeting. Fenneran said he had guessed as much, and suggested Bowie just go home and forget the whole thing. I walked my sad friend to his car past Alf, whose squad was no doubt well deployed to kill again if necessary tonight. Bowie put on his glasses.

"I wasn't just sucking up, Gabe. I did see Chitto try to kill him. Jesus, I heard the man's dying words. Like Wild Bill Hickok in the picture show." In his car he stared at me through shooting police lights on his glasses. "We all heard Chitto say Seminoles believe Fenneran's the Devil. Old chief said Fenneran, from Georgia, resided here with his bride's clan like an Indian, just to mock folks like the Devil do."

That touch of burr head, in an effort to sound slightly less haughty about swamp superstition, probably tasted as servile to him as had his apology to Fenneran, because Bowie flinched. I lamely punched his shoulder. W. H. Dildress was leaving, and Fenneran's writer too. So was Judge Wilmont heading for his

car in the clanging departure of the ambulance. I was glad to see the police cars leave with reporters driving off after them for the story. Commissioner Fairboro was obviously decoying them away for some specific reason of Fenneran's.

The remaining men headed for the canal. Fenneran, Christian, Polsen, Hogan, they stopped there at the sight the opposite bank presented. Mrs. Needles was in place on her chair, her back to us. But something unusual was planted in her garden. Facing us on a stake, the monstrous head stared, slack-jawed, with ghastly primordial ferocity. Chitto had erected it ritually. That was plain, and so was Fenneran's reluctance to let it out in the news.

"Teratogenetic," Professor Hogan observed. "You may be onto something, Tate. A teratoid progenitor, quite possibly. There must be others that she gave this one up to protect."

"As her grandfather," I put in, "gave himself up to protect."

"Precisely." With an ingratiating nod at Fenneran, Hogan said that did fit his theorem of altruism genetically induced for the purpose of group survival. It seemed remarkable to nobody that Mrs. Needles would let Chitto take the head from her freezer. Hogan stayed at the barest edge of my comprehension with something about Seminole religious practice conforming to the evolutionary purpose of Chitto's self-sacrifice to protect at least Josie.

"That purpose," Fenneran proclaimed, "protecting maybe more existing monsters, is clearly an open declaration of war."

He meant Josie's war, and nothing in my deep sense of her animosity disputed that view. I knew Tate calculated the logistics of her war in a multiplication of crocodilian beasts that reached procreative maturity at ages like six or seven, which posed a terrifying algebra of monsters proliferating year after year in the sheltering swamp. Yet, when he challenged my credulity with the cunning of his smile, I wondered if Hillary had not cracked that formidable mind of his at last and driven him to visionary delusions. Perversely, I said, "Chitto didn't die for Majosee. He did it for twenty thousand dollars you paid him."

Thus I left them for my workshop where I had better games

to play. Polsen came right behind me. He didn't speak, he just wandered around the walls to examine my work once again with that critical reticence all artists love so well. Soon he began to loiter before a big one. I fell back on my leather couch.

The collage that held his attention was made from an Italian packing crate, the boards stenciled ALTO and BASSO severally, with futuristic electronic parts and antique desk sets mounted with shots of a civil war burial, sports immortals, and a solemn violin virtuosa. Collectors were frequently taken with that work but found it too expensive. "I like this," Polsen said. "I'd like to make a thing like this myself. I think I will."

"You? Where the hell would you get alto and basso? Boy, the doctors I put up with who accuse me of diagnosing if I say aspirin but find art a field they have a perfect right to pontificate in. Now it's Sheriffs."

"Haven't you been getting in my act? I never complained when you went snooping around Swamptown."

"That was social. Even Tate socializes, between his maneuvers to build and destroy. I'm glad to see him in better company than the KKK now, studying sociology."

"Sociobiology is Hogan's thing." Dexter held me in his gaze a while, then said, "If Josie's never sexual, not even with her husband, why would she want to change the beast into a beauty like you for that? No, it figures she thought you were the Devil she turned into a human with her booze. She's told Price, and so has Junn, that she thinks the Devil came to her in one of those five boys, and *then* put the crocodile to her. Thinks it takes both the Devil and a beast to impregnate her with monsters."

"What do you want from me with that preposterous backwoods diabolism?"

"Just your intelligent cooperation is all. If you don't clear out while the clearing's good."

That sounded like a threat, and I had come out of the war feeling just a little more American than anybody who didn't fight in it. I said, "I'm not clearing out," though I felt like doing just that, and resolved instead, right then and there as Christian strolled in, to construct some kind of outflanking facility from which to use my shotgun for an ambush in case of assault by

rednecks like these. "Any bastard who tries to lean on me—"

"Don't throw yourself into a fit," Barry cautioned me.

"Glad you don't scare easy," Polsen said. "I told you once before that you're in danger of Indians. Not the Seminole tribe. Just one squaw who won't sign a peace treaty. Surely never end her war now with ole Chitto killed. She could be breeding monsters. Or is that your gazebo in her?"

I steamed at that. They had apparently won Polsen over. "What is this? You going to have Price Fenton describe more obstetrics in the Gulf Glade Playhouse unless I get you Josie?"

"You may need police protection," Fenneran said in the doorway. "It appears we're in this together, Gabe. The Devil's messengers."

"Chitto could have killed me long ago if he wanted to. I don't need police protection, and I'm not luring any more victims over here for you."

Christian said, "I told you he's smarter than he acts."

"But no saner," Polsen had to add.

It infuriated me. "I blame Hitler for my head. What do you blame? The spell those morons cast, biting off a frog's head?"

"Doesn't matter what I blame. Nothing depends on that."

"You were right, Gabe," Fenneran placated, "about the effectiveness of Chitto's sacrifice. It inhibits any measures we might have taken to neutralize the understandably embittered woman. But we no more want to make public your relations with her than I wanted that chief to outmaneuver me by immolating himself."

He was simultaneously humoring and threatening me. The man was shameless. He would stop at nothing that coaxing, flattery, blackmail, or violence might move out of his way. And Christian carried the drive ahead for him. "We want you to influence your liberal friends in our mushrooming cultural circles. But only to keep them from interfering."

"Not to make a civil rights issue," Fenneran added, "of the destruction of ferocious animals that could devastate all our careful accomplishments. Including your Harvester Mall."

I fumbled with a phenobarbital and swallowed it. Breathless with resentment, I said, "I care more about human life. To me that supersedes everything else in value."

The Sheriff's laughter startled me. "We head cases care about people, and aren't standing still for any harm coming to them. Right, chicken? So if monsters start showing up in numbers, they just have to be destroyed. And we hope you'll be sensible enough to discourage your civil rights cohorts from deciding to call such monsters human beings."

I said, "They are, if they have human blood. And you don't need crocodile blood to be a monster. There are plenty of them down here already, treating people as less than human if they have black blood in whatever degree. And you three swamp witches can get the fuck out. I've had all I can take of this racist hoodoo."

I ducked into the shadows and got the shotgun I kept loaded between my file bins for the very beasts I now found myself defending. Polsen, ever the cop, started in after me. But Barry held him back and shook his head in dire warning. It meant watch out, I could be dangerous in the dark, I was crazy enough to take Dexter out with his neck snapped the way we used to do the Nazi sentries. That scared the Jesus out of me. I was some case, all right. The future whispered in the shadows of the eaves: I had one choice of a side to take, and had better get my sympathies over on it fast.

I hid the shotgun again. Back in the light I said, "I'm not forming anything you can turn into a posse. But if it becomes necessary to keep my friends from interfering, I'll do my best."

"Good," Fenneran said. "I hoped we could enlist your soundest judgment, Gabe. To influence Hillary especially. You might remind her of the marvels we have yet to create between our kind and the wilderness." He let me ponder that hint of his detachment about any relation I might have to the susceptibilities of his wife, then added, "Habitat is everything."

"Fuck your habitat." I walked outside.

With a single blackball he had shocked me over to the active side of his game—for the sake of which he seemed willing even to manipulate the mother of his children into the arms of a lover, if that was what it took to influence the power of her ethical family. For all I knew, he might have smoothly used her to bend Dex and Barry too his way, defender of justice and champion of the people to serve as preservers of his property. So why not

me among the other chance contributors to a destiny of monsters he foresaw?

Across the moonlit canal, Mrs. Needles sat on her patio chair in aromas of breezy night air. Indians could use her house for magical arbitration, an employer could use her body to purge his anguish. The Snake Clan could convey a severed head through her, and a chief could retrieve it to erect a stake of challenge in her garden. She was like the lowlanders who once cheered our advance with small British flags they found to wave out their windows, then produced black swastikas to flutter instead as we were retreating from a massive counterattack.

She was like all the people in the world, for any faction to use in any way it pleased. Her loyalty was free for the asking. Old age itself could make her bear it as a devotion with her cadaver of a husband. She was all the inertia of a human race I once cared so deeply for in her, and I knew the grotesque head of retribution was staked in all our thriving gardens.

Fenneran, smarter than us all, cared little for law or the human race as more than pawns in the game he chose to play. People came and standards went. Habitat was everything.

PANORAMA THREE

THE DISBELIEF OF CHRISTIANS

ONCE UPON A LIFETIME I woke from a nap on the beach unable to place myself in time or space. It was only for a moment. But a feeling just like that is quite protracted now, washing over me in waves of fatalistic impulse as I ponder what to do next with my guns.

Around four, that day a few years ago, my wife went inside with the kids and left me to doze. Waking later, I found myself alone with a distant standing figure and the endless surf. I thought I was twelve in Coney Island. Or twenty, next, in East Hampton. No, more likely thirty at Antibes. Then I remembered: my God, I was fifty on Banana Beach in Great Gulf Glade.

All of that took place in one sunstruck moment of my mind. I could fully believe I was twelve, twenty, thirty—fifty. And the most remarkable part of it was that my sense of self felt exactly the same at every different age.

It still feels the same at fifty-five, even though the world has turned upside down and Marissa thinks I'm the one that's gone mad. Inside I feel the same though it's hard to believe my wife has another husband now, and my son is lost like me to war, and my daughter is deranged.

I have guns to settle up with now, and that too feels the same.

COLLAGE 14

No animals of monstrous abnormality came out of the swamp for law enforcement to eliminate. In all the time of Fenneran's anxious expectations, there were no signs of danger to the flourishing metropolis. Tate was wrong about that. But on the constructive side of his vision, he had foreseen the future with clarity.

The Key Coast shoreline evolved into one unbroken park of leisurely commerce, which swept inland as well in many places. Wastelands of clapboard storefront housing and fallow tracts of sedge gave way to that salutary encroachment. Transplanted verdure replaced the desolation, creating endless groves piped with music, the settings utopian, as if all the splendiferous shopping malls of America were thrown together. In this vast greening, the limits of Harvester Mall became indiscernible.

The restaurant itself was a dining ideal. Just about everybody ate there most of the time. Success had advanced the gazebo's policy to the entire Harvester, and the larger it grew, the greater

was its wholesale buying advantage. More and more wings had to be added in this self-augmenting process, which eventually blanketed nine landscaped acres with fine international cuisine at prices not much higher than equivalent ordinary meals would cost anyone to prepare at home.

More spending resulted, more jobs, a prosperity that leaped both bays to each new beach hotel and back to the shops and theaters and other restaurants, which thrived in their appealing differences of atmosphere and a competitive need to maintain the highest standards. I benefited personally from architectural design assignments that kept supplementing my income. People all over, from workers to professionals, were gracious in their relative affluence. Outside of infrequent sociopathic crimes, no hostility was apparent in Gulf Glade by the time our second daughter, born in those years, entered the Cypress Shores School.

The lively arts were bustling in Gulf Glade. The cars flowed like wine, the avenues poured color in the night lights. At concerts and ballets, the musicals, the plays, everywhere we went there were friends who joined us in the crowd. Yet, with each passing year of quiescence, Fenneran grew more apprehensive that Josie, cunning in her unregenerate hate, was patiently conspiring against the lives of everyone, including the Indians.

He had her fixed in mind as the deadliest of misanthropic enemies, despite assurances from Deputy Fenton that grief over Chitto had left her as retiring as a possum, somewhere in the swamp with her husband and her son.

I found pleasure in watching Marissa shop gracefully through the spotless white malls of department-store elegance branched out from New York and Chicago. In her turn she pleased herself with the driving when we dined out, to permit me an appetizing drink without risk. Endearing in the earnestness of her concern, she always managed to find me witty, one cocktail high.

We had come to share an easy sense of fullness reminiscent of our earliest days together, an irony in that now it centered on four children who weren't there back then. The domestic sounds of afternoon delighted us. For me the best was of Lissa

coming up the driveway on her bike. I'd hurry out in time to see her standing on the pedal in her floppy hat, sweeping toward her little sister and hopping off to scoop Amy up on the rear fender for a spin around the cul-de-sac. My boys made me as happy when they played some ball before supper on the big back lawn where I could watch from my drafting table. An enthusiastic athlete before the war, I loved to see them experience what visual impairment kept me from thrilling to ever again.

I favored my wife's environmental conservation group's opposition to polluting Shark River. I didn't mind Honey Baines telephoning for Marissa's support against sex discrimination in hiring. Even Terry Peacham had mellowed for me somewhat on his TV pulpit of bias, referring to the "criminal class" rather than blacks any longer, though that was plainly the racial code term throughout his tirades for "law and order" in a city with one of the lowest crime rates in the nation.

One evening after the Harvester, I sat laughing at that Neanderthal former Sheriff with Amy in my lap. When Marissa took her off to bed, leaving the others busy with their homework, I went to sing a little in my workshop. My wife had let me have two cocktails this time, because Polsen had shown up to come over and handcuff me to my chair. Sometimes Deejay could not get him to release me until they were done at their table. The Sheriff got crazier every year.

Cutting selvage from some photos at my table, I mused on poor Deejay. All the gallery work was falling to her because of Hillary's preoccupation with her sister in their current work of founding a museum that would rival the Windgate up in Riopunta. Dedication seemed to be wearing Deejay out while making Hillary sanctimonious instead of aging her. Though she often remembered to thank me for dispelling her guilts by not submitting myself to destruction like a brother, she never got in a heat with me again, not even back when I was still pathological enough to be tempted.

That she had quit "promiscuating" bothered me less than her objections to the innocent Christmas cards Donny enjoyed sending out, like the one of a hugely pregnant Madonna beatific in her halo. And that bothered me less than her occasional remarks

about Deejay, which were beginning to take on the alienated carping of stale marriages. What bothered me most was Jennifer. Her settling in Glade meant two Brisburn sisters terrified of Vietnam in spite of Fenneran's guarantee to keep their sons safe from it, and one more to whose fey beauty I had all but succumbed.

Her misnamed husband, Royal, was so gauche in his flirting that he openly propositioned my wife. I was ashamed, after being told by Marissa, to find myself letting his wife seduce me all the way up the ramp to my ambush alley, the girdling catwalk I had built high above the floodlights in case anyone came to harm me in my workshop, back when I thought my friends dangerous.

But I was too devoted a husband to go all her way, my collages were selling so well that I even wore suits for Deejay's sake sometimes, and all that decadence was behind me now. There was not even a Mrs. Needles left to steam my obscure yearnings for Hillary into a mirage of some objective meaning in the world. Tate Fenneran's pensioned secretary might still exist, for all I knew, but not in sight any longer since workers' bungalows went up across the canal over tracts sold off on the county side.

I was glad her house had vanished with the tragic one. Puttering at my table, I sang to celebrate the obliteration of sweet garden flora amid which a monster's head was planted to face across at me, the tender roses and hibiscus out of which a hideous living face once blossomed to capture my lust at the embankment. I could not believe my eyes, next, when I saw that very face at my window.

A bleat of horror escaped me. I thought she was blooming in my imagination on devil's eye those cocktails had siphoned back from my system. But it was Josie I reached outside, maneuvering to keep the moonlight off her face while electric sparks rippled all over my scalp.

Nothing remained behind me—the years of respite were the illusion. That was Mrs. Needles maturing in my house, not Marissa. Those were the McFees, not the ageless Brisburn sisters, between whom I was clinging to my marital fidelity.

Josie was dressed in swamp rags, and so was the sweaty boy

she had with her. About the size of my thirteen-year-old Toby, he looked Negroid but had skin as light as mine. Her greeting gibber was unintelligible, not on account of her tipless tongue alone, but also because the boy she was introducing seemed too old for the one I deciphered her to mean by, "Dif my fun."

Human, not a beast, he had to be my son too. She had likely come to confront me at last. That was my shocking first reaction to fathoming her impeded sibilants. Then the age disparity confused me—her child by me could be no more than six or seven. But afraid to ask, I let her speak, and counted on his probable racial difference to disassociate us.

I seemed to hear her say there should be no more draining by big machines in the swamp. Repeating words to make sure I got her message, she demanded that all work on the new international airport be discontinued. I thought she meant me personally when she said I went to Africa for slaves, only to jail their descendants now to save my streets from their retaliation. She meant all of us, all her enemies, but in my discomposure I was not sure till she called me by the Indian honor name Storyteller, as her ghost had once.

She said I drove the Seminoles deep into intolerable swamp, then found the very swamp too valuable for Indians and cornered them in mean reservations. Not yet satisfied, I made Seminole minds over to the image of mine, to banish and destroy her. But she was not destroyed. She had multiplied, and was multiplying still. I was to tell that to Mr. Fenneran, she stated, and took my hand to feel her swollen belly.

Her rag clothes were wet. It was not an alien sweat I had noticed on the boy but slough water. I followed them back to the canal, interpreting her careful enunciations.

I must do as she said, she commanded. Her people must not be driven from their swamp haven as the Indians were driven into it and the Africans stolen from their farms across the sea.

Were her people not Indians then, I asked, not blacks?

They were, she responded, a kind the swamp bred as rapidly as the beasts that roamed, and with the abundance of its plants. As countless as the blades of grass underfoot, they would have no place to go if driven out by the giant pumps and dredges.

Her face turned into the moonlight. I saw the most horrible sight: the wisdom of delusion, the calm of insanity. She wanted me not to believe her, I saw that too. She wanted Fenneran not to act. His failure to stop the machines of progress would incite the war she had always yearned to launch across the landscape of her madness, and with all the justification every war was based on by the lunatics who brought it on the world.

As I was sure I knew everything in seizure, Josie was sure she knew everything always. So did reactionary Bull Peacham, and Fenneran too. Maybe that was all that madness was.

But I could not discount the fetus Josie was carrying, or the boy who sat now with his back against my wharf block and his elbows resting on it. I said, "Who is this baby's father?"

Josie pointed to the smiling boy.

Dizzy, I felt ridiculous saying, "How old is he?"

"You," she replied, "hepped me make him deven year ago."

I, as the Devil, and a monster she eventually killed. Her eyes told me more—that she had just implied a challenge, one too important to have let fear keep her from this visit to the metropolitan side of the canal, that it no longer mattered if Fenneran's people killed her: her war was won.

She slipped over the wharf block and swam away. I asked the rising boy, "Who's your father?"

"Muddabudda."

He dropped away without a splash to swim off with his mother, the mother of his unborn child if I were to believe her. But I didn't have to believe, and dropped away myself. I didn't have to tell anyone about the poor scarred face of spite and debase myself again to save the insensible city. I felt no duty to assure Barry Christian's election as President of the Metropolitan Council. I was not eager to warn Fenneran against a swamp freak invasion that he could leak to distant newspapers as casually as he admitted, at last, having leaked the annihilation of a Pinebrake family just to attract an influx of taxable new arrivals curious about monsters. And nothing could make me report this to the Sheriff. He would only handcuff me. I just got my arms around my wife whose face looked so patient above me on the star-spangled night.

"Toby called me," she said. "You passed out on the grass. Have you been having these again?"

"What did I say, what did I see?"

"A whole bunch of crazy animals in Pinebrake. Monsters all over the industrial complexes and entertainment centers of Gulf Glade."

"You're putting me on, but I love you just the same."

"That reminds me, you mentioned the amusement parks too."

We rolled a little in the grass. I knew I had not been hallucinating, but allowed myself to believe that Josie and son were just a seizure dream threatening to spoil all the fun.

And later on I refused to associate her visit with the mysterious murder of Chuck Stowell, found scalped in his surplus store up in Naples.

Whereas I used to take my phenobarbital only upon auras of warning, a more successful regimen of four pills a day at regular intervals had kept me seizure-free for years. The smart doctor who had conceived that simple epileptifuge no longer served at the Veterans Administration. Still, I trusted its hospital clinic more than the private physicians I sometimes consulted, and always returned to the VA like someone going home.

But that security was deteriorating in the changes that occurred with the Vietnam War. New technicians and doctors from Asia seemed all right, but I really didn't like the blacks who came down for jobs from the north and brought its pseudorevolutionary arrogance with them. It took the form of a smug exclusionary superciliousness that would have seemed blatantly racial if the clerks who practiced it were not despised by black VA old-timers as much as they were by me. I was reminded of that whenever I reacted with a temper that aroused the guards to stave off a fight. Most of those offensive guys were Vietnam veterans, so I could hardly throw my combat status up to them. I didn't feel much at home anymore at the Veterans Administration.

The same mixed sense of frustration, alienation, and anger crept over me when intrusive choruses of bongo drums began to sound nearby with galling regularity. It was impossible to

THE DISBELIEF OF CHRISTIANS

work conceptually in that repetitious rhythm. The players were thought to be Swamptown Negroes at first, the idle or helpless kind that had lived on welfare for succeeding generations. The bongos seemed just another seasonal affectation typical of them, like skull caps or spats or cheap transistor radios, just a noise from the shacks, too remote to be annoying. But they soon gathered to bang out those plaguing drumbeats in Hammerhead Park, and the police had to move them out.

They appeared to care no more about the police than about the citizens they distracted. Driven away, they would return and thump incessantly into the night. Marissa was afraid I might go into seizure. My lie about a VA doctor ruling that out had not convinced her, and she noted the power we could tap in friends. Unwilling to impose on anyone over such a matter, I agreed to telephone a simple complaint to the police instead.

An officer who sounded frustrated said there was little he could do. "Those swamp people keep swarming back like rats. They don't even care if you hit them on the head."

I didn't want anyone hit on the head. "Aren't they from Swamptown? I didn't know they're Seminoles."

"Who knows what they are? I just say swamp people because that's where they seem to come from and go back to. Those that don't squat in the abandoned shacks."

Nobody applied any measurable pressure. I guessed it was the fatalistic nature of human trust to shrug off intrusions not too painful or menacing. Some people resented the beer cans left behind on benches, and some were irritated enough to say we never should have integrated the park. My aversion to that obtuse kind of prejudice might have been what kept me from taking the step Marissa suggested.

After all, it was not every day the bongos were to be heard. And my work sometimes required long mechanical periods of no more than pasting, soldering, and carpentry of parts already laid out. The drumming didn't really bother me then, except for the tedium. It didn't really interfere even when I had punctilious juxtaposing of images and machine parts to accomplish with sensitive attention to design. It was while conceiving the ideas, and recording them in complicated annotations, and projecting them in various dimensions articulable only by means of

symbols and drawings, that I suffered personal feelings of imposition by obnoxiously inconsiderate intruders.

The notion that they were swamp people began to wear the
face of my dream that was not a dream about Josie visiting with
her son by me or monsters. I didn't want to burden Barry
Christian with deciding how to meet her ultimatum at such
great cost to the advancement of Fenneran's habitat. I didn't
want Tate fitting all she had said into prophecies he had made
long ago. But, sick again since her reemergence, I was starting
to have fantasies about the women Marissa did her club work
with, whose liberated posture it was to tempt her half-assed
celebrity of a husband, and I feared subversion by swamp bongos might reduce me to foolishly succumbing. So I telephoned
Polsen about Josie, disgusted with myself for giving in once
again to a civic responsibility that could only repay me with
further misery.

Dexter listened respectfully, then said, "Let's go to Mexico."
It sounded like deliverance from this base reversion to susceptibilities I thought I had subdued once and for all. "Let's take
our wives on a real holiday for once."

The roads through city parks were blocked to automobiles
after the morning rush and before the evening repetition, so that
people could freely ride their bicycles in those elegant settings.
One breezy day of sun in Hammerhead Park, a girl named Clara
Huxton was struck on the head with a golf club and killed in the
sight of witnesses who did nothing to intervene. She was white,
the two boys who ambushed her and got away with her bike
were black. Terry Peacham's fury focused on that point as he
analyzed the incident on television. So did everybody's seem to,
wherever we went the week after our return from Mexico. I
tried to keep my own rage from attacking me in that narrow
way, and it took careful thought. It was going to take even more
careful thought to resist shooting down every supercilious black
who looked like a threat to my children.

The feminist movement had opened Yale and Harvard to
Lissa, but she chose the university that would keep her home.
New England held little as a substitute for the theater activity

of Great Gulf Glade, its stadium and water sports, the rich art of its museums and galleries, the fine beaches and marinas, the array of hotels, restaurant bars, and movie palaces. She insisted her family played a large part in that decision, but it was obvious the largest part stemmed from her warm hometown attachment.

Though Armistead, with the superior academic reputation it boasted even when smaller, had over the years come to stand with the Ivy League schools in size as well as scholastic quality, most important for Lissa was the reality that all her friends were here. All the intimate sharing of good times. All the thrills and surprises of young love. I hoped the new times would never hurt her. Fears overtook me whenever I saw her toss her hair in that unconscious manner girls had at her age. It was just about the age at which all the promise of youth was pillaged from Majosee. That plain fact always gave Lissa's face an Indian cast for me in my anxieties about her, as if she might somehow be punished for crimes that others had committed against Josie.

Donald Brisburn Fenneran and his brother Bill, handsome young men both taller than their father, flanked their grand-mother in the static sun that palled the afternoon at Loker Brisburn's graveside. Faith was just as attractive in her age, thanks to fortitude and face-lifts, no older looking than the ruddy minister robustly extolling her slain husband.

He sounded just like the principal two years back at Cassie's high school graduation, making his speech of platitudes about the labors of our generation to fulfill the dream of Great Gulf Glade. Donny had said in my ear meanwhile, as mothers and fathers beamed and Loker Brisburn heartily applauded, that Vietnam and similar genocides were the fulfillment Dr. Cafrey stood there celebrating.

Now the mothers and fathers wept with Cassie, home from her junior year at a college up north, which, according to her mordant brother Don, specialized in shiftlessness, called individuality in the framework of the sexual revolution. She was almost the exquisite copy of her weeping mother. Her Aunt Jennifer wept too, but Faith did not.

Mortuary procedures kept Fenneran occupied. Back when

Donny was still an Armistead student, Tate had agreed to join the Brisburn board of directors only as an inducement for his sons to adapt their educations strategically toward key participation themselves. By the time Don had graduated to Harvard Law School, the corporation was reshaped as Brisburn-Fenneran Industries, with subsidiaries that operated far beyond the Key County limits Tate once set for himself. His expansion from sponge marketing and agriculture included an enhancement of his own commerce in real estate, as well as utilities, investment banking, hardware, construction, oil drilling, coal mining, insurance, textile merchandising, and even a charity trust.

Only a shade less golden than her younger sister, Jennifer smelled as sweet. Her son and daughter whispered comforts by her cheek. Her husband had stayed out of town making Gulf Glade the hub of his Kearny Department Store chain, a lesser chore than cementing industrial agreements abroad, from which Fenneran had inconveniently returned for the funeral arrangements.

I didn't know why I found that funny, and funnier still my pal Don's early surrender to his father's distrust of fine art, but laughter threatened the sorrow. Using one surreptitious hand to choke myself as Polsen once did me promised to work. Until the Bocaleons foiled it. Because her husband was another who had pressed too coarsely at Marissa, I had nearly let Liz lionmouth me in wooded Sunset Bayou. That very subject had won me some frontage there as a gift from Faith Brisburn for my drunken gallantry at the Causeway Lounge. Now Clint and Liz, so rednosed in their turgid grief, bubbled up my laughter, and just in time I disguised it as blubbering with my breastkerchief. Marissa patted my villainous arm to comfort me; Marge Christian made me feel even worse, dabbing like me at tears, but sincerely, in the Buenaventura graveyard.

Even Honey Baines looked nicer than I felt, laughing at the pink she wore in mourning, her festive garden hat in the enormity of Loker Brisburn's murder, as she guided a television crew to discreet shooting position. Publisher now of the *Gulf Glade Times*, she was currently heading up a women's rights

campaign with inane arguments that amplified the laughter in my handkerchief, even with Carl Meyerberger sitting among his numberless kin in a wheelchair, looking like time.

County had to approve integrated housing to get the Bayfront right-of-way from him at last. He had also held out on ceding Swamptown for a fairground until city agreed to develop only half the land into Big Cypress Amusement Park while keeping the rest open permanently to squatters too poor for better than its shacks. Now he could only rue that proviso, since the marauder who had cut his old friend down was a Swamptown youth. Still, wherever Meyerberger sat in all flat Florida, his long years heading for a hundred, he seemed to make a hill of the spot.

Everyone seemed worthier than me, even the nihilistic pop artists paying their respects really to Hillary—or to the power of the Brisburn Museum she was establishing. Tate hated them more than I did, and that almost made me laugh again. Where he only found my old substantial kind's idealism tedious, he detested the shallow stylists being mass-produced by our schools. The funny thing was that he himself had lured their progenitors here among the morbid affluent, making a city planner's dream come true by merely insinuating into far-flung journals a notoriety of monster attacks.

But that manipulation of the news did produce a major new center of the arts, elaborating Buttonwood Levee into a citywide marvel that made Gulf Glade world famous as the cultural center of the South. And today the heightened tempo of art life was grieving at Buenaventura. As well as artists, writers of a stylish prominence equal to the dash of TV personalities had congregated to venerate their supreme commercial patron at his passing. Their loss had me in tears I was sure Mrs. Brisburn saw through as laughter when she beckoned to me with a finger. My handkerchief mask had failed me.

Faith wanted me over on the other side of the grave, but on my way somebody whispered, "I was supposed to visit your studio."

Knuckling my bleary eyes I saw Stephanie Wilmont sadly smile, and whispered back, "I guess you died and went to Congress."

With breasts brushing my arm, she faced away to an apparent undertaker who turned out to be her husband instead, shining on top of his head. The vicissitudes of Fenneran's enlightened nepotism had sent her to heaven, not her husband, who had risen only to Chief Judge, reviewer of all court decisions. Barry Christian had risen to President of the Metropolitan Council and, needing someone close to watch over his law firm, elected Donny a junior partner. Bill Fenneran had risen to drilling engineer. I reached Mrs. Brisburn choking with laughter in my handkerchief, until she said, "Were you my husband's lover?" A TV camera eyed us. I was thankful she spoke too softly for audio between Fenneran's sons as their aunt and mother flanked my sickly conscience. Miserably, I said, "I beg your pardon?" "Only lovers weep," she continued, and all my laughing stopped. The saddest thing to hear was Faith Brisburn saying, dry at her husband's grave, not sighing, pale and expressionless, "We weren't lovers anymore."

"Was not a *shvartze* killed him," Meyerberger said when the TV camera moved off, "was a *bahayma.*" Nobody comprehended him but his clan and I, the members of our tribe.

I saw us later on my screen, grouped with Christian in a pan from Wilmont, who had just said, "Despite the eminence of the victim and the race of the suspect, a fair trial is guaranteed."

Phyllis Chalfonte explained that *bahayma* meant herd animal in Hebrew, though we both knew it to be common Yiddish usage. She was Meyerberger's granddaughter. I was an animal hiding from Mrs. Brisburn as she herded the wake home, Donny grimacing at my tears while Bill seemed touched. His grandfather had lived to see him strike oil in Big Cypress Swamp, so went the talk in that agony of senseless murder, but nobody recalled Loker's disgust with our youngest generation. He deplored the lascivious dancing and callow humor of his grandchildren. "I would leave," he said once at a Buenaventura celebration, "if I didn't live here."

Because she had witnessed the slaying, Mrs. Chalfonte had no choice but to attend the wake with family. Forty or so, she was youthfully hale, with a freckled look of wholesomeness that a wide white headband touched off. Her screams had alerted Ar-

mistead students who ran to overpower the cutthroat before he could flee the campus that spanned vastly reclaimed swampland.

He had slipped into the car park that evening for no better purpose than to move along snapping off antennas. It must have escaped him that anyone might be seated in her car. When Loker got out to ask why he was doing such destruction, the boy slashed him and stabbed him and ran.

The sky did not change, no thunder cracked it open. As casually as that, the leading life of Gulf Glade was terminated. The crickets were rising. Birds sang in the sycamores.

Everyone seemed confused about the assailant's age and the reason Hillary's father was a mile across the campus from his car. Phyllis said she had taken him there (his chauffeur following) from her grandfather's estate to prove her driving ability for a managerial position with his charity trust. That was how Police Commissioner Tolstadt had it. In the drawing room where mourners chatted softly and picked at the tables of fare, Sheriff Polsen deemed it more likely they had just returned from a day out of the county together and were making plans for their next rendezvous before driving on to meet his car.

"Why do you posit that?" Christian asked as Marge drew away.

"Don't you know," Polsen said, "that everybody's a fraud?"

Fenneran smiled. Deejay led Hillary elsewhere, both of them looking back askance. Nobody ever bothered to dispute Polsen. He would parry everything with the same stubborn irony he employed when justifying as American tradition his often violent solutions of difficulty in his police sphere. I never argued when he handcuffed me in Mexico and refused to unlock my wrists till our wives decided what to do that day. Or when he brought up Josie's visit to me as soon as they got out of earshot. I regarded that as more of his wry needling, but now at the wake I learned that the Indian woman had earnestly preoccupied him.

"Something about her kid's precocious size," he said. "Like she was up to establishing that more than to stop anybody from building an airport or pumping oil."

Commissioner Tolstadt said the killer was smaller, yet looked mature. The connection eluded me until he said "Muddabudda"

was the name they used for him, based on the only recognizable utterance that came repeatedly from his incoherent patois.

I had no heart to ponder that strange sound shared by those two boys, or the swamp rags they wore in common, and turned away to mingle in the wake. But Barry stopped me, saying, "This young criminal has extensor muscles that stay in tension like Wiley's."

I was too scared to deal with that, and resented Polsen asking me, "Did you happen to notice anything about the forearms of Josie's kid when he relaxed them on your wharf block?"

"Who can remember?" I said to shake him off. It was not that we didn't get on well. The man was just a trifle stranger than it seemed a little brain damage should make anyone. In all our travels from Taxco to Tepozstlan and back to Acapulco, I never saw him take an alcoholic drink. Finally in Oaxaca he confessed having tricked me into believing he drank devil's eye, with the sole intent of addicting me enough to give myself away in case I was a paid assassin sent to finish Fenneran off.

I was searching for my buddy Don when Honey Baines caught me to serve us shrimp fritters while explaining widowhood and sex objects. I didn't understand a single point, so I said just two kinds of men were bred by a society like ours, those who knew they were sexists and those who didn't. She could not understand a word. We were meant for each other.

Honey contemplated me thoughtfully, then spoke the only complete sentence I had ever understood from her. "I like you."

To stay out of trouble I looked around for my wife, but instead found Mrs. Brisburn, beckoning with a finger again. People were bringing her their commiserations; I tried to withdraw, muttering my way past with the others, but she made room on the couch for me to sit and endure the maudlin rambling of her grief.

"Our civilization must be nearing its end," she remarked, gazing aside at her daughters as they approached with an angular gray man. Faith took whisky for us from a servant's tray and said, "There used to be mystery. Now there's only sex and drinking. I hope you never divulge why you wept. I know it was not in mourning."

She was apparently high, to indulge this laconic display of courage so unabashedly while acknowledging her murmurous quick visitors. Among them came Hillary and Jennifer with their guest. Suave as an actor, he deeply bowed. Faith raised her slow aristocratic gaze and said, "Dr. Ryerson, I presume?"

My drink went right to my head. Bowing to her bereavement, if not to some foul gluttony my loathing projected, he acknowledged me with a slightly drunken search, and expressed his overwhelming regret. He had bestowed his peculiar ministrations on others I knew about from Speed Byrd, a few so young they had frightened off even that friend who, dauntless at my age, had experienced the sweaty palms and inorgasmic kinks of riper girls set free the Ryerson way.

For years I had avoided meeting the fulsome quack in fear of killing him. Likely his presence at the wake was to bring Hillary through this tragic day, maybe by putting it to her behind the window drapes. Jennifer took them both away after a whisper to her mother, already scheming to pay the analyst back. Without a sign of anything ulterior under way, they were soon to use me a little in punishing Ryerson for more misprisions than I could ever imagine.

"Naïveté," Faith said, "once lent life mystery. My daughters still have it, but theirs don't and their sons don't. There was magic," she added wistfully, then thanked some solicitous people. Her resuming comment startled me. "I thought Loker was a freak, the first night, because of his pubic hair. I was a virgin of course. How wonderful the mystery. Your generation surrendered that. You thought our advice merely prudish, but what we were trying to save you for was joy."

I had always liked her, but now her defined jawline and hooded eyes, the prominent blade of her nose, fascinated me as she said, austere in her black lace, "I never dreamt men grew hair where women did. He looked ghastly thereabouts. Loker was a horrifying sight. I ran away, hysterical, from Buenaventura."

I felt the excitement of that bridal naïveté and blurted, "What was so terrific? That sounds precisely like the sexual ignorance your generation helped mine escape."

"Leaving a void. Now your generation is further enlightening its own children—and robbing them of more mystery, more magic, filling the void with confusion. Loker Brisburn charged off half naked to retrieve me. By horse, by God. And raced me back, not to this house of memories and treasures, but to the slave quarters that still existed here."

I drank with her as Faith restored for me the slave quarters a fire had consumed years ago. "He shackled me to the whipping post and tore off my clothes. How thrilling to scream where the slaves once had their souls torn out like my virginity. He ravished me. Ah, magic. Oh, rhapsodies of passion I never imagined in my simple masturbations."

Drunk, I heard myself say, "You're bewitched by romance."

"By mysteries. As you know mine, I know yours."

She was young in the vivid pictures of my mind, staring back across the years at me—and across the Pinebrake canal, suddenly white again with age, resurrecting the fear of exposure I thought I had outlived. I saw her nod to acknowledge condolences with a glance back at my seduction by an Indian in screams of slaughter. How thrilling, she said without speaking, and nodded to the whispers of unwidowed wives who had bid to know me in the flesh. How mysterious. What magic in the devil's eye, from old reservoirs of which my whisky drew.

"I loved only Loker. Until he sent my child to war."

"We're not letting our white sons go to Vietnam."

It came from nowhere in my own voice.

"How could you know I was thinking that?"

"Epileptic magic."

"I never stopped loving him. We lived graciously ever after at each other's throat. Rescue me from this."

Thrilled, I helped her rise and sailed her through the smiling mourners. She whispered a destination. Then we were out of noisy guests in still corridors, Faith and I, and then a small vestibule as mute and frightening slowly levitated us, and she had me alone to ply with the Wildean audacities so popular in her youth. Following her to an immaculate isolation of alcove doors, I hoped this autocratic widow, beautiful but seventy and capable of violence, had no illusions about fulfilling with me the

equation of sex and whisky that signified the end of civilization for her. She led me into darkness, and shut a heavy door to enclose us in stale odors.

We stood in an actual restoration of the slave quarters, right down to the mustiness and mildew and carbide lamps she brought alive with sparks from a flint as I went around opening windows. A whipping post dominated the room, a hewn cedar log that stood thick and phallic, with shackle chains hanging from the top like doom. A bullwhip snaked across one wall, and cots lined a longer wall in vertical tiers, like the hammocks of a wartime troopship. There were even rocking chairs for old slaves and mammies to appreciate in the magnanimity of their masters.

Very drunk, I took one and rocked, unable to fathom why Mrs. Brisburn had enticed me here except for punishment. She let her hair fall silver in the dancing carbide glow, and slid a chair around to face mine, rocking, glaring at me with bedeviled eyes. My voice, more disembodied than before, echoed back from a lost old side of myself. "You want me shackled to the whipping post."

"Oh, mystery." Her voice soft as a purr, she rocked. "Oh, magic of the human mind, how could you tell?"

"You know I'm epileptiform."

"And usually wrong. I can see why Marissa remains Marissa, beyond mystery. With her charity work and children to watch over. One man and one existence and wanting nothing more. Why she spells paradise that way." Faith spoke in the rhythm of her rocking. "Her charming children, her comfortable home, the vapid conflicts of her friends. I asked her once if she realized all men are polygamous. She said not you. She said you are her children's music lessons, their humor and athletics, when in fact you are nothing but your art. And they and she and everyone else are mounted in their places on your one ongoing collage." It shocked me awake, next, to hear her say, "That's Hillary's assessment of you, and of your wife that she's like Tate."

"Tate," I cried out to break the inauspicious spell, "haw!"

Faith rocked faster. "They're the same in that they both accept the inconsequence of life. If you die, Marissa will grieve.

If you betray her, she'll suffer pain. As Tate shapes reality to his will, Marissa shapes her will to reality. Thus, mystery and its antithesis are ultimately alike."

I was thinking Hillary was right, when her mother said, "Tate is right, you know. Order cannot be introduced to human affairs. Only to habitat. Orderly streets, and buildings that function. By removing human interference. To protect people from themselves. I have become pathetic."

"Don't say that," I pampered. But Faith just spoke and rocked and rocked and spoke about reality shaped by individuals on a circle of destiny she meant to show me soon. I was too stoned for symbolism, and tried to sleep, when a knock sounded softly on the door to make her spring up with my wrist in her bony cold grip.

"My rendezvous—don't spoil it!"

How magic and mysterious, she floated us through the eerie light, she stood me at the punishing post of the slaves, how thrilling. *Art News* should hear of this, I thought, the Pinebrake pervert brought full circle to face his ultimate worth. But with much relief I saw a camera materialize large in her right hand, where my blind side had kept it absent on my left.

"Come in," she sang as I let her slip my wrists into shackles above, which brought the handcuffing Sheriff to mind. I hoped the gold star mother had not rewarded me with that Sunset Bayou lot for suppressing the truth rather than a vicious lie at the Causeway Lounge years ago. She flashed a blinding light to capture me on film, a slave in necktie and formality suit. Two people came into blurred view as she said, "This will make a great collage."

My hands slid out of the shackles like melting butter. "I didn't know you make collages."

"These shots are for your collage, not mine. Jennie?"

Her daughter took my place in the shackles as Dr. Ryerson shadowed forth with somber eye to say, "Such therapeutic activity is exemplary, Mrs. Brisburn, at a time like this."

As soon as the flashbulb flared he hastened, no doubt already tutored by Jennifer, to take her place at the whipping post for Faith's recuperative game. It was hard to believe anyone could

remain unaware of what Mrs. Brisburn was up to, yet Ryerson smiled voluptuously as she slipped his wrists into the shackles one by one above his head. His face a blithering ecstatic phenomenon, it fell wooden with apprehension when she deftly snapped one cuff after the other to lock his hands in slave chains.

I looked for Jennifer in her mourning lace. She was gone. I wanted to slip away too, but Faith rooted me there by taking the bullwhip down from its hooks on the wall. "Burl Brisburn died here," she told Ryerson, "chained like you to compulsion." I was horrified to hear her add, "There's no difference between the pitiful insect who debases others for pleasure and the wretch who destroyed my feckless husband for maybe saying nigger."

The odious lecher screamed, "Help me!"

"Faith, you can't!"

"You're absurd." In her spidery black lace she rushed at me raising the bullwhip. When it cracked I was out the door. I was racing down the corridor to find my wife when Ryerson's first shriek sounded to the lash.

Sharks swam across my TV screen with repulsive company names like Essdee Stores and Hemmorhelp and faces nobody would believe, urging my patronage. But not even commercials could help Marissa extract me from my workshop. Patiently I waited for the news breaks to continue celebrating our most illustrious murder, and soon I saw the white race on parade with all its traits in living color, while ancient lace and upswept hair kept Faith in black and white as the camera picked up her crowd.

I saw us wend toward the mansion as Marissa, who had urged me to follow the gold star mother, now urged me to leave my TV. Oh, what a big parade. All the politicians were there for interviews. I saw the Zoning Commission marching. "Fifty million in public funds," said the head, "no corner cutting necessary in the foreseeable future."

But Donny had told me federal income-sharing funds for sewage-disposal plants were used instead to finance tennis courts and yacht clubs in the rich communities, while his father admonished us not to be simplistic: "Such buttering is necessary to keep things turning in the real world."

Bongos thumped in the real world as I watched United Insurance Underwriters troop across my screen, Hal Swayzee leading with his wife, a local celebrity humper bent on making a trophy out of me. Her friend, my forbearant wife, begged me to come watch better things inside with the kids. Marissa called it morbid to relive the funeral. She knew of no visit by Josie and son that placed me close to this murder. She only knew I was drifting away. My wife said she sensed we were parting, but she had no sense of the wake, or the whipping meted out in a grandmother room where every mansion holds its most disenchanting keepsakes entombed.

Marissa wept as I relished the sad televised faces of the snobs and fops a blackball had allowed me to avoid with grace so many years. The bankers who stooped to filching devices like niggardly landlords. The doctors who comported themselves with the vacuous conceit of dress designers. The lawyers whom success had rendered as pompous as prosperous shopkeepers. I loved them all, because I never had to see them. My screen ran over. Loker's parties had always been the best around.

Over sweeping shoreline vistas of the urban highway arteries, the shore length of shopping malls, industrial complexes, and retirement cooperatives, the TV reporter's voice said, "Few millionaires live to see beauty and contentment wherever their glances venture." As her camera was finding the sports parks, hospital plants, research centers, and great marble libraries, she told the viewing public, "Only a decade ago, all this was still mostly a disconnected dream, and a mere ten years before that, just a scattering of rural towns in a gulf tidewater county."

She knew Loker's good works extended well beyond his personal wealth and power, but not that he was unhappy in his life. My wife said she was unhappy in mine. But I saw no need to listen. I saw no black face on parade to Loker's annihilation by a black, and wondered if calling people nigger could really kill so nice a man. I had to conclude it was not a nice man who said nigger and not a black who killed. It was the same beast in both, and I was sentenced to see it in the swamp of TV faces while the bongos outside drummed warnings in my head.

The profiteers of Great Gulf Glade lived in guarded harmony like the insects and snakes and mice that shared the airplants of

the wilderness. I colored them white in my one ongoing collage until Deejay came around to express concern about incomprehensible turns she saw lately in my work. That inspired me to paste the insects to the snakes on a gigantic board I erected, never to leave my workshop again because of Deejay and Faith.

For weeks I pasted up my pictures of the world and kept the world at bay. Marissa had instructed the housekeeper to let no one intrude, but could not eliminate the bongos. I eliminated Jennifer, avoiding her calls after an urgent one she made to explain there was much more that Faith had avenged in Ryerson than his depraved use of her daughter in distress.

I didn't want to know the details, not from her any more than I ever did from Hillary, who was only partly right about my never having cared about anything but my art. What she really felt was that I never cared to understand her willingness to spend my life on solving hers. She was wrong about my family.

I cared plenty for my wife and kids. Marissa had it all the time —no hassling with clandestine affairs or other complications, a casually orgasmic woman pleased with all life let her have, including a few insignificant pretensions. She had no use for other people's values unless they fit her sentiments, and I had called that rigidity, obtuseness, a poor sense of proportion, by that means to blame her for my degenerate experience with Josie and all my loitering at gluttony's brink thereafter. It had to wait for an eccentric rich widow to sardonically focus me on the moral imbalance of stealing more than life had to offer.

I needed time to knit the sundered months into collages Deejay might find more consistent with her patient understanding. Marissa accepted that too as her portion without complaint, and it helped. I began to dress immaculately once more, and to think of good times with her again in the theaters and dining arenas of Great Gulf Glade. I was returning from all the disorder Loker's murder had fanned in me, when Marissa packed off for Mexico to get a divorce, citing my distrust of the good things, the simple beauty of life.

The simple beauty of Jennifer reached me while I was reeling. My defenses down, her urgency got through, but not to extenu-

ate Faith's vengeance on Ryerson. That had slipped her mind like the death of her father. She came ostensibly in need of architectural finishing touches for her museum, but forgot that too, with a self-indulgent blushing I once mistook in her sister as the endearing humility of women blessed with allure.

Genuine mysticism allowed Mrs. Kearny to believe her sibling rivalry romantic, whereas it was really just aphrodisiac, exciting her imagination up the ramp and all over my ambush alley until, at word as we rested that my wife had left me, she vanished in a pitch of anger that seemed the first sincere emotion she had expressed all afternoon.

What happened? I had no idea. So, Marissa, ended my first trust of the good things, like our marriage and Loker Brisburn's life, in pure bafflement.

COLLAGE 15

What happened or did not happen exactly? Who ever really knew? People were too preoccupied with themselves to believe in objective particulars. Did a monster really happen? Did Jesus? Did my wife really say she waited till I was well before facing up to the necessity of separation? Was my behavior really a manic burden she had to endure for years? Things came through one's consciousness and were forgotten with the passing of time. Like the decrepit old woman the Needles couple kept. Like Josie's son and the killer who also said "Muddabudda."

He ended up in an asylum for the criminally insane, far upstate. I cowered in my workshop. Or fled from the bongos to my troubled sleep. Till Fenneran telephoned to pity me over Marissa. Of all people. I had liked it better when he scared me over Hillary. So, without a life left to protect, I let him take me high in his glider above the habitat he rarely had to oversee, hovering always above others in his array who ran all his vast creation for him. We sailed like a two-assed bird and I had no fear, until he confided the deepest secret of his life.

Realizing that only his own emotions could hurt him, he had disciplined himself to hate not even evil, and to love not even his children. So he maintained; as if that left me not sick enough, he added, "Now will you believe it was nothing personal, back when I wanted to tear that fetus of a monster out of Josie?"

I said, "I can no more believe her kid's a monster than I can believe you don't love your children."

He laughed. "It's human, all too human, to disbelieve."

I was good and sick. It was too silent up there. "What's your real purpose in bringing me up here, Tate?"

"Something is clogging up our sewers. Or somebody. And desecrating every surface of our malls, the statues in our parks."

"Kids. Is that unusual?"

"More and more. Some new phenomenon is filthying Gulf Glade. I'm asking everyone I know to be observant, and try to believe we're in a growing danger."

He was graying nowadays, like Polsen, and getting as crazy. It felt scary as hell to think a man beyond emotion had unseen presence everywhere, all the time, manipulating everything.

But even that felt better than being pitied.

I was adjusting to everything but the bongo drums and an increase of violence in the news, when Toby announced that his mother was getting married. She had only recently left me to doze on the beach; I had no idea it was forever. Who could know anybody? Who ever tried to, really?

Jennifer B. Kearny went out of reach just when I needed her, confessing she found single men unprovocative. Dex Polsen arrested the bike-stealing killers at last in Swamptown. At the Harvester he told me they spoke in the same incomprehensible swamp argot as the people who were overrunning the Indian reservation and the boy who had murdered Loker. Then the Sheriff handcuffed me to lift everybody's spirits a bit, and I let Baldy Haverstraw take me to a clandestine dogfight in Armistead Hammock.

We saw Faith Brisburn there with Dr. Ryerson.

Hobart Harnett, my wife's husband, was a handsome actor of wide TV fame. He waited something like three years for Ma-

rissa to feel secure enough about my seizures being under control to leave me and marry him. I doubted he ever got past her conscience to her body. But I could have been wrong about that. Who ever knew anybody? There was no mystery, however, about his accepting all my kids because his pretty gamin of a wife wanted them with her.

That required the purchase of a high-rise condominium on Ceremony Key, with a bedroom for the boys and another for the girls whenever they were not with me. Interested in acting, my twelve-year-old Sam had his stepfather always taking him to watch from the studio control room as the shows were being taped. Hoby frequently did Amy's homework. I was sure he'd nurse me back to health if I went there to have my seizures, which had recurred, though not to any intense degree, when Marissa finally moved out of the house and was gone.

Until the phone calls began, I worked harder than in all my married years, when celebrity humpers often tempted me but to no avail beyond fantasy. Mrs. Bocaleon and Swayzee, now I joined up to learn how country club wives were as self-indulgent as their husbands in beach cabanas and the cabins of their cruisers. Mrs. Herlihy, Hooton, and Glunn, I had liked them better as fantasies.

Another disadvantage of being single was that I never got to watch television anymore. All I had time for was ballet and theater and movies and gallery parties with friends old and new. My eminence in the arts started to expand. Not, however, from all that mingling but from the warm place my exhibitor Deejay found for my labors at the great Brisburn Museum, where Jennifer turned out to be provocable by single men in surprise engagements on bolsters as strange as a bannister, piano, or Byzantine Saint Peter's chair.

The sexual revolution was real. Fun was out of the closet. True love was out of my life.

I knew it was bad for my head to worry about my kids and miss my wife so much, but I couldn't help it. I was able to control it better before the unsightly strangers began to mass in

Hammerhead Park to idiotically thump away on their bongos. The staccato drumbeat persistence was almost constant now. I detected an acid of racial scorn in my malice, and was ashamed. Yet I somehow found myself reaching for my shotgun, relic of that awful time when a nightmare came alive to visit death on my neighbors over the canal.

With workers' bungalows now obscuring the serene house that could seduce me once to delusiveness, my sunstruck reveries just took me on creative flights of mind. But the haze of swampy doldrums came to have more of its original effect on me in the torment of the drums. When they shattered my abstractions of the afternoon, an obsessive mania stole close to damaging my brain like Nazi gunfire again. Daydreams floated me over the water to the war again, to myself lying dead of gunshot again. A sniper had killed me the day we rolled over the river Rhine.

I always thought of myself that way, wiped out till they wiped me in again by presenting me with the bullet from my brain for a souvenir as I lay blind and comatose. Little by little they brought my vision back from zero to a functional blur. But they never gave me back the trench knife someone stole from my body. Violated once more, I would see myself rise with that sleek weapon safe in my hand again, to stalk every trespass on my life right to the persecuting drummers in the park.

Afraid I might act out those murderous impulses as I used to my obsessions, I contemplated wisely getting myself out of earshot. What with increased property values, selling the Pinebrake house would enable me to build a really superior one on the bay acre I acquired from Faith that year of my conflicting urges to help Majosee and advance myself with her adversaries.

But now, in the same mire of contradiction, I was reluctant to abandon Pinebrake. I wanted my familiar workshop to roam in among the files and memories. Even though my children's family was asunder, I wanted that house to be their rock, as the house of our next mayor's childhood was still his. I had always envied Barry Christian that security.

*   *   *

Bahayma came to mind whenever the bongos kept me from my work. Their rhythms always threatened to set off the same beat in my head and induce seizure. I could accomplish little until they fell silent, hours after midnight. Idiotic drummers had me on the night shift.

One evening Honey Baines phoned just as the bongos started. Upset, she protested that no one was being responsive to Seminole complaints about industrial activity all over Big Cypress driving throngs of swamp derelicts onto the reservation. Then said she had a petition for equal rights legislation that she wanted endorsed by men as well as women of distinguished professional standing.

"Women are supposed to drink like fish for promotion," she came over to plead at my bar, "and submit to humiliation, so when men become aware there's a light in the tunnel, so to speak."

So to speak, I thought, would set women back a hundred years. But I saw a light in the tunnel of her mouth, and the children were staying at their mother's, so I patiently explored Honey's cacology about obligatory company parties and other degradations women had to endure for their only chance at job promotion.

"Do I understand you're forced to drink?" I asked over some Chinese food I had suggested she bring. "And to endure ribaldry, and submit to even worse in utter humiliation? But you want the freedom to drink all you please, to make bawdy jokes and advances of your own, and to submit without humiliation?"

Honey had trouble comprehending me in the bongos, and I comprehended little from her. But a woman under forty was a budding flower in my goldening country club. So I let her drink and petition me suggestively and joke around all night.

I was just coming to trust the rain of good things, Marissa, when the simple beauty of life began pouring.

Hillary was as happy as I'd ever dreamt she could be, working to rival the great Windgate Museum with the newer Brisburn. So I accused her of having driven Tate crazy at last, and she smiled demurely, as at a compliment. So I confronted her with

the fact that Marissa no longer stood between us, and she said Tate was taking her to Europe that week. It had taken me all those years to realize she was something of a nitwit. I just couldn't decide if that was what qualified her to be the museum's curator or if being curator had made a nitwit out of her. One only had to observe the catholic juxtaposing of genius with banality in most museums to realize that practically all curators were nitwits. Still, I agreed to host the Monet show she hoped soon to mount, since I held the same hope regarding her.

It was not bad having the publisher of the *Times* as my good friend living with me off and on at her place or mine. Hers was a professionally decorated but livable duplex on Keyport Park Avenue, where plane trees shaded the benches. Her manner was appreciative, due to a fear of men that she attributed to her tragic first taste of sex the night of the Bayfront fire. Her presence was unobtrusive, due to liberation and incomprehensibility. Her body was superb, a model of bashful preservation that spoke well for early wrath. She just talked too much when we made love.

I didn't mind her telling me what to do in her enthusiastic spirit of discovery. That was the sexual revolution. It was just that I could seldom make out what she wanted. When Freud reached the same conclusion about women in total, he may have had no more than an incoherence problem with the whole opposite sex.

One afternoon Honey came home and woke me from my sleep. She was depressed over Bill Fenneran's pretense, in reacting to her phone call, that he could not grasp what she was saying about the Indians. At length he quit stalling and said there was no way to stop or reduce the oil drilling unilaterally, and advised her to see if his father would consult the other companies about some sort of readjustment when he returned from abroad.

I said Bill was one of the finest people I knew, but nobody cared about anything in Great Gulf Glade, and told her to relax with a bath while I telephoned the Council President to see if he cared. The Fennerans were in Europe, exploring ruins and

relics of antiquity, and Barry was in Keyport Station, the ornate city hall that went by its old railroad name to memorialize our own relic of antiquity. We rarely met any longer, now that his wife did her consciousness raising with Marissa Harnett, not Kogen.

Barry would occasionally telephone on some pretext to show me I was not forgotten and could reach him whenever I wished. When he took my call, I pretended not to hear his greeting and made him repeat it. I persisted in blaming the clatter of the drums.

"Cut it out, Gabe. How come you never call me? Afraid I'm too busy? A City Council to run? An election? Nah."

"You have strikes, budget crises. You have noise pollution going off on innocent taxpayers like drums in their heads."

"The tom-toms again. Yeah, people are complaining all over the east end. Hammerhead. Armistead."

"Pinebrake. They're effectively putting me out of business."

"Oh, Gabe. We have a bit of a culture conflict on our hands. Blacks on the Council like your friend Bowie Pratt are defending the right. Or should I say the left?"

"I'll try to hold my breath till you and Bowie resolve the question. Is it the same swamp rats that are invading the Indians, and is there any way to help the reservation?"

"Swamp's a county matter, Gabe. How are the boys? I understand Toby's a real tennis flash."

"Right, right. And oil-drilling companies operate out of city-zoned buildings. How are the girls?"

"They're all fine. Emmy's with Lissa right now at the library. And oil drilling is licensed by the state."

"You can help the Indians if you want to take the trouble."

"Listen, soldier, it's more serious than you think."

"How do you know how serious I think it is? The invasion of Seminole privacy is outrageous, and this assault on my very own ears is worse. Who are those swamp people?"

"They're extremely primitive. I don't know where they came from into the swamp, and I'm afraid to speculate. Tolstadt views the police posture in this as one of avoiding riots now and real assaults later. Like housebreaking, juvenile violence. Rape."

History touched his voice, an Indian girl persecuted by people —her own included—of goodwill and constructive drives. "Dexter says he lacks the manpower to enforce the laws of trespass for the reservation. And to be very frank, Gabe, there just isn't enough public concern to back up a call for troops from Fort Copeland."

"And you're not about to drum up any and distract the public at election time."

Barry sighed. "Gabe, I'm expecting Tate back next week. We're anxious to consider that exchange you had with Josie and her son some years ago. Would you like to join us with the Mayor?"

"No. And stop calling me Gabe. Don't you know it sounds political to speak someone's name so much? I've taken all the punishment I can for submitting to my public spirit. I want no part of that anymore. You run your workshop and I'll run mine."

"See what I mean about public backing?"

Winter was the wrong season for it, the slough runs were too shallow to hide the victims of slaughter. The floating bodies of men and women snagged in the fishing lines of sportsmen and piled up against the drainage pumps and oil rigs. Donny heard about it from his brother. Bill suspected the Indians of killing swamp derelicts who intruded on the reservation. But there was no possible way of ever proving a thing like that.

My friends were Donny's too, so at his wedding one sunny Buenaventura afternoon they met the Publisher (as all of them referred to Honey). Her conjugal relation to me made the groom's aunt blush and his mother pale. His father was occupied buying an upstate newspaper from the bride's. Her mother had friends who were polluting the artistic quality of Glade, including a TV producer who thought it captivating to ask audaciously how I ever understood what Honey was saying.

"I just smile when she smiles," I replied, not smiling at this smiley, scalpy Milton Kindbor. He had a solid reputation for plagiarism, and I had no interest in sharing with him my discov-

ery that Ms. Baines could be comprehensible. She was, after all, a gifted journalist. That equipped her to recount anything effected in the past. The present, however, was too close upon her to sort out, and the future just outraced her mind.

"Hold it, hold it," Baldy Haverstraw said when Kindbor tried to join our lawn table for cocktails. "Let's face it, baldness is all we have in common."

I heard bongos in my head. It made me sad to see even a known welsher like Kindbor slink away in such mortification, it made me feel as low as rejection by Marissa had, it made me see an iridescence pulsating in my truncated perimeter of vision. I resented being tipped over the brink toward seizure by sympathy for a person of Kindbor's ilk. The man's a *bahayma*, I thought, and took an extra phenobarbital.

"They stripped down the plumbing parts from an entire construction site," Honey said after her first sip. Something stagy about her apartment always inclined me to have martinis ready at her return home on days that I was driven there to work out my compositions far from the bongo torture. "It was going to be a school for handicapped children, but they surely put an end to that. No funds left to replace the spigots and what-all those awful nigger boys stole."

"Say Swamptown boys."

"They're not, in their filthy rags they aimlessly loiter in."

"What's that, Honey? I didn't understand that."

"Oh, shoot, they're swamp rats. They sleep in the marsh. They also beat up and robbed a sickle-cell anemia patient today."

"What race was the victim?"

"Black. A Negress. They don't care what color."

"Who's they, Honey?"

"Them. Whatever they are. Let's eat in tonight."

They. A breed apart, whoever they were. They came on cats' feet, unnoticed at first. Then, as if overnight, we were infested with a destructive rabble from the wilderness. The fabulous revitalization of habitat was civilizing the population just as Fenneran had hoped, when jungle people stole

into every corner of the swampside and ranged deeper west. They were changing the polished aspect of the city with spray paint. Graffiti covered the benches in parks and avenues. It ridiculed the monuments to heroes, and smeared entire store windows with strange alphabetical designs. Not in my time here had anyone heard so many sirens wailing through the nights, not since the Bayfront slum was redeveloped. They fought each other with knives. They broke into shops for all they could carry off. They swarmed in Hammerhead Park, lining the footpaths to rest their beer cans on the buff limestone walls. They clustered in the groves with their bongos, wiping out my work days. Evenings were no better. Tom-toms, as Barry once called them, thumped away into the dark late hours. The pasting and construction, which could not be done at Honey's, I had to execute around dawn.

Dexter complained that he was too occupied with crime to do much about small matters like noise. They had just murdered poor Guy Helker, who had never harmed a soul but Majosee and me.

Like human vampires in dread of the Cross, *bahaymas* never came to such places of culture as the Brisburn Museum and few Glade denizens ever sought the pleasures of its gardens. To discuss the Claude Monet show Hillary enfolded me in the romantic dusk of nooks and promenades full of towering art.

We were alone when night fell. She whispered my name with a shiver. In one moon-dappled bower we enjoyed a statue of gentle planes, where I learned how familial was the passion of her sister for desktops and office commodes. Oh lips, the tiny bikini Hillary whisked away, the flush of excitement that kept her so young. I dwelt on my fear of her husband to stem my nervous haste. Oh, the broad moonlit alabaster of her magic, one could feel one's life rippling away and slipping back in opposite directions.

Oh at last, at last I had Hillary Brisburn Fenneran's sweet bird. But I wished it were my wife's.

Divorcees of the world, he's crazy but go back to him.

*   *   *

They came with filth and lived that way in flour sacks and old bedsheets or just as slovenly in the apparel they contrived to steal. The men never shaved, the women went uncombed. They spoke in an awkward dialect no one else could quite understand, and communicated with each other in loud vulgarities. They were abominable to hear and worse to see, yet I often found myself defending the *bahaymas*, resisting Honey and Hoby and anyone else who generalized about them as criminal or odious.

They had no regard for self-improvement or family bounds. Tracked down for shoplifting or burglary, they were sometimes uncovered in the act of fornicating with relatives that included siblings and parents. But logic insisted there had to be some who never burglarized or drummed on bongos or profaned against nature.

Right on Pine Ridge Road they forced a crippled man to watch them sodomize his sixty-year-old wife. Yet I argued in their behalf against Bill Fenneran and Marissa Harnett and everyone who said exactly what I usually felt about them. My pity for Guy Helker was sick with personal guilt over striking back at a miserable halfwit like him, but I protested that the pair apprehended hatcheting him to death should not be regarded as an example of them all. In the process I completely eliminated myself as a voice of protest against their atrocious bongos.

I was too busy seeing that nobody got away with accusing them of stealing at every chance and never working till the need became desperate. Because some of them did get menial jobs and took up permanent residence in Swamptown. And the whole thing just sounded too much like the prejudice of fifteen years ago against the Negroes.

Nor did I feel right calling them *bahaymas*, though everybody did by the time the first to do so was a hundred years old.

Carl Meyerberger's centennial was a municipal event. Now that he was close to death, the leading citizens came from their country homes to be seen tolerating him on TV. The cameras found them celebrating, plush with all I knew about them, all over his gently sprawling lawns on Seashell Key.

The smiles were rabid. My talkative newslady had admitted that these people strode rough-shod over the world by the grace of Tate Fenneran, who, by licensing them to prey, controlled them like the children all people were to him.

Clint Bocaleon milked utility customers by counterfeiting fuel costs and swallowing tax rebates for his company. Judge Cheatham cheated widows and orphans by skimming legal fees paid to his relatives and associates from his Surrogate Court. Bill Dildress gouged excessive rents from workers housed in the bungalows of his widespread realty developments. I could imagine them all exulting in the words of a TV director I had heard just the night before, stimulating his crew as it filmed a commercial across the Pinebrake canal: "Shove it up their ass!"

I could imagine Claude Monet shouting it too. The Brisburn Museum's grand exhibition of his works had been a scandal. The language of art had plainly said fraud. I could not condone such pretentious sham, but had given my word to host the gala opening with Mrs. Fenneran, so I simply had to expose it.

Every kind of important person came. Many thought I was Monet, familiarly calling me Claude in their praise. Milton Kindbor called the show great, with a beaming smile that called his TV shows greater. I told him none of the paintings was really by the late artist; he flattered me with laughter and offered me a part in his latest situation comedy.

When I told my VA psychiatrist that every one of the hundreds of works had to be by a Monet student or servant, he said he could give me an hour on Tuesdays and Thursdays.

I told Marge Christian it was beyond the great French painter to counterfeit morning mists of the woodland by means of a milky surface veneer, or to forge the delicacy of a Japanese bridge with curdled house paint. She promised to tell Barry, but instead brought me Marissa, whom I asked, "Why would Monet have maintained three huge studios on the estate of his thriving old age, if not to sign mass-produced daubs while laughing at the dilettantes who bought them after spurning his impecunious youth?"

She said, "To keep a different mistress in each studio," her eyes flashing a pent anger that told me she still cared, even

before she added, "because some men are like children. They just can't believe in anything good until they taste it."

I was encouraged when Donny showed up with his wife. But art had left him, I discovered when he laughed in my face and said I must be crazy to think the great galleries of America, which had lent his mother that plethora of works, could be so roundly duped. Only Baldy Haverstraw could be persuaded that the paintings were all spurious: he volunteered to burn down the Brisburn Museum.

I rejected that only because of Marissa, whom I couldn't seem to find at Meyerberger's celebration. Had I let Baldy do it, half these racketeers, including Tate, would not be here. Honey herself, though she worshiped Tate as a demigod, had told me he owned a broad percentage of votes with which to command these politicians through nothing more respectable than old Bayfronters whose pit-fighting interests depended on his state-wide protection. But he had helped her advance as a person rather than sex object, and Honey enjoyed an uncomplicated view of life that distinguished between good and evil strictly in terms of how she was personally served.

"You can't help liking the man," I always told her, and not entirely as a sarcasm.

The champion buzzard of them all arrived, our erstwhile congressman, Bo Traggan, currently a lobbyist for overseas interests with State Senator Fairboro's support. Two barefaced crooks. Carl said he would never forget Bo solemnly asking him for campaign funds to help promote democracy, and I believed him, having heard the story a dozen times myself. Though he sat shrunken to the size of a child in his wheelchair, the old man seemed as sound in mind and uneven in wit as ever.

"Money is honey," he said to entertain the Publisher. "I used to think so. Now I think Honey is money. Don't laugh."

To rescue her I said, "You used to think money was funny and Christian was Jewish."

"Yeah, yeah. I used to be senile, but I got over it."

His grandchildren laughed, but his children were old and only smiled politely. I saw Phyllis Chalfonte roll her eyes upward to signal she knew how boring her grandpa must seem. I

wondered what anyone ever got out of fawning on the world with such gratuitous ingratiation. Deejay was at least subtle in that; I didn't have to love her less for replying, when a Meyerberger scion asked, that Nola was teaching school in an Albuquerque blue-collar district with the ignorance of bigotry mired deep in its grain.

Dexter said, "Like she never left Glade. Right, Carl?"

"Never mind."

"I just said something smart."

"If you said something smart, you changed."

His great-grandchildren laughed. His grandchildren were too old for caustic banter, and only smiled at the gathering media crews. I left Honey to meddle there and drifted over to the Brisburn table of Fennerans and Kearnys just as Tate's sons got up to follow him away. A chilly glance from Hillary sent me off with them. She had managed to interpret my exposure of the Monet fraud as a disparagement of the master's actual genius, but I had never known her to bear a grudge so long.

Her mother cut me with the same gelid glance, but Jennifer earnestly whispered something I missed as Donny said to his father, "I know the airport's drained and ready to go—"

"Then you should know I can't stop it."

Bill said, "The Indians are just killing those derelicts that stray onto their land."

I got into it saying, "They asked both Glade and Key to hold those people off, but nobody cared about an overrun reservation."

"Did you care," Fenneran faced me to ask, "when I tried to stop this pollution at its source? Did the Sheriff?"

I said, "You can't mean Josie's the source of all these—"

"Monsters," he said quite soberly. "A breed worse than I anticipated back then. I tried to convince the environmentalists, everybody, that she had to be sterilized. Only Barry had the common good sense to weigh the danger in her bitter hatred."

Don glanced quizzically between us. Bill said, "The flooding from blocked sewers after a rain is nothing less than monstrous."

*　　*　　*

The future Mayor of Gulf Glade approached the TV taping of centenarian Meyerberger to review spheres of power with Fenneran. I saw Judge Wilmont smiling, his scalp aglint in a cloud-breaking flash of sun that soon faded. These men really were all gangsters. I realized each one of them had his own array of power, which merged only sometimes with the other's.

Fenneran's extensive complex ebbed and flowed in constant fluctuation according to his skillful manipulation of events. Bill probably had a political mob of his own, though I doubted that about Don. Dexter sure as hell did. I could tell from his resistance to Fenneran in the past. And the presence of taciturn, cold Price Fenton at a party like this told me he was a bargaining element of Polsen's in the coming election.

"It's all mine own teeth," Meyerberger said for audio. "I paid every cent on delivery." Everybody laughed. Sparkling, he added, "This year my company gave up ladies. Because the directors forgot what to do." The laughter increased. He searched for the black face of the sound girl and in his waning voice said, "I'd like better to say *bahaymas*," while the mini-camera recorded the last sight of him that remained to us. "We had our own *bahaymas*. We never liked them. Every Jew on the earth is a citizen of Israel except our *bahaymas*. Not allowed. Can't come in, the crooks and murderers. The black people, they protect their *bahaymas*. Call them brothers. So go respect them." The media stayed with him, presumably to edit later as desired. "They'll soon see what brothers. Right away they'll find out."

The black girl held steady on the mike, a good media soldier brightly smiling, not mortified like all the whispering onlookers. At the edge of the crowd around the crew, Marge was overseeing the careful work of a woman putting makeup on Barry. "The bahaymas," I heard him tell Fenneran, "are people blind to the intrinsic wonders of life. But I can't say anything like that on the air."

Marge looked like a secret Barry was sworn to keep. And he like hers. They shared a private confidence. How rare that was. What fun in life. Marissa had said it didn't matter, finally, if my blindness to intrinsic good was congenital or a result of war

wounds. Like a child, I would always have to take a lick at simple beauty to believe it. That was the major reason she left me with the secret I had to keep that during our marriage the only beauty I ever really touched to believe was poor disfigured Josie.

I looked for my wife with sobs of longing. Where could she be with the children? "It doesn't matter what bahaymas are," Tate was reacting, in his voice an impatient quaver that surprised me. "What counts is what they do. Unto others, not just themselves."

Something was wrong. Emmy Christian had it in her sky blue eyes, coming under the sycamores as the camera found her father and the media crew obscured him, drawing the crowd around.

"Lissa," Emmy said, and searched for a way to put what she had to add. Her kid sisters were both kissing Tate, his chauffeur Alf closely watching. "She didn't want to leave Marissa, Gabe."

"Come on! Out with it, out with it, what's wrong?"

"It's Hoby, Gabe. He might have scabies."

That was nothing to laugh about, so I turned away to laugh, glad to hear Emmy say next my boys were safely playing tennis somewhere. "The way they're spray-painting this city," Fenneran said, "is like the willful, mean desecration of a shrine."

I said, "I can stand graffiti better than the bongos."

"All of it must end," Tate responded. "They absolutely must be stopped from this degrading of our—"

"Habitat," the Sheriff said behind Meyerberger's wheelchair under the windy vast sky.

"They are committing murder," Fenneran said, "and worse."

We all glanced at each other, some of us back a decade to monsters. The sun drew sharp lines from Tate's eyes. In praise of him, Honey used to ask if I ever heard of a bank robbery in Gulf Glade, or prostitution, or any other hint of organized crime. She no longer asked, because all of it was happening in disorganized bahayma fashion, with any number of other crimes more sophisticated than ordinary street depredations and sadistic assaults.

I asked Price Fenton if bahaymas were continuing to commit sodomies and other sexual abominations. He replied with a sim-

ple nod, and added, "Lam Cordhall been murdered out on Cape Tulip. Scalped. Like Chuck and Guy."

Fenneran said, "I can't believe the smiling amenities around us, as if this insidious pestilence is not growing worse, and to everybody's conscious knowledge."

"Did anybody scream in the street," the old man piped in his wheelchair, "that Hitler was alive in the world?"

A silence fell among us. Into it laughter floated from the TV taping crowd. I didn't know Guy Helker had been scalped. I thought bahaymas were caught hacking him. I thought I was dreaming. Long ago I thought Fenneran had brought the problem of Josie to me alone, and only now it came clear that I was just one more among all the clowns he had tried to alert against monsters.

Did he honestly believe the bahaymas were Josie's offspring? And did my natural skepticism reflect shortsightedness? I didn't know how to take him. Or his kin of wanton Brisburns. He said, "This country is feebleminded."

The sun came out on us all.

Snide and swaggering, they started to affect the most egregious concoctions of clothing style in which to shout obscenities at one another from all the mall benches. To see them strutting with beer cans around their bongo players, conglomerating unkempt in garish stripes and plaids, one almost wished they would revert to the foul, muddy rags they brought with them out of the swamp.

They crowded the jails. Yet their vicious outrages multiplied beyond the power of civil control. Unsolved crimes were laid to them. Although gain was their purpose most often, they were identified in Great Gulf Glade by inhuman crimes of brutality, of sheer meanness, and set apart universally as bahaymas.

Under the unwashed muck of the swamp, some captured felons were perceived to be more Indian than black. On TV news I saw a grinning pair that seemed Oriental. Arraigned for hurling acid at children in Hammerhead Park to steal their bicycles, they spoke in the crude jargon of bahaymas. So did a housebreaker who, in custody for shoving an old woman to her

death from a tenth-story window, was unmistakably white. He
had raped the victim first.

Another bahayma, with blond hair, murdered three children
in their sleep at a girls' camp. After that, even Terry Peacham
quit insinuating color into the crimes. Their skin tones definitely were various; their abuses were peculiarly bahayma. No
Negro violator had ever been cited for throwing down a tomb-
stone, or defecating at the door of a church. Blacks as well as
others who stooped to such abysmal animal depths always
turned out to have the speech patterns of bahaymas from the
jungles of the swamp.

Yet Negroes of Armistead Hammock and the bungalows of
Pinebrake continued to give refuge to bahaymas evading arrest.
Even after two such fugitives threw a six-year-old black out of
a high window and slashed his grandfather's throat while rifling
the sanctuary that poor old man had provided them.

My middle age flowered in Buttonwood Levee. I was young
again on the open sea. Fishing and dining and laughing on the
new boat Honey bought us, I did my best to appreciate the
happy days with her more than I had the rich devotion I lost
with Marissa. And taking similar pains, Honey grew more coherent.

At plays and movies, at the opera and ballet, her judgments
were astute, her interpretations sometimes brilliant. We swam
at Banana Beach, often with my children. Honey loved to take
them afterward to Big Cypress Amusement Park or the dog
races. We even took in jai alai, which excited her so when the
gambling paid off that I reaped the sparks at home.

She stayed there most of the time, as the children tended not
to. I saw them more than ever that way. With Marissa. And
Hoby. He never came down with scabies, but did reveal one
enormous aptitude for hypochondria, and an even greater one
for histrionics, sometimes falling into the persona of Moses,
suddenly, or Peer Gynt, without a touch of makeup.

On our motorized sloop we took them all out from the marina.
One weekend we sailed down to Key West just to snoop around.
Nothing existed there that Gulf Glade lacked. We took our

friends out too, with their wives and families. Thank God no-
body sang. Great Gulf Glade filled my cup from the Tarkey
Meadow Sports Complex to the stake matches down Wildcat
End, and all the galleries of Keyport that led to the Brisburn
Museum in Buttonwood Levee.

My work lured viewers and collectors there. My fame was in
the newspapers. Honey radiated good cheer in her glistening
teeth and grateful eyes. I enjoyed her alluring clothes. I expanded in her glow. But my cup ran over when Lissa told me
she was in love. Since she was little, I had never met a friend of
hers I didn't like, boy or girl. So it bothered me not in the least
that her young man's mother was good old Phyllis Chalfonte. I
was only glad I had grown up in time to resist the notion of
seducing her back when mourning over Loker made her ripe
with loss.

A girl in Bayfront Park was doused with gasoline and ignited
to die there. Passersby saw three bahaymas running away from
the blaze in laughter. A pretty TV newswoman said so on my
workshop screen before she smiled to add, "On a happier note,
the threatening bus drivers' strike is near settlement tonight."

Reporting a fire in Cedar Ridge, she called it vengeful arson
by bahaymas. That was Councilman Bowie Pratt's district. So
was Armistead Hammock, where a new school for disruptive
children was being dedicated on my TV screen with scenes of
the spacious grounds and the multicolored faces of the students.
Boys and girls, black and white and whatever, they all looked
alike to me with their hollow bahayma grins.

"They do not all look alike," Bowie came on to say as if
reading my mind and the communal one as well. He had cul-
tivated a mustache and wore bolder glasses now. Into the mike
he said, "Some are tall, some are short. There are fat ones and
thin ones, average and bright ones, just as there are among the
rest of us."

He expressed flat resentment of the term bahayma applied to
distinguish not only criminals but even those who, finding
work, abandoned Swamptown and the thatched lean-to shelters
of the marsh. He was voicing my very argument the evening

past with Honey, yet I had no sympathy for the indignation he displayed while working bahaymas took their leisure outside my home to keep anyone else from working in their clattering clamor of tom-toms. Bowie sounded false and tedious, yet I was bound to defend his position against others again and again.

The young newswoman announced more stories to come after a station break, late developments in the trial of a salesman alleged to have murdered the housewife he raped while robbing a Tarkey bridge party, the arrest of ten Bay Slope boys for clubbing some homosexuals who roamed their park, the death of Patrolman Brick Murphy in a bombing incident at the airport under construction. A yogurt commercial followed, with jingle singers costumed in silly joviality. To think a nation's taste accepted that convinced me Fenneran was right and we were feebleminded indeed.

Then came a newsbreak to precede the promised items. Late last night, three women were raped in an industrial park office and grotesquely murdered. There were no further details.

I dreaded learning them when the Publisher got home. I checked to see that all the doors were locked. I telephoned Marissa to ask if our children were safe.

COLLAGE 16

The Mayor's wife believed no human being should ever be
called an animal. It was one of her many sentimentalities. Barry
told me so to stir my self-doubts by saying she reminded him of
me. But I was too fond of Marge to be bothered by the compari-
son.

We were getting ready for the inception of some new commissioners at Keyport Station. I had helped select them as a member
of his official planning board, fully aware he had invited my
participation on a hope that I could talk Donny into serving as
Police Commissioner. When my effort failed, I asked Barry
never to involve me in civic affairs again.

I reminded him of that. Seated at his elaborate desk between
the state and national flags, he said, "You placed yourself at the
center of involvement forever one day on the Gulf of Mexico."

That reference to my admission years ago still stung, though
I told him the fight with my conscience was over, Seminole
philosophy was my salvation at last. When the sight of red-

headed bahaymas in custody made me breathless with guilt, I decided once and for all to blame every mistake and misdeed of my life on the corrupt twin of my righteous soul, even the unlikely possibility that I was the forefather of numberless bahaymas.

That was when he threw Marge up to me as an example of my bewildering sentimentality. "Nobody can believe the violence one sees in the TV news. Twenty-five fruit pickers buried by one murderous bahayma. Two others torch a priest for interfering in the rape of a nun. To see such felons laughing at the camera next, you just can't think of them as human beings. Then why, why do you argue when people just as horrified as you call them animals?"

I didn't know what to say, so I said, "Because you cage them like animals before proving them guilty beyond a doubt."

Barry rose, handsome as a movie star. "The jails are packed with repeaters, born criminals, because we simply can't hire sufficient judges to try them."

"You can if you fire the party hacks that Met funds support."

"Now you sound like Donny. He resigned from my law firm just to address that very issue. A sensitive position I may have to fill with my playboy nephew."

"Fill it with Lissa," I jumped up to say.

He met that with a broad grin, one hand on the elegant brass doorknob of his office door. "Want to deal?"

"You can go to . . . what's the deal?"

In reply he opened the door, and in a flurry of white faces came the black one of Councilman Pratt in his glinting eyeglasses. Bowie grabbed my arm as Barry grabbed my other one, and they escorted me down the corridor like someone who might try to break free as soon as Bowie said, "See Junn for us."

Young thugs were taking over entire schools in Bowie's districts. I didn't know that until he told me so on the way downstairs, with Barry greeting lackeys to stave them off. Money was being extorted from students for passage through the halls in Pinebrake and other desegregated boroughs that bahaymas had reached. I thanked goodness for Marissa, who had long ago

transferred the second of our four kids still in lower education to a shore school.

Where we gathered for the swearing in of Price Fenton as Commissioner of Police, Bowie told me the bahaymas themselves were uneducable. The Sojourner Truth School for disruptive children would be a joke if it were not an institute for the training of future terrorists. "I'm just glad we didn't name it after Martin Luther King, Jr."

He crossed himself right there in the antechamber crowd of politicians, a man as agnostic as me, so I crossed myself too in Martin's name and said, "Then why are you always defending them in the media? Just for the headlines and exposure?"

"If I don't speak up for them, I lose my constituents fast as clicking a light switch. Lose them, and I can't help them."

"Or yourself." It amazed me how barefaced every politician was. "I know how you guys think. I watched him for years."

I indicated Barry, who was leading everyone into the Council Chamber, Polsen smiling with other dignitaries heading for the rostrum, just an entrenched old Sheriff now, getting his man the city peace-keeping commission for whatever it meant to him politically. Some of my best friends were whores. I wasn't about to let them make one out of me even to launch my precocious firstborn into prominence as Barry's advocate at the company in which, as Mayor, he could no longer legally participate.

"You may have watched him," Bowie said, "but you sure haven't heard him. Barry's a sincere public servant, Gabe, and so am I."

"Yeah? So how come you send me to Junn? I don't even know why anyone should go wherever he is. But in any case, you'd be the logical one, you're his old buddy."

"He turned me down, and named you. The only one he trusts not to shoot him in the back. I'm the big sellout to him."

"Want the truth, Bowie? To me too."

I turned to go. He caught my arm. "You've got no cause to say that, but this is no time to argue the point. You coming in?"

"Every time I get Barry to forgive me for having a plate in my skull, he starts tapping on it. Now you're doing it."

"Gabe," he said, chasing after me, "it's of the utmost impor-

tance. She's living in Swamptown, preaching mad sermons to the bahaymas. I doubt they understand anything, but they revere her. Haven't you noticed they even talk like Josie?"

The shock was physical. It seemed impossible that bogs and forests full of people could reflect the mutilated tongue and mind of one woman. But I could not deny the similarity.

I had stayed above the suspicion taking hold around here that the whole pestilential breed was Josie's spawn out of five rapists and a crocodile, and out of swamp fugitives of every race in succeeding generations. There were actually growing numbers of people who speculated with that fantastic view—at Fenneran's instigation, I believed. It was based on the single essential that crocodilians of every species reached procreative maturity at six or seven years of age. That accounted for the mature look of Loker Brisburn's killer five years ago. It threatened my stability right now. I took a phenobarbital.

Bowie said, "Somebody's got to remind Junn he's black and tell him in spite of what black people think bahaymas are not black. They went to the Seminoles and got themselves dumped in the slough, so they tried the blacks and found them easy. Tell Junn bahaymas prey on black loyalty, the way Josie preyed on his. Tell him Chopka's teaching them to plunder and kill."

"Not me. I'm not telling him. Who's Chopka?"

"Muddabudda."

It shook me to my soul. Because I knew. It came crashing back together all at once. They spoke her crippled tongue. "Muddabudda" was the honorific "mother's brother," used for Josie's actual brother, Chitto Jumper's nominal grandson.

"Chopka," Bowie said with icy animosity, "is their warlord."

"I'm not boating into any swamp to find Junn."

Bowie said the old black man seemed the only one Josie was ever bound to heed with anything approaching reason. And if she refused or proved unable to goad those ugly hordes away, then Junn must come and preach the truth to all the widespread black community—that blacks numbered largest among the victims of bahaymas, and must stop protecting them.

I said that seemed ridiculous. Who was Junn any longer to the black people, many of whom were from out of state? He was just

a marsh native sixty-five or older, who had probably not set foot in the city for twenty years. People would ridicule his swamp accent and laugh at his rags, without the first notion of his depth, wisdom, and vision of mind.

Bowie waited for some people to go by, and said, "Every Negro would recognize his strength of soul and believe him at once. Like we all did Martin Luther King." He crossed himself again. So did I, which I had never done for Jesus, the most crucified member of my own tribe. "I believe that, Gabe. It's the only hope we have. We're trying to avoid severe official measures that would make you as well as me ashamed."

He was giving me the business, good old persuasion with a curve or two. I resisted, though I knew Fenneran had the power to enforce harsh city measures against all bahaymas, guilty or not. I refused to believe they stemmed from Majosee via animal myth, though I had no answer for the mystery of their presence in the Everglades, so close by without detection, likely for generations and maybe centuries. An agnostic could live without knowing. I refused to go into the swamp after Junn.

Great Gulf Glade was stunned by the news that five bahaymas captured in the Key Industrial Park atrocities never reached the jailhouse, but were killed in a shootout when they seized a police officer's revolver and fled into the pine woods at Barrens End Road. Civil libertarians thought it incredible that none of the policemen was hurt, and expressed flat doubts about the whole story. Among them Chief Judge Harmon Wilmont was the most outspoken in the press, and people began to take sides on the issue of police policy under the new commissioner.

Out of the contentious developments a very tough young civil rights attorney emerged as a partisan of criminal bahaymas. He regarded them as human beings damaged by the inequities of a ruthless commercial society whose depredations had driven them from their indigenous habitat. This ardent lawyer was Donald Brisburn Fenneran. He and associated counselors left the lesser violations like burglary and shoplifting to government-provided legal defense, and took on the serious cases of violent mugging, rape, and murder.

The reactions were strong enough to Don's courtroom argument that the brutes who threw acid at children to steal their bikes were themselves children a civilized society must care for as sick unfortunates in the polyglot family of man. But even our friends the artists, liberals all, were no less than shocked by his defense of the bahayma who had murdered sleeping children at a girls' camp.

Someone had to defend them, he told his father. I myself found it unbearable when he took the case of the three who had raped a girl and laughed while burning her alive.

The Fennerans just took themselves off to Europe again, mostly in pursuit of his business affairs. Personally, I was glad. I admired Tate's ingenuity but feared his ruthlessness: he was sure to destroy me one day over his wife. As for Hillary, I had no patience for the chaste curator's mien she was refining, and she seemed without further need to redeem her long-ago risk of my life, after using me as an atonement object on a statue, a fender, and her own sister's Byzantine Saint Peter's chair.

I just hoped she and Tate would return in time for Lissa's wedding. I looked forward to seeing my parents there too, the families of my sisters and brothers. But I worried about bahaymas. With the likes of Donny ready to defend them, they had taken to robbing people at gunpoint in their homes, as well as their stores or offices, and lingering to rape and torture.

In sunny Courthouse Square, after he pleaded the Cedar Ridge arsonists incompetent to stand trial, I told him the wedding was to be a modest one on my own Sunset Bayou grounds, though Justin's people preferred something more in the tradition of the groom's great-grandfather. I said, "Carl Meyerberger loved the grand old American splash he learned from your grandfather." That reminder of Loker's murder by a bahayma seemed to quicken Don's gait, and we scattered pigeons as I hastened after him saying, "But Justin wants it Lissa's way. At her father's new house when it's completed. They both imagine that to be my sentiment."

"Whereas you wish the Chalfontes had been graceless enough to insist on having it their Meyerberger way."

I was not about to let him twist away that crudely. "It's not

like you to state the obvious, Don. Construction is taking longer than I think I can endure Pinebrake. I see them with their bongos now. They're moving in across my canal, those bungalows. Grinning savages, who have reduced me to that natural inertia no artist can resist without continuous struggle."

"Then why are you always arguing in their defense?" He sought no reply, answering that himself. "For the same reason I do in court. To protect individual rights, the most important principle of justice in a free society."

Thereafter I took the individual right, over his objections, to pace my wharf with the shotgun to let them know I owned one. But it never won me respite from the imbecilic drumming. I was returning the gun to my workshop, one evening, when a car drove up. Bowie Pratt got out, his glasses white in the floodlights.

"Tell Junn," he said across the driveway. "Tell him a fifteen-year-old was just shot. A black girl of fifteen was shot dead by black bahaymas on a joy ride. Walking with her black friends in Armistead Hammock. Tell him she was my girl. His old friend Bowie's littlest."

I almost suffocated in Bowie's grief. But I had four kids of my own to protect from the very kind of bereavement he was suffering. So I insisted the new Police Commissioner was closer to Junn and Josie than I had ever been. Bowie said the years had swept that away, it was no longer so. He even admitted that Junn had chosen me in the belief I lacked the nerve to pull a gun and shoot him. I wept with Bowie. We held each other's hands like children in a game. But I said no, and he left in mortal despair.

At Connie Pratt's funeral, I whispered to Christian in our pew that it was all very well for Fenneran to start a superstition taking hold and then leave for Europe, but conjectures not worthy of reasonable people ill became the Mayor. Barry confessed suffering moments of estrangement from familiar sanity. Still, Shawn Hogan, the realistic scholar of sociobiology, had told him in the presence of the Sheriff's ironical smile that life held

more surprises than were ever dreamt in heaven or hell.
The preacher was making everybody weep. I said, "If Junn
agreed he has something to say, why is it not to Price Fenton?"

"Raping Majosee was one thing. Becoming Police Commissioner is apparently beyond forgiveness. Price says he'll escort
you to Junn."

It was useless to talk. I wept with Honey and the rest. I
marched in silence to the dirge.

Before Honey left for her parents' big celebration of a wedding anniversary in Homestead, she confided that a defensive
impertinence, stemming from her rape years ago, had disrupted
every relationship she had at its outset.

I happened to be trying, then, to bring the same order to my
quandaries as I often could to the complexities of my art. I was
climbing chairs and ladders to reach the highest points on a
huge collage of collages while searching every cranny of my
conscience, relevant to my children on the one hand and Bowie
on the other, to make a decision about visiting Junn.

Honey thanked me for my tenderness, and said my sensitivity
had provided the fortitude she needed to come sexually alive at
last. It sounded ominous, as if she never expected to see me alive
again. After her farewell address, I drove home and listened to
Terry Peacham in the rataplan of bongos.

As ever insolent and smug in his limited perception, he had
turned quite scholarly, with religious overtones and diction as
immaculate as his whitened hair. In lofty tones he delivered
statistics now. Only 2 percent of the Swamptown population
ever committed atrocious crimes. Most of those violations were
against the rest of Swamptown and other black communities.
How could anyone say, he demanded, that poverty was the root
of crime? It was an insult to the other 98 percent, to the entire
law-abiding, hardworking colored population, when judges just
moralized and turned senseless criminals loose to prey brutally
on the innocent again and again.

"How can anyone argue," he harangued nasally, "that murderers and butchers of human beings are not made differently
in the womb? I submit that one who can shoot down a young

girl as a boyish prank was born that way. I submit that he is not altogether human. He has, we had better believe, crocodile blood in his veins."

His face white as death, his eyes insanely distorted by the thick lenses that magnified them, his lips drawn thin with ancient hatred, he was explicating the very concepts of my friends. And worse, he was giving expression to my deepest hidden emotions. To be put over on his monocular side of consciousness by the bahaymas was in itself ample reason to hate them.

And hating them, I felt morally bound to help save them from the genocide he was subtly preaching. The conflict was maddening; responsibility for my children aggravated it. My sense of having failed Bowie overwhelmed me. It was impossible not to feel blame in the murder of his child. Lonely in my tom-tom-haunted house, I went to stay at Honey's, and that was where my family rang me.

Amy, my baby, said, "Mommy wanted me to call you myself, so you'd know I'm okay." Eleven years old, she said, "I was mugged in school today, Dad."

Before I could faint, Marissa took the phone to say, "She wasn't struck or injured in any way. They just stopped her in the hall and took her watch and money."

"I'll kill them! How'd they get into Cypress Shores School?"

"Walked in from the woods. Girls. Confirmed bahaymas."

Our children's memories of school would be bolted doors and padlocked windows. I said I'd be right over. But first I telephoned to have Barry call Price about escorting me to Junn.

The bulldozers of industry had driven Junn out of the swamp with everyone else of that habitat. So we were spared the journey there. Nor was Junn staying in Swamptown. But Swamptown and the swamp were everywhere now around the east end districts.

In an unmarked car, Price Fenton drove me through streets lined with bahaymas drinking, sneering, laughing in their gaudy anomalies of costume. As if by a perverse absurdity of style, the women's hair was mostly tangled in foul neglect, and many of the men wore denim swamp hats despite the evening

heat. The clamor of their voices was an insult to the ear. They had brought their jungle habitat along.

Black people passed among them, self-consciously different in the neatness of their sensible hot-weather clothes, the women mostly graceful, the men erect instead of bent to every swaggering display of themselves. From Pinebrake through Cedar Ridge to Armistead, we traveled no street that was not scabrous with bahaymas, and passed no building of brick or glass that was not grotesquely disfigured with graffiti.

Armistead Hammock, once a lovely open suburb of cottages and trees, was dissected by fences of various hastily constructed types. Junn was living there. Not with Josie any longer, Price explained. That was over. He stayed now at the cottage of his second wife, the last surviving McFee. Price made it clear she had brought Junn into legal wedlock now that no sisters existed between whom to hide irreligious feelings.

The Commissioner explained more on the way. Burly in his well-cut light suit, he was a cool prime student of Polsen's, almost a reflection of the Sheriff in his taciturn aloofness from the kind of subjective expression most people were given to. He made no jokes about the McFees. He said nothing about his personal history with them and Junn and Majosee.

I appreciated that in my misery of conscience, visiting Junn too late to do Bowie any good, and listened without much heart as Price told me indignant phone calls were flooding all his precincts. People were saying clean out the impassable streets and malls full of bahaymas or they would do it themselves. But the police could not satisfy them with arrests for minor infractions like loitering. Crime was out of control in Great Gulf Glade, because the courts were overcrowded.

I said he sounded like Bull Peacham. "I know," Price granted. "We get our information from the same sources." The laws were against us, he went on in educated fashion, a mature far cry from the vulgar slum brat he once was, even from the shy yet menacing young deputy when I first met him. "An inspector has to review every arrest. Every criminal has to be supplied a lawyer. Then a judge has to review everything the MA can't dismiss. Prosecutors can't give every case full attention. Getting a con-

viction's almost impossible anymore. Nowhere to lock people up. Jails stuffed with them just waiting for trial. Then the sentence is up to the judge. Most of them are political bums who don't give a shit because they live on the keys where it's safe. Less than 3 percent of crimes are prosecuted. Less are punished. Information's public for the looking."

I thought nothing could be more upsetting until, describing a bank embezzlement by twelve-year-olds, he said there was a kind of genius inbred with the heartless idiocy of bahaymas, and that incongruous mix had the primitive children competing for street fame by stabbing people to death. Civic groups were frustrated in their attempts at rehabilitation. Religion given to bahaymas did nothing for their morality. By law, no one under sixteen could be tried for murder, and by statistics over 50 percent of the murders were perpetrated by bahaymas under sixteen.

I was amazed that Honey had never taken me that far into the horrors she brought home from her city room. Price said, "She's no doubt sparing your mind." He parked on the district's main avenue to avoid drawing attention to the cottage of Junn's wife. "We're glad there isn't the room to print it all. Vigilante gangs already stirring, Gabe."

"Why don't *you* spare my mind?" I asked testily.

"Because you have to speak these things to Junn."

"Why don't *you* go speak them?" I said, growing tense by quick degrees in the crowded midst of sweaty, loud bahaymas. "Why has Junn turned against you?"

Price thought a while in the thump of bongos, then said, "He never did more than use me. I was always the enemy, aside from what I did Majosee. So are you, an enemy to use somehow. That man's as smart as Mr. Fenneran. Remember that." Price rolled up his window and had me shut mine. I immediately began to sweat like the hostile faces leering in. "Do you want a gun? I have one for you, license all made out."

"No. I'd have to use it." I blamed them all for shooting Connie Pratt. "I'd have to kill them."

"Funny. Exactly what the Mayor was afraid you might feel."

That added anger to the hate and fear that bathed me. "Let's

get going." The hot night was cool in contrast with the car. We locked our doors and met on the sidewalk to go shoulder by shoulder among blacks and bahaymas all eyeing us suspiciously. "People," I said, "I don't see any whites. They all move out?" "Those with good sense did." Sirens wailed remotely over the bongo tedium. "Tell Junn the whites've started taking vengeance. Could kill anybody. To save his people he's got to wake them up to the bahaymas, or get Josie to drive them back in the swamp."

He didn't seem to sweat like the bahaymas and me. In an airless pall we crossed toward the park beyond which Junn lived with his wife. A gray-skinned woman was shrieking obscenities at three abysmal louts who were drinking on the pedestrian island of the square. Bahaymas drank everything from soda pop to whisky in wrinkled paper bags. Speed Byrd claimed he once saw a mother feeding her baby its milk bottle that way in Hammerhead Park.

One of the three suddenly made a threatening gesture at me with his covered bottle. My dejection over Bowie stopped me to say, "How would you like that bottle shoved right up your cloaca?"

He showed me his teeth, but reeled away as Price peeled me off the other way toward the park. "See how you react with your own store of violence? That's the ripple effect. Victims got dogs, then guns. Now they're going out after muggers, trying to track down killers and just getting in our way."

I was barely listening, preoccupied with a curiosity. Still shaky from the scare, I realized I did hate that ungainly sloven on sight, and wondered if it could be that he had sensed it, to turn on me that way unprovoked.

We passed other loitering bahaymas without incident until at the dark mouth of the park Price thrust a gun on me, looking around where not even bahaymas dared to venture. I heard a muffled groan. He had probably heard it start. But I kept my hands in my pockets and said, "Where's my license?"

"Take it, take it!" A yelp sounded somewhere.

"Give me the fucking license!"

A yellow slip came up. I took it with the stubby gun. Price

went pounding away at a dead run. This is a setup, my mind warned, but I ran, jamming the steel piece into my belt beneath my flapping sportshirt. A gunshot blasted over the bongos. A siren broke, deep in the park. I reached Price with a hop over the body of a cop with undone pants and saw the Police Commissioner fire his second shot, right into the head of another policeman on top of a gagged black girl with bulging eyes of horror. The siren became an approaching chorus of them screaming at the night.

A police car leaped close to brake with a screech. Another arrived the same way, splashing us with light. In it I inspected my license, official with stamps and seals. Carefully I folded it away in my pocket while they pulled a bare-assed corpse off the outspread womanly legs of the girl and loosened her gag to let the vomit gush. Price was addressing me. A police officer was bending to untie a young black man from a tree he was hugging. A second cop freed a child lashed to the tree. As soon as their gags were removed, both began to yell in their snot.

No one could set up such a nightmare. Yet how could I believe Price had arrived just in time to kill white bahaymas impersonating cops to rape a young mother? And before the eyes of her husband and child? Right in a public park? I wanted to ask how much Fenneran had paid those bahaymas to get themselves killed like that, but knew my thinking was fractured. They had handcuffed and dragged that whole family into the park with no one interfering.

"You just shot them in the head?" was all I could get out.

Price looked insulted. "They pulled a knife on me. You saw what they were doing. Yet some judge would've set them free."

What if he had been shot without a trial years ago for the same abomination? Then this pair might have got away with it tonight. I didn't need him to tell me. Nor would I have to tell Junn what happened here. It happened constantly. That accounted for our timely arrival. Fenneran didn't have to be in the country. He had set this up long years ago—and the enmity of Josie —by simply tampering with justice to manipulate it.

Junn's greeting was polite in the attractive McFee parlor I remembered well. His wife led me there in a vague fragrance of

soap. Miss Daisy, as he called her, had grown ampler on the long legs I imagined bare in the game she once shared with a sister or two. When she padded away to make some tea, Junn offered me a drink and I accepted, eager to wash out the taste of evil.

He drank devil's eye with me. What little hair remained had turned white, but he was still lean and seemed fit. He had me sit with him on the couch, a small television portable on the tea table before us. Against TV chatter and the bongos outside, I delivered the statistics of precaution for the welfare of the blacks.

Junn scarcely listened, until I insinuated vengeful reaction by an aroused white population. He said, "They won't do much. Whitey gotten like the blacks. Take shit. That's all folks is, long's they can cheat each other."

That was true. A time had come when everyone doing business in Gulf Glade was a cheat or rabid profiteer at the least. I reminded him the Seminoles took no shit and gave no quarter to the invading swamp people. Without interest he poured more devil's eye and stared at the TV screen. I spoke Chopka's name to see if that would stir him. Junn said, "Shhhhh."

There on video was Terry Peacham, scaring me in the company of blacks. Because all at once I saw, I felt, the ugly pastiness such whites must typify to people oppressed by them for ages. But Junn just laughed. I asked him what could possibly be amusing about a vile reactionary like the former Sheriff known as Bull. Junn tittered. "He keep us informed how bad you all suffering in this here paradise of yourn. You recall Olata Micco come back from the dead and tell you crocodile blood go take over?"

Alarmed, I said, "You heard that term from Bull Peacham."

"Shucks, ole Injun said that. No longer be true leaders, no longer hope for nobody. Just shit, piss, and corruption. Blacks come to be like whitey in that. Everybody and the brothers just a crook anymore, everybody just a goon."

He proffered more devil's eye and gracefully allowed me to decline it. I tried again, saying, "These people who came here from the swamp—"

"Bahaymas. They likes that name. Because they all be children. You all got the cojos to kill them to survive?"

"We don't kill children. Price Fenton just killed two bahay-mas out there for raping a young mother. A black girl."

"They was children. He killed children. Sh-sh-sh."

"The victims have no rights," Terry Peacham indignantly declared on TV, and Junn laughed out loud. "Justice is a plati-tude, a myth that protects only the vicious. We're told that children are bludgeoned to death because of an ambusher's pov-erty, and discontent drives a human being to rape and worse." Junn was beside himself with laughter. I thought paroxysm would choke him when Peacham shouted, "Don't believe it for a minute! It's not unemployment or an unhappy childhood that creates an animal! It's crocodile blood!"

Junn and I both said the last words with him, the old man wriggling with hysterics.

I said, "Junn, the victims of bahaymas are mostly black."

"The victims of everybody," he was barely able to say, "is mostly black."

"Bahaymas are their own victims too. As many of them are violated as blacks. Brutally robbed, raped, murdered."

Laughing on, he wheezed. "Well, you know," he tried, and waved me off to wind his laughter down. "That prove they ain't racist like the cops."

"They killed Bowie Pratt's young daughter, Junn."

Abruptly he quit laughing and faced me. "Bahaymas six years old. Right, that's all they was. But you too smart to believe."

"Your old friend Bowie. You must have loved him, and his wife, back when they put their lives on the line for you."

"I'mo tell you something about love, turkey. You ain't know what love is till you knows what hate is."

He drank in sodden addiction. Hopeless, hollow as the bongos outside, I said, "The city wants you to urge Josie to take those people back into the hammocks of the swamp."

He regarded me with bleary incredulity. "Where you expect they go?" While Peacham yapped an affronted harangue about invaders, Junn began to drum on the tabletop in deft cadence with the tom-tom thump outside. In the same rhythms he said, "Ain't no swamp no more but what them big machines you got there go pickety-pockety-pick-pack. Ain't no way to live in that.

Ain't no way to pick a peck of fruit or pack a crate and lift dat bale. Go pick-a-peck, go pack-a-pick, like to make a body sickety-sockety-rock."

I remembered the gun in my belt and thought of firing it at his mouth as blithely as Price shot monsters in the park. A hand touched my shoulder and I jumped, smelling vitamins in place of soap. But Junn kept rapping and paid no attention to his wife behind us in the darkness spooked by TV colors and bongos that he accompanied to drill them in my head. "Arpeika Sam Jones, Tiger Tail, make black kill black like Asi Yaholo he shoot ole Micopotokee dead."

She beckoned behind the couch. What the hell was going on? Was I supposed to be frightened and confused? I was frightened and confused. "He go into history." Breathing hard, she took me by the wrist. "War party chiefs, that be his way." She wiped a work-worn hand across her mouth and, sounding horny, said, "Come on, he be going on a while, I give you some cheese and jelly."

"No, no." I yanked my hand away.

Junn kept tapping, reciting wrongs—Andy Jackson enemy of the Seminole, the Indian Removal Act—his drugged mind weaving him among threads of time and tragedy like someone lost in hammock jungles, and in his bongoform clatter Miss Daisy drifted away. He suddenly told me Josie was insane, then said in the abstracted ramble of narcosis, "Cut off some tongue, some nose, her little ears, but you-hoo-hoo can't cut off her bahaymas."

"Junn," I said, making one last effort for Bowie's sake. "Someone, a friend, to see his kid shot down by—"

"Bahaymas. They man side the evil soul, not crocodile side. No punishment for rapist, punishment for victim. That be your own reward, now, white folks." Sirens shrieked. Junn ignored them, drinking. "Snip her tongue for Chitto murder white man, she still preach war. Taken some nose off her for monsters born, she still swear to divide the whites between your two souls." The sirens were raging outside, the drummers too. "Cut down her ears for murders by her beast, what you think she do now? No swamp nor Injun ever did stop Majosee, and you expect me

tell her stop crocodile blood for you? City that ruin her expect she send these children back? To pickety-pack, to swamp go pickit-lickit, shoot a black man down, shoot a red man down, shoot a croc man—"

"Junn, for Christ's sake!"

"Hooee-dahooee, this here howling too be after them into the swamp, and you expect her send them backity-back, hickety black, a-hooee-dahooee—"

"Hey! Hey!" He was right. The sirens were howling and the machinery of progress meant upheaval to the swamp. But one more minute of his ironies and I'd surely pull the gun and kill him. For Price? And Christian? And Fenneran across the ocean? I had to get out of this. I had to phone headquarters if I wanted a police car to pick me up according to plan. Nothing could move Junn to cooperate; he made that unmistakable.

"Go back and tell your city. Tell Bowie Pratt, he taken to your ways. Tell them it took my whole life long, but at last I knows what Seminole Wheel of Life mean. Wheel mean your chickens always come home to roost. Paradise? You all live in Goonland now."

I ran to escape his impenetrable narcotic trance. Miss Daisy, her scent back to soap again, tried to entice me into the kitchen for hot tea. But I kept running, and she overtook me in the passage hall, so I asked for a telephone. She breathed a passion of vitamins at me and went ahead swinging her broad bottom like a temptress until we collided in a doorway full of breasts, the boudoir too pink, too perfumed. A seizure threatened now.

Watching me bend to phone the police for a car, she sat down on her fluffy bed and heaved a tyrannical bosom. "Opportunity knocks. Junn ain't come find us in here no way."

"Listen." I just couldn't take the McFee game now, I took a pill. "I can give you some nice pictures to hang on these walls."

"We never studied no fancy stuffs like white folks."

"That's true," I conceded. They never knew a boat basin either, she meant to insinuate, the light on her glasses quivering, or the pleasure of ballet. "I get your point. I know." They never knew the thrill of flying over the earth to Europe, or sailing on a yacht, or fishing for marlin. "I care, but it's not my fault. I'll send you a couple of nice pictures to hang."

"Don't need them dirty nekkid white gals," she muttered angrily, seizing me by the hips, "Come on, I give you what you needs." Her glasses glaring in my eyes, she was forcing me down on my knees before her. I couldn't believe this. I never had this while in seizure and a powerful curiosity tempted me when she fell to her knees beside me, suds her aroma once more. "Come on, you troubled man."

"No, no," I resisted, but she began to breathe even harder, kneeling with me at the lacy pink bed.

"Lord, thou art three, we be three, have mercy on us." Her elbow shot me in the ribs. "Pray!"

"Jesus mercy," I prayed. She could mean we three in the house or two more sisters still alive with her in arch deception between their nutritious and detergent odors and getting ready to pounce. I had a gun in my belt. I didn't have to submit to a gang prayer. Yet I held still for it in pure mortification, thanking God that only one Daisy used my soulful body so before the police car came and delivered me.

I found Mayor Christian waiting in his dimmed-out office at Keyport Station. When I finished speaking, he admitted having expected no better report on Junn than I was able to make. "Now I can appoint Bowie Met Attorney. He needed this proof that Junn has written off not just him but the whole black race."

I agreed a good black MA was a constructive idea for the city. "But that can't be the only reason you committed me to such a bellyful of racial pain and vengefulness."

"No," Bowie Pratt said, seated in the shadows without my knowing till now. "It concerns Honey too. Better to hear from her how she fits in. It's that sensitive."

I had not been eager to hear his broken voice, and was willing to pursue the question no further. But even more remained to it, Barry said in a voice nearly as damaged as Bowie's.

"I know you just went through something. But one patrol doesn't win a war. Everyone's in this one."

"Not many," I said, "who live where the streets are safe. You're in Glade Park and I get out soon to Sunset Bayou. Wave that flag at Pinebrake or Cedar Grove, not at me."

Barry said, "I'm worried about my parents in Tarkey. They

won't move out, they want nothing from me but the pride they take."

"Bahaymas be everywhere soon," Bowie put in.

"My brother's grandchildren," Barry continued, "had to hear a bahayma call her old man motherfucker as a casual affection right in a Bay Mall garden. Okay, just a culture difference. But Chester could only hate them for disrespecting his. He told me, 'I can't stand to look at them.' We were brought up to love everyone, but the bahaymas have made a bigot out of my sweet big brother. Chalk up one more revolting crime by crocodile blood."

"Barry, Chester's a widowed, lonely man. Life is tragic."

"It never had to be this tragic," Bowie grieved.

To keep from bursting out in tears for him, I found the temper to say, "What do you want from me?"

"I want Don Fenneran," the expediential Mayor leaped in. "To convince all his idealistic, inspired, and talented colleagues that all this crime is interconnected. If only for the sake of innocent working bahaymas who are brutalized every day, Don has to despise the criminal ones and stop defending them as social victims."

"Nobody can deliver Donny. Neither Bill nor their father can. I can't. Not even to help Lissa get the job of assisting you to undermine the Bill of Rights for Tate Fenneran."

"Then get ready," Bowie said, "to protect your Honey's right to free speech against your Donny's assault on that same Bill."

I dreamt of war, Bowie in a steel helmet, weeping. In his helmet Barry led us to an assault on a trellised porch house painfully familiar though we had never attacked one in reality. A shot from inside struck me right in the forehead. Oh, the treachery—to be tricked back into the goddamn army right after being shot in the head from behind. Then to be shot there frontally—the sheer treachery woke me. Honey, home beside me fresh from her bath, was a garden of relief in which to celebrate until she ran to shower again.

Returning apprehensive as a child, Honey told me her part in sending me to Junn. I had to hold her while she explained that

one purpose of my mission was to get me behind an editorial the city and county administrations had asked her to articulate. "I said not if you object. I phoned Italy to tell Tate that."

"What's the piece about?"

She took a deep breath, and said, "Civil rights abuse."

It smacked me in the brain like my dream—in Tate Fenneran's voice years back under the floodlights of my workshop. I could see why she and all of them, from Bowie in his sorrow to Fenneran thousands of miles away, felt I might take exception to it unless confronted with Junn's recalcitrance and the multiplying danger it posed Gulf Glade. I had undergone considerable danger myself to advance this tactical maneuver in our crisis, and wondered if offering me to it (like the expendable Hillary once made me) was courageous or cavalier of Honey Baines.

I was dreaming war again when she woke me, smelling like fresh meadow air. Aghast beside me on the phone, Honey said my prospective son-in-law was dead. It was high afternoon. We had slept away most of her day off. My older daughter's fiancee was gone. My older son was a ravening avenger lusting to murder all bahaymas, not only the one he had beheld killing Justin.

We drove right out to Ceremony Key. The police, Hoby whispered, had brought Toby home and would be returning to question him further after the family pulled itself together. Marissa had a brunch ready for us, but all I could touch was some coffee until I had seen Lissa.

Amy was comforting her sister in their room. Sam was trying to calm down his brother in theirs. Lissa got up to embrace me and lay her face by my neck. "Daddy, why don't I cry?" she asked, then really broke me down, answering herself with another question. "Because I never cried over you?"

I ate some eggs with Honey while Hoby filled us in. Toby had been helping Justin move some belongings from his dormitory to his car this morning, for transportation to the new apartment he and Lissa had rented down the Key. She wanted to live near her mother. I had to ask Hoby to stay with the main events. It was simple, he said. The young men found a young bahayma

taking things out of the car, right on Racquet Club Boulevard in broad daylight. Two tall youths confronting a little bahayma, they took pains to be polite. Toby asked him what he was doing. The bahayma said he was ripping off the car. Justin pointed out that it was his car. A knife flashed, the bahayma fled like a hare, and Justin Chalfonte lay dead in the street.

At the cemetery Justin's Meyerberger clan was overwrought. His parents seemed distraught with guilt as well as grief. I could not shake off that notion in the dreadful mourning. They appeared to be stunned by a sense of divine retribution. Even if that was only in my mind, what terrible shapes grief took. Phyllis Chalfonte's wholesome white headband and agonized red eyes were too sad to bear in the livid overcast. Lissa wept as though her heart would break, and so did poor Marissa.

There in a graveyard where the past seemed to die and the future to stagnate, I found a title for my current big collage. In pathos I named it *Lifetime*.

COLLAGE 17

The world had changed. Life had become abnormal because of the horrible infestation from the swamp. Children were no longer free to roam in their innocent packs. Young people could not go about lighthearted after dark. The elderly were trapped indoors day and night by savage miscreants. Still, Donny blamed Terry Peacham's diatribes for the growing public reaction against the bahaymas as animals incapable of profiting from rehabilitation to find their places in a civilized world.

Then he read Honey's editorial and it drove me wild to hear him lump her with Peacham while citing abstractions like prejudice and alienation as the roots of crime. Unstable family life, he cried to prove us all wrongheaded, the frustration of poverty amid affluence. I would have thought Don an imbecile had I not known him to be discerning, brilliant, sophisticated, and profound. Echoing an observation of his father's, I said that to argue why was to waste the lives of victims on analysis, while synthesis, or what to do about it, was the urgent necessity in crisis.

He dismissed me with an impatient wave of his hand. I felt like kicking him in the ass.

HOW WE ABUSE THE ABUSED

Government agencies are pouring funds into rehabilitative programs for the muggers and rapists that live among us. But we have not been able to find any way to redeem their devastated victims. Scarred for life, crippled in wheelchairs, the prey of violent criminals must often depend on financial support from relatives and friends.

Of the multimillions we spend on all the aspects of crime, less than 1 percent is allocated for the victims. Confronted about that callous neglect, the Mayor told this newspaper, "We simply lack the funds." Asked the reason for such disproportionate expenditure on the criminals, the Chief Judge could only say, "Civil rights."

Civil rights are as vital to a free society as antibiotics are to our bodies and tranquilizers can often be to our minds. But, as even the best of drugs can be abused, so can a noble essential in the structure of democracy. We are witnessing a most insidious abuse of civil rights in our time.

Civil rights abuse is destroying our bodies and our minds like the deadliest of narcotics. Decent citizens, normally passive but forced to arm themselves for the protection of their families, are being driven to roam in vengeful packs against murder in their neighborhoods, interfering with police investigation, intent on gunning the predators down like animals.

To worsen the situation, purely ethnic attacks by bigots generate a smokescreen of sympathy for the brutal thugs. The effect is a murk of moralistic sentimentality that maligns every cry for law and order as a racist conspiracy, even though the invaders from the swamp represent every human skin color and are called bahaymas only because of the lawless, wanton, irresponsible and destructive culture their way of life represents.

Thus, conflict multiplies among well-meaning people. Public speculation on the origin of bahaymas becomes extreme. Educated people who live distant from the robberies and rapes and senseless murders cannot accept a genetic heresy as credible. Those in the midst of the pillage, however, we who personally see this ragtag proliferation of evil incarnate all over our once-peace-

ful streets, have no choice but to believe in the impossible and insist on legislative action before we are swept into the bowels of chaos. Whether human beings or animals are besieging us, we must confront the issue of civil rights abuse.

This newspaper submits that it is an abrogation of our own civil rights to surrender our freedom of the avenues and parks to criminals. We hereby request the Metropolitan Council to call an emergency assembly for legislation on this specific issue.

It is civil rights abuse to place the concentrated attention of society on the criminal instead of the victim.

It is civil rights abuse to hold an idealistic quibble above the protection of citizens as a society's first responsibility.

It is civil rights abuse to defend the constitutional right of treatment as a citizen for those who answer their needs by means of bloody, premeditated crime against the law-abiding.

It is civil rights abuse to support a chronic offender with welfare funds provided by the offended taxpayer.

It is civil rights abuse to provide welfare support to continuously pregnant women who abandon their children.

It is civil rights abuse to withhold publication of the names of serious criminals under sixteen.

It is civil rights abuse to barricade any rapist or murderer of any age against the full weight of the law.

The very freedom of licentious women to bear children at will, after conviction for child neglect or mistreatment, is nothing less than civil rights abuse.

Donny hated that editorial. I thought she wrote it very well. Terry Peacham loved it. After it appeared in the *Times*, he vilified the "bleeding heart" judges who passed light, if any, sentences on the vicious and the cruel. He berated everyone of "the liberal persuasion," as he distinguished us in his knack for exclusionary bias, and with seething, pompous sincerity he said, "We did all right in the old days. We didn't need this progress."

I could just imagine the black and poor-white thousands cheering in his good old skull-cracking days as Sheriff of a jobless, decaying eyesore of a county. But he next created another kind of picture—of a whole population, with a long history of fatuous indiscretions, gaping unprepared when the bahayma invasion struck. He sounded inspired in this vision

of the brainless fatalism that served the meek as faith.

"Terrorizing our schools," he shrilled, "they have just raped a young teacher at Bayside High, far from their swampside hovels."

Adding that zonal hint of scorn was plainly racist. We didn't need Bull Peacham listing all the assassins and butchers the media featured daily, but he presented every crime of the week, with bahaymas apprehended in each one that was solved, and found the very evil of those offenses reflected in the epidemic of broken antennas on cars in every district of the city, in the unremitting increase of smashed store windows and irreplaceable religious stained glass, in the obscene spread of litter and graffiti.

Peacham raised his voice to call each and every bahayma a son of a crocodile, and unreservedly wished them all dead. Then, right there on television he shouted, "Sickle-cell anemia," forgetting it was an exclusively black disease, "where are you?"

I felt like kicking him in the ass. Yet much as I detested Terry Peacham, he forced me to believe that violent crime was committed by people who were not people. That followed me to sleep with all the rumors of bahaymas thronging to Josie's mad harangues. In my dream she exhorted her spawn to avenge her persecution. By the thousands her bahaymas were the children of injustice, in spite of Bull Peacham's disbelief.

Honey woke me to say Barry was in my workshop. She looked disturbed but not alarmed. In my drowse, as I drew on my robe and went down, I wondered only about his arrival in the hush of night.

It was graying to dawn in a rain. Police cars were in my driveway. I turned on the workshop lights, and switched them right off. Christian sat at my work table in a rain cape and hat, looking like Roosevelt at Yalta. But the Mayor of Great Gulf Glade, combat officer in five European Theater campaigns, veteran of years of political infighting, was weeping in his hands.

I shook with an electric charge of fear for his three daughters —then a thousand shock waves of alarm bolted through me because any harm to my own children would reduce him just this way. "Barry," I said, "what happened?"

He looked up wet in the face to say, "It's Mr. and Mrs. Lucci. They've been bludgeoned to death in their home."

The name was vaguely familiar. "Who are they, Barry?"

"Such lovely old people. A stonemason and his wife in Tarkey. I knew them all my life. My parents are inconsolable."

I put my hand on his shoulder, ashamed of the relief I felt. He knuckled his wet eyes like a kid. "We must legislate safety. We have to dismiss the spineless sentimentalists who shrink behind false morality. Will you come if I call an emergency meeting?"

I was awed by people like him who could mix heartache and expedience that easily. My old friend, Fenneran's best pupil, he had come to soften me up for that report to the Met Council on Junn. I felt like kicking his ass too, but agreed to attend and invite friends. The situation was really that desperate.

Everyone I telephoned had someone close that was missing, hurt, or killed. Yet those who lived on the bay side or the keys, where crime was not frequent, had previous appointments.

With all the courageous aplomb of station, Chief Judge Harmon Wilmont came on television to debate the redoubtable Peacham, who was calling for an expansion of capital punishment to cover all crimes that employed deadly weapons. With the pride of eagles in the light of his eyes, the judge countered with an excoriation of capital punishment and demanded its abolition as a disgrace to the moral dignity of civilized people.

"Your Honor," Terry the Bull responded, "in Armistead Hammock just last night, a girl of seventeen was raped and slashed. When she was dead, the bahayma raped her again. And your working bahayma, your family provider, a beneficiary of your moral dignity, I say, slaughtered his wife and two children in Cedar Ridge, *and* the poor garageman who had come to repair their car. No, my dear Judge, I submit that there is no room on this earth for such beasts, and no obligation of human conscience to protect them."

"I don't know about your conscience, Mr. Peacham," retorted Wilmont, "but I would not want the life of a human being on mine."

"His Honor does not seem to mind having the innocent lives of murder victims on his conscience by the hundreds."

"There is no documented evidence to prove that capital punishment has ever been a deterrent to murder."

"I have evidence here, documented by no less than the Federal Study Commission on Crime, that for each released murderer eight more victims will die."

"That is a conclusion drawn, moot at best, and there remains no established reason to commit murder in the mere hope of deterring murder."

"Then let me establish an unassailable one herewith. Capital punishment will most assuredly deter the murderer from ever repeating his crime. And the rapist. And the armed robber."

"By that logic, sir, we should electrocute the pickpocket and sneak thief, we should hang the shoplifter and truant."

"Yes, Judge Wilmont. Leave out the truant—that is facetious —and you have my blessing."

Narrowing his ferocious eyes for the cut that kills, Harmon Wilmont said, "Would you personally pull the electrocution switch, Terry Peacham? Would you volunteer to drop the hangman's trap?"

As if any father of children would hesitate to kill with his bare hands any of the savages Peacham had mentioned. I dreamt of catching up with Justin's killer. I thirsted to crush the bahayma porter who raped a rabbi's daughter and then crammed her in a furnace to be hauled away later with the trash.

Wilmont, my fellow liberal, disgusted me, until I pitied him as the epitome of idiotic political inertia when Peacham said, "The people will be forced to pull the switch and drop the trap by themselves, if our vaunted judges continue to circumvent the law by refusing to commit for capital crimes."

"Why didn't she state as specifically that the accused wait too long for trial?" Donny demanded in the antechamber of Council Hall. He was endlessly furious about Honey's editorial.

Beside him on the bench at Keyport Station, I said, "Leave me alone. My son's so mad, he's going to kill someone if Justin's murderer is not caught soon. My husband-in-law's so sardonic about Lissa's anguish, he's breaking my feet."

"She practically admitted every offender is a juvenile, but wants those that are so-called bahaymas deprived of all rights."

Several councilmen were congratulating Judge Wilmont. They said he had handled reactionary old Peacham very well. Heads I felt like kicking here more than asses. By contrast these blandishing frauds made the Police Commissioner look faultless in the deputy Sheriff's uniform he still liked to affect. His benefactor, Polsen, was due to attend, but his liberator, Fenneran, was still abroad. Distant too were my parents and brothers and sisters, with the wedding murdered. Glad they were far away from this demented public tolerance of jeopardy, I nonetheless felt abandoned by them as I did back when I returned from war all changed, and they went right on with their lives.

I sensed just such a resentment of me by Toby—not Lissa but Toby, somehow—and didn't understand.

The Sheriff arrived in uniform, with a handsome young man as blond as Cassie Fenneran, who came clacking down the corridor between them like an apparition of the younger Hillary, choking my heart. Polsen introduced Evan Brisburn, the son of Dexter's sister Nola and Hillary's late cousin Burl.

At once Donny began to proselytize Evan over the sins of Honey's editorial even though it scored the bigots who held all bahaymas responsible for the criminals among them. Councilmen greeted the Sheriff with awkward jests about his bringing advice from the peaceful countryside, and he riposted with the audacity of calling for the return of police brutality.

Dexter's reputation for irony being famous, everyone reacted with nervous laughter, until Cassie stopped it with a sob. I quickly realized what Don and I had both failed to—that she, Evan, and Dexter were all as grim as plague.

"It's Grandma," she wept, just as Barry had while saying, "It's Mr. and Mrs. Lucci." More of that echo washed over me as she went on to say, "Faith's been bludgeoned to death. They ransacked the slave-quarters chamber."

That obnoxious room—I was too shocked to feel sorrow. Everything seemed a repetition. Our lives were being smeared with violence like the graffiti that covered Gulf Glade.

Yet Don, in the very pall of his stunning grief, stubbornly opposed all attempts to postpone the emergency Council session

due to death in the aristocracy. He was a fanatical game player like his parents. They were all as crazy as I felt.

The public was poorly represented in Council Hall. No one I had notified showed up, not even Baldy Haverstraw, so devoted to antiviolence legislation that he had sworn to kill every obstructive councilman.

Cassie had departed with her visiting cousin. The others I knew sat at long Council tables between the public gallery and the rostrum. Barry presided there with Council President Tolstadt, who was singing long-winded cajolements all around to get the meeting under way. He put me to sleep.

I was sleeping a lot those days, as I sometimes did in the old time of seizures, and feared their possible return. Barry woke me taking a firm stand against councilmen helplessly afraid that any projected measure would inevitably be escalated. "We must dare," he held forth, "to impose severe legislative restraints against specific outrages. That need not mean the sudden end of our hard-won civil rights. We must not be so insecure and ignorant as to misinterpret such bills as a means to harass those who merely resemble violent offenders but commit no crime."

A black councilman rose to inveigh against code-word terminology behind which to hide everything from elitist privilege to racism. Barry had failed to win over the black opposition with my report on Junn. Dozing, I imagined Tate Fenneran ridiculing any hope of reasonable negotiation of differences among infantile windbags, and woke to Judge Wilmont bestowing his measured words of sage, self-serving caution.

"The principle of increased severity of punishment," he said from a council table, "is in itself a dangerous escalation. Simple ethics dictate more realistic bills in what is essentially a crisis of the courts. I call on this responsible body to legislate more youth counseling, more rehabilitative facilities, and to legislate above all the power to appoint more judges."

Though he spoke that side of my mind, it rebelled, as the other side rebelled against the narrow punitive approaches to crime it often favored. In this personal crossfire I suspected Wilmont of opposing all protective legislation as a threat to shady sup-

porters of the cynical cheats most politicians were. Imposters pretended to represent liberals like me, I brooded in a clamor of applause for the judge from a few at the Council tables.

One of them stood up to be seen by constituents saying, "It used to be the Negroes. It used to be the Indians. Now the same racists are threatening in every park and mall to burn out the shacks where harmless swamp folks live and work."

A woman in the audience yelled, "Bullshit! Don't start that! Who goes in the parks anymore but fools and bahaymas?"

As Tolstadt banged his gavel a man cried, "Angry! Bahaymas, everything they speak—a question, a joke—they say it angry! They make life sick!"

"Neighbors try to admire our lobby," a stout woman shouted against the banging gavel, "the doorman has to lock them out. The whole city is locked up tight!"

In my mixed sympathy and revulsion for the privileged, I saw Barry throw both hands high on the rostrum. "Overwhelming fiscal problems face us. Ladies and gentlemen. This great city is threatened with a shortfall due to retrenchment in federal aid. We can hardly pay our police or protect our teachers."

I had to be dreaming. No, I was awake to Donny's anger. "Bahaymas never misappropriated public funds," he asserted with a vibrato of passion in his voice. "They never put federal income sharing into tennis courts and marinas."

"No, no," Barry cut in, "I mean to say this city, we really could have worked out all our problems if not for the bahaymas. And with legislated relief from them, we still can, I'm sure."

"We can't even work out pollution," Don rejoindered, "which bahaymas never gave us. Or industrial cancer and war, which these people never produced. Or the decadence we inherited from slavery—the pillage of the public trust, the adultery and deceit that are our way of life despite all the platitudes about our work ethic and dignity. We must not persecute these people to avoid confronting the defects and gross inequities of an industrial oligarchy that reduces them to crime before they can even mature."

Bowie Pratt, whose child was dead of immature bahaymas, caused a stir when he stood up among the councilmen to say,

"Why are some of you called bleeding hearts when you are so heartless? Without any feeling whatsoever for victimized, brutalized old people and small children. Sanctimonious egocentrics, you pamper yourselves with noble ideals at the expense of the meek and helpless, at the cost of their very lives and the emotional survival of their families. If you had hearts, they would bleed for the ordinary lives destroyed by senseless violence. They would bleed for the human mortality mocked and demeaned by the tolerance of such unessential agonies as bahaymas in our midst."

"Mr. Pratt," someone interrupted. "Bowie. Friend." It was Donny. "To kill murderers gives us nothing but more dead people."

"That's better than nothing," Bowie reacted, "even if murderers were people. Your idea that more is worse is not a premise but a dogma. We are not brave, we are not kind, we are not generous to the future, if we fail the power a free society possesses to legislate any counterattack on evil it deems fit."

Our bereaved Metropolitan Attorney sat down, his echoes resonating in the silence that fell like a stupor over the hall. Presently a crackle of applause sounded, and rapidly increased. In the attending awe the Mayor spoke, Wilmont, Bowie again, and I could not believe my hearing. One side conceded that society simply must be willing to suffer great stress over the imposition of strong restraints on vicious, homicidal barbarians. The other side reciprocated by calling for sound and equitable judgments by the Council. Each side had influenced the other to do nothing as usual. Life—social, political, economic—was just too complex to structure a clear resistance to evil.

Everything was being repeated over and over. Government had run completely out of credibility. Nothing was to be believed any longer, not a solitary political leader any more than the most avaricious TV commercial. With the possible exception of Polsen.

Drifting off in hopelessness with sorrow over Faith, I almost missed witnessing the Sheriff exploit his reputation for irony. He too, Dexter got up to say, deplored capital punishment as a

degradation of civilized law. But he deplored even more the criminals who forced that on us. In the absence of legislated means, someone would simply have to bear the burden of finding other means, no matter what, against the wanton destruction of our lives and liberty.

That, softly spoken, was a formidable challenge, offering the Council its last opportunity to enact legal measures before he, the toughest, most irreproachable man in Key County, staunch proponent of justice all his life, was forced to personally accept the onus of bringing violent bahaymas in on a slab.

It was not lost on Donny, though he seemed distracted, sunken low amid the seated councilmen. His grandmother's sudden death had apparently caught up with him full force. His head turned ponderously toward the public seats. "Statistics are in hand," he averred in even tones, "that prove young murderers can be rehabilitated into productive citizens." Letting his gaze pass across Price Fenton on its way to Polsen at the next table, he added, "Just as young rapists can."

The Sheriff spoke up. "Who can disagree with sincere people like Don Fenneran? Understanding and rehabilitation are of course the best way to save people from the worst in themselves. But I also have to agree with Don that we can't even take care of ourselves. Where, then, do we come off trying to take care of animals?"

That was the famous irony of Polsen. He drowned a murmurous flurry of controversy saying, "Nobody has any use for reformed bahaymas who have killed productive human beings. Not even those selfsame bahaymas, who are worth nothing to themselves. I know they're worth far less to the rest of us than the enormous cost of supporting them in humane, uncrowded prisons."

That was the famous hard nose of Polsen. He walked out of the hall, leaving the Met Council with a choice of actions and a warning that the choice had better not be given back to him in the sloth of politics of personal ambition, or he would never be able to discourage the rapist transformed into Police Commissioner from bringing the savagers of people in too dead for the cure.

THE DISBELIEF OF CHRISTIANS

INHUMAN SAVAGE MURDERS FAITH BRISBURN

Donny called the *Times* headline maniacal and, to judge from his manner on the phone, was mad enough to kill the Publisher for such a brutality. Without lying, I said I was too busy to see him. She was working on my misery over Lissa's Justin, maybe not with sensitivity but the best way Honey knew. As police were arresting the leader of a homosexual murder ring on my TV screen, she charged me with doing funny heterosexual things to her, and dug the evidence out of my pants to pickle it in her martini. She swizzled her drink that way, laughing on the rug with her back to crimes of compulsion by white folks.

A student killed off his entire family in its sleep as Honey lionmouthed her whole martini, unable to laugh when another kid sent a pipe bomb to blow up his grandmother and save the world. I was sure the newscaster said that, in spite of my preoccupation with Honey. Before she was through the screen turned gruesome with the point-blank murder of six patrons at a Keyport bakery, and I climaxed without learning if anybody knew the killer's breed. The war in Vietnam exploded. We lacked for nothing in our parlor. Honey sat up as winded as the boy soldiers livid with fear in the gunfire.

"Why are you panting?" I asked. "I did all the running."

"That's what you think," she said happily, and offered me marriage to a total woman, the latest media canard.

Each evening of our wait for the Fennerans' return to attend Faith's funeral, Bull Peacham hacked away at the conscience he was winning over from me, while the Publisher hacked her own way and Donny hacked his. If the tragedy of his grandmother did not keep him from assaulting Honey, then the Swamptown fire would have. It left him too exhausted. Or Josie did, screaming in the smoke.

He phoned to invite me along with Bill and their cousin Evan, who was interested in Josie's infusion of the Seminole wars into her charges of arson. But another cocktail time had come, and by catching the fire live on TV I could avoid hearing Don lay it to Honey. I lost no time in blaming it on old Terry.

Another spirit of fun, and the fire raged before us. Honey straddled me with her skirts raised as Josie came on screen to chill my soul screaming, "Yo-ho-eeeeeeee!"

That, a voice announced over the scene, was the ancient Seminole war cry. It used to strike terror into the soldiers of Zachary Taylor, the reporter added, coming into view against the blazing backdrop active with firemen. Josie struck terror into me, sweeping into the picture red in reflection of the shooting flames and half mad with shrieks about crocodile blood.

She was no harder to comprehend than the next media female. Some were as delightful as Honey purring in my ear, but most lisped or gibbered in giddy falsetto, and the same mystery of electronic transfer that made them comprehensible seemed to be doing the same for the lunatic shrieks of Josie, whose butchered nose weirdly stirred me in Honey's warm butter of kisses. Whose mutilated tongue lashed at the camera while Honey palpated my excitement. Whose violent eyes bulged as hot wonder engorged me, Honey absorbing my soul with breathless whispers to stay me.

Josie intensified the horror of crocodile blood by crying out that anyone could have passed it into the human race long before her rapists did through her. Explosive cuts to Vietnam supported her tirade while Honey sounded intimate cannon with her breathing.

In the flames of Swamptown Josie screamed that Africans along the Nile could have been lying with crocodiles for all the centuries that beasts in human form ravaged the meek.

I felt man and animal struggling in the bush. I heard warfare rumble in her proclamation to the viewing public that soldiers could have fathered bahaymas right in Big Cypress Swamp during the Seminole wars, and Indians like Osceola and Billy Bowlegs and Coahoochee when they were driven deeper and deeper into the morass by the crocodile blood that made war.

Generals Zachary Taylor and Winfield Scott had plundered her life with Fuse Hadjo and Micanopy and Wildcat. She inculpated them all behind Honey's back, screaming Andrew Jackson and John Tyler too and current national leaders who must have crocodile blood in their veins, for anyone who na-

palmed helpless civilians in Asia had to be less than human.

Terrorists who slaughtered children, she shouted to the world on fire, must surely be bahaymas to act so without human shame.

And it was Majosee I loved, it was Honey grotesque in my arms, while as many as two hundred victims were dying in Swamptown.

That was the rough figure Donny gave, stopping off on the way home to tell me humorists at the fire had suggested busing more bahaymas in from other districts to hinder the rescue work or to apply for city jobs as fuel.

He believed the Sheriff's Department was ignoring testimony from survivors who said arsonists had come racing through in cars to throw torches, calling them sons of crocodiles as their shacks ignited. Though as always reluctant to praise his father, Don admitted that all disaster plans in effect this night were said to have originated with Fenneran. But I recalled other fires that singed that name, and got sick with genocide coming to mind.

I took Honey aside to tell her something was happening to my head. She giggled, expressing the hope it was nothing she had done. I went upstairs for a phenobarbital, forgiving Honey when Don brought his somber resentment of her along. He said she was being sucked in by a force of entrenched bigotry that the region had never expiated. It was growing like ringworm, he insisted, so I told him to depend on Dr. Polsen for a cure of anything against the law. Don called me naive, and said he dreaded Polsen.

"He had people hosed in their cars, he had deputies breaking windshields to force cars out of there. He made me sick."

"You make me sick." Who could convince a legalistic fanatic that Polsen had just saved lives? I let Donny watch me take a pill.

"You don't believe me? Neither will Barry. You have to tell him Dexter is bringing bahaymas in dead. The word is out. He's doing it through his worshiping automaton, Price Fenton. The Police Commissioner is Dexter Polsen's cold steel tool."

That was impossible to dispute. "You don't believe me?" I said, and threw up in the toilet bowl, all the cold soy sauce

chicken I had delectated with the Publisher before Don arrived. "I marinated that three days for nothing."

"They brought in the kids who killed the Luccis," Don said as I washed and gargled. "Alive. Twenty years old, of Italian extraction. Had they been bahaymas, they would be dead."

"You ever stop to think of all the work there is in running this city?" I could barely see him. My mouth felt like varnish. "Barry can't run it properly on account of bahaymas like you."

Don was enraged, as incoherent as Honey could be. I took another phenobarbital, the first one gone in a wash of Chinese chicken. I was really very sick, vague and throbbing at the peripheries of my vision. But as he followed me from the bathroom I had to tell him. I said his defense of atrocious beasts had become idiotic, and climbed into bed. He accused me of being too obtuse to listen, and told me something Polsen had shocked him with when he confronted the Sheriff about overstepping his authority.

"Life has forced me," he quoted Dexter, "to come to terms with the fact that I am, after all, not a saint."

Passing time had taught me something too, that artists were useless to the world. It was too fucking dumb to pay attention. Or too smart, as smarter Junn once put it. Oh, I was sick and Don was smart as all Gulf Glade was dumb. All of us were wading in the blood of the dead to argue the piss of ethics.

Still, I thought I might find a solution by fitting elements of worth to my floating brain. Sweat needled me. I pasted faces side by side to bring back the dead and missing. I tried to explain the collage to Don, but my brain turned over in its grave.

The three white suspects in the Lucci murders were dead. The radio gave it, next morning with the rain, that they had tried to escape a court-bound prison van and had to be shot by police.

The news put Honey in a state. She ranted on the telephone because her newspaper had failed to bring out an extra edition to headline the story. I was still sick, but not too sick to understand that this put a hole in the theory about Polsen that lots of people shared with Donny. They would have to acknowledge

the killings as honest police work or concede that the Sheriff and Police Commissioner were not biased.

I tried to call Don the next minute, but didn't. When Honey gave up the phone to hurry off and dress, I turned to reach for it, but my brain rolled the opposite way. I sank to rest, and fell out in a sleep so deep that Honey couldn't wake me in the evening. I remembered her trying anxiously, and laughed at the importance she attached to eating on time.

Whenever I turned my head one way, my brain swam the other. It went oozing all over itself in my skull each time I turned to answer the phone and tell someone I felt fine. Marissa called in the morning, hysterical. Toby had been arrested for murder.

Our son had killed someone for snipping off the radio antenna of his car. He had beaten and stomped a bahayma to death at the Racquet Club car park. Marissa was terrified that bahayma crowds would lynch him before we could release him on bail. At the moment I was taking deep gulping breaths of gratitude that the flash of a knife had not swept Toby away like poor Justin.

We buried Faith in the rain. The Buenaventura graveyard seemed on the wrong side of the manor to me. I shouldn't have gone. Lissa stayed home on Ceremony Key with Toby, who was still saying, "It's gone too far. It was just too much to take anymore."

Fenneran told me my son would have to stand trial. Hillary said tenderly I was not to worry. I wished it had been the other way around. I wanted their son to take the case, but he refused. Not Toby but the poor people needed him, Donny said. It was his grandmother's funeral after all, I told myself, but with misgivings in the black mushroom field of umbrellas.

Everybody seemed to be facing the wrong way, though the open grave was alongside Loker's simple stone where all of us had gathered, back those short years during which some of our children had grown up. This reversed quality had hovered in my workshop that morning, but as a vague sense of disorientation, nothing so frightening as this phenomenon now. I had

tried to work while Honey preened herself for mourning. But *Lifetime,* my towering collage, loomed over me with the colossal scorn of indifference. I had recalled the importance of visionary insights that reached me down my misty life, but not what they were.

It was all for nothing. So said the tears of Jennifer Kearny. What did she want from me? Lots of people were divorced like us between the murders of her parents. The Glunns and Cheathams, the Swayzees, Hootons, and Hogans. All were in the mourning crowd. Even the Mayor's sister Etoille was no longer married to Winfield Scott Prescott. Some had even remarried, as Honey suggested I should with a whisper at the graveside beside Fenneran and his weeping wife. All my work was for nothing, I whispered with the rain, all that laborious construction. All that love of children, I thought beneath the umbrellas of gloom and nostalgia.

All that selling out, my wife thought back at me with a handkerchief at her eyes. What a fool you were, Faith sang in my mind, and the Sheriff's eye said look where all your fun got you. The sharks of commerce swam in the rain, faces no one would believe selling real estate and grieving. The Publisher always smiled at funerals. The parson iterated. The Sheriff whispered, "Bahaymas never serve on juries. Your boy'll be tried by his peers. They'll knight him, not convict him."

That was easy for him to say. How could I take the word of someone who expected people to believe that three educated boys of Italian extraction who had killed the Luccis would attempt a senseless, suicidal escape from the police? They were young murderers of good family background, like my son.

"They were bahaymas," Dexter said.

Had I asked the question aloud? I used to behave that way in the devil's eye of seizure. Or was that a dream? What did he mean? That the Police Commissioner was his tool was what Don meant. That was clear. Dexter was bringing killers in on a slab through Price Fenton. Over his shoulder Bill Fenneran asked me, "Have you noticed that Dr. Ryerson is not here?"

With that he wheeled off and ran. The Sheriff turned to watch Bill speed away in his golden Ferrari. I hoped the Christians and

Fennerans had not heard Dexter's comment, afraid it might be just an irony in which he regarded Toby as a bahayma. I was sure Judge Wilmont did when I saw his presuming eyes, and the narrow craving that always glinted in them.

I was far too sick for anyone's burial but my own, yet had to parade in this one's wake through the rain. Many had perished that way, feeling deathly ill but ashamed to admit it in public. I felt like General Arthur MacArthur, who once raised every heart by stating heroically at a regimental reunion that, though advanced in age, he was as ever ready to die for his men, and dropped dead.

I just faded away like his famous son Doug, yet witnessed everything. Faith's wake unfolded for me through the magic of TV. Only this time I was the camera, fading out, fading in, dissolving. Dexter faced my lights for comment, calling it wrong to dwell on race, which flashed me back to Josie saying in the flames that even the President of the United States betrayed the crocodile blood in his veins by napalming children.

Tate condescended to say a few heartfelt words about genocide, but first had to take an alarming call from Mrs. Dildress. On the same couch I once shared with Faith, Jennifer resembled her in my lens, her former husband bowing with a condolement. She nodded in gracious acknowledgment, and turned to face me for interview.

"The speciosity of Dr. Ryerson's therapy," she read from an open scrapbook, "is revealed in its helping my poor Hillary to remember seeing an incestuous sister voluptuate in the ancient dirt with bloody Burl, whereas that was really her mother."

Something was wrong. As Jennifer sat reading her mother, I saw Faith rage so young, bullwhipping Burl for corrupting her son, then redeeming the nephew with love until Hillary found Todd screaming in the house and came running. "That was I, not Jenny," Jennifer spoke from her mother's book, "that Hillary tried to kill with Burl and herself, burning down the slave quarters in her delusion of incest. He was only my nephew by marriage after all."

And there came Burl's son into focus, telling Jennifer, "Your

father taught mine that a Jew's children are everything to him."
Then he faced my lens to say, "Is that true?"

Behind him Shawn Hogan bent to console Jennifer. "The
bahaymas," he said, "blame society for their hopeless conditions, and so feel justified in assaulting more fortunate people."

What a cockeyed way to pay their last respects. Something
was wrong, something was wrong. Fenneran was paling at the
phone. "Are you saying," he was saying, "that Bill is dead?"

Everything was wrong. The show was on, but the screen was
blurring, teardrops were falling, audio was flooding with sound.
"Do you feel," Judge Wilmont said in camera, as the courts
called it, "that your son was justified in killing that youth?"

TV wasn't there any longer, my own eyes and ears were, and
my speechless mouth with my heart in it. Donny said without
tears for Bill, "Did you say Toby committed less a crime than
his victim did?"

My friend was turning against me, his brother Bill no longer
available for comment and bereavement already like salt in my
nose. Strobe lights were flashing. The system was breaking
down. Nazis were privileged to rally against victims of the
Holocaust, bahaymas were allowed to throw beer cans on the
walks, their women to defile the malls, the ugliest hookers on
earth.

The system protected abusers against being abused by legal
restraint, and in my grief over Bill Fenneran his Aunt Jennifer
handed over the book of large photographs and confessions,
saying her mother had willed me to collage them. Faith had
bequeathed me shots of Ryerson shackled half naked to the
whipping post, and there he came live before me in tow on Bill's
leash. Bill was live too! He had the quack in a dog collar, all
bruised and bleeding.

It was not Fenneran's son Bill who had perished in Mrs.
Dildress's terrible phone call but her husband Bill. And that was
not television, that was real, Tate Fenneran quoting her report
that bahaymas had clubbed the President of the Chamber of
Commerce to death, while Bill Fenneran told us of clubbing the
lascivious psychiatrist all over his office with the heavy suitcase
Ryerson had packed to leave Gulf Glade forever.

But what had told Bill he was Faith's killer? It was all coming too fast amid my inherited photos of Burl shackled too for punishment and love, so the answer had to wait for another episode. In this one the fury of Bill's brother was directed at a police bulletin that said the four murderers of Dildress, caught in the act of raping his secretary, were shot dead while trying to escape arrest.

"Why were they not brought in on leashes but alive," Donny stormed, "like the lily-white inhuman savage who murdered Grandma?"

Police Commissioner Fenton well knew the political importance of never answering a question directly. "Wish I'd thought of dog collars at the Swamptown fire. Looters weren't poor, they were animals. Fruit pickers, most, earning much as a hundred a week."

"Enough to support any hovel," Donny rejoindered huskily. "To resent living like a dog doesn't make anyone an animal."

"You don't have to live like a dog," the Sheriff told Don, "to have animal blood." I had them in a two-shot, their wives discreetly grave alongside at a buffet for Don's rebuttal: "Nor do you have to be Marge Christian to love the socially sick."

"It's socially sick to love evil," Dexter parried, "which is all that makes a person different. Not race or creed or place of national origin. Nor politics or philosophy. Just inhumanity. Just crocodile blood."

In livid color Donny watched uniformed police lead Ryerson out, babbling and bleeding in his dog collar. This was the next episode fading in with Bill's narration. Granny's killer betrays himself by his failure to appear at her funeral. Bill, knowing she had promised the shrink Brisburn Manor, only to assign it instead as the city's future residence of mayors, rushes away to catch the quack packing off, and exacts a confession. That's entertainment. Bill is praised by his father, his brother faces Polsen to plead, "Must we relish killing even monsters?"

"No, I grieve over bahaymas the cops have to kill. But I'd sooner mourn a twelve-year-old animal than some old lady

with maybe six months left to live that he smothered to rob and rape."

"Why mourn either? Why not save the victims of society before they're reduced to making victims of their own?"

"Given those choices, I'd take them. But we get only one. So I choose to mourn your victim of society, over his choice to butcher the innocent."

Donny looked around at the mourners. All the faces of his life were there. Every eye met mine through the magic of seizure as he spoke three words that blew my mind at last.

"Who," Donny demanded of us all, "is innocent?"

The raped old woman deserved it? Them that gets their throats slit asked for it? I tried to protest, but had no voice, sweating in and out of coma. Still, the show went on, the only difference being the charley-horse pains and some nurses entering the scene. From Kearny to Herlihy, I panned over men whose industry had lent their wives to my loneliness. Then I zoomed in on Mrs. Christian's covetous impatience to take over Brisburn Manor.

Not even the Mayor's wife was beyond reproach. Oh, what blame I found in the present and the past. Marissa got us out of London before the smog deaths, Honey saw the oil spill with me on the Costa del Sol, and maybe we prated about our travels to glow in refinement, maybe we flaunted the haute couture stores in which we sometimes shopped, or the tributes to our accomplishments. But to equate our guilt with a murderer's—how could Donny say such a thing in the presence of his mother, the curator of a great museum?

She was in my viewfinder with her gentle Deejay. What sinners we were, what dull adventurers. We coveted and lusted, but never cracked a citizen's skull. None of us was a lethal beast of prey, and Donny, that made a difference!

Even Marge Christian, her point of view over endless Brisburn gardens, said, "Airline crashes, fires, diseases. I must admit we don't need crocodile blood adding to the tragedies so common to life."

How excited her color was. Audio caught her voluptuous gasp

of yearning to occupy the sumptuous tall chambers we dollied past down marble halls that satisfied her passion much as a seat in Congress had fulfilled Mrs. Wilmont. Cut to Stephanie's beaming flush. But domination of Courthouse Plaza had done something less for her husband; I could kill him for the danger I felt his monumental disappointment aiming at my son.

"Bahayma," he judged my Toby as the lens dimmed, dissolving Wilmont into Terry the Bull Peacham. Wherever it was I had faded out to, head ballooning and heart set to spill, the bullterrier Wilmont stared down into my face as bug-eyed small as a Pekingese dog, yowling, "Your son broke the law and must pay!"

My son reacted, I cried without voice. The bahaymas act! You excuse them of breaking the law but condemn their victims!

"You're insensitive to social injustice!"

"Nurse! Nurse! Get my gun! Get everybody's gun!"

COLLAGE 18

All the collectors who frequented this gallery of my confusion, the chaste, the wanton, kept dissolving into one tiny bullterrier above me, and I kept yelling for my gun. Until the nurse explained it was only a compact TV over my bed on a boom.

Oh, shit, the hospital again, vilest of all war's degradations. Terry the Bull hung over my face, spewing, "It's finally the liberals who are crying our values have been rendered extinct! Liberals, don't you know! Let them now confess the political idiocy they contributed to the breakdown of society!"

Who could deny it? My own friends were changing their tune. Some were afraid Baldy had a hand in the Swamptown fire. They said so visiting my comas, thinking me alive. I knew I was dead when Faith kissed my cheek and said Mrs. Brisburn had destroyed Ryerson by making him kill her. No, that was Jennifer fading out like her lost mother. Oh, crazy, depraved, the lives he must have ruined, I was willing to mourn him as a sick doctor for the Sheriff, who kept searching for my hands to

cuff under the sheets. No, he said, it was to see if I had my gun.
I said, "I'm not you, nobody's coming to get me in a hospital."

He said they might try to use me as their only way through
the intricate security of Fenneran, who would not see anyone
alone anymore, not even Donny or Bill. That made me die away
in sorrow. My brain floated off. So many visitors were touched
by murder, Dexter by life. Or wife. Or sister somewhere far. He
seemed to say her son had beaten her as Evan was battered by
Burl, himself a battered child, poor Nola.

At a bleak house, a tricycle rested in puddles riddled by rain.
Bahaymas had murdered two young mothers with point-blank
gunfire after robbing and raping them. The women were white.
So was one of the bahaymas. Price Fenton put a service revolver
to his head and fired, dressed as a county officer like the Sheriff,
who watched and mourned in the needles of rain.

Price handed the gun back to one of his metropolitan policemen as black as the other bahayma, and a second shot exploded.
The killers had tried to escape in an airboat, ladies and gentlemen, you can read that in your newspaper. Polsen told me no
one was to be given this mercy on hearsay or hate. Only those
caught in the act of inhuman cruelty, a principle the Met Council had refused.

Or I dreamed him speaking on a screen with that cold smile.

"This society has been turned into snail shit by pompous,
sanctimonious judges who hold themselves above taking a fellow human's life but not above sacrificing countless innocent
lives thereby to unleashed criminals of every stripe."

Someone was kissing me with intimate affection. It made me
happy to see my wife and smell her precious aura. It felt like
years since I had her so close. But that was all just a hospital
dream, I could tell by the familiarity so moist in her eyes. Nothing had changed. Oh, what a relief. All that anguish and horror,
just the hallucination of one grand mal. It came on cats' feet,
unnoticed at first. Then we were infested. It had seemed so real.
Incredible. Who ever saw a monster? What a joke. But we were
back to life, thank heaven, just a young couple full of little kids,

poised at the turning to rest and ponder a while, my baby and me. I slept again in paradise, smelling my Marissa. What joy.

Suddenly I was up in the world and my kids were all grown. Even the baby was twelve. That was okay. I could work that out with Marissa. But I saw her husband and died.

It was all true. Eagles were near extinction as a species. The fish they savored were dying out in mudholes. Great Gulf Glade, at the height of its fabulous municipal development, was overrun by a destructive rabble from the wilderness. Could this be reality? To find out I said, "Is Dr. Ryerson dead?"

Bill Fenneran put his hand on mine and said, "Yes. He attacked the Sheriff and tried to break free. It's all right, Gabe. We don't get broken antennas in this city anymore."

Hoby told me Toby had been acquitted. Marissa watched me in tears. Okay, I thought, it's okay. You take Hoby, I'll take Toby. The Publisher came over to kiss me too, very tenderly. I loved her profoundly, I played with her hair, but I couldn't remember her name. She whispered it, blushing, and told me it was all right. I had suffered a mild stroke.

No tubes were in my nose. I had no paralysis. But I knew it was not all right. Marissa had swollen eyes for a reason. Only Sam and Amy were there, not Lissa and Toby. Rain filigreed the window. It just felt like a dream because I was seized, or stroked. All of it had really happened.

I said, "Is anyone hurt?"

Everyone's head shook to humor me but Donny's. Noticing that, Sam said, "Lissa had a breakdown, Dad. It's all right, though."

I rolled over, and the jelly slid in my skull. I knew it was not all right. Lissa was at Seashell Key Retreat, a sanatorium that employed theater therapy. Sam told me she had been cramming for her law degree when my stroke occurred, and she decided I was a computer that broke down. Marissa said it was no joke, Lissa meant it. Her Justin was dead. So was her father, killed in the last Mideast war. That was her belief, and it was hardly a delusion.

All that remained of me was a data bank dripping crocodile

blood, with readouts of boys and girls murdered for their bikes by judges, people butchered by lawyers. And Don stood there thinking he looked resolute, not supercilious, not decadent with pretension. I asked him if Judge Wilmont was dead, and he looked angry, and everybody disappeared, leaving me alone with a bahayma in my room.

It had to be TV because he came over as coherent as Josie, saying, "Yeh," with a grin, "I kill dis guy wit his crutch, but I be out quick. Dey can't do nutting, I'm only tirteen."

They had to be called subhuman or we would die with all that civilized life had promised the future. There was no other way.

I watched boys die above my bed in Asia, the data bank drinking more blood from the tiny TV. I saw the funerals of cops in American flags who were ambushed by bahaymas consequently killed while resisting arrest. I heard the bitterness of taxi drivers vowing at the burial of a brother never to accept fares again to Swamptown, Cedar Ridge, or Pinebrake. It was all so heartbreaking. But Lissa's breakdown cut me deeper. I thought nothing could be worse. But there was worse.

Driving me out to see Lissa, Toby told me he had waived his college deferment and enlisted in the marines. The blood slammed into my ears. It was done. It was doom. The firing squad, the blow I couldn't take. Slow sparks danced across my vision. A burning in my chest was so intense I feared a coronary. He took no apparent notice, speeding us over the causeway. I didn't think I would live.

The impenetrable facade of my Lissa hurt too much. Not only did she imagine me electronic, she could not decipher my sounds. The doctors had asked me not to correct or contradict her. There was no danger of that from Toby. He and others were all human to her, and communication was possible, if difficult. My daughter assured us she would recover once her grief subsided over loved ones lost. Her condition convinced Toby I was to blame for his trouble as well as hers. He told me so driving us back.

I had permitted the situation to develop that took Justin's life and made my son homicidal. I had objected to violence on TV,

but accepted it. I had marched in the great Washington demonstration against the war in Vietnam, but allowed it to continue. And worst of all, I had argued the rights of bahaymas while citizens were shot in the streets without reason.

I had let them move into my street while more provident people were abandoning their fine big houses there. Though bahaymas had abused me with inconsiderate filth and noise and obscenity, I tolerated the imposition of their nasty way of life on our pleasant life of decency, which advanced technology and progressive economic planning had endowed on the hardworking and law-abiding. The bahaymas had turned it to rot in our mouths, and I defended them. "Then," he finished me off, "just in time to avoid my trial, you conveniently got sick."

I thought I remembered arranging with Honey for his lawyer, but wasn't sure enough to say: he had no idea how sick I had conveniently made myself. The sea wind whipped my eyes. Toby berated me for my fame. How beautiful the shoreline was beneath giant clouds. He skimmed the surface of the world, accusing me.

"You live for glory. In newspapers, magazines, but not in your own family. You artists are as fake as politicians. It's not enough to just see through fraud and corruption. If you love your children as you claim, it's not enough to just identify evil. It has to be met. You have to *do something*."

Now he had to do something for our way of life in Asia, he said, before vengeful bahaymas caught up with him here. Driving us through downtown Keyport, where they lounged in unsightly bunches, he felt them closing in. Dexter had told me bahaymas didn't care enough about themselves to make any such effort for each other. But without much more hope of convincing Toby than I ever had of stopping this war with Speed and Baldy in Washington, I said, "What have you got against your mother, to do this to her?"

"What did you have against her to feel up an Indian whore behind the house when I was a kid?"

I went straight to hell in the irony of her doing this to us. Josie was notorious in Gulf Glade. I could not explain that single glimpse he misinterpreted as a child years ago without relating

myself to her. Now she was adding my handsome athlete of a son's suspension of his college studies to his sister's illness. She was sending my Toby to war.

There was no rest from life, and bahaymas made bearing it impossible. I longed for the devil's eye of another stroke to relieve me, the maze of hospital visitors, Cassie and her mother describing hills they had rolled across lately through the Black Forest where I left the part of my brain an artist needed the most. Stop wallowing in self-pity, I had imagined from Barry in his steel helmet by my bed, the Met Council listening to him tell war stories in the lamplit murk. Then I woke to him framing bahaymas in the memory of his experience among lethal children, admitting bahaymas were all children, but deciding that to spare them for that would mean he should have allowed those World War burp-gun babies to kill the men for whose lives he was responsible.

With typical arrogance the noisy bahaymas crossed slowly before us, and Toby made each of them leap for safety. None forgot to curse us in obscene outcries of hate. "The German kids were people," Barry had said into my daze. "The bahaymas are beasts." And Bowie beside him said, "People could never commit such harm." Then he looked at me to add, "Outside of war."

Unable to speak, I couldn't thank him for the afterthought. But we were beasts. War turned kids into beasts. Poor Bowie. My despair over a daughter was little compared to his. Yet Barry was in another sense carrying more. Heavily bent over in the darkened room, he had hoarsely said, "The bahaymas must be stopped dead just as those blond kids with burp guns were. Not for Fenneran's habitat or even Polsen's law. For survival."

Toby's eyes were wet as he stopped for a light. "You're the one who did this to Mommy." The big serve killer's term for Marissa was too much to bear. I had to get out and hail a cab as he said, "It's too late now to change anything."

Everything was too late. I had clung as long as possible to keeping my workshop intact, waiting too long to put the house up for sale. Pinebrake values had plummeted because of bahaymas brimming over to the city side of the canal. Daylight mug-

gings were not unusual. The sirens were constant. We always heard screams in the night. Commercial streets were as crowded as the shopping malls with vociferous, exhibitionistic bahaymas. Litter piled up in their wake. Benches and monuments and even the great bulging royal palm trunks were vile with disfiguring graffiti.

The best price I could hope to realize for my house there was preposterous. Money, a long-time no serious problem, had become one again due to the suffocating expenses of Toby's legal defense and Lissa's care. Her brain scans alone cost a few thousand that our health insurance failed to cover for some reason that left me hating the entire medical profession as just one more self-pampering pack of greedy wolves in Samaritan clothing.

Like politicians and artists, Toby might say. The medical-industrial complex, as Donny would. "Health care costs are climbing so rapidly," he had argued with his father by my hospital bed, "that only the rich can afford vigor any longer."

I was half in coma then, but remembered. Don had condemned landlords and bankers as the basest traffickers in evil, who had corrupted productive industrialists too in a cult of manslaughter subtler but more pervasive than the bahaymas. "Mr. Dildress herded old people under crumbling wet roofs. Without bias Mr. Meyerberger invited blacks and whites alike into squalor. Do their souls rest in peace, or were they beasts without souls?"

"The young oversimplify," Fenneran reacted. "They expect human affairs to be organic, and can accept nothing less. But social growth is synthetic. Bill may have been a vulture, but Carl just didn't conceive that kindness could kill."

I was still half in coma, but had to go up in the air and glide with him in order to explain a plan I had devised for a man-made key above Seashell where bahaymas could be attracted to live. He thought the idea feasible, but too late to resolve the predicament. "We need a more immediate solution. I'm considering something."

I begged him not to ask my participation in odious steps I had hoped he might avert by implementing that island refill plan.

"It's just like you," he said in a soft, complimenting tone that

disarmed me for what followed, "to hold yourself above the dirty work of Gulf Glade's security. You've obstinately rejected the possibility of monsters for years, with a stronger and stronger tone of intellectual superiority."

"That sounds mighty strange, coming from you. I was shot in the head. What made *you* smarter than everybody?"

The absence of his smile was scary in our silent climb on upcurrents over the hot city. "I meant for you to share the joke of being insinuated into my utilitarian school of art. You could have prospered from it long before this. Instead you underestimated me, just because I was willing to let my wife have a hobby."

With that ambiguity he swept both my souls away in a steep, long bank over the landscape of a splendor I could have provided my family as Barry had his with a stubborn faith in the better of Fenneran's souls. But I kept my fright from steaming me off to a vindictive self-betrayal with respect to Hillary, if that was his purpose finally. His smile had returned.

It enraged me by the time we landed. With smooth urbanity Tate offered me the killing kindness of a loan. I refused it, shouting on my way to my car, "As for Donny, he undersimplifies!"

My sleep was miasmic with war. Waking was no relief. I had to consider selling the new house that had reached completion at Sunset Bayou while I lay hospitalized. Whatever our state of incohesion, I had designed a mansion for my family, maybe too hopeful it would restore us somehow, but surely as a priceless utilitarian work of art for the children's future. I had mortgaged the valuable frontage; with that cash and other equities gone, I had to get all I could for the house. The highest offer came from someone most distasteful.

Former State Senator Duncan Doran, now a high-priced counsel for politicians with grins like bahaymas, was currently defending three nursing-home operators indicted not for avaricious neglect of sick old people but for cheating the federal government of Medicare funds. Nothing had ever humiliated me more, not the nose-tweaking belittlement of rejection by the

Key Country Club, not even the adjustment to physical handicap and divorce. What could I do but sell to Duncan Doran?

Toby knew nothing about shellfire. He'd walk right down the city streets smiling at the noise, just a big kid who didn't know enough to be scared of explosions on the flat sidewalk with nowhere to take cover. I could no longer face the horror of bombardment, but always had to run in and get him safe. Then I'd wake up jabbering his name in the bongos, and make Honey mad.

Then I'd go down and work to stay alive. I had that going for me thirty feet high. I had to reconstruct the workshop roof a bit to make room for that obsession. My best friends thought me crazy, but that collage fused everything I had gathered since Chitto got guards to kill him in my floodlights. Everything but the album of Faith's illustrated confessions her daughter gave me at the wake.

I had to put that off. I could more easily face incoming shells than my stolen glances at passages like, "Burl married to release us from the bondage to which Hillary's fire addicted us, but, craving for its revival, he begged me to resurrect the slave quarters the night the Bayfront burned."

What tangled impulses drowned even Faith in crocodile blood. Everyone in the world was gone it seemed but bahaymas. I snapped secret pictures of them to blow up and mount on the big collage with industrialists they resembled. Terry Peacham began resembling them too in pictures I got of him yelling from the TV screen that single-residence houses were making slums of the residential neighborhoods and millionaires of the slumlords, and anyone who killed a threatening bahayma had money coming, a kind of bounty some people around him were offering for violent resistance to crime.

That seemed loathsome, contemptible, even though the disgusting faces of bahaymas made me weep for my contaminated older kids. Even though bahaymas played bongos at my door, and were always trying the locks. The Police Commissioner told me they had learned there was no legal penalty for entering without breaking.

I had telephoned to complain about bahaymas soliciting me right on my own street, for sex or handouts, depending on gender. Price said judges had his hands tied. It made me thirst for confrontation, a destructive appetite that Terry Peacham whetted bawling, "Welfare is our hard-earned tax payments. Animals used to work for people. Now people work to pay animals not to work!"

Honey wanted us to live permanently in the decor of her apartment and have a baby instead of a workshop. But I had an obsession to obey, though the bongos kept me from it most of the time. Price Fenton said, "Nobody can slit a throat while slapping bongos, Gabe," and I said, "The gun you gave me may not deter all bongo players, but it sure will a few."

"No killing allowed. Unless you catch them right in the saddle of a crime, Gabe. You want more rights than a cop?"

Indulgently, he sent police around to take some bahaymas away in dog collars, which he usually reserved for purse snatchers and muggers. Such brutes were often seen on the leashes of cops, but numberless more remained to get drunk in the streets and spray their names on every surface. They decorated the whole length of my wharf block with spray paint, and stole the boat my children played in as kids. One day I saw my grocer, Tom Gomez, lying dead on the sidewalk, shot down by robbers he had pursued with his gun.

Every storekeeper on Humphreys Avenue had a gun he still wished he could use on bahaymas, and so did I. On speeders too, and other drivers who stopped for lights on crosswalks, and other creeps who dispensed dogshit in their wakes. They shaved and dressed like me but looked just like bahaymas.

One rainy noon when the bongos drove me upstairs I could tell Honey had left me by the absence of her clothes. I started to phone the *Times,* but could think of nothing to tell her. She didn't phone either. Those who did were sorry.

I told Sam the less Lissa saw me the sooner she'd be well, and Amy wept with him. I asked Marissa if she thought Lissa would stop mourning me before I stopped computing, and she wept too. I told Donny I'd have to kill some bahaymas if his cousin Evan wanted to come admire my work when he returned from

Miami, and Don said I was crazy, he said I was extreme. So I told him to go fuck himself.

Then I asked his mother to come do that to me for old times' sake before she could tell me she had called to say Deejay Polsen, who had only just sent me a small advance for work I might never deliver, was undergoing a mastectomy at the moment. Instead of blubbering, I said, "Does that mean you're not coming?"

Cops and cabbies kept dying. Captured felons too. I wore the handgun in my belt, a little wishful for trouble. When a hag with hair like old mops and a face like dung said, "You wanna git in my meat?" I said, "It'll cost you twenty dollars." When a beggar I refused got hostile, I showed him my teeth. As white as me, he said, "I'mo go home git my *pitoo* and *koo* me a white man."

He meant pistol and kill: I had come to understand their violent dialect. "Go on," I said, "I'll wait right here for you."

He fell into a sheepish grin-and-dance routine, others in plaids and stripes smiling on. They sensed my gun, and plotted. I saw it in their eyes. With mine I invited them to try my ambush alley, but gave them no smile. I gave them shit. We didn't have enough with friends getting cancer and loved ones turning away. We needed bahaymas too, and kids driven nuts by them. They'd never know what hate was, because they never knew what love was. The poor bastards, I felt like putting them all out of my misery.

Marissa wanted me to see a doctor. It really disturbed her to feel the gun in my belt when she embraced me at the chapel services for Jennifer. A bahayma in a car had hit Mrs. Kearny and run on Royal Palm Drive. It proved no one should live alone, the Publisher said when she came to get me for the funeral.

Congresswoman Wilmont gave me the knee in our pew, and I whispered, "It's too late for that."

I had just said that only a while ago at home to divert Honey from my high excitement about Brady Wiley. No newspaper

was out yet with the story, but she had all the details to lighten my grief over Jen. Short hours past in the night, as if leaping through a gap in time, the most monstrous of the five who had raped Majosee plunged out of nowhere into police headquarters without a scalp.

Eyes bulging in the spurtle of gore, and before anyone could learn who had peeled his skull so bare and split it, Wiley just dropped dead. "Like Arthur," I observed, "MacArthur."

Honey admonished that farce was out of place at a time like this and suggested we make love to calm me down before departing. So I suppressed a remark about Josie's five gaining a lap on the Brisburns in their race to the grave and instead said it was too late, as I later told Stephanie Wilmont in our pew. The secular eulogies were starting. On my other flank Honey whispered, "Shhhh."

"Democracy," Fenneran led off at the pulpit, "is a noble ideal, to be cherished but improved. For in our time it has grown too fat. Its lard is costly in lives by the thousands. This disastrous excess obscures every premise of democracy, let alone its virtues. All the honest, altruistic proponents of democracy are becoming absurd worshipers of fat, and the ideal at liberty's center grows hollow. No longer is democracy the fiber of life, or the muscle of liberty, or the bone of happiness."

The Congresswoman gave a decorous gasp, then murmured, "In my view it's people that grow too fat," and I thought she wanted more room till she added, "for the improvement of the system."

I had her wrong? She used to seem just a psychological daredevil with loose political morals. It surprised me to hear myself say, "Greedy people *are* the system. Their *politicians* won't permit improvement."

Stephanie wore a breezy scent. I stayed at her ear, smelling it while past her Wilmont pretended not to see. She still had her high breasts instead of children. We brushed eyelashes, turning for her to whisper, "I surrender. Politicians are beyond contempt. All espouse good over evil, but do nothing about it."

She sounded like my son. I loved her like one, until she licked my ear. It shook me like a virgin, whereas Stephanie had never excited even my mind before. She glowed in this Florida foun-

tain of our youth. No Hillary (weeping up front between daughters-in-law), not even a Jennifer (rest her souls), she was still a gray-eyed beauty at her age, with a broad gluteal agility I suddenly coveted at my age. I whispered I worked late at night when the bongos rested, and we pressed thighs as Fenneran went on mourning his sister-in-law's death by quoting Shawn Hogan's proofs of a subhuman species with genetic compulsions to pillage and kill.

We needed no more convincing. I tried to leave, but Honey pulled me back down. "This isn't a show," she whispered. "You can't just stand up and walk out on a funeral."

Eyewitnesses had come forth with testimony. Don left the chapel with Judge Wilmont and the Sheriff, Dex going directly to arrest Chopka Emathla for the murder of Brady Wiley. Honey led me out with Stephanie's breasts pressing my back. Amid magnolias that bowered the exit I kissed most of Hillary's wet face.

Outside her brother-in-law tried to kiss mine. Jennifer's estranged widower was drunk. His devastated children drew him away, but not before he sobbed, "Wildcats. Animals driving cars in this city. Raccoons, elephants, skunks. Imagine!"

Marissa kissed my tears. Neither of us had heard from our son at boot training in North Carolina. Our daughter in theater therapy liked a role Hoby had devised about computers. With his hand holding mine amid the crowded cars he began to praise my other kids, but Stephanie double-barreled me spongily ahead.

Because her husband had gone with their car, the Congresswoman squeezed me, ribald but qualmy, between her and the Publisher, who drove with suspicious glances at my lap, and by the time we reached Buenaventura Wilmont was back to get the devil behind me in place of his wife. The Sheriff had returned to his wife at the hospital. The Chief Judge had set Chopka free on bail at the demand of his attorney, Don Fenneran, whose sister told me so, radiant in plum rainwear on one of those lugubrious treks to the grave that mingled people strangely under a motley of umbrellas. Her brother had apprised her on the drive out. Cassie introduced me to Dexter's sister, who had

come from the west to grieve, though she had never done that for Jennifer's parents.

Nola Polsen Brisburn had some gray but was vivacious late in her forties like Marissa and other local women. Fountains of youth were not Ponce de Leon's exclusively. Apparently New Mexico had its own. Imagining that Nola goosed me at the grave, I almost fainted. But to my relief it proved to be Cassie. This was her aunt's interment. Crazier than them all, she galvanized my old heart anyway in this unending collage of bereavement. I felt unwholesome.

I felt infirm, and thought her father was sermonizing from the police blotter in the absence of both minister and Sheriff: taxi driver fare thugs at the airport, the incredible proliferation of murderous drunken drivers. All were bahaymas, Tate repined in the rain, their prosecution was no longer possible, civil rights had become a code term for victim abuse. "One begins to wonder if the vigilantism of the old West was not slandered by safe, smug historians into an unjustly pejorative term."

"Then why," Don wept over the grave of his aunt, "has crocodile blood not spread? What has contained the weird phenomenon of bahaymas to Great Gulf Glade?"

"Good lord," his father prayed. "Who do you suppose blew up thirty passengers waiting at a New York airport if not a bahayma? Can you really believe human beings capable of that?"

"Can you really accept as patriots," the Mayor sorrowed, "those who bomb department stores to indiscriminately cripple children, and neighborhood taverns to dismember their parents? God knows only bahaymas can do that, not human beings like you and me."

"Eggheads," Royal keened while Jennifer's son and daughter tried to subdue him, "they spill their rotten odor on people while monsters come from the jungle to do this to us."

As workmen lowered the bier with tackle, Honey cleared her stricken throat to eulogize a movie director's wife slaughtered pregnant with friends. "Can you open a newspaper," she wept hoarsely, "without someone raping a little baby? How abominable must animals be for the son of Tate Fenneran to defy and defend."

"Nobody's perfect," I lamented in defense of her syntax.

"And the industrial gougers?" Don wiped tears from his glances between brother and father. "Are they human, considering their mortal crimes against the poor? The food-supply profiteers? Are they all not putrid with crocodile blood?"

And he called me crazy, he called me extreme. A lash of rain chattered across the umbrellas. This was war, not just a graveside debate among eccentric kin. As if struck too by that, his heavenly mother fixed her sorrowing green eyes on me like a benediction. "And the utmost crime? Is war started by beasts or human beings?"

That was her elegy to us both as hopeless casualties of war. My sad, my lovely, it had taken me all those years to realize Hillary was a genius who understood everything but art. I could not bear her heartbreak, and faced across her sister's grave where Stephanie invoked the name of Hogan, who was with us only in spirit this day. "According to Shawn, genes that dictate behavior are changeable. In time, bahaymas can adapt to new social conditions."

She held me, not Fenneran, in a gaze fiercer than her husband's as Tate, his whole application of sociobiology contravened, faced not the Congresswoman but his wife to say, "Even the belief in a genetic reason for barbarism is irrelevant in our emergency to eliminate it." That laid everything to rest but Donny. Obviously exasperated with him, Fenneran placed his hand on Don's shoulder. But it was me he addressed, and I was scared. "Would you say I did my very best with this guy?"

Something dire had to be hanging over my life for them all to be wanting me always at the center of their conflicts. If bahaymas didn't kill me, these overweening nobles would. I said, "You did very well with Donny. I'm convinced he's right and you're wrong."

Everybody sadly smiled but Don and Honey. She didn't get my joke. He got his father's threat.

High with rain, the watercourses swallowed more victims of crime and retribution. Everyone knew a missing person, a storekeeper at least, a cabby or a cop. Some were dredged up dead

from the brackish mangrove bayous down below, but many more such corpses were plainly bahaymas, regarded by Don Fenneran as the persecuted in revolt, struck down by the police without due process but with the tacit encouragement of his father.

In it all, outrage rumbled over the release of Muddabudda. Barry Christian fed that widespread public distemper by turning down the bahayma warlord's demand of a swamp sanctuary for his people between Seminole land and the city. The evening news featured our Mayor refusing to encourage terrorism by negotiating with it, then showed irate citizens who supported his stance and disappointed ones who believed no opportunity should be lost that could rid us of bahaymas.

Both sides of the question had my sympathy, and all I could do was work. With rot in my mouth, to term it my son's way. There was no word from Toby in reply to Marissa's plea for an invitation to visit him at camp, and I dreamt of nothing but war. Mourning my death in it, Lissa agreed to converse with the computer next time I came, her progress slow but hopeful. My other son sensed that I hoped only to die before Toby, my other daughter wept as much as I denied ever having such thoughts.

Honey could not understand why I declined the last chance she brought me to live instead of die by honeymooning with her all around the Gulf in her sloop. Sensitivity was never something you could win in an argument, so I just said no matter where I went in the world it looked like Keyport to me. She had learned to blame everything on my head, and spared me to work in the bongos though my head ached with all that crowded it.

That included the fright of Evan's mother when he suddenly arrived at Jennifer's burial and picked up wet earth to cast in the grave. Did I dream it in stroke or had Dexter visited to say watch out for his battered nephew? It was not Nola across the grave but me that Evan showed his dirty palm, ecclesiastically intoning, "The sluggard will not plow by reason of the cold; thus shall he beg at harvest and have nothing."

What did everybody want from me? Now it was Josie, raging on the TV screen to entice me. This scarred victim of us all made me squirm with more swampy urges than Mrs. Needles

used to send me over the canal, but I hesitated to make a sex object out of Honey for such a capricious lust. So I complained to my congresswoman instead. Guessing she worked late, with a husband like hers, I reached her at the office, and as a pretext asked how come Mayor Christian was keeping bahaymas out of the swamp if Fenneran wanted them driven there. I appreciated the straightforward duplexity of her reply: "It's too complex, I can drive over and explain, but wouldn't need a chaperone at my own office."

"In that case I'll drive right over and listen."

"Tomorrow. This unrest has forced Harmon to convene a review of the evidence against Chopka Emathla. If you come, I'll explain Barry afterward in the privacy of my office."

I doubted the kinky itch would last. So I took it to the Publisher and, swallowing my integrity, tried to imagine she was Josie. But in vain despite her shrieks. Honey's bottom was just too robust. So I made Stephanie the fantasy, though her tempting seemed so extreme I felt the recurrent foreboding of contenders who kept luring me to their side of danger. Hoping to learn which side she was on at the hearing, I went after her congressional seat over Honey's strong opposition.

Liberal Don didn't balk at discrediting two black laborers. Calling their testimony inconclusive won a routine dismissal for his client from Judge Wilmont without necessity of trial. So much for the scalping of four sick unfortunates in the polyglot family of man, with only Price Fenton remaining for Chopka to finish off.

Earlier, Mrs. Wilmont had told me a lot of Hogan about being genetically programmed to behave as we do, the individuals of a species sacrificing even life to preserve the common genes. So, bridling as we left the court, I turned it back on her. "We've just seen a permissive judge preserve his crocodilian genes by favoring the criminal over the victim, and it seems a crocodilian crime for Tate to have placed your husband on the bench deciding the fate not of criminals, but of all us multitudes of victims."

"Chief Judge is an elective office," she reminded me.

"Bullshit," I said. "The party selects and the sheep elect."

"Don't blame the party on Tate. He needs it as much as it needs him." In the morning sun we were crossing Courthouse Plaza through a magnificent stone park of sculptures full of graffiti. "The question is, do the people need Tate?"

That sounded ominous. She took the instant of my disquiet to say Tate was intent on having his own man in the White House. "To answer the question you asked last night, Barry refused to negotiate with terrorists, as he put it, because he's to be the presidential candidate who took no arrogance from savages. The ultimate proponent of law and order. A modern Andy Jackson. There's more to explain. Shall we do it in my office?"

Even self-sufficient women depended on their allure to tempt men, and resented them as sexist for responding. "I suddenly need sleep. You sound as if you could use some too."

"Oh, Jesus, if you don't believe that, you surely won't believe your friend Barry is about to bring such massive destruction down on the bahaymas that survivors, if any, will escape in terror."

"Yeah?" I said irritably among the sunny passersby. "How?"

"That much hasn't reached me yet. In any case you wouldn't be convinced until it happened. Christian genocide. Will anyone believe that?"

"Ah, you're crazy, Stephanie." I hurried, but she came striding along. "Why me? Why bring a disinterested, bongo-crazy individual like me, with probably depraved genes, into this extravagant defense of your politics?"

"My politics need help, not defense. The country deserves it. And you're in a peculiarly essential position to provide it. But I knew you wouldn't believe. Not until you saw the holocaust."

She turned away as broad as Daisy McFee, exciting me. But her intensity had really worn me out even though it was not yet quite my morning bedtime. That vast fatigue, along with a sense of escaping from disaster, made her easy to resist.

It was another matter, however, to resist her fears about Barry that I had suffered about Tate for years. Nor could I confront either of them about it without placing myself in jeopardy. She was smart enough to know that. But I was not. I was exhausted. I was burdened by familiarity with the influence Fenneran had

over Christian. I was surprised by a message from the Mayor when I got home.

I returned the call. It seemed a perfect convenience to learn if such stupendous fears as Stephanie's were justified, so I asked straight out if Barry was regarding himself as presidential timber these days. "I'd say not," he replied, "after this call."

"That sounds fraught with significance. Clarify it, please, and let me get some sleep."

"To be President, you need the gall not to tell even your old, old buddy to keep his kids off the mainland this week. Good-bye."

"Wait!" It held him. "You didn't even call me Gabe several times, so this can't be political. Barry, some of your closest associates are expecting you to overreact. Don't do it."

"You don't do it, soldier. Don't be a pious halfwit like them and defend an enemy culture that's either at war with us or breaking our laws, while we neither meet it in battle nor arrest its atrocities. We're just letting it destroy us. Keep Sam and Amy at Marissa's all week. That's an order."

COLLAGE 19

The great swing of hips in her breezy frock taunted me, her stalwart breasts. Stephanie was coming to my workshop at long last, and I could hardly wait. Meanwhile, in my congresswoman's defiance of her age I was in love with Faith in the album I inherited.

It kept tempting me to skim her tantalizing notes, though each would end up stinging me like the photos I tried not to see of her chained with Burl to the whipping post. One such entry said, "How glorious the human imagination, to sublimate as romance the functional spice with which nature tricks us into propagating the race. That exemplifies our magnificence. Ah, boundless magic. Eventually, chained to that whipping post, Burl died in bliss."

Ah, carnal knowledge—who shot those photographs of her and Burl? If her message was really carnal ignorance, what were the leaders of the people but mad exploiters all coyly blending off to absurdity in mutual tolerance? My Toby was right, I had to do something. But I didn't know what.

All I could do was collage, until Stephanie phoned to say she was coming over, now that the weather was lovely. I told her the bongos were fierce, the natives were restless, she would be taking her life in her hands, driving into treacherous Pinebrake. She said not to worry, she would bring a machine gun along.

With the rains ending, no radio station carried anything more than smug weather reports, but a sudden news break announced animals amuck by the hundreds in our streets. Somehow every cage had been thrown open at Big Cypress Zoo. I told my congresswoman to quickly tune in her radio and hung up to switch on TV.

The prime-time shows were not to be preempted for any news short of strike arbitration. That was TV. But the radio kept blaring on-the-spot bulletins with barking sirens and gunfire. County and metropolitan police were out in force. Among the hungry predators, normally docile beasts had turned ferocious with fear and confusion. Soon the evening shows were over and Bull Peacham came in view with a tirade that uncovered the real proportions of this weird event: the all-out war against the bahaymas had erupted.

I was too staggered to understand that yet as Terry fulminated, glasses white with flames of hate. "Crime must get worse at this rate. Nothing stands still. Stop it now in the pornography explosion downtown as well as the mugging, murder, and rape in swampside. Stop immorality of every kind, I say, and do it now, or be devoured by animals, animals!"

The news followed. At last I saw the squad cars race in full howling color, young reporters shrieking into their microphones that jeopardy prowled the city as never before. The police were asking everyone to calmly remain indoors. I was amused to see an old soldier like Mayor Christian admonish citizens not to arm themselves and rove in cars. It was like the order to avoid Calvados that he passed down to men embarking for the Normandy beaches. Drink anything but Calvados. We drank nothing but Calvados, and lay all over the cobbled streets of Carentan like the bodies we left in the surf.

I got my shotgun down from the high catwalk and understood all at once. Barry was no longer amusing, no longer an innocent

young lieutenant but a pragmatic old general prosecuting Fenneran's great counterattack against the hordes of Majosee.

Everybody in Great Gulf Glade was getting down his shotgun at Barry's entreaty not to. Stephanie's prophecy of holocaust leaped back like a slap, waking me to Tate's (hence Barry's) comprehension that once people realized dangerous animals had to be shot down, momentum would keep them right at it, shooting bahaymas until every mall and park was rid of them. My kids were safe, living on Ceremony or mending on Seashell or militarizing in North Carolina.

I telephoned Marissa anyway but got a busy signal. I thought of the handgun up in my bedroom but had no time to waste getting that. TV showed people running with their weapons. There was already gunfire outside, where the bongos had stopped dead.

I unlatched the door for a look, and jerked it shut at once. A civilian car had just hurtled past spitting buckshot at the night. Not animals but people were fleeing. Not people but animals. Bahaymas had murdered three Brisburns with heirs left in discordant agony. They had desolated Justin's family. The grocery remained sealed with its corrugated metal night shield, Tom Gomez's partners in shock, his orphaned family forever shattered. My daughter, my son, we were skinned alive by bahaymas. I slipped outside to kill bahaymas. I saw them racing for the large house they had transformed into a brawling slum across the way.

They were trampling over refuse heaps where the weeds of wrath grew tall all over the deep lawn. I leveled the shotgun to litter the place with as many bodies as the repeating magazine of five cartridges would bring down at the easy range of fifty yards.

Obstreperous, obscene, those animals vomited themselves on the rest of us with plunder and rape. They blared vulgar music into our heads on the avenues, turning up bottles to drink from in our faces, offending us next with crashing glass to cut the knees of children who stumbled at play. They suffocated us in their garbage, they tortured us with tom-toms, they murdered life. They were a pollution to eradicate and now was the time.

I had them in front of my gun, but I couldn't murder the bastards. An atrocious lawlessness had descended on us like plague. It was the most inconceivable catastrophe ever to befall a society. Barbaric aliens had invaded civilizations before, and so had actual plague, but there had never been anything like this in the world. There was never, anywhere, the sudden emergence of a people so deviant, cruel, and irreclaimable. Yet my finger just would not pull the trigger.

Nor could I believe other fingers would. Yet Baldy said it was happening when he telephoned to enlist me. It got him mad to hear me say I couldn't chance hitting an innocent. "An innocent Nazi?" he shouted. "An innocent virus? You son of a bitch, you think you're better than me that I should shovel your shit? Get the hell out there and carry your fucking weight!"

I hurried up the ramp to put my shotgun back in its place. I hurried down to telephone the Mayor and heard my yapping voice cry, "Emmy? Gretchen? Beth? Put your father on, it's Gabe."

Their mother came on to say, "Barry's at Keyport Station, dear. We're moving to Buenaventura this week."

"Oh, how nice, Marge. Guess what's happening tonight. Mrs. Wilmont told me all hell was going to break out, and lo—"

"Oh, don't mind Stephanie, Gabe. She wanted the mayoralty so, and now Bowie Pratt is to run in Barry's place when he—"

I depressed the button softly to let her enjoy speaking. All over the east side foxes and zebras ran in circles, tigers and leopards searching for jungles of the swamp. I saw them in the news, the nets and fierce faces spotlit on my TV screen. I heard my children weep in fear and pity, the two that telephoned. They wanted me far from swampside. I had to decline because of company I was expecting. Marissa took the phone in a pique that sounded like jealousy so I said it was a collector coming and asked if any word had come from Toby. There was no word. But she had just left Lissa smiling. I promised not to go outside.

As gunfire crackled and animals roared with fright, it hurt to feel so thankful for the safety of everyone but Toby. For a postcard from him I would gladly have run outside shooting among the bears and lions, the gazelles and elephants and wom-

bats and wolves that were shooting back with handguns and dying like dogs all over Gulf Glade.

When she arrived I called Stephanie crazy to have braved the hazards of this balmy wild night. She said she had congressional immunity and I laughed with bawdy fawning, sick of my own jokes on the theme. Then my best hope sank at the sight of Evan Brisburn checking to see that her car doors were locked.

The gunfire and shouting were distant. The bongos were still. But Evan, implying the two had spent a clandestine evening together, said they had watched it all on TV, the news special reporting armed citizens on the loose in car packs long after the zoo beasts were all rounded up or shot.

He had something in a paper bag like a street drunk. He didn't fit with her. I latched the workshop door, resenting Evan's lean youth and pinched little eyes. "For Tate to understand impetus so," Stephanie said as the remote gunfire continued to murder monkeys and jackals and goats, "proves him not only lethal but incredibly cunning. Opening the zoo cages has to be the most ingenious single idea I ever heard of."

I said, "That's about how he once praised my gazebo plan."

"I know. You had imagination back then."

Rather than acknowledge that audacity, I got back to work. "Okay, it's genocide. Are you really sure it's Fenneran's doing?"

Evan laughed. Stephanie gave that salacious little gasp of hers and said the scope of my huge collage amazed her. That stirred my vanity, till she added, "It's perfectly insane," and clacked away in her severe dark business suit. "Your work is as unexacting as your character has led me to expect."

"My work," I returned her insolence, "is your Rorschach test. My art is to intimate contradictions as allegory. People sense that and bring me personal things they want put to use."

"I sensed that," Evan said from the leather couch. "I brought you something personal I want put to use."

It looked like booze in the paper bag, so I shook my head when he asked if I was curious to see what he had. Nor did I care to hear, I said when the testy Congresswoman offered to tell me, how Tate had manipulated the zoo. "I'm an agnostic," I said,

climbing my ladder high before the collage with a tack hammer. "We're able to live without knowing."

"You can die of ignorance too," Stephanie quavered in a kind of controlled fury. "With all you've personally seen of war and greed, of monsters and corruption, you still don't believe. Do you have enough sense to believe this?"

She peeled back some of the paper bag on Evan's lap, and I could feel the adrenaline strike through me. The crazy woman had really brought a machine gun. It bristled, though small and shiny as a toy. Slowly, as calmly as I could, I descended the ladder, hoping they realized that, with my experience as a combat sergeant, if Evan dared to point that thing at me I would die of fright. I tried to toss it off with a laugh, but nothing happened. Now I was sure Dexter had told me this kid beat his mother.

Like a mind reader he said, "Tate has been coming to my mother in New Mexico for years. I know his ways like a book."

I had to nod. Even Christian knew Fenneran worked in ways too complex for anyone to comprehend, but I would not argue the point, or any point, with Evan. Because gunshots knocked you kicking. They shattered bone and tore nerves apart. They shocked, they excruciated. Only cowboys could tie up a gunshot wound with a bandanna and fight on, kissing girls. Evan had a machine gun full of bullets, so I believed. I was willing to believe anything, as long as these people didn't kill me.

Another mind reader, Stephanie said, "Evan won't use his gun on you. Unless you force him to, of course."

He said, "I'd like it full for the guests at a luncheon tomorrow, the very scum of the earth," and that was all right with me. But not when he added, "Although I have two more magazines full, right here in the bag."

I attempted to work, but only private detectives could show that kind of intrepid scorn for a gun while rationally obeying the gunman. A headache came and ballooned to nausea as Evan explained the interdependence of practical and conceptual knowledge in dialectical materialism with its long-range perspective on the interrelation of all facets of life.

I could not help but agree. Terry Peacham remembered no longer the hot menace of a gun, the paralyzing wallop of his

shots at Negroes, or he would less often call for open warfare by other people's sons against the oil sheikhs and small Communist nations. But I did remember the shot that sledged me right out of the jeep on my face, blindly yelling "Hey hey hey hey hey" into oblivion.

So I found it as easy to concur in the position Stephanie took, that Fenneran's materialistic democracy was an undialectical failure visible in any public facility of unproductive union workers. I had known the obnoxious clerk all my life, and my guests had a machine gun. I dreaded finding out what they could possibly have on their minds, to come out of this night of slaughter with that weapon and all that Marxist rhetoric.

"Christian knows he's being groomed for the Presidency," Evan said, "but doesn't realize it's for Tate's final war."

"Not against bahaymas," Stephanie elucidated. "You can be sure that's just a code word. He's consolidating multinational industries for his final solution of the socialist question."

I didn't say, Bullshit, you're just bitter about losing the Mayoralty. I was content to hear Evan say they had a good use for me. Until he told me what it was.

His mission was to murder Fenneran. Earnestly polite, he said I was necessary to the task. "Tate has been a father to me. Yet he's never willing to see me alone. Aside from the Mayor and the Sheriff, you're the only one."

I sweated, pretending to work. My voice shook shamefully as I told him, "No better man for it than your Uncle Dexter."

"To kill my mother's future? He'd promptly shoot me right between the eyes if I approached him."

Stephanie's eyes narrowed. I had dug Polsen's distance from their scheme out of Evan. He didn't kill me for that, so I said, "I'm never alone with Tate. His chauffeur, waiters. Bodyguards."

"Not in a two-seat glider. He's going up in the morning."

"Oh. Yeah. Well, I can't take a machine gun up there."

"No, this is my gun. You take your gun." (Who told him I had one?) "Afterward, just walk to your car and drive away. No one'll notice he's dead in time to detain you."

I was really perfect for the job. In a way as close to Tate as

his family. Even drawn by him and others to this very epicenter of their conflict. I could admit all that, but Evan talked and Stephanie talked and I felt like kicking both of them out with their tedious evangelical jargon. Instead, as he drew the shining machine gun from its paper bag, I went to my file bins for a folder with Evan coming along into the dark. "The war was long ago," I said. "It's hard to see myself killing a guy." Back in the light I asked him, "Why did you bring all that firepower?"

"You have a shotgun up there, Gabe." Dexter, my mind ticked off, knew nothing about my ambush alley to have told his nephew. The pointed gun was back in its paper bag. Watching me spread pictures out on the work table, Evan said, "Artists are natural dialectical materialists, and bahaymas sit in the high seats of American power. I'm surprised to see you balk at such a rare opportunity to serve the human race. This gun is a Chinese *Svau Ji-ch'iang*. I'm a Soviet political officer."

"Haw-SHEEE!" It burst from me like the sneeze I then disguised it to be. That one was just too much for me to believe even with the guns of Stephanie's breasts suddenly pressing at my back. The headache rearing, I said through my teeth, "Where would you two be while I'm up there gliding with Fenneran?"

"Harmon thinks I went to Washington," she whispered. "It's not too late for that stuff. Unless I must visit Seashell Key."

Expedience, the soul of congresspersons. She was probably echoing Evan's party line just to humor his bloody activism for her own ends. *Tick-tick.* Because Tate was frustrating her politically as he had always done her husband. Very near hysteria, I turned around to belly with her and embraced her girdle. She heaved away; both of them looked appalled, a pair of scandalized assassins. "The world's on fire," she snarled, "and you just want your little twiddle twaddled!"

"It was just my way of asking what's on Seashell Key?"

"I thought you'd never ask," the Congresswoman said, pacing.

"You don't have to be Jewish," the foreign agent added, "to know how vulnerable someone's children make him."

"I'll be at the Seashell Key Retreat." Stephanie flashed a hand-

gun and let it fall back in her purse. "Who would suspect a congresswoman, whose husband just died at a luncheon, when your sick daughter drops from her high-rise sanatorium terrace?"

Maybe I screamed, but I was deaf, I was blind, I didn't even see her go. I was alone with Evan, his deadly toy of a machine gun glinting at me when I said, "Am I to understand that you're *commanding* me to kill Tate Fenneran?"

"The choice is yours, but only to pick up the phone. Say something Tate'll invite you to discuss, gliding over his spoils."

His gun was aimed not at me but at my broken kid. What did they want from Lissa? His Aunt Jen was dead, but someone else also knew about my catwalk *tick-tick* where we returned to *tick tick-a-tack tick* and that was Liz who Bocaleoned me up there with Freudian jokes about the shotgun and could have mentioned its presence to Price, the first to discover that great talent of hers in Sunset Bayou. Could Price be this killer's ace against my baby? *Tick-a-tack-tack*, the bongos were starting somewhere far, and a nearer set replied as the barred owl used to in these parts. I said, "That's the whole trouble with you crusaders, finally. You just don't understand that nobody's allowed to tell anyone else what to do. People just can't be that way to people."

"We can. We have the power. To set agents on all your kids if Tate should survive your glide after I've called off Mrs. Wilmont at the Seashell Retreat."

I was supposed to kill for them, then live on in the hope they'd never find cause to harm Lissa, Toby, Sam, or Amy. I had dreamed this would be my last collage, my most comprehensive. Then I'd be free to sailfish with my friends out on the Gulf, forever. The void at last of search and stress. The VA psychiatrist had called such dreaming suicidal, and said I had to quit fighting World War II or it would eventually kill me.

My *Lifetime* was just about finished. I wished it luck. Evan's massive firepower guaranteed me instant death rather than the painful mere probability of it in a single shot or two. Appreciating that, I slipped into my one hope in the file shadows.

"Gabe, don't be stupid and go for that shotgun!"

Old soldiers, we faded away. Artists, we worked in tennis shoes. What a mistake he made. Dancing to one side, I stopped

in the darkness where Christian once kept Polsen from pursuing me as if I were crazy enough to murder him as a Nazi. With any part in this, the Sheriff would have warned a nephew not to give me that chance. Polsen had come to learn the simple trick we had on patrols. We hid in doorways. We looped the forearm around a passing sentry's neck and pressed it to his throat while thrusting that shoulder hard against the back of his head. The pitch of my breathing, a typhoon in my ears, always drowned out the sound of a cracking spinal cord. The bongos silenced Evan's.

Could he have expected bongos to endure in a morning concert for his cover, should gunfire become necessary? I doubted that any foreign government agency would employ a young desperado like this one. For over twenty years Fenneran had been taking precautions I couldn't even guess at to stave off vengeful underworld forces. The wily Organization had found its consummate hit man at last in Evan—close to Tate, trained to move an opportunistic politician to help execute his mission. I had not just now killed an alien despot for abusing human rights, but oh, well, the thought was there.

This skinny kid was heavy as hell in death. I stretched the body out on the couch and ran to latch the door. Stephanie had thoughtlessly left it ajar in an unsafe neighborhood like this. Was she Evan's dupe or exploiter? Drop such a doctrinaire liberal politician into Mississippi, and she'd be preaching racism before her parachute was off. My skull base ached with pure hatred, but I didn't kick Evan in the face for plotting violence on my Lissa.

I remembered to mourn him instead. So young a man. He could have been rehabilitated after killing my poor child. I telephoned the retreat director and told him to let no one but immediate family near Lissa. Still emotional about the calamity of animals last night, he believed when I said she was in serious peril. No police, I had him repeat, no political figures. Nobody but us.

Early as it was, Marissa had only just got home, but I didn't want to hear about her hospitalized husband. Get Lissa, I said, take her with Amy and Sam to the boat basin. Don't tell me now,

at least Hoby's alive, just take the kids and get on Honey's sloop. Lots of people must have suffered such attacks last night, a lot of people died. We don't want Lissa to. We don't want harm to Amy or Sam. Hoby'll be all right, nobody uses gall bladders anymore. Marissa stop crying and try to understand. They want to kill our Lissa. No, no cops. Don't tell Dexter either. I don't know who's after us. I know how this sounds, just do it. Maybe it's not just in my head. What's there to lose if it is? I don't know if Honey'll go with us, I'll see. Sure I'm taking my pills. Will you get the fuck going? There may not be much time!

I had to get going myself, but didn't know what to do with the body in the dawning light of day. I sat with it at the brink of seizure, shuddering. Full of phenobarbital, aspirin, caffeine, phenacetin, my head felt strange. I couldn't drive this way but had to. I had just killed the Sheriff's nephew, a Brisburn no less. I felt a desperate incapacity to face Polsen with that, or Fenneran, or even Don or Hillary or Bill.

I could not even be sure no one among them was in alliance with Evan and Stephanie—and Price. I had little doubt he was the accomplice who provided them with all that background on me. The moment he heard from Stephanie that Evan had failed to contact her, Price was sure to overtake me with all the killing power of his police force. I had to get out of there.

But I couldn't A sudden gunshot exploded the latch from outside. Terrified, I scooped up the machine gun on my way into the darkness of my file bins. Into the workshop they came. A pair of laughing bahaymas. In stripes and plaids and high-heeled ugly shoes. Dragging Stephanie Wilmont by the arms. Her girdle was gone with her skirt. I saw her bare legs and belly with the hair, she looked so tender. I saw her blind gray eyes and bloody face, the teeth pearly in her open mouth. She was dead but they were still lusting, their pants undone. They had caught her departing and raped her in the car until daylight drove them inside. I could see all that before the shot rang out, one of them firing point-blank into Evan's face as the bongos thumped outside. In immaculate peace on his back, he had looked so saintly that they thought him merely asleep.

I went up the ramp to old ambush alley for my shotgun, and watched them below in the floodlights. They folded Stephanie over the back of the couch across Evan grotesquely. One had a bottle that they drank from in its paper bag while arguing in amused whispers for possession of her. They stood in perfect range from the high girdling catwalk, beautiful at the end of my shotgun, but too near the bodies for me to open fire. Then the first put his handgun to the second's head, which inspired him to point the whisky bottle at his partner's head, and they fell to reeling laughter that spun them to the distance I required.

One threw the bottle crashing at a wall. The other fired a shot into the collage of my life as if I were a grocer named Tom. Two sweethearts, I blew them away with the shotgun. Mourning, I blasted them down with a second shell. What a loss. Donny could have done wonders with them. Government clerks. Even school teachers, once rehabilitated, to educate more such youngsters.

Bahaymas were two-legged people, I once heard Donny argue in court, not animals on all fours. He deplored brutality of course but understood. They were made that way by life in this society.

When I descended, a third bahayma came in with a can of spray paint. He could not see me beyond the light, but saw the carnage and turned to withdraw. I was prepared to let him go, not having caught him in the saddle of a crime. But my *Lifetime* attracted him. He stopped to gaze critically over the immense composition. Then, having judged it, he sprayed his name on my art. So I silhouetted him on it with a blast of shot. That seemed only fair. No doubt they had been spray painting her car when the Congresswoman fled and with a stunning punch had dragged her into it. Her husband would understand.

Judge Wilmont blamed such behavior on the absence of equal opportunity, on racial bias and a socially distorted sense of values, but never on anything like hate, viciousness, or evil. To me he was not a judge but an undertaker drumming up business. He was Death, masquerading all his life as Florence Nightingale.

Why should his wife not die of that? After all, a child at play uncovered a well and died of that. A family went boating, and

drowned. Why shouldn't this deprived person's fate turn that simply on his bad luck of going out to desecrate with spray paint? You cross a street without looking? You get killed for that. It wasn't your fault, you just weren't thinking. But that was life. You willfully kill somebody? You are killed for that. It wasn't your fault, you were just born a bahayma. Why shouldn't that too be the hard reality of life? Why shouldn't it be so for the false revolutionary who could justify killing children? A plane crash killed the unlucky. That was life. Let murdering and raping and all human harm be that dangerously unlucky to the perpetrators. And to their guilt-ridden, pious defenders. And call it life.

I was crazy, dialing with five dead people around me. I had shot myself right in the collage, and to keep from screaming my lungs out in the horror, I was eating. My children, my children, and poor Marissa Harnett. The Publisher didn't answer at home, but her secretary did at the office and said hang on, the boss was there early to leave early for a luncheon.

Stuffing fruit and cheesecake in my mouth, I told Honey my workshop ran with crocodile blood. To hear me say bahaymas had fired on me overwhelmed her with love. She assured me I was too distraught to call the police, and said, "I can't expect you to take me to the luncheon."

I was inclined to agree, though unable to recall a luncheon appointment other than Evan's (*tick-tick*). She forgave me for always smiling but never really listening, and said she would report my bahaymas directly to the Police Commissioner for me. That sounded fine. So did her inability to come comfort me, having to tie up the terrible news of the night and then go make ready for the luncheon. Convinced survivors of the terror would be disposed to shoot us on sight, I didn't want her in Pinebrake. Nor did I want her around to get hurt in case Price came after me.

I stuck his gun in my belt. Honey knew three bahaymas had forced me to kill them, but I had told her nothing about Evan (maybe because of the luncheon she had echoed him to announce) or Stephanie (by the habit of never mentioning a female

visitor). Price might go after Lissa to repay me for Evan and Stephanie, but I would be there to confront him. If he showed his face, he'd never live to spend the first thought on my other children.

I faced up to telling Polsen, but his home phone didn't answer. Taking a deep breath, I dialed his office, and learned with relief that I didn't have to tell him his nephew was dead. A deputy who seemed to know me reported the Sheriff away on vacation. "Always promised he'd show Deejay a mountain," the man said, voluble with youth. "By now they must be on top of Ole Smoky."

My car packed and ready, a clean sportshirt over the gun in my belt, I drove away noticing Stephanie's Mercedes covered with graffiti like the camouflaged Volkswagens the enemy drove in the war. The day was clear. I saw bodies for old Bayfronters to skin nostalgically. Surviving bahaymas shoved pushcarts full of paper bags, escaping the carcasses that remained for the sun to spoil until buzzards or sanitation trucks could reach them.

Snooping bahaymas, lured into my workshop by the shattered door lock, would be driven out by the cadavers at least until the police arrived. Thanking God for Fenneran's highways, I kept reminding myself to remember my blind side and raced all the way to the marina. But I found no sloop there.

I stood on the pier like a fool with the paper bag in my hands. I sat on a bench amid pigeons. I paced in the sun. It was too late to catch any of my family at Marissa's. I thought of telephoning the Retreat, but didn't want to stop them there. I wanted Lissa out. Nor did I trust myself to be there with Evan's loaded machine gun and extra magazines if enemies came to the Retreat after Lissa. My wife and children could get hurt.

Not a bahayma was to be seen in the bayside malls where I roamed with my paper bag. Early on a new day, one sometimes saw work crews scrubbing everywhere to expurgate the tall white walls of graffiti. They had already been here, I could see amid whistling shopkeepers and shoppers wending at their leisure. I bought fresh fruit to eat from a short man with hair on his nose whose smile made him handsome. An excited big dog ran up and licked the hand I gave it.

The piped fare was not tinhorn but chamber music after the fashion of the Harvester. Not for years had I enjoyed so many young fathers shamelessly acting like fools to amuse their tots while girl mothers laughed. A greater ethnic variety of nice people than I had ever noticed ran most of the shops. People cleaned up after their dogs along the palmy decorator walks. It felt as serene as times past, and I longed to keep this melodic celebration going forever. But the missing sloop was sure to end it. And just when I could see the simple goodness Marissa said I never recognized. Afraid to guess what the boat's absence meant, I located a phone stall and called up Commissioner Fenton.

Price asked what police I was talking about. He had sent no police. I asked if he didn't believe the three I killed had crocodile blood, and he asked what three did I mean. I tried to keep cool. He saw them born, I said, he must know I meant the bahaymas I shot in my workshop.

"Gabe, I didn't know. No report ever reached me."

Was that a nascent code term for sweeping away the genocide of bahaymas last night? "You son of a bitch, I reported it. I personally telephoned you." I really believed I had conveyed it to him directly. "My God, I'm insane. Excuse me, Price, it was Honey. I know *she* phoned you for me."

"What, about the luncheon? She just phoned to ask if I'd be there today. Gabe, I've never given her a second look, you know that. I told her I'm not going. You know the night I had?"

"She forgot what she called you about, that's all. Too much on her mind from last night. What luncheon is that, Price?"

"Duncan Doran's, don't fish with me. Listen, get some rest and don't worry. I'll take care of everything with the captains."

In the rush of blood to my head I could not even hear my own good-bye. A luncheon at my own house in Sunset Bayou, and I forgot she told me? The house I built and had to sell? To a political shyster like Doran? And I forgot?

She had called Price only because her secretary heard her tell me she would, her question about the luncheon just a hasty contrivance. Instead of informing him, she had gone straight for the sloop. How strange that I had excluded her from those who knew about my ambush alley and the shotgun up there. She was

the one who had briefed Evan, right down to my handgun from Price.

Leaving the phone stall, I saw Marissa with her suitcase, I saw my family with one son missing. But it thrilled me to see Lissa there in a brimmed straw hat like her mother's. All four of them were waiting on a bench, watching the empty slip, the water burbling in the sun. I felt like ordering them to get five yards apart, as I always had to remind my men under fire. Even in risk of shellbursts, soldiers were as gregarious as cows. Could they get to Toby at Camp Lejeune? They.

The scumbags, who were they? I had to tell myself finally. They were poor Honey Baines. They were misguided saviors like Stephanie, and avengers like Evan. They were the manipulative forces that twisted dupes into such shapes, ultimately the fortune builders like Fenneran. "I feel no more like a murderer," I told Marissa, "than I did in the war."

They were everyone but us. She led me aside. "What's the matter with you? What's in that bag?"

Gifts from a computer like me had disturbed Lissa once before. I said it was just some spare parts and magazines. I told her Congresswoman Wilmont had brought Evan Brisburn over last night and threatened to kill Lissa unless I killed Tate Fenneran for them. "Then some bahaymas broke in and I had to kill them. Now it turns out that Honey was part of this plot against Tate. Her sudden disappearance with the sloop proves it. No one but she and I had the keys, to say nothing of her failure to tell Price."

Marissa in the sun, her face. It disintegrated into the severest pattern of anguish I had ever seen.

"I must have been suspicious, to tell Honey so little. But the first sound of my voice told her I took care of Evan. I should have known she hated Tate, overpraising him so blatantly for years. She wants him dead, and me too. Who knows why? Maybe for raping her with Brady Wiley's dick way back in the Bayfront fire."

"Let me," Marissa said, "take you to the hospital."

She smiled when I smiled. "See, baby, nobody's going to believe me." Not if she didn't, she knew I meant.

"How come you always called me baby?"

"Because I always loved you."

Teeth showed in her painful grimace. Muscles tensed on one side of her neck to start her hand flying at me. But she restrained herself, and said, "You always loved the kids, and now you talk murder in front of Lissa. Toby's going overseas."

That was her crack in my face. I accepted it, grateful they were all safe now, if Toby and I weren't. I slapped her back by saying, "Marissa, I had to kill him. I killed Evan Brisburn. Then three bahaymas killed Stephanie Wilmont and I killed them."

She said something like an echo about devil's eye giving me horrible delusions. I shook my head in denial, yearning to hold her close. Amy came over and kissed me, but only on the cheek. She said, "Lissa's doing great in theater."

Lissa came over and said, "You're to be Amy's father today. How do you do?"

That was the language of her therapy. The computer was being allowed to pretend for her theatrics. Softly firming my voice, I said, "Then I'm to be your father too? And Sam's?"

Nodding, her pale eyes intent on mine, she said, "The nurse looks in at night. If I dream, she feels my brow. She's very sweet. My father always liked sweet people." The sun in my eyes swarmed with passersby. She said the doctors worked with her in theater, they were very sweet. An Indian cleaning woman came each morning to talk about her grandchildren. She was very sweet.

Lissa kissed me on the cheek. A computer embracing her would have been too upsetting even in pretense. She took something from the pocket of her voluminous white smock, and handed it to me.

A picture postcard from Toby at last. The writing was blurred, but I didn't care. Marissa smiled when I smiled. She was sure I had finally gone out of my head. Sam looked at me that way too, slowly coming over. I wanted to tell him never fight in a war. Don't die for them. If you come back hurt they'll hate you. For your suffering. For your valor. Don't ever believe different. Tell your brother. Tell him. Would I lie to you?

But I couldn't tell my son. He might think me theatrical. It would surely embarrass him as self-pity. It wasn't that at all. I was pitying him and Toby, which felt much worse than feeling

sorry for myself. I was pitying a billion chumps yet to come, and fight, and die for Duncan Doran.

That was who I had to visit, though Marissa wanted me in the hospital. She would take me there herself, she said as our kids drifted back to the bench. I touched the short coiffured ends of her hair and said she just wanted all her husbands in one manageable place. She smiled to humor me, and whispered, "Sam can take her back to the Retreat. Gabe, you don't know how you look."

I offered a quick deal. I'd go only if she had Sam drive both his sisters home. She didn't argue, knowing she could later get Lissa to the Retreat. That was okay with me. Later it would be safe. I went to the kids with the fullest sense I would never see them again. "Sam, take care of everything."

Marissa came over, murmuring instructions. A computer, I couldn't embrace her in front of Lissa, I couldn't grab my Amy and Sam. Lissa smiled, the first time I had seen that since Justin's murder. She looked at me and said, "Come back, hear?"

She was a southerner, my daughter. Thus did the clans blend in the great tribe of man. I walked away laughing. My wife came with me. But I had to catch up with Honey.

Marissa drove, afraid to let me. "How positive you once were that Barry, Dexter, and Tate were conspiring against you."

"They weren't. Okay. But Honey was. It's good I built that catwalk. It's good to be suspicious. That's not paranoid."

"Oh, Gabe. How could you think she'd ever harm you?"

"She has the blood for it. Crocodile. Whatever her reasons, wherever she's headed, I'm sure she can justify herself, just as Evan and Stephanie did with their revolutionary cant." Marissa was looking really scared, but I couldn't stop. "Politically, she's their opposite, but they're the same. So is Terry Peacham. They simply aren't people. They're bahaymas."

I smiled at her, like someone with gas. She pulled up at the VA hospital, where I could leave my car in government care. She wanted me to agree that I'd be best off letting them admit me to inpatient care for a while, so I smiled for her again, figuring I could ditch her there. But she refused to hail a taxi or give me the car keys. I had to let her come in with me and watch

a check-in clerk disdain me. I had another set of keys in my wallet. She forgot I always took that precaution.

Right in line at the contact desk the clerk upbraided me for not having brought my patient data card to show him. "What do you think it was provided to you for?" he demanded, a punk half my age. "Well, answer me!"

"Who the fuck are you supposed to be?" I answered him.

His eyes flashed. I had never known so black a face to blush, but it happened. And it was my placid wife who shouted at him, "If I had a gun I'd shoot you dead!"

Tempted to offer her mine, I was glad she had forgotten I carried one in my belt. "Lady," the guy said, "if you think you can talk to me like that just because I'm a—"

"Motherfucker," I finished for him, and along came the guards, two big black men with revolvers on their hips. I might have killed them with him on the spot but for the danger to others, especially Marissa. Then I was glad Evan's gun stayed in its paper bag, because they sent the clerk right off for a break and told me he was crazy from grenade wounds in Vietnam.

As another black clerk apologized, checking me in, I was glad I hadn't let the poor veteran make one of those berserks out of me who blow strangers away in public places. I let Marissa take me with my routing sheet to say good-bye at the elevators, where she told me they were operating on Hoby's gall bladder that afternoon and she had to be at Todd Brisburn Memorial soon.

I wished him luck. She saw me trying not to wish he died, and kissed me. Marissa told me not to let any of the creeps here bother me; I promised not to shoot them. She laughed with worried glances of recollection at my waist, and reminded me our children needed their father. Like the hole in my head, I thought. It was hard to believe she didn't realize I was going to leave right after watching her go off in a taxi. It was hard to pull apart, our mouths kept returning to suck at each other and I got half hard to her.

But nobody paid attention. The veterans all had too many problems of their own to care that we were saying good-bye forever.

COLLAGE 20

Gilded cloud banks floated high over Sunset Bayou when I showed up at the luncheon with my paper bag. As if they knew me, a pair of cops saluted my way right in the tall hedge entrance while Mayor Christian was addressing the tables incomprehensibly. More uniformed police watched over the lawn from a wide limestone façade between the double picture window of the house I built.

Important people were there. Rising in her garden hat, Honey watched me with concern and hurried to alert the officers. To see her do just that was why I had carried in the paper bag. Only my camera was in it. I had left Evan's machine gun where I could quickly reach it in the car, and parked that on broad Shore Road so it would not be closed in by other cars in Doran's driveway.

Knowing the land there, and how a boat arrived from the bay, I had watched Honey's sloop tack in. What the three gingerly cops approaching meant to me was that she likely knew the bag,

and now could be sure Evan would not be along as she may have expected.

"The grim puzzle of their origin," Barry orated, "demands a reinterpretation of psychological and sociological beliefs to adapt the biological view Shawn Hogan propounded." Who could understand him? "A new concept of human standards must be devised, a new reality accepted in the world: that violence is born, and we must no longer harbor reptiles in human form."

I smiled when the policemen smiled, and let them inspect the contents of the bag. Honey smiled when I smiled. Guests smiled when she smiled—until I took out the camera. Smiles returned only when Marge got up to accept with a kiss the photo I shot of Barry speaking beside her, these community leaders realizing I had a Polaroid that stored nothing for media reproduction.

They were "the scum of the earth" for whom Evan had wanted his gun full. As Barry spoke, my camera caught judges with the lawyers who practiced before them. I shot legislators at table with commercial lobbyists like Bo Traggan, who whispered he had heard of my gazebo and laughed when I whispered I had heard of his. I handed out fresh photos to city commissioners seated with the realtors and entrepreneurs they regulated. State Senator Fairboro smiled wistfully with Clint Bocaleon. So did Judge Wilmont, who imagined his wife to be in Washington. He must have won an adjustment from Fenneran to be so compliant with adversaries like Duncan Doran and Judge Cheatham.

The audience applauded, but Barry wasn't through. He just needed some water, so I continued shooting the grafters and filchers of the public trust, wishing my camera were Evan's machine gun instead. I had saved their terrible lives by taking his. Had Stephanie not said her husband was to die here? It was time to quit just making pictures like an artist and do something for my son's respect.

Holding the camera over my head, I spoke up, loud above the babble. "Shawn Hogan discovered that bahaymas evolve into people just like you. We didn't have to kill them last night. Stronger restraints, anything law could devise until—"

"They killed themselves," Dr. Larrup stood up to shout.

"Mass suicide. As a social protest. Nothing new about that."

Father of Donny's friend Pete, he was another lovely client of Doran's, just indicted for running an abortion mill in elegant Key Medical Center to exploit women not even pregnant. Honey tapped my shoulder, her smile an inflexible mask through which she said, "If you believe I love you, Gabe, go home."

I wouldn't believe you, I crooned in mind, but said nothing. Barry was saying enough, and there from the house with Hillary came Tate, smiling like a puppeteer.

"Get away from here quickly," Honey said on an urgent note as Fenneran watched us past the toadies gathering to him.

"Does he know," I asked Honey, "that you sent Evan to me?"

Of course he knew, I realized as she rustled away in her garden fluff, a string on his finger had her send Evan. But what human being could understand why? Tate approached in a casual stride like his meander in and out of my workshop shadows, years ago as a younger strategic tactician. He dressed like a prince. He looked like a grinning crocodile.

"I'm guessing," he said, "that Honey just tried to save your life. She thought you'd have more sense than to come here after refusing Evan. But I rather expected you'd come finish up for me. Indirectly, of course, I did pay Evan twenty-five thousand dollars to go get his neck broken in your workshop."

Stammering with shock, I managed, "Why, for God's sake?"

"Inflation."

"Ha, ha, Your Majesty." I trembled with fear. He had programmed me? He was programming me still. "Methinks Stephanie said you want Barry as your own man in the White House."

Turning, he watched TV crews negotiate to film Barry glossing into statements for advantageous public consumption, and faced me again to say, deadly suave, "Not until he learns, as Governor, a warmer smile and colder heart."

Citizens were murdered. That was everything to Barry. He had condemned the bahaymas only to save his people, who were nothing to the habitat Fenneran had decreed a genocide to preserve. I said, "Stephanie also said you want her and Harmon dead."

"Keenest observation of her ill-fated career." With a farewell

smile, Tate said through Barry's concluding rhetoric, "My lingering fear is that stupidity will finally destroy us. Like the Wilmonts, this country is feebleminded."

With that powerful reiteration Tate walked away from whatever his programming had laid out for me. Around the cameras, Hillary came drifting over like a sunbeam in her divine jade frock. So radiant still in her fifties, with all her Brisburns gone. How fabulous the boundless magic her mother knew. I said, "Barry. Just listen to him."

"Just look at you." She kissed me with petal lips.

Bo Traggan laughed irrepressibly. I had the notion he had gone straight from Congress to jail or South Africa, but did not remark—he was old. Fenneran was not much older than me, though he once was, and Wilmont too. I resented them both for eluding the war by years grown so few between us now.

Four men, apparently bodyguards, accompanied Tate and Honey toward her sloop, moored in swamp milkweed scarlet at the shore. He turned to wave Hillary on. People gave a little cheer. She said, "We're supposed to sail the inland waterways to Washington for Cassie's wedding."

Rumors of a senator for Cassie once circulated. I was not invited. Tears burned in the eyes of the country club madman wearing my skin. Tate beckoned again, impatiently, but Hillary shook her head at him, her skin translucent, the lines delicately endearing, magical. What power. "What about guys," I said, "who don't become drunken slobs over imprudent wives like you?"

Kissing me again, she licked my lips. "They devour the world. They destroy to build and build to destroy. Prudence has a yellow streak down her back. I'm staying with you to the end."

I couldn't grasp that, until I saw Barry take Marge inside. Fenneran waved once more. Hillary must have heard him plotting with Honey, and just lacked Barry's progressing nerve to sacrifice me at last with the others. "Nobody can be all bad," I said, "who would exterminate the vermin present here, but Evan's not coming."

"I think Tate knew and left that to these police. It's to happen as soon as he's gone. Is this how simple the afternoon looked

when you were killed? Was that too half a joke to you?"

I couldn't tell if she meant me or Todd, but, plainly insane, she had chosen to end the war for us at last. Her inquisitive eyes, the tender mouth, together they said nothing would ever be meliorated in the world, and so her beauty broke my heart at last.

I recalled the simple crackle of gunfire the afternoon they wiped me out. I saw Judge Wilmont's scalp on fire as he chatted in the sun, smug with the power of the courts to bend even Tate his way. Didn't he realize that was the very power Fenneran had resolved to destroy with him, the sanctimonious cretin, and all of us with him? Did he really expect his opposition to win him a senatorial bid from Tate, the little dunce?

Smiling Fenneran turned away to the sloop for good with Honey and his bodyguards. The simple sunny afternoon was witnessing his final solution of the Hillary syndrome, his conflict of love and hate that masqueraded as pragmatic detachment most of his life.

I had lost my mind in the enormity of everyone carrying out Tate's game plan, which never did include getting his "liberalistic" wife out of harm's way. "He's killing you!" I heard myself shout at her like someone in a dream. "He sent Evan and Stephanie to my house this morning so bahaymas could rape her and kill her and shoot Evan too!" Men cried out, I saw women swoon, police were closing in. "He killed the Congresswoman," I yelled. "He's killing you all like bahaymas he slaughtered who never harmed a soul!"

Someone's face shot forth like a blood clot, Harmon Wilmont yanking a cop's holstered revolver and aiming it with all his teeth bared. Stephanie had told him Washington but picked up Evan instead, so the justice who would have no killer's life on his conscience, his eyes floating in a sea of borscht, was shooting me for exposing his wife, not to abomination by crocodile blood but to scandal with a Brisburn and the mad lecher of Pinebrake.

The shot exploded; I saw the flame flash red at my face. I had heard of crazy people shooting judges, but never of judges shooting a crazy person. And right in the forehead like the worst of my dreams. He got me right in the head while I was reacting

with the licensed gun in my belt. I blasted him full in the chest, the son of a bitch, the reports multiplying in my brain like my voice yelling "Hey hey" etcetera in Germany the first time I died of this. With the blood pouring down in my eyes I barely made out cops running at me, so I whirled around and ran.

I was shot in the forehead, so what did I know? People were after me, so I ran. Disoriented though I was, I knew the land and reached my car, scooping Evan's machine gun from under the seat. But there was simply too much blood running out of the hole in my forehead to see anything, so I just drove away.

Everybody ran from me in Armistead Hammock. I couldn't tell if it was the machine gun or the blood. I couldn't tell a bahayma from a person until Daisy McFee got busy with my head as I wailed, "Hide me," in the soap of her smell, "I think I killed some guys."

Junn said, "Must be white guys, you say hide."

"Half and half. They shot me in the forehead. Am I dead?"

I could not make out all the people that replied in the smelly vitamins Daisy was sure would pull me through as another woman somewhere said, "Never seen nobody bleed so much."

"Sorry, sorry," I said, gagging next because that was castor oil she spooned me. I thought I must be comatose to imagine TV calling the Vice-President of the United States a jingoistic hypocrite just indicted in disgrace. How could that be? How could Daisy want my machine gun while plugging up my head? I would not surrender it. "Bahaymas out there. They'll kill me."

"You hates them so," said Majosee. "What you expect?"

"I hates them so, what they expect?" I had to be dead to understand Josie so clearly. "Not just the killers and rapists. I hates them all." Dead wasn't bad, at least I could say what I meant. "They spread filth, they think spitting's fancy, swagger and curse for status. They're so different, they're ugly."

But dead or alive, the pain was awful and screaming still scared me. I shivered to hear Josie shriek, "They got a right to their own ways. Who you, say they ain't?"

"Sorry, sorry, you're right, they're not different. We are."

I tried to rest in peace, but Terry Peacham would not allow

it. He was after me with some money. No, he was debating Josie on TV, that was why I comprehended her. And it was a turbaned Seminole he was trying to pay as Junn laughed in the soapy blood and vitamins. The Indian said politics, not religion, was the biggest business in the world, and he was Chopka Emathla. I knew by the letters beneath him on the glaring screen when Daisy washed more blood away. He said politicians labored only to be reelected and steal more, not to represent the people they flattered.

"That's not true," Milton Kindbor stuck his flexuous nose in to say. "We have many wonderful people in Congress."

Wonderful? They weren't even ethical, or credible. Dead or dreaming, I knew that without Chopka saying, "Find someone defends politicians, you found a crook or a fool."

Kindbor wore the obsequious grin of a usurer. He had acquired a curly gray moderator's wig, but was still a bald panderer to me. Well, he had always striven to be all things to all patrons, the jackass media dispenser of a gullibility called entertainment. And all at once—Eureka! In death I knew the secret of life. Not religion but entertainment was the opiate that kept the people from rebelling. Bob Hope. The Marx Brothers. Barbra Streisand. Sammy Davis Jr. Terry Peacham!

"This is the richest country in the world," pontificated the Bull, "yet the most crime-ridden. Our poor are better off than the middle class of many nations. How can anyone say crime stems from poverty?"

Junn wheezed with laughter, but it was me in shrill disgust they had to calm down with devil's eye. Daisy said, "They machete you, them nasty boys? This some cut, on up into your hair."

On the screen Terry was entertaining Chopka with a thousand-dollar award for using his ax in the swamp on bahaymas he caught using his wife. A raped wife had driven their warlord to kill bahaymas—why had it driven that stupid judge to kill me? And why did I save those other leeches again by shooting him after killing Evan? I'd have shot myself for that, if I weren't already shot.

Terry displayed the ax with respect. He understood the emo-

tions of Mr. Emathla, whose lips were trembling. He sympathized with Mrs. Emathla's reluctance to appear, and said, "Please tell, in your own words, sir, what came over you?"

I was dying, even though I was dead. "Well," Chopka began with a vein bulging at his forehead, and suddenly all hell broke loose and they pronounced me dead and shaved my head some.

Wrong again. Not I but Terry was the one pronounced dead —killed live on TV like the guy who shot Kennedy. Junn said nothing could bleed like a scalp but, seizing the ax, Chopka had chopped deeper than Peacham's scalp for the viewing public in the screams and running and strobing till the color went blank with voice-over screaming, "He's dead, my God, he's killed the former Sheriff!"

Junn guffawed and drank from his jug; there was no other sound in the room. But soon a low, maniacal laughter blossomed into hysterics. It was coming from me.

They revived me with devil's eye, which also kept me from being scared back to death by Josie's presence in the flesh. But all she did was comfort me with memories of girlhood to keep Junn from going on about the murder of Peacham. It kept collapsing him in asthmatic laughter that took devil's eye to control.

Her stories made the swamp friendlier than I imagined it to be. She called me Storyteller to honor my good soul because I had killed white men as her brother had, and offered me his chickee there for a hideout. It would be easy to find down the marl road from Big Alligator Show on the Tamiami Trail.

She said they had refused Chopka bail and it promised to be a long time before they could provide a jury of his peers as his lawyer demanded. His wife had enough of open chickees, and had moved into the closed shack Junn had long ago made of his. Junn said they'd never think of searching for me at Chopka's, and should they blunder upon me, I still had all my firepower.

I was none too comfortable about that, though glad the old soldier in me, skull creased deep and painful, had held onto the handgun after blasting Wilmont. It would make a welcome backup for the machine gun and shotgun in keeping bahaymas

at bay. But I promised to shoot no one who didn't threaten me bodily and thanked them all for their kindness. Promising too that I would go right to my doctor as Miss Daisy insisted, I left with her beret over my bandages, and a vengeance in my heart for the crocodile blood that had cast my children into sorrow, impairment, and danger.

My car was conveniently in full camouflage, someone had spray-painted it in the night that had fallen. As I drove away the radio news theorized that the only remaining bahaymas had fled back into the swamp. Next I learned that many dignitaries had perished indeed with the Chief Judge as I fled from the luncheon of swine, the gunfire real, not echoes in my mind. The report called it a crossfire between police and "armed intruders." Shocked by that prevarication, I was even more horrified by an apprehension of Fenneran's undeniable preternatural power, his capacity to have made me the instrument of eliminating all his political opposition including Evan and both Wilmonts and, perhaps, his faithless wife as well.

Her name came in the painfully slow index of those killed or wounded. Millicent Dildress was dead with Traggan and Larrup and Doran. Hillary and the former MA were in critical condition at Brisburn Memorial. Speeding home to pack clothes for my getaway, I nearly crashed on the highway in anguish over Hillary and fear of her omnipotent husband though he was sailing on to Washington with the Publisher. I thought of killing Honey, and knew I was mad.

They had driven us all as mad as the boy soldiers of war. They would say I had overreacted in firing back at the judge. I should have merely restrained him after he shot me dead. They.

Price's police had sealed up my workshop effectively. I heard no bongos, eating practically everything in the house, showering, shaving for disguise where my great red mustache had flourished. I found a nice satchel for my sweet shotgun and machine gun and fell out in the radio rebroadcast of the Mayor's voice pronouncing the great truth of our time, that racial discrimination had died in the wide difference that existed between human beings and bahaymas.

I uncovered other great truths in my sleep. Dreaming someone crept in beside me smelling of soap and praying, I guessed
there were still several Daisies and was sure women had played
their deceptions as long as men like Fenneran. But my greatest
truth was that all that sex I had to taste, all that time in fact and
fantasy, was really just a gun substitute. I loved not women but
guns.

That was why I had saved mine though shot smack in the
head. Junn laughed in my sleep as the Mayor's oratory swung
the political pendulum of guile. Bigotry was dead, humanity
was in, but all I wanted was my guns, despite or because of
Christian saying and saying and finally saying, "There are, in
all Gulf Glade and the world, only people with, and people
without, crocodile blood."

Early next morning I drove away to get my money in Peacock
Square. No more bahaymas were evident in Gulf Glade; at last
the people could move freely once more. With others I stood
waiting for the bank to open. When it did, a woman rushed in
to be first, and knocked an old man off his crutches. Without
even pausing to help him up off the floor, she only tittered a
flighty apology and filled her shoulder bag with money. I too
made haste to a window, and filled my satchel with mine. I had
seen the smile on her.

It was familiar, a bahayma grin. I followed her car, laughing
at the cops. Were Dexter not on vacation, my home would have
been his first place to track me, my bank his second. I followed
the dumpy blonde out to a tag sale. Full of cash for bargains, she
smiled as I approached her from my car, the only other smart
early bird on that country road. But she frowned when I tipped
my beret to reveal bandage and said, "That was no accident at
the bank, that was violence. Lady, you have crocodile blood."

She gasped with affront, and violently thumped me on the
chest with her fist, or wrist. So I pulled the gun from my belt
and shot her in the shoulder bag.

I didn't feel half bad. Cedar Market bustled in the sun. The
troughs flowed over with almonds, cheeses, fruits. News head-

lines said the Mayor had narrowly escaped assassination. Scanning a copy of the *Times* in my car, I learned that an "armed assailant" was suspected of "terrorist retaliation" by bahaymas.

Anticipating the outrage of Donny at such political pot stirring, Honey's paper had compensated him with a by-lined column that allowed all the free expression he had probably demanded. The range of his asperity was bound to satisfy the biases peculiar to everyone from Tate to Chopka, with me included.

"Evil," he wrote even before his mother was shot at his father's luncheon setup, "gorges the richest arteries of power. The ultimate bahaymas occupy Washington and Moscow and the highest corporate seats. Crocodile blood is what makes authoritarian people different from the rest of us. We are their natural prey."

I still loved that boy, though he was yet to see the blood of the mighty offender and abysmal thug blended to quintessence in the workaday creep who made ordinary moments stink for other people. Even as I sat pondering so, my reverie was shattered by a sudden blast of the loudest rock music. It was blaring from the news vendor's radio right outside my car. A new ordinance to outlaw that particular nuisance had just been passed with a law against dog litter. To remind the man of that, I had to shout over his noise, and he shouted back to suggest I drive away and stop making a pest of myself. Passersby shouted too, the avenue crowded. I yelled I'd never find another place to park. In that case, he screamed, I could just get lost. I knew that sneer. So I yanked my gun and shot him in the radio.

That left me feeling much better. Until, pretending it was long distance, I asked after Hillary. Bill said it looked bad for his mother. He urged me to return for a routine inquest, with little doubt of an acquittal according to Donny. I said I no longer trusted the mechanics of democracy, which gave us bahaymas in human clothing by now, all over our normally troubled lives.

A heavy rain fell on me as I left the phone booth. When I attempted to cross Armistead Road, someone stopped his car for a traffic light squarely in the crosswalk before me. Even in nice

weather I never understood why some people had to breach the law and inconvenience pedestrians that way. In heavy rain it seemed nothing short of a crocodilian inconsideration.

With my face splashing, I asked the driver if I was supposed to climb over his hood to reach my car. Arrogating all the power of his car, he let me know he didn't give a shit what I did, a pencil-mustached fuck in a paisley jacket. Beside him the female of the species looked just as indignant in her shelter. So I took the key out of his ignition and tossed it away. By the time he retrieved it and raged after me, I had Evan's darling machine gun out of my trunk. No one else was out in the rain to watch. It was lovely. The crosswalk crocodile started to swoon, and as he went down I just had to let him have it, with a smoky rat-a-tat-tat, right in the motor of his car as his consort ran screaming in the rain.

I had never used that gun before. How delicious to break it in on a motorist. I even hated myself as a driver, sometimes— and was almost killed that very moment by the kind I hated most. A speeder came screeching around the corner and I leaped aside just in time to see his leering grin in the downpour. On a swift inspiration for the quick draw, I pistol-shot the bahayma just once in the gas tank that a machine gun volley might have exploded in flames. The sleek yellow roadster died easy up the street. With my snub-nosed .32 in one hand and Evan's shiny rapid fire in the other, I went singing in the rain to my car.

Excited, I drove with the satchel beside me—who knew what new sport lay ahead? A minute later I knew. It loomed in the blaze of lights as I approached Keyport, a huge trailer truck driven right into State Square with no better purpose than to tie up the city in gridlock.

I discovered a small alley of escape and stopped there to get out with my shotgun. Carefully I leveled it and, confident the product damage would be invisible, blasted the SWISS CHEESE KING, INC. right in the immensity of its van. Then I peppered it with a second shell to leave the trapped onlookers cheering.

* * *

It was true, herds of bahaymas now lived in bathed disguise among us, and I zested to leave every parasite who undermines life transfixed with the same look of perdition I had enjoyed in each creep right up to the gridlock goon who personified his arrogant tractor-trailer. But with such passion threatening to include as further targets the foppish art mongers and fey dilettantes and repulsive slaves to fashion, it began to seem excessive. I really felt programmed to escalate, even kill. With an awful sense of danger, I hid in a movie house to gather my perspectives and restraints.

After all, nobody was forced to dine at the exorbitant "in" spots for professional snobs without palates, or to mince through the galleries full of pretension and vernacular. Why couldn't I let those groupies fake each other out in peace? It was the well poisoner I hated, the spoiler of other people's time on earth. Those were the beasts who sent me to war. Those were the monsters who broke my children's dreams.

My heart was full of Marissa's belief that the movies ruined innocent lives by dispensing impossible romantic expectations, and though no film demanded attention, with most conducive to sleep, I suffered an overwhelming urge to shoot Hollywood right in the screen then and there. It felt like time to leave town before I became a bahayma for Fenneran. Because of him Honey was gone, Hillary might die. Both had tried to save me. They were the opposite of bahaymas. I should have been more sensitive to them. And to a goodhearted guy like Hoby, instead of coveting our wife.

I could drive straight out to the airport for a couple of years with my parents. They would do my bad soul good, though we were cultures apart. I could tell them a head like mine had to be bandaged from time to time. I was perfectly set up for travel with clothes and money and a car trunk in which to leave behind the armaments not allowed on planes. But I slept through two movies, and when I got to the car it wouldn't start. I had left my lights on since the rain. The battery was dead.

Famished, I picked up the evening paper to read as I ate. In addition to the Vice-President, the President of the United States had been busted. So where did I, a lowly artist, get off

thinking I could just buy a ticket home without getting nabbed?

To call a repair service also seemed a sure way to bring the police collaring me. I could send a Seminole from the Trail to jump my battery in the morning. Eating a Greek souvlaki, I looked again at the news, and my heart took an alarming leap. Hillary was not expected to live out the night. She had the local headline, second to the President's. I crumbled in shock. I might never see her again. My parents were old, I might never see them, my brothers and sisters. People in the Thessaloniki Gyro Rest wanted to help me but spoke only Greek, gaping at my beret and bare lip. I didn't even know I was weeping with my cheeks full.

I kept weeping and eating souvlaki right into a taxicab I hailed to load with the suitcase and satchel from my car. I gave a location on U.S. 41 where I was to find Chopka's chickee down a swamp road, then blubbered in my hands. Tate hovered over me, the son of a bitch grinning, and all I could do for Hillary was weep. Her children, her grandchildren. The driver, a chunky redhead like me, tried to be comforting and did relax me, speaking about his native Floridian status so much that he put me to sleep.

Unfamiliar skirmishes wounded my dreams. I woke up crippled on the causeway to Banana Key. Big Cypress Swamp was in the opposite direction. I asked where he was taking me. The cabby said Big Alligator Show on the Tamiami Trail, and suggested I lean back and enjoy the ride, he knew how I must feel. I dug in the satchel for my handgun and stuck it in my belt. Then I leaned back and enjoyed the ride.

Great Gulf Glade was a bejeweled vast metropolis of activity and magical beauty. It was habitat supreme, demanding admiration for Fenneran and bottomless loathing for the parasites born with crocodile blood to give every such magnificent creation an underside putrid with corruption. This animal thought me a mourner some plane had carried in for him to haul around town running the meter up in my profound and inattentive bereavement.

He was every predator who read obituaries in search of the grief-stricken to swindle, every ghoul who sold fake cures to the

dying, every slum plunderer with double-weight scales to bleed the starving impoverished. I got out the old shotgun. This monster I was not just going to shoot in the meter.

After a wearisome ride sixteen dollars long brought us to the deserted wilderness, my cabby announced a "swamp tax" of twenty-five dollars over the meter to make the bill forty-one. "Us Injuns had paradise here," I said, "till you white folks came looking for it."

Then I told him my plan. I would be a cab driver for a while, and let him be a swamp derelict living on game and fear in the morass of Josie's history. All the tourist stands were closed for the day, the Indians withdrawn to their chickee villages deep off the highway. The crickets had it all to themselves. We were alone in the night, yet the guy thought I was kidding. He grinned until he saw my face in the moonlight. It caused him to dilate his nostrils and say, "You Jew?"

"Yeah. You bahayma?"

He gaped, offended just like the woman I left with a bullet in her money. Then he bent away for a big monkey wrench to shake at me, furiously growling, "Okay, get out the fucking cab."

That sounded like a threat of bodily harm to me. I didn't mind getting out, on the far side to make him come trotting around to an abrupt stop with the moon behind him. I wanted him to see the round mouth of the shotgun grow larger and larger like his eyes. "You ran my ass down the keys," I said, "instead of swinging me up to this highway a few minutes' drive."

"Ain't go do that no more, nosir." He gently laid the heavy wrench down on the taxi hood. A plane sawed overhead. "Was a Captain Levy come up in the Seminole wars, yessir."

"No shit. Was eagles too, back then. Till crocodile blood like yours made life sick."

"Make it up to you, sure will. Just you put down that gun and tell me how to make amends. Now, you don't want to hurt me."

"Sure I do. Get going. There's only one chickee before the Indian village, down this little road. That's yours."

"Portuguese and Jew, Captain Levy was. You full-blooded?"

"Jew between," I said, and he nodded sagely with a glance at

the wrench, but gave up any impulse to try it on me when I raised the shotgun level with his face. He licked his lips, he rubbed his thighs, and headed down the marl road in moon glow.

The Seminoles were likely to deliver him in the morning. But gunfire exploded. He was in ambush. I saw him struck and lunged for cover against the taxi. I saw him hammered down dead in my place and sudden light pinned me to the cab door. Headlights from the opposite roadside trapped me. "Put down the shotgun, cuckoo bird. We know you're crazy, not dumb."

Sheriff Polsen strode into the haze of light. With tremors I dropped the gun and cried, "That chickee was staked out for me?"

"For Chopka, don't flatter yourself. Your friend Donny got him out of jail this afternoon, to maybe scalp ole Price."

"You knew that wasn't Chopka! That was a cab driver! You let him just walk into that!"

"What's the matter, can't you take a joke?"

"That was no cab driver, that was a bahayma." Commissioner Fenton appeared in his deputy's hat. "No city needs them. They have no right to pollute us. We have a birthright to live free."

Without my mustache I looked like a plucked chicken. Polsen said so, taking me into custody. Chickees burned in the hammocks. Swamp fire, it happened all the time, though the season was not yet dry enough for that, he allowed as we got in his car. Chopka's cutthroats were burning in the crackle of guns. The Sheriff admitted that too, once alone with me, speeding through the night. "Four out of five serious crimes go without even an arrest."

Taking me in was the first reason he ever really had to handcuff me, and his failure to do so felt like doom. It seemed a ticket to oblivion for me, as if he wanted me to attempt an escape in the swamp, like the salesman who drowned in the slough after murdering a housewife he raped at her bridge party, or the Bolivian couple who were torn up by wildcats after enslaving a child for five years. I said, "Everybody saw Wilmont shoot me in the beret."

Dexter nodded. "Understand you bled like Foxy Christian."

I was afraid to ask if that meant Tate had let Barry get it after he taped his speech at Duncan Doran's. Polsen's holstered gun looked invincible. His men had taken my two heavy weapons but overlooked the handgun in my belt. I drew it slowly, his eyes on the road as we floated darkly through the swamp. Tate, he told me, once employed an opportune injury of Barry's to keep him from serving in another war, back when they all had to keep giving blood for their Sheriff. Slowly I slid my gun out of sight.

"Foxy left the hospital so weak from giving blood he fell and hit his head. Blood just gushed from his scalp. So he returned to the hospital and made them give him back his blood."

Tate was just, the Sheriff said, and I shuddered, thinking Fenneran could well have manipulated me here to kill this nemesis, or this friend to kill me. Good and scared, I said, "It wasn't the bahaymas that killed your nephew, Dex. Tate manipulated him to it in my workshop. Honey engineered it."

The Sheriff was preoccupied, slowing down to stop off the highway that traversed the swamp Josie's simple stories had changed into a mystic forest, a forgiveness she gave me to hide in while actually sending me to the ambush she anticipated for her brother. Dexter turned and faced an unseen gun cocked behind my leg to punch him out of the world at his first deadly act. I was soldiering again, the Jew between friends who were enemies.

"His father killed Evan," Polsen said, "or his grandfather, whoever started hitting on himself in the flesh of his kid. It made a professional gunman out of Evan. Imagine someone always beating up on his mother. Evan was bad-ass. That's life. Just one way left for crocodile blood when government fails to defend. Somebody's got to cut down every Chopka set free on a technicality by some Donny. We're obliged to burn every chickee full of technicalities armed with handguns and knives, so long as legal fetishists dominate the courts. You don't need any Donny to defend you for knocking a pious bahayma off the bench. Most everybody admires you for that."

All he had stopped the car for was to tell me so. I admired him too, for admitting the error of his early skepticism by personally

counterattacking the monsters Fenneran had foreseen. Polsen was not my enemy, poor Josie was, even considerate Daisy McFee, in her hopeless heart. And wise Junn, whose kindness was as nothing to the vengeful hate that made him save the infants of monstrosity. Just as I was about to ask a crucial question, the Sheriff answered it by enunciating a life-or-death logic in the stolid inaction of the Council. "Shave them," Dexter said, "and bahaymas look like most anybody. So it just has to be the nature of the crime that determines the presence of crocodile blood."

"Okay. So what the hell are you taking me in for?"

"What do you think we came down off Ole Smoky for? Don't you want to see Hillary before she goes to heaven?"

When we reached the hospital everyone was there but Tate. He had the decency to abide in Washington with Honey, making ready for the wedding though Cassie had flown home to be at her mother's side. In the corridor I heard her tell Donny how useless his newspaper column was, her other brother watching over with all the powerful reserve of their father.

"The interest of politicians is politics, as the interest of artists is art." So Cassie had grown up existential. "Scientists research only science, and crusading journalists expose only what will sell newspapers. That's why industrial piracy fears no social outcry against anything from windfall profits to dogshit."

It was like hearing Hillary say dogshit, their resemblance that striking. But what Hill did say in her room was worse, after Dexter came out to tell me she wanted only my forgiveness. With tubes in her arms and nose my poor pale Hillary whispered, "Who are you?" Then, assured it was I, "The museum will buy your great new collage only if you cut it down by a third. Take it or leave it."

Then she died. Deejay erupted in hysterics, but I couldn't help comfort her because Polsen had handcuffed my wrists behind me. He knew Hillary could laugh. I didn't know he could cry.

The Sheriff's handcuffs remained on me till I was booked for inciting to mortal riot. Bill Fenneran came to go my bail and

told me it was excessive even for a judge killer. His sister came to ask if she could hang around my studio sometimes like her other brother used to, and scolded me for sexism when I said she had to go marry and I had to disappear. Then came the toughest of the three kids Tate gave Hillary, to ask how it felt being held for society's crimes against me.

"The polluters made you do it," Donny said. "*Someone* has to defend you frustrated fortunates."

"People come in five beautiful colors," Bowie Pratt eulogized at the grave, "coping with fire and storm, paying with privation for their disasters, then going on, improving life as they can."

Who could guess what he wanted, electioneering like a white man as if anything could keep him from becoming our next Mayor?

"I have just quoted the courageous Hillary Brisburn Fenneran of civil rights days long ago. More recently she said, 'Bahaymas too come in five colors, but are not beautiful,' meaning they, unable to live without harming others, impair the quality of life. Who can afford to wonder any longer what heights of injustice they resent enough to monsterize other victims of history?"

Sobbing, I couldn't afford to listen anymore, but in my ear Don claimed the same mystification as Bowie's, but over monsterizing profiteers and polluters.

It seemed he had, in his grief for the downtrodden, come to have as little for loved ones as his father. Tate had the indecency to attend with Honey right in front of Nola Brisburn, and stood between them over the grave of his wife, seemingly without shame or remorse in his impression that everyone was Hillary's lover down the years. He wept with me no more than Faith had, saying at Loker's grave that only lovers weep. Either that was wrong or Tate was right about his wife, because Barry stood weeping with Dexter, Bowie, Speed, and half the City Council as we buried Hillary without her spleen.

They had removed it trying to save her. They had removed her generous heart, and the one unriddled kidney, for use in saving other lives. A donor, she had willed her lungs and crazy

brain too for scientific research. If I asked for the part I wanted as a keepsake, they might think me crazier than she was. They.

The bahaymas were gone from the malls and silenced across my canal. But they kept proliferating on TV, grinning in the guise of government figures tolerant of joblessness and pollution as the prices of freedom in an open, democratic society. Running for Governor, the Mayor had already learned to say as often as a senator, "That is what the American people want."

All I wanted was my guns, which my friendly Sheriff returned. All he wanted was for me to enjoy them now and mourn later, like Price Fenton upon the death of Chopka. The warlord passed on while burying his mother in swamp ritual. Price mourned later because Josie escaped from the small funeral ambush attended only by bahaymas, who did not escape. It was a brutal assault of the kind I had learned to deplore but understand. The abdication of other responsible officials made war a peace officer's job.

Even Milton Kindbor came to understand, right after Judge Wilmont's will was made public, turning his Armistead house into a sanctuary for bahaymas. Declaring them not animals at all but a human product of life in this society, his document blamed their conduct on social abuse, the physical deprivations of poor housing and undermined family structure, on the insecurity of a community that just didn't care enough to provide them a sense of their true personal value. So Milton, his wife raped in Armistead by bahaymas who then initialed his bare bottom with graffiti, disguised himself and Baldy Haverstraw in curly gray moderators' wigs and burnt down the Wilmont house as a tribute to my job on the Chief Judge.

That lucky shot I had fired was not going to accelerate my daughter's recovery, or bring my son home from the everlasting war bahaymas made, or encourage me ever to work again, but people did say I had set an example that inspired citizens to go out and shoot such a judge now and then for better diversion than having their brains washed out by the TV opiate called entertainment. They were also inspired to shoot civil rights

abuse legislators, to the horror of Donny though I said, when he visited me to complain, "Rent-gouging landlords too. Wherever there's a little pleasure."

Of course I deplored all that, I told him, but understood. Indignantly, he accused me of having been coopted by his father, utterly failing to recognize his own courtroom jargon I had just turned back on him in mockery. I continued with a touch of Wilmont's, paraphrasing him to say victims were made that way by life in this society, the hardships of bodily abuse, the social deprivation of being locked in at night, the insecurity of enduring a government that just didn't care enough to provide a sense of personal safety, or even ethics legislation by Congress that a child might find convincing. Victims were human, after all, not animals.

Don left in a fury of obtuseness. As a victim myself, facing possible imprisonment, I could no longer support the prospect of a large artistic undertaking, but kept my faith in the American way of gun worship. No substitutes for me, not even Donny's sister.

When not in Washington as Senator Hathaway's wife, Cassie kept after me. But I was afraid the anarchic lawmen her father might send would interfere with the plans I had for my beautiful guns, so I couldn't let her hang around. I flatly refused even after she shot her husband in the ass for speaking to her exclusively in stentorian baby talk instead of normal congressional pomposity. Life in this society had made me crazy, not dumb: I wasn't about to get shot too in the ass as a sexist.

Mrs. Hathaway's weapon was a pearl-handled .22, she told me on the phone. "I'd like to come right over and show it to you." Little Cassie, she had it to show me now. Only I couldn't risk that, not even when she added with a naive enticing reminiscent of her mother, "We can put our guns together and shoot some fine art."

But who could argue with chance? Our paths crossed in a lingering fragrance of rain during my first stroll in renewed Hammerhead Park. Placidity had come back to the lanes. She glowed violet in rainwear and it was romance at first sight, which crazy Cassie compounded saying, "Gabe, did you ever

dream in your wildest seizures that you might one day be Tate Fenneran's son-in-law?"

What a laugh she gave my flattered old age. All I needed was her father's dowry of my house bought back from the widow Doran for my kids. Cassie took my arm. We were dressed so nice. It felt like the good old days when parks were safe.

But, with crocodile blood spread wide among the masses now, law enforcement was always absent in its pursuit of atrocious crime, so I had to use the gun in my belt on a big fat guy about seven feet tall. He had a big fat dog on a leash, and it was taking a big fat shit against a playground fence. There went our romance.

We watched to see if the guy had a scoop to use by law, but he brushed us off with a glance of contempt and just walked the waddling hound away. Mrs. Hathaway said, "Oh, sir, kids'll soon be playing here, after the rain."

"You soon take a flying fuck to the moon, white cunt."

Cassie whipped out her .22 to shoot him in the ass, but I stopped her, whipping out my .32 to shoot him instead in the dog.

We moved on in existential nausea. "Poor fat dog," I groaned. "First thing I ever killed that didn't threaten my life."

"That guy's worse than just a sexist and racist!" Cassie was really angry. "He's like every spoiler—just constitutionally unable to conceive of others being quite as real as himself, the big bahayma! How deadly that is!"

How marvelous she was. "You just explained everything from rape to reckless driving." On that her murdered aunt came back, I sobbed for her mother too, but now had a theme worthy of a major collage, the very project that had waited so long for my dread of work to subside. So I invited her to come help me plan a caper against commercial jingle producers I hoped to blast in the sound console, and promised to help her blast all verbal abusers of women. "But not in the ass."

"Then I'll have to hit yours with an artistic talent equal to Donny's. That is, superior to all the painters in current vogue."

"Don't make me laugh," I said.

But she showed it to me that drizzly afternoon, and boy, was

it good! Exhilarated, I learned all night not to be so judgmental, not to jump to conclusions without evidence as most people did.

Thus, as she cooked for us in a Hammerhead mansion, I stopped blaming her father for anything I didn't know as a fact, and rendered unto Tate what was Fenneran's, including the Publisher. For all I knew, maybe Honey was always his agent in my closest intimacy and now it was Cassie, bringing me breakfast in bed. Such riddles possessed me by the hundreds. But a suspicion like that could divide us, so I had to meet it head on. Only I didn't know her well enough.

"Thank God," I hedged, "as an agnostic I can live without knowing what resources you inherit from such quaint parents."

Cassie said, "Billy got the oil and Donny the steel."

"And you?" I poured some of the wine she had served.

"Wouldn't you like to know?" She had this way of saying no more than the patience of her whimsicality allowed. I was sure of that next when she dismissed my long-winded recalcitrance about the unavoidable inquest as "a fear of other people's speeches."

And there came my title, *Faith in Other People*, for a new collage based on Cassie's exquisite theme and her grandma's album. We already had several scales of one to ten for judging, on evidence, the harmful degrees to which some are born incapable of feeling others to be as real as themselves. It was fun to regard drunken drivers as worse bahaymas than litterers, while seeing less crocodile blood in narrow snobbery than in grudging selfishness, with a drop or two even in rudeness.

Inspired at last to face the ecstasized agony of Faith in a complex work, I was also ready to drown in oratory at the inquest, and awaiting it, I sometimes dreamt my savory partner was the young Majosee, full of a love that Josie had lost to forgive with.

"If we can learn to recognize crocodile blood, we may really become that wonderful nation that nobody owns," our next Governor and future President testified for me from the viewpoint of his own partiality. But all I could dwell on from mine, as Barry went on to blame the Chief Judge's death on misguided

liberalism, was what Tate Fenneran might have in store for me, to show up at my inquest.

A *Times* editorial had told me he was back at work. It admonished the public not to emulate false heroes who took the law in their own hands. I knew my Honey's blithe opportunism as well as Cassie knew the voice of her ventriloquist father. She felt he was manipulating logic to defend property values against inevitable anticriminal riots exactly the way our Federal Reserve manipulated the money supply to control the national economy.

At the inquest Marge Christian dispensed with the central issue by testifying she had seen Wilmont fire a policeman's gun at me. My lawyer then exhibited the resulting scalp wound. That was not only his introduction to a self-serving speech, it was also our future Mayor's, and reading Honey's editorial was my only diversion. Earnestly it warned that citizens were amateur gunmen already mistaking each other for armed criminals in shootouts that hit passersby too.

It had saddened Cassie to see such logic offered as the sole guiding factor for a people motivated by more danger than mistakes could ever produce, and by absolute disgust with a court system of hollow moralities that continued to render law enforcement helpless. It saddened the Sheriff too, but the speeches tried his very souls. He rose to begin one of his own with a simple metaphor.

"Evil is not man, it is monster." That was the metaphor my war-torn head had always longed for. "We can abolish capital punishment," Dexter went on, "in favor of a better way to deter crime. Honey Baines named it the first time and I'm telling you for the last time. We must employ it or perish. That way is to reserve constitutional rights for human beings only, and rule all violent crime punishable by the denial of those rights. If I never say another word," the Sheriff added for emphasis, and dropped dead before he could finish.

To live, one tries not to die, and hopes tomorrow will bring a postcard from one's son. Mrs. Hathaway paints sublimely whenever we're up from the spicy function her granny called magnificent. I have a *Lifetime* to cut down by a third for the

means with which to pay my Lissa's therapy bills and stay in ammunition.

That's life, or what Marissa calls selling out. I think she resents my having the Hillary I love with the Donny and Majosee of my conscience all in one gun-toting divorcee to face the future with, hoping that Junn, hidden by the shadows of the swamp, is not sapient in believing us cast eternally into Goonland. I hope too that Deejay, sour with her beloved Dexter's death, is wrong in believing that leaders like Fenneran have eliminated compassion from the dawning times. After all, Tate has also produced children who are proof that having heart when wiped out will wipe one in again.

As Honey arrived breathless beside him after the inquest, he faced cool Cassie beside me with his flat pragmatic gaze to say, "The choice is yours."

I knew my Tate's genial deadliness: that was to call me a madman and a fool not worthy of her. The man seemed right, until his daughter said, "Like everyone else, even heartsick editorial writers and pontifical judges, you can attitudinize as logically as you want, but there's only action and reaction in this world."

Then she kissed perhaps the killer of her mother, and gave me the heart to go on with her forever popping spoilers in their bongos, predators in their double-weight scales, machos right in the motors that drive them to kill. We know what fun is.

And we know faith in others to resist the social creeps who twist the hearts and shrink the souls of people. We know what games are, we know which are played by those with a soul or two, and which by bahaymas without soul, with only the mean streak it takes to brutalize.

We know how to recognize crocodile blood.